WINDS OF CHANGE

The Timekeeper Chronicles

The Chivalrous Welshman
Time to Kill · Tick Tock · Windup · Stopwatch · Free Time · Leap Second
Imminence · Synchronization · Turning Point · The Eleventh Hour

The Fifth Horseman
Famine (Winter 2026)

The Hands of Time
In the Hands of the Enemy · The Hands Pulling the Strings
The Hand Holding the Knife

The Lone Wolf
Wolf Pack · Alpha Wolf · Lone Wolf

The Akari-Bearer
Bearer of Bad News
Right to Bear Arms (Summer 2026)

Singles
Of Saints and Sinners · Chasing the White Bear · Winds of Change

Winds of Change
A Novel of
The Timekeeper Chronicles

Brooke Shaffer

Black Bear Publishing

ISBN:
    Hardcover: 978-1-953113-46-7
    Softcover: 978-1-953113-47-4
    eBook: 978-1-953113-48-1

For Joe, the bank robber turned pastor

February 2, 2016

To: Fianarantsoa, Madagascar
From: Charleston, West Virginia, United States of America

Dear Lalao,

I have a lot of explaining to do, and I know it. Unfortunately, this time it is not so grand as running off to fight evil spirits and slay dragons. I don't know how much you've heard, if the news has even made it back home, but I trust you to know me.

After we last spoke, I tried to get help for my seizures and discovered I was being poisoned. The only available treatment at the time was total cessation of all pharmaceutical interventions while my system tried to flush out the poison. There were many lonely nights of pain and fear, and just as many days I do not even remember because of terrible spasms and seizures. What's worse, because of it, my eyesight, what little remains, is beginning to fade.

The dragon fled, but it is not defeated. It used such chaotic time to bring law enforcement to me, to lay on me all of the crimes the others committed. I was arrested and accused of many terrible and treacherous crimes, including a number of deaths, most of them police officers. On these charges, I was found not guilty. For this, I am thankful, and I believe the ancestors favored me that I should not suffer such terrible injustice. I was, however, found guilty of kidnapping a boy and attempting to murder his father, who also happens to be a police officer. These are the facts, and they are the only facts that matter now. Truth does not matter. The reasons why do not matter, and they sound preposterous to those whose eyes are closed to the spiritual world. How could I make them understand the things I know, show them the things I have seen? I know I could never show them the dragon, for it would only hide itself in order to make me look the fool.

I have been sentenced to sixty years in prison, and I write this letter to inform you of my new residence and how you may reach me there. Regrettably, correspondence may have to be in French (as you will note this letter) or English (which I know you do not know), so that all the hands it passes through (and there will be many of them) can read it and ensure we are not discussing anything questionable. We could use Malagasy, but the time between sending and receiving would only be that much longer as they search for a translator. If you are comfortable with international calls, and if time differences permit, I will call you and we may speak freely in Malagasy. Calls are recorded, naturally, but it will be great hassle for them to inquire of a Malagasy interpreter. This is all, of course, assuming you even wish to speak to me.

Do not worry about how I am being treated. American prisons are luxury resorts compared to the hell I have experienced. There are three meals a day, and they are more than just cold rice. There are even protection considerations for my seizures and impending blindness. This does not mean there are no hardships; simply being here is stressful enough. But I expect this will be easier to endure than hard labor in the hot sun (and there are fewer pickaxes).

Perhaps you are wondering why this happened, why it was allowed by either the spirits or myself. We know that fate is fixed. And we know that I was permitted the ability to choose, to defy this fixed fate. Part of me fears that I have chosen poorly, although at what point I made this poor choice, I do not know. I expect I will have plenty of time to think about such things, and to consider what to do now. Further accommodation laws require that they provide me with necessary materials to reasonably conduct religious observances. If I am able, I will build a shrine and pray there and hope the ancestors choose to hear me.

My activity options have shrunk to include simply food, chores, and doddering around a small cell. This provides limited and yet limitless opportunity to consider my next steps. In the small jail, a volunteer group brings a book cart around like a small, traveling library. Unfortunately, with my failing eyesight, even this meager respite and oasis of knowledge and entertainment is becoming lost to me. The group has no braille books, and even if they did, I do not know how to read it. I suppose I should learn. If this encroaching blindness is the punishment of the ancestors, I do not expect it to be short-lived. I must learn how to read the bumps.

Of course, this does not bode well for written letters between us, and I cannot very well dictate to someone who does not know Malagasy or French. Nor could I expect you to learn braille, whether English or French. I expect the answer will manifest itself once I get to that point. As expected, the guards here care little for what happens to us, but the government agents and social workers take a nauseating interest in our lives and rehabilitating us back into society. I suppose this is not a bad thing. I am simply unaccustomed to such interest in my well-being, especially from a government entity. But without their understanding of the ancestors and the spirits and the way of things, I do not expect I will make much progress with them.

As I stated before, my options are quite limited and yet perfectly limitless. In the jail, I am left alone for many hours at a time and then herded here and there like cattle on the farm. I suppose once I reach the prison and am no longer the new toy, things will settle down and I can establish some sort of personal routine.

Even if you decide to cut off contact with me over these events, please let me know so I am not kept waiting. On the other hand, that would be a kind of poetic justice, wouldn't it?

Ever yours,

Rivotra
981436

One
Intake

Rifun had only ever flown a few times in his life, and it had been miserable each time, leaving him retching with nothing to give and so weak he couldn't even stand. Bouncing along in the back of the armored van as it swerved helter-skelter around the twisting mountain roads of West Virginia, it was all he could do to not get sick. The armed guards had placed a bucket at his feet once they saw the nausea start to take hold, but he knew that once he gave in, it wasn't going to stop easily. The back of the van had no windows through which he might attempt to focus on the horizon, and the best he could do was stare at the bottom of the bucket and pray that the trip was over quickly.

He very much preferred portal travel. True, it could be physically taxing to rip open a hole in the universe from here to there, though it was but a minor, momentary inconvenience compared to this hell he'd endured for over half an hour now. Unfortunately, with the Safe Earth Defense System in place, his ability to conjure portals was blocked.

The van jerked to the left, swinging long and wide around a corner. Rifun was locked in place via his wrist and ankle cuffs; he was prevented from falling over, though his head certainly protested the sudden catch at the end of the chain. One of the guards, who was not so attached to his seat, banged angrily on the metal plate separating the back of the van from the front and yelled at the driver to watch it up there. The driver made some retort Rifun did not catch, if only because he was more intent on not losing the contents of his stomach.

He could feel the van roll around a longer, gentler curve, slightly uphill, before suddenly cutting back the other way. The guard on Rifun's right side, caught off-guard by the maneuver, bumped into him, breaking his concentration.

"This isn't going to be good," Rifun commented as everyone righted themselves once more.

He'd barely gotten the words out before he leaned over and retched. Breakfast hadn't tasted especially good going down, and it was worse coming back up.

There were four armed guards in the back of the van. Whether it was because of their own nausea or solely from the sound and smell of his vomiting, two of them joined him at the bucket. One retched twice and apparently felt much better, while Rifun and the second guard spent the rest of the trip, about another forty minutes, passing the bucket back and forth.

By the time the van actually slowed down and it was announced that they had arrived at their destination, Rifun had absolutely nothing left to give though his body still went through the motions and his abdomen ached something fierce. Only when the van came to a complete stop did some of his muscles relax. He dry-heaved once more, then, mercifully, stopped. He rested shaky elbows on his knees, hands on his forehead, wishing only for sleep. He rubbed his eyes and blearily looked at the guard with whom he'd shared the bucket. Young kid, maybe twenty-five years old, white as a ghost and shaking like a leaf.

"You all right?" Rifun asked.

The man, lips trembling and crusted with stomach bile, just nodded, barely able to meet his gaze.

The rear doors of the van swung open, and Rifun was momentarily blinded. The light probably wasn't any brighter than a standard lightbulb, but his head wasn't having it.

A new voice outside the van cursed. "You kissing or giving him a blowjob or what?"

An armed guard approached from the front, laughing as he fiddled with the key to unlock the cuffs from the seat. "Naw, we got Dirk for a driver."

"Shit, man."

"Jenson," the guard with Rifun's cuffs said, nudging the pale guard with his foot. "Take the bucket to go."

The sickly guard, Jenson, spat once more into the bucket, then nodded wordlessly, grabbed the bucket, and slid, almost crawled, toward the back of the van. One of the new guards outside helped him out so the bucket didn't spill, saying, "All right, man, go get yourself cleaned up. You look like shit."

Rifun felt a tug on his cuff chain. He let out a breath and staggered to his feet. Just one step at a time. He was on solid ground now.

He didn't know whether it was the nausea and ensuing migraine or his own failing vision which ultimately distorted his depth perception as he exited. Whatever it was, he severely misjudged the distance from the bumper of the van to the concrete below and swiftly fell to his face, barely able to catch himself so he didn't get injured.

A few of the gathered guards found this quite amusing, but the one with his chain and the one in charge of the new party just sighed with exasperation and hauled him to his feet.

They were in a fully-enclosed garage. There were no windows, not even in the two bay doors at either end of the room. There was one steel man door leading outside and one, which they walked toward now, leading into a large building made of block and concrete. By the time they closed the twenty foot distance from the van to the man door, Rifun managed to regain some of his composure, at least enough to walk on his own two feet and not stumble into anyone else. His head still pounded. Every light was too bright, every sound too loud.

Welcome to Mt. Olive Correctional Complex, the only maximum security prison in the state of West Virginia. It was completely isolated deep in the mountains, and fully self-sustaining with its own power plant, water treatment, hospital, post office, and even courthouse. Once inside, there was no reason any inmate should need to leave. Perfect for containing the worst of the worst: serial killers, rapists, drug kingpins. Or, in Rifun's case, cop killers.

He hadn't actually killed any cops; he'd been found not guilty on all those charges. But the kidnapping with intent to use as hostage and the attempted murder of a police officer, those he had been convicted of. Add in a few minor charges and he had been sentenced to sixty-three years.

As the metal door opened and he was marched inside, the fluorescent tube lighting doing nothing for his migraine, he knew he wasn't going to last that long, and it had nothing to do with his age. It didn't have much to do with his

7

seizures or blindness, either, although that was working against him. Rather, it was the simple fact that those who wanted him dead could basically do so at any time. They had the means to conjure portals in spite of the Safe Earth Defense System. They had the means to Disguise themselves as anyone or, in rare cases, anything. They had access to all of the abilities he'd lost in the last year which would allow them to manipulate the fabric of reality and cause him to die in tragic agony, while the best he might be able to do was a little conjuration of Time.

He wasn't going to last long, he thought as they took him down a narrow hallway to an office. All these formalities, probably some big speech about his lengthy stay and what would be expected of him during that stay, and he didn't expect to last a year. Three months, tops.

The office was as dull as could be expected: block walls; gray, industrial carpet; a whiteboard with some notes in varying colors; filing cabinets in every corner; a couple chairs straight from the thrift store bargain bin. A couple of working inmates sat at computers; one took a manila envelope from one of the guards as they entered.

Across the room was a man in uniform. Rifun was not well-versed in American corrections, but judging by the crispness of the uniform, to say nothing of the chevrons and patches, he guessed this was the man in charge, if not the warden himself. He was talking to the other working inmate, steaming cup of coffee in hand. He looked up at the new arrivals.

"Welcome, welcome," he greeted, taking a sip of coffee. "How are you this morning, Trevor?"

"Better than some," the guard with Rifun's cuffs commented.

"Any trouble?"

"Only with Dirk's driving."

The uniformed man nodded as he took another drink. "All right, then. You boys know where the break room is. Help yourselves before you take off."

The guards who had accompanied Rifun on the drive left the room, though not before undoing his wrist and ankle cuffs, and the guards who had met them in the garage filled the void.

Rifun might have expected the uniformed man to start into a speech, but it was the inmate who had taken the envelope who spoke next.

"Full legal name?" he inquired.

"Rifun Felix Ndolo." Rifun spelled it out.

"Birthdate?"

"March 13, 1987." That was a lie, but no one was going to believe he'd been born in 1897.

"Previous occupation?"

"Military."

The inmate paused in his work for half a breath, then resumed without a word. No doubt that little tidbit was going to make its way through the population by the end of the day. Let them make of it what they will. Just like no one would believe he'd been born in 1897, they also wouldn't believe that he had led intergalactic armies into battle across multiple worlds.

Rifun was then made to stand in a certain spot so his picture could be taken for an ID card that was printed right there. While it was printing and the inmate searched for some sort of clip to thread through the slot, a new prison uniform was brought for Rifun to change into. Dull gray scrub-type pants and matching shirt. The pants had regular front and rear pockets and the shirt had one breast pocket. The back of the shirt was adorned with a large "MOCC" in faded black lettering.

"This is your ID," the uniformed man said, launching into his speech as he handed Rifun the ID card. "You will keep it on you at all times. You will produce it when asked. If you fail to produce it, there will be disciplinary action. If you are caught with someone else's ID, there will be disciplinary action."

Rifun took the card and clipped it dutifully on his breast pocket. He saw that the man's ID badge on his chest read "Capt. Eric Mann".

"Your file says you've been in prison before, albeit another country," Mann went on, taking a step back and another sip of coffee. "So let me bring you up to speed on how things are done here in America." He gestured. "Me and my guys, we're not 'guards.' We are 'corrections officers.' You will address us as 'officer' or 'CO' or 'sir.' Our job is only to ensure you stay inside this facility. Your job is to see to your own damn self. You are responsible for your health, your entertainment, your education, your life. You want to hook up with a gang so they watch your back, that's your

9

business. But don't come crying to us because a rival gang beat the shit out of you.

"You will be expected to pull your weight around here. This place is only as clean as you guys make it. Your clothes are only as clean as you guys make them. Your food is only as good as you guys cook it. If you are upset about the quality of life around here, you can look in the mirror and take a number. If you want to actually try to make something of yourself while you're here, there are plenty of opportunities for you to participate in college classes as well as more demanding jobs around this facility. Once you're out of intake, you will be assigned to a neighborhood and a social worker. It is their job to get you connected to such programs and opportunities, not ours. Understand?"

The captain did not wait for a reply. "Finally, there are plenty of ways that you can get in trouble around here, and we'd be here forever if I tried to list them all. Like anything, it's only illegal if you get caught. If anything does come up, you get to wait in the Hole until your court date. We handle everything internally here, so don't think you can call up your lawyer and whine to him. Outside lawyers are for outside matters. In here, we have our own laws and our own lawyers. This is our own little world in here."

Captain Mann shifted his stance and took another drink of his coffee. "Any questions?"

"No, sir," Rifun replied simply.

Mann raised a brow, but turned his head and nodded to the three guards—ahem, officers—who had been waiting by the door.

"You'll spend thirty days in the Fishbowl," Mann said. "If you can survive that, well, what's a few more decades?"

The three officers took Rifun out of the office and down the hall to a large, open, concrete room. Cells lined the wall in front of him and to the right on the ground and an upper level, about sixteen in all. The doors were solid steel but with a window about six inches by twelve. To the left was an open shower area. As Rifun was led there, he noted faces started appearing in the windows. Most were quietly curious, but there were plenty of others making lewd comments or suggestive noises, mostly muffled by the heavy doors.

Rifun would be lying if he felt no discomfort at being made to strip down and shower publicly, but the faster he got this done and over with, the faster he could get to a bed to lie down and quiet his head.

"What happened to you, man?" an inmate from the nearest cell asked. Rifun could tell he was speaking loudly in order to be heard through the heavy door.

Rifun ignored the man, though he did glance down at his body at the mention. The last time he'd been in prison was after the Uprising in his home country of Madagascar, right after World War II, and he'd spent nearly ten years being tortured almost nightly by the French. Burning, flogging, electrocution, waterboarding, beatings, and more, for no greater sin than opposing the French occupation. They'd left his face, though. He could wear long sleeves, cover up the mutilating scars, but he would always know. He would always remember. And never forgive.

On the other hand, the question could have also been directed to his two missing fingers, the index and middle fingers of his right hand. That had happened in the final standoff with police a couple years ago, one of the officers getting in a precision shot that took them clean off his hand and nearly took the thumb, too. He'd been too focused on escaping the area to think about grabbing them in some hopes of getting them reattached, and now, here he was.

After the shower, Rifun was permitted to dress, then taken to an empty cell on the ground floor where he was locked inside with hardly an, "Enjoy your stay."

It was a standard cell, he figured. Six by six feet, bunk bed, toilet-sink unit in one corner, small emergency window at the top of the wall just big enough to pass inspection but not actually big enough for any full-grown man to wiggle through in an emergency, and a security camera in the corner.

Grateful to be alone at last, Rifun crawled into bed, put the thin, starchy pillow over his eyes, and tried to sleep.

He was woken up maybe an hour later by the lunch call. Reluctantly, with his migraine eased to only a moderate headache, he sat up on the bed. As the food cart rolled in front of his door, the officer accompanying the inmate waiter barked at him to get up to the window for count. Sighing, Rifun stood and turned toward the window. Only then did the slot in the door open so he could take his tray of food.

It wasn't much. A sandwich, some kind of pasta salad with tomatoes and leafy greens, a small, semi-solid blob of something he could not identify, and a cup of water. That was all right, he figured. Using Time not only extended one's life, for most users, but also reduced the need for food. And, actually, it didn't taste all that bad. The bread was not stale, the meat inside wasn't rancid, the pasta salad was crisp and fresh. The semi-solid blob he guessed was what Americans called pudding. He wasn't impressed, but it was sugary.

He presented himself at the window again when the cart came by about ten minutes later to collect the trays. He was informed that everything that went in was expected to come out; if even one tine was missing off a fork, he'd regret it.

Then he was left alone again to sleep, at least until dinner. This meal was slightly larger, deceptively tasty, but no less stringent about ensuring everything he received he gave back. He never responded to the officers' warnings or threats. On the one hand, he still had a headache and just wanted a good stretch of uninterrupted sleep, more than just a quick nap. On the other hand, what were they going to do to him? Oh, he had no illusions that they wouldn't burst into the room and forcibly subdue him, but that was the easy part. The hard part was torture, and they weren't going to go that far.

Rifun might have hoped that after dinner he would be left alone again, perhaps until some nightly count before bed. Instead, it was time for a little walkabout apparently. The doors were opened, the inmates informed that they had half an hour to get out, stretch their legs, walk around the room, and take a shower.

Given that there were eight showerheads and more than eight inmates, showers were either quick, uncomfortable, or both. Having already gotten his shower for the day, Rifun just watched from the doorway of his cell, trying to calculate how he was going to fit into all of this the following day. Time would let him stretch out his shower time as long as he desired. He could turn a single millisecond into an entire day if he so chose. Unfortunately, it would not increase the volume of water coming out of the pipes, nor would it keep any of the other inmates away from him.

Another inmate approached him. His hair was wet, as were certain spots on his clothes where he hadn't gotten completely dry before dressing. He was a middle-aged man, soft in the belly, hands calloused from years of hard work, graying hair rapidly receding in the front and thinning in the back.

"You never answered Ant's question," the man said, stopping a couple feet from Rifun. His posture indicated that while he might be in intake for thirty days, he was no stranger to the prison system. "What happened to you?"

Rifun glanced around the room, struggling to distinguish one man from another until he thought he saw one who might have been the man who actually asked that question. He looked back at the inmate who had approached him. "Well, that's Ant's question, isn't it?"

"And now it's mine." The man shifted his stance, trying to intimidate without looking so threatening as to attract the attention of the officers. "You some tough shit or what? And what's with the accent?"

Rifun let out a breath. "The accent is Malagasy, from Madagascar. I did spend time in their prisons, yes. I was sentenced to hard labor, torture, and even death. Those things tend to leave marks."

The man studied him for a long moment, still holding his pose. If he were about twenty or thirty years younger, Rifun might have believed there was something to the posturing. And while he wouldn't discount the possibility that the man still had some good strength left in him, he wouldn't have the endurance to last long in a real fight.

After another minute, the man relaxed a little and took a step back. "Word of advice. Drop that fake-ass accent. You ain't black enough to be African, and some of these guys in here will eat you alive for disrespecting them."

Rifun gave the man a look. "There is no fake accent to drop, and I am more African than they could ever hope to be."

Now the man laughed, garnering attention from several men nearby. He shook his head and huffed an amused sigh. Before he turned to leave, he said, "Your funeral."

No one bothered him after that, though several of them looked like they wanted to. He could not see many faces well, but posture was easy enough to read to tell who was a veteran inmate and who was brand new.

13

The half hour timed out and the inmates were herded back into their cells. Then, after another hour and a half of doddering around, the officers came around for final nightly count and lights out. This was a bit of a misnomer, of course, because the lights never truly went out. The best they did was dim to about twenty percent illumination. It would be enough for an officer making his rounds to see that someone was still inside and still alive.

With his naps throughout the day and the progressive lessening of his headache, Rifun was unable to fall asleep right away, however much he might have wanted to. Instead, he stared at the underside of the top bunk and all the scratched images and words thereupon. Most all of them were obscene or profane, but he also found the first few lines of The Lord's Prayer, a few psalms, as well as one-line prayers asking various saints to save whoever it was had etched into the metal.

He did not hear an officer walk by so much as he happened to be generally looking in the direction of the door and saw movement on the outside. The officer stopped briefly, glanced in, then moved on.

Rifun looked back up at the underside of the bunk and closed his eyes. Though they no longer hurt, his eyes were still tired, but his mind was awake. It demanded something to do, even just a problem to mull over and try to solve. Well, he figured, his biggest problem was going to be just how he was going to survive. Except he didn't have a good answer, or any kind of starting point. There was nowhere he could run or hide that Julianna wouldn't find him eventually, and all she had to do was wait for him to have a seizure or just induce one herself. Once he was down and helpless, cut his throat. His use of Time was no match for her use of the Akari. He was too weak, too vulnerable.

He rolled onto one side. Now that his headache had taken a backseat priority, his body was starting to voice its displeasure with the state of the mattress.

He was going to die here. Maybe not tonight, maybe not tomorrow, but at some point very soon, Julianna or one of her henchmen would come for him. And they would kill him.

Stars and monsters, kingship and treachery, a destiny walked on the edge of a knife. He scoffed and mentally shook his head. A prophecy about his life given long ago. That knife had been used to stab him in the chest once already. Used again to stab him in the back. Only one thing left to do with it now.

Gradually his thoughts faded into sleep, but it proved to be no respite. Because of his progressive brain damage, he no longer experienced visual dreams. He couldn't remember the last dream he had, if there was even an audible component to it.

It made for some lonely nights, but it helped to bridge the gap between lights out and morning count. Once the officers were satisfied everyone was where they'd left them last night, everyone was permitted breakfast. This proved to be a light meal consisting of a bowl of oatmeal; either an apple, orange, or banana; a tiny portion of scrambled eggs; and a cup of milk. Fifteen minutes were allotted to eat before the officer came back around to ensure everything that had been received was given back.

This was followed by half an hour of out time. Similar to the night before, they could walk around, stretch their legs, or take a shower. Before Rifun could get more than ten feet from his cell, the door to the hall leading to the front office opened and an officer approached. He was not the captain from the day before, but his chevrons still indicated rank. When he got close enough, Rifun saw his nametag read "Lt. Remy Oswald".

"981436?" the lieutenant inquired. "Ndolo?"

Rifun presented his ID card. "Sir."

The lieutenant indicated another lesser officer with him. "We're going to take you to the clinic for a medical workup and then do a little orientation."

It wasn't as though he had the option to say no thanks, he'd rather hang out in the concrete box for half an hour with the others.

Lieutenant Oswald handed him a winter coat which he put on, then led the way, the lesser officer walking behind. They headed down a short side hallway to a door leading outside. After adjusting to the sudden splash of morning sunlight and winter chill, Rifun could see a large building directly ahead and a couple more to his left along the secure perimeter fence.

"Captain probably already told you, but this facility is entirely self-sufficient," Oswald was saying. He walked like a man who was confident in his physicality and did not feel the need to show it off every second of the day. "Power plant, water treatment, hospital, courtroom, library, gymnasium, church." He pointed. "Baseball diamond over there, got a couple teams forming up in the next couple months, if that's your thing, keep you out of trouble." He dropped his arm. "Got football, soccer, tennis, even boxing in the gym. You get in trouble, sports privileges are typically the first thing pulled, so keep that in mind." As they neared the building directly ahead, he changed topic. "Medically, we have the small clinic and the larger hospital. Hospital is for big shit and emergencies, and the clinic is for everything else. Regular checkup, dental, vision, go to the clinic. Fall down a flight of stairs and break an arm, go to the clinic. You get shanked in the middle of the night and wake up with your insides on the outside, hospital."

They arrived at the building and Oswald pulled open the heavy door. The three of them filed inside.

"All medical personnel are contracted workers," Oswald went on, walking up to the desk. "They're considered civilians. You fuck with them, we fuck with you. Got it?"

"Understood," Rifun answered.

"Help you, lieutenant?" the receptionist inquired. He was a man about thirty years old, glasses, nothing remarkable about him to Rifun's eyes.

"981436, Ndolo, intake workup," Oswald said.

"I'll let doc know."

The receptionist stood and left the desk. The lieutenant turned his attention back to Rifun. "While you're here, you are your number and your number is you. Anything you need, you ever have to identify yourself, number first, then name."

Another door opened and the receptionist motioned them back.

Linoleum, block walls, and fluorescent lighting, the only alternative to concrete and stone, and the clinic was no different. Walking into an exam room, Rifun noted that every drawer and cabinet was locked. He didn't expect there to be any drugs in the rooms themselves, but someone lashing out like a crazed lunatic looking for his fix might not know that.

He had just taken off his coat when the doctor walked in. The doctor was a forty-something man with thick black hair, thick-rimmed glasses, big ears, and a bandaid around one finger, carrying a clipboard. His nametag

16

proclaimed him to be "Wallace, Peter H., M.D."

"Morning, Remy," Wallace greeted.

"Morning, doc."

"Intake workup, eh?" Wallace looked at his clipboard, then at Rifun. "Number and name?"

"981436, Ndolo, Rifun Felix," Rifun recited.

"And your birthdate?"

"March 13, 1987."

The doctor nodded. "Excellent. Now I have here...your medical records from some tests you had done during your trial, and some other reports. Looks like you have a traumatic brain injury to your occipital lobe which has resulted in occipital epilepsy, is that right?"

"That's right. The initial injury resulted in blindsight, but with my seizures getting worse, the last doctor told me I might have a year or two before I am completely blind."

Wallace nodded, still looking over the papers. "That's what it says, yup. It also says you have been responding well to medication, so I'll get you on the schedule. Have you taken any medication today?"

"No. The last was yesterday before I was transferred."

"All right, I'll have a nurse bring some before you leave. Tomorrow it will come with breakfast." Now the doctor set aside the clipboard. "Occipital epilepsy can be managed with surgery; did you know that? We could theoretically stop the progression of your blindness."

Rifun frowned and found himself actually considering it. His vision wasn't great, but it was better than nothing. If the seizures could be calmed or less frequent, maybe he would have a chance at surviving longer than a few months.

"I'll let you think about it," the doctor said after a moment. "But if you've only got a year, I would advise you to think quickly. Now then, is there anything I need to know before we do a physical workup?"

Rifun indicated a long, precise scar down his right arm. "I have rods and screws in my arm and wrist from a previous hostile encounter. Obviously you can see I lack two fingers. Other than that, nothing that might make a difference."

17

Well, nothing he thought would make a difference. Given the short sleeves of the scrub shirt, his torture scars were glaringly evident, and the doctor demanded to see them. Reluctantly, Rifun stripped down to his boxers as directed so the man could investigate further. He came to the same conclusion everyone else did: they looked horrendous, and they probably impeded some manner of temperature and pressure sensation, but were otherwise nonlethal anymore.

They also impeded the doctor's ability to get accurate vital signs, whether it was a standard blood pressure or a reading of his heart. In the corner, Oswald and the lesser officer were growing bored and annoyed.

The last part of the workup was a simple hearing and vision test. The audiologist concluded that while Rifun apparently suffered from mild hearing loss, which the doctor attributed to his military background, he was otherwise fine. As for his vision, while his eyes were physically healthy, his LogMAR was 0.5.

"That means you need to be twenty feet away from something a normal person can see at roughly sixty-three feet," the optometrist explained. He leaned back in his chair. "Unfortunately, because this is from a brain injury, not necessarily natural decline, I don't think glasses would do you any good."

Rifun shook his head. "No, I don't think so."

With that, his intake workup wrapped up. Just as soon as Wallace dismissed them, Oswald was on the move again, the lesser officer following obediently with Rifun between the two. They made a quick detour to the hospital just to show him where it was, then headed back outside.

They ended up on the opposite side of the building on the interior of the complex. It was here that Rifun noticed multiple identical buildings arranged in an arc formation along the perimeter fence. Oswald walked out into the open area enough that he could point to each building in turn. "That's the rec building, got the gym, the library, any and all classrooms. Over there is general population or genpop, where most guys go. That there is acute medical segregation; honestly, that's probably where you'll end up, with all the other sick bastards. That building is the court building, includes punitive segregation, lovingly called the Hole. You get in trouble, you wait in the Hole until we figure out what happened and how you need to be punished. This here is the chapel. That wing there that's attached to the main building, that's the extra good behavior barracks. You do well, keep yourself clean, do classes or get a job or whatever, you get certain privileges, including bedding down in there. Inside the hospital is the psych ward where all the crazy fucks go. You decide to try and off yourself, you get placed into special management. And way over there beyond the fence where you probably can't see, that's the work camp. Low-risk, low-maintenance guys over there. You'll never make it there, so don't get any ideas. They're the ones who do most of the actual work and maintenance around here, try to work their way out of here through apprenticeships and applied skills."

Oswald pointed out several other buildings, and mentioned the location of such places as the post office, maintenance garage, warehouse, cafeteria, commissary, laundry, and so on.

Then they were heading back to the main building where the intake cells awaited. But rather than going back to intake, Oswald took Rifun to a different part of the building. This section was comprised entirely of offices and staffed by civilians; Rifun knew this because most of them were women. Some of them greeted the lieutenant, and he replied in kind. They approached a particular office, the door already open.

"Morning, Remy," the woman greeted, looking up from her computer.

"Got a tub for me?" Oswald asked.

"Number?"

Oswald looked at Rifun who recited his number followed by his name. The woman nodded and reached under her desk for a yellow plastic tub, its lid slightly ajar. A label on the tub and the lid declared to all that it belonged to 981436, Ndolo, R. It was slightly larger than a sheet of paper and about six inches deep. She held the tub out across the desk. Rifun glanced at Oswald who nodded once.

Cautiously, Rifun took the tub with a mild, "Thank you."

"You want to give the speech or should I?" the lady asked of Oswald.

"I'll let you," Oswald told her.

She nodded. Then, "This is your tub. It is labeled and marked exclusively for you. You can put whatever you want in there—food, extra pair of socks, stationary, et cetera—but anything found inside the tub is presumed to be yours. Someone gives you drugs to stash, they become yours if they're found in there. Inside you will find papers detailing your crimes and sentences, length and dates, concurrent or consecutive, definite or indefinite, terms of conclusion, terms of parole, and so on." She made a vague gesture around the room. "This is administration and records. Something happens to your papers, we can print you off a copy, but we can't answer questions about the content. If you have questions about your trial or your sentence, things like that, you're going to have to go to the courthouse and talk to the lawyers."

Rifun peeked inside the tub. True to her word, there were legal documents within, lying at the bottom of the bin. He sealed the lid, then followed Oswald out of the room.

The lieutenant pointed out a few places of interest on their way back to intake: the social workers' offices, the interior visitation room which resembled a cafeteria, and the offices of the higher officers like the captain and the warden. But he wasn't a "warden," he was an "administrator." Oswald rolled his eyes at that.

"If the social workers ask, it's 'administrator' or 'officer' or whatever politically correct title you were told to say. Where the social workers can't hear, not too many people give a shit. Warden, guard, asshat, we hear it all."

Rifun did not respond to that, and the next thing he knew, they were back in intake.

"Keep the coat," Oswald said as Rifun walked into his cell. "You last thirty days here, you'll still need it."

Then he closed and locked the door and wandered off.

Rifun sat on the bed, opened his tub, and brought out the papers. Evading and eluding, five hundred thirty-three days. Illegal possession of a firearm, two years. Kidnapping with intent to use as hostage, thirty years. Attempted murder of a police officer in the second degree, thirty years. Because a deadly weapon had been involved, he was required to serve at least one-third of his sentence before coming up for parole. Earliest possible date, some time in 2036.

He put the tub back together and slid it under the bed. Not going to happen. At the same time, if he was right, at least he'd be dead before he completely lost his vision. That had to count for something, right?

He sighed and rubbed his face. Without his headache to distract him, the loneliness of the cell directed his thoughts elsewhere, to less friendly places. How did it come to this? How had he allowed his devotion to blind him? Had he disrespected the ancestors in some way? Had he offended the Author? Was it possible that some miracle would come about to deliver him from prison a third time? Was there any chance of regaining his Akari abilities, or had he exhausted all of his chances?

Probably exhausted them, he decided. Once, he had a chance to reunite with his family on the farm in Fianar, stay with his grandmother, his *nenibe*, and get to know the side of the family he'd barely been aware of while under the lash of his stepfather. Later, he'd had a chance to marry a smart, beautiful woman, even raise a family. Both times he'd abandoned the family on some mission of the stars, intent on slaying a demonic spirit.

Now, he waited here for the dragon to slay him.

Outside, the lunch call went up. Rifun stood and went to the window to be counted. The tray slid through the slot in the door, and he sat to eat. Tomato soup with a grilled cheese sandwich, a banana on the side, water to drink. Fifteen minutes to finish, then back to the window to ensure everything was exactly the way it should have been.

The afternoon passed uneventfully, then it was dinner. Meatloaf, fries, another dollop of pudding though a different flavor, and water. Back to the window. Then half an hour to stretch legs and get a shower.

If there was any benefit to military training, it was the ability to take quick showers. Rifun waited until the last three minutes of free time before ducking under a free showerhead. Between his training and slight use of his Time abilities, he was in, washed, and out in exactly two minutes. No one was impressed, but at least he'd discovered a method for bathing without needing to share a showerhead.

An hour and a half later, nightly count, then lights out. Rifun again lay on his mattress, staring at the things etched into the metal, his eyes drawn repeatedly to The Lord's Prayer and the various psalms.

"Yea though I walk through the valley of the shadow of death," he whispered. He closed his eyes. *I will fear no evil.*

Except I do.

March 8, 2016

To: Mt. Olive, West Virginia, United States of America
From: Fianarantsoa, Madagascar

My dearest Rivotra,

Oh, you have no idea the joy it gives me to hear from you! I had worried for so long! The only reason I even knew what had happened was from one of my contacts at the university in Fianar. She teaches political science and keeps up on news in other countries, and she just happened across a news article about your trial. She doesn't know you, but I mentioned you a few times to her, and she asked if the person in the article was the same. Lo and behold, it was you!

I knew what had happened immediately, even without them telling me. You tried to destroy the dragon, but it somehow slipped from your grasp, scurried away from death and plotted its revenge, bringing to bear such mighty physical problems so as to stop your work on spiritual matters. How predictable! And the lesser evil spirits under the dragon's command have swayed the hearts and minds of foolish men to lock you away where you will not interfere in their plans. The exact details matter not. You are correct. I know you, and I believe you. I know things are not what they seem, and I know too well that the media is the enemy. Why wouldn't evil spirits take advantage of such broadcasting to a large audience?

I do know you, Rivotra, and I do trust you. I believe you have done good work and been so terribly punished for it. I also believe it is the evil spirits who are dogging you now and stealing your sight, stealing what the ancestors granted you so you could fight the demons.

I am very glad to hear that you are not being mistreated. Zanahy is caring for you even in this trial for you have served him well. I would suggest that your first prayer at your shrine be one of thanks. I understand that few people would do such a thing, thank the spirits for being in prison, but it sounds like a much softer landing than it could have been.

Tomas is rather upset by the whole thing, which I find a bit surprising. You met my other boys only once, I believe, so they are a bit aloof regarding your disposition. If they are upset, it is only because I am upset. But you and Tomas know each other better, perhaps not as friends, but acquaintances. I was surprised to hear him voice a rather strong opinion about the situation. I think it is because he is the youngest and spent less time in fear of the communists. He remembers the time well, but imperfectly. His clearer memories have more to do with the communist overthrow and our celebration of a democratic government, and he projects this liberation onto the United States as a perpetual reality.

Suffice to say, he believes this somehow politically motivated, and he has become a bit obsessive over American politics in the last couple weeks. He is convinced that overtly racist privileged white Americans sent you to prison. He does not understand the spiritual aspect of things, how men may be swayed by good and evil spirits. He does not realize that such selfish, narrow-minded pride is also evidence of evil—well, he does, but he applies it only to others, rarely to himself. If you are able to build your shrine, please pray for him, as I do, that he would see this for what it really is and examine himself in the process. Although you are far away, you are a chosen shaman, and you are of this family. You have the power to direct the spirits to and away from him.

But regardless of the cause, what matters now is the current situation. Your seizures make you vulnerable and your blindness even more so. If written letters become impossible, then please do call. Do not worry about the cost to me. Madagascar may still be only a developing country, but we are not so savage that we do not have internet or inexpensive methods of making international calls. Fianar and the Betsileo have always been ahead of everyone else in the country when it comes to learning and innovation. I am certain my contacts at the university would find some way to make it happen. If you like, and if it is possible, I could see if they have any materials on learning Malagasy and French braille. We will learn it together! That would be such fun, I think! And I cannot expect that my own eyesight will remain so pristine forever. It may become necessary for me as well!

It is not lost on me that sixty years is well beyond what I am capable of achieving in my life. Although Tomas is rather zealous over American politics, he did mention that not all sixty years need be fulfilled before you are released. Please, you must let me know just as soon as possible so I can make lunch plans again. Tomas tried to take me to our usual spot in an effort to cheer me up, but I could not find joy that day. All the years my husband and I waited for the communists to come and arrest us for dissent, all the days I worried that he would not come home from the university because he had been apprehended, and it is you who ends up in prison! What a path you must tread for the demons to come after you so! I cannot even begin to fathom the things you have seen and done on this marvelous quest of yours! And it certainly is not over yet!

Do write to me as often as you can. And call as often as you can. Whatever language we must use, whatever medium, I do not care. I must hear from you. I must know you are well. I forbid you from leaving me again! If anything happens, I must know about it!

Yours,

Lalao

Two
Thirty Seven Days

Nineteen days into his stay in the Fishbowl, Rifun received a cellmate, or a "cellie" as they were called. He was a twenty-two year old who had apparently made an appearance at his teenage sister's party—the kind their parents either didn't know about or else entrusted to their responsible adult son—and proceeded to rape eleven girls between the ages of thirteen and seventeen. His claim was that they consented and only got upset when they found out he'd slept with other girls at the party. Rifun was trying to figure out how any man, however hot-blooded and well-endowed he might be, could get it done at least eleven times in two hours.

However cool and tough the kid might have pretended to be during the day, however nonchalant he tried to be about his crimes or the crimes of others—euphemistically called "setbacks"—at night Rifun heard muffled whimpers and stuttered prayers coming from the top bunk. This went on for days.

"Eventually," Rifun sighed, "you're going to end up with a cellmate who isn't so tolerant of your weeping."

It was the night before he, theoretically, moved out of the Fishbowl.

"They're going to kill me," the kid, Laurence, blubbered. "They're going to label me a pedophile, kill me, and use a steel pipe to rape my corpse."

"And if you're lucky, it will be in that order."

That did not help the situation.

"What am I going to do?" Laurence wondered.

"You're going to do whatever you have to in order to survive," Rifun told him. "May I recommend something along the lines of following the rules and going above and beyond to prove yourself thereby earning yourself a safer place among the staff, before you run off and join a gang?"

"Gang would just make me their bitch." Now Laurence rolled over, peeking over the edge of his bunk to look at Rifun. "What are you going to do? How are you going to survive? How does an epileptic blind man survive a place like this?"

Rifun gave him a look. "Extenuating circumstances aside, I probably have better odds than a pedophile."

The young man spit on the ground beside the bunk. "Fuck you, man!" He rolled back onto his mattress. "You're no help."

Rifun opened his mouth to speak, but there was a tap on the window. He looked up to see the officer standing there on his nightly round.

"Lights out," he said. "Go to sleep."

Laurence said some kind of affirmative while Rifun just put up a hand of acknowledgment.

"A few words of tough love are probably the nicest thing you're going to hear, so listen good," Rifun hissed. "If you're that worried about the rectal chastity of your corpse, you might as well kill yourself now before that news hits the general population. If you intend to live, well, you got a few more weeks to decide what you want to make of yourself here. I can't tell you what that is. You want to defend yourself, work on that. You want others to defend you, I might start working on a good story. But the more you live in fear of yourself and what you did, the more it will control you, and the more others will notice. Don't act like a pedophile, maybe you won't get treated like one. But above all, what will be, will be."

Laurence did not reply.

Rifun let out a quiet sigh and considered his own words. He really hadn't given too much thought to any plans, long-term or short-term. He wasn't overly concerned about who he was going to associate with, activities and free-time pursuits. He was basically preparing to walk out of the Fishbowl in the morning and fall over dead. But what if that didn't happen? What if he did have a few months, a year, or longer? Was he just going to sit and stare at a wall all day? He couldn't say he wasn't a little depressed, but he didn't have to stay that way, sitting under his own personal thundercloud.

Maybe he could enjoy life a little before Julianna finally took him out. No destiny, no armies, no wars, no obligations. Maybe he could engage in an activity solely because it interested him, not because it was part of a cover for some strategic maneuver. That would certainly be an interesting change of pace.

This never-before-known curiosity carried over to the next morning. After breakfast, during the half hour of free time, a lesser officer approached him and told him to roll up, basically grab all his stuff and be prepared to move. Rifun shrugged on his coat, grabbed his tub, and followed the officer down the hall to the exterior door. Once outside, the officer handed him a slip of paper and pointed to a building.

"Genpop, down that way, that building there on the left."

"Genpop?" Rifun questioned. "I thought I was being sent to medical."

The officer shrugged. "Not my call."

Then he ducked back inside, leaving Rifun standing there with a slip of paper that proved to be a transfer notice. He was to give it to the desk officer when he arrived in genpop.

He was outside the building and hadn't fallen over dead. No one was attacking him. Rifun knew a moment of pure humiliation even as he told himself to not let his guard down. The Fishbowl was fairly high security and tightly controlled. The rest of this place, probably not so much. As the captain had said, the officers' job was only to keep them inside the fence. What they did while inside the fence, that was up to them. Even pretending that he didn't have someone out for his blood already, it wouldn't take much to make enemies here.

First step then was just heading down to genpop. He made his way toward the blurry thing the officer had pointed out. Post breakfast, there was plenty of activity going on around the complex. Rifun watched the general flow of people and determined his most likely entry point. He could feel a few stares as he approached the doors, but no one called him out.

Once inside, there was a desk officer to his immediate left and right and a short hallway to his right and another straight ahead. Rifun approached the desk officer to his left.

"Don't recognize you," the officer said.

Rifun just handed him the paper.

The officer looked it over and nodded. "All right." He set the paper aside and tapped something on his computer. "You're going to be lodging in

Neighborhood F, House 14B."

"Cellblocks" were called "neighborhoods" and "cells" were called "houses." The immediate area outside the cell door was the "porch." And the officers were not immune to picking up the slang of their charges.

The officer handed him a new slip of paper. "Give this to the neighborhood agent."

He gave Rifun directions to the appropriate neighborhood. Rifun thanked him and went on his way.

The complex as a whole could house around a thousand inmates. When everyone was in, the place was probably pretty stuffy. Now, with everyone out and about, the place was massive.

Each cell housed two inmates. Each block housed forty cells. Each floor contained six blocks. Rifun made his way to the last block on the first floor. The heavy steel doors were open and he stepped inside.

Cells lined the walls on three sides, seven on the left, seven on the right, six at the far end. The same was true on the second level. A catwalk above the second level allowed two armed officers to keep watch and snipe any inmates being disruptive. To the right was the office of the neighborhood agent, or the officer assigned to desk duty for that block.

"You looking for something?" the officer asked.

Again, Rifun just handed him the paper. The officer looked it over and nodded. "14, right up close to me here." He pointed to the cell closest to the office. "B means you're on the bottom. Or it would if it mattered. How you two work it out is up to you. You get your shit in there, get settled in, then come back and I'll have some more paperwork for you to run around with."

Rifun nodded once and headed for the cell the officer had pointed out. These cells were slightly bigger than the ones in the Fishbowl, about eight by eight, with a bunk bed, a toilet-sink unit, and a security camera. Another yellow tub sat under the bed, belonging to "961145, Gallagher, Francis L." though the man himself was presently away. Rifun slid his tub under the bed, laid his coat on the mattress, thought better of it, and returned to the officer.

The officer handed him yet another slip of paper, saying, "And you thought you'd never need a hall pass after middle school." He leaned back in his seat. "But before you go, a little housekeeping. You might notice that things are a little more lax in here than the Fishbowl. Morning count is at six o'clock sharp, then you're pretty much free to come and go as you please. You want to head to the cafeteria for early coffee before breakfast at eight, fine. Want to get in a couple more hours of sleep, cool. However, you will not be a freeloader. If you're enrolled in some college or vocational activity, you follow that schedule. If you're not, you'll be put on a chore rotation.

"Your good behavior time is linked primarily to that rotation. You show up on time, you do the work, you don't cause trouble. It's up to you to figure out how to manage things. The social workers can help you with time management if that's a problem. Lunch runs from about eleven to three, to accommodate the many varying schedules and rotations. Dinner starts at five, runs to about eight, same reasons.

"Bathroom and showers for this neighborhood are down the hall here." He pointed down a short hallway on the other side of the office. "Feel free to use them whenever; you don't need a hall pass for that.

"Now, unless you're on night kitchen duty, where you might spend a little extra time washing dishes or mopping floors or whatever—or maybe there's the rare late-night baseball game—you are expected to be back here before nine o'clock. After nine o'clock, this door—" He indicated the main door into the neighborhood. "—closes. You come in after, you better be on kitchen duty or have a slip. Otherwise, it's counted against you. Got it?"

"Yes, sir," Rifun said, nodding once.

"Good. Lights out is at ten o'clock." He vaguely gestured to the slip of paper in Rifun's hand. "Now then, you're going to take that slip and head down to talk to the social workers. They'll explain all the amenities."

He gave Rifun directions to find the social workers. Although the main complex offices were in the admin building, social workers were always available in the building in the event of an emergency. Granted, it apparently wasn't more than two at a time, but it was enough.

"Good morning," one worker greeted. "Help you with something?"

This social worker was a woman about thirty-five years old or so, still had a figure, her styled hair not naturally the blond color it was at the moment. She wore glasses and a huge smile that was a little too excited for the environment.

As had become routine, Rifun just handed her the paper.

"All right," she said, still grinning. "Come over here and have a seat."

He followed her to a desk where a laptop was set up and took a seat. She tapped away on the keyboard for a moment, inputting various information from the slip. She read something on the screen, then finally looked at him.

"Okay, so, my name is Tina, and I am just one of the many social workers here at Mt. Olive. Any one of us can help you if you're short on time, but it looks like you are going to be assigned to Andrew. He's not here right now, but I can go ahead and get you started."

"Started on what?" Rifun wondered.

"Figuring out what you need, what you want, how to make the most of your time here. According to the records here, you have a high school diploma and a...license...?"

"*Un licencié ès Lettres dans architecture et ingénierie d'université de France à Versailles,*" Rifun finished. "I believe you would call it a Bachelor's in Architecture and Engineering. I also have an equivalent degree from the Architectural Association School of Architecture in London."

Tina blinked. "And you were in the army in Madagascar?"

"Yes."

She let out a breath and leaned back in her chair, expression frank. "You know, the majority of people who come through here don't even have a high school diploma, can't read, can't write, can't do math." She made a gesture at her computer. "You've got all that. You are more than qualified. How many languages do you know?"

"Malagasy is my native language, with French being close enough to native. Although I never studied it, Malagasy is somewhat mutually intelligible with Indonesian and others of that family. I also speak English, some Irish and Welsh, and a scattering of other European languages."

"So, I don't think we have to worry about putting you in a GED program. If anything, I think you could teach the program." She frowned. "Tell me about your time in the military. What was your specialty?"

Now he chuckled. "The army of Madagascar is not nearly as big as the American army. There really aren't any specialties, at least not to the degree that I understand it here. Everyone does everything." Now he frowned. "I was deployed to mainland Africa to assist American and European forces hunt down insurgents. We were ambushed and I was captured. I think it was about a year they held me, and they tortured me every night, or close enough. When I was freed and sent home, there was time still left on my contract."

"They didn't," Tina cut in.

"Mental health isn't a thing in Madagascar. Feelings don't matter in a developing nation that can't feed its people. And sometimes, those people get upset with those in power. I was put on a security detail for the president, but it was too much. I ended up switching sides, siding with the protesters. I was court-martialed and sentenced to hard labor in prison. It was after that when I left the country to pursue my education."

Lies, most of it. But again, who was going to believe that a man who looked just thirty years old had fought with Malagasy nationalist groups in both the 1920s and 1950s, or that he was a veteran of World War II?

Tina nodded, expression sympathetic. "Have you ever been evaluated for post-traumatic stress disorder?"

"I don't need a doctor to tell me I have it, but I have no desire to be on medication. Bad enough I need medication for my seizures."

Her head continued to bob. "I see that, too. And your progressing blindness, which can make things difficult."

He shifted in his seat. "I was told that I would be sent to the medical segregation. Yet here I am."

She finally stopped nodding. "The acute medical ward is honestly more of a nursing home for some of the old heads. It's also for inmates who are unable to care for themselves for whatever reason, who might be undergoing cancer treatments, wheelchair bound, things of that nature. But you, you're here, walking around, talking, you can care for yourself just fine. Epilepsy sucks, but it doesn't really impede your ability to live and work. As for the blindness, I mean, blind people can get along very well. You might need some assistance, but you don't need a nurse."

Rifun grunted and nodded. "I understand."

She shifted position and again changed topic. "It also says here that your preferred religion is pagan animism. Is that correct?"

"It is."

33

"By law, we are required to make reasonable accommodations for you. This might be iconography or setting aside a certain day or time of day for religious activities. In my experience with pagans, it tends to be different for each person, so you have to tell me what you need."

He just shook his head. "That is what I picked when given the options, but I don't know how much I believe anymore."

"Okay." Her tone and expression said she didn't quite know what to suggest. "Well, if you change your mind, just let Andrew or one of us know. Or we can introduce you to the other pagans here; I think there are one or two. Or, I mean, if you want, you can always meet with the chaplain or one of his understudies."

"I'll think about it."

He wasn't sure what to make of the meeting. It was at once a psychological exam, at once a job interview, at once a scheduling for college classes, and at once a simple conversation. Eventually he assumed it ended because she printed off a piece of paper, then wrote out a couple of familiar slips.

"For the time being, I'll start you off easy," she said. "In the morning, you'll be on chore rotation, starting in laundry. In the afternoon, you'll be working in the library." She handed over all the papers. "The slips will let them know that I am sending you there for rotation. The large paper is just for you to keep. It's a printout of your schedule, a small map there for you, and who to talk to." She wrote out a third slip. "And this pass is for you to take to the social workers in the admin building so you can get a psychological workup done, maybe see about some kind of treatment for PTSD." She added quickly, "It doesn't have to be medication. There are other therapies you can try if you want." She leaned back in her seat. "Go ahead to the admin building first and talk to them. If you're out before lunch, then head to laundry. If it's lunchtime or after lunch, go to the library and report to laundry tomorrow morning."

Rifun looked over the paper and slips. He had no idea what to make of everything. Wasn't he supposed to be in prison? Sure the barracks were a little cramped, but this was almost like going to university again. Dormitories, part-time job, courses of study, sports teams, social workers and aids. What was all this? Where was the hard labor? Where was the violence? Yes, there were officers around, but they weren't lording over him from horseback. He honestly didn't know what to do.

Well, apparently his first step was going to see the social workers in the administration building. He guessed that Tina had sent an email or called ahead because they were ready and waiting for him, and he reluctantly entered the office of the prison psychologist.

The psychologist didn't tell Rifun anything he didn't already know. He knew he had PTSD. He knew he had some manner of depression, but what new inmate didn't? He knew very well that he was stressed. No, he didn't have uncontrolled anger issues, no history of or desire to abuse drugs or alcohol. He might have been sexually frustrated in the sense that he hadn't gotten any for quite a while now, but he was no predator. If anything, he simply fit a neat little mold that the psychologist deemed satisfactory to sum up what happened to get him incarcerated: A man with no good father figure, growing up in a culture that looked down on mixed race children, desperate to prove his worth before gods and men. He tries men first, in the army, fails as he is captured, tortured, then expected to defend the same entity that abandoned him. He tries the gods next, as in the Cult of the Akari, and his devotion to the group sucked him into something just short of terrorism.

It was a perfectly logical little bundle, Rifun thought, and wholly inadequate to describe the situation. The good news, though, was that because the psychologist was able to package him in this neat bundle, he did not insist on medication dependence. He fully believed that if Rifun could come to a more rational view of the world and himself without resorting to extremes, he could be rehabilitated just fine. Having a normal, steady routine around the prison and regular counseling sessions with a group for those with military-related post-traumatic stress disorder would be a good start. He recommended medication anyway, but did not outright order it, and Rifun refused. Instead, he was given yet another slip which he was to take to the prescribed counseling group that met twice a week; the next meeting was in two days.

He didn't want to go to the group, but refusal would be considered noncompliance and he could get in trouble. He only had all of one day of good behavior time that could get wiped out, but even so, he just didn't feel any real sense of oppression. There was no torture here, and the other inmates were more likely to beat him bloody than the officers. Hell, even the officers seemed pretty hands-off compared to what he was used to.

The psychological exam had run long and he arrived in the cafeteria on the tail end of the allotted lunch time. Just like university, he grabbed a tray, got his food, and chose a table. This late, he was able to find an empty table and just look around the best he could, try to get a feel for the place. If he were intruding on anyone's territory, no one said anything about it.

Afterwards, he headed to the library. He tried to give his slip to the desk officer, but the man pointed him to the head librarian in his office across the room.

The head librarian was a large black man with short gray hair. By appearance, he might have been sixty years old or so, but Rifun knew prison had a way of aging a man. He offered up the slip. The big man took it, looked at it a moment, and muttered something resembling, "About time."

He lowered the slip, leaned on his desk, and regarded Rifun. "You know how to read?"

"In multiple languages," Rifun answered.

"You know how to count?"

"Yes."

"You know the Dewey Decimal System?"

"I might need a refresher."

The man wore an expression that said he'd been around the block more than a few times, seen it all, done it all. Rifun silently guessed that he was also probably in for life, no chance of parole, and had made this place his life. Finally he nodded and straightened. "Call me Typo."

"Rifun."

Typo indicated a cart containing about fifty or so books sitting outside his office door. "Take that cart. Make sure the books are clean, no spills or stains or tears, and especially no contraband. You find damage, bring it to me. You find contraband, take it to Jim at the desk—" He indicated the desk officer with whom Rifun had initially interacted. "—then let me know. Clean books, just put them away."

36

The head librarian then returned to whatever he'd been working on before Rifun interrupted. Rifun waited half a second more, then went out to grab the cart.

The library was a respectable size, Rifun thought, for a prison. Whoever was in charge of acquiring books at least had good taste. True, the trashy romance novels and swimsuit editions of *Sports Illustrated* were the most abused, but there was a good collection of mystery, science fiction, fantasy, and other fiction. The nonfiction section was also well-stocked with informative books and tapes on a variety of topics.

Although he knew where he was, Rifun couldn't deny that he was still a tad surprised when he opened up a book and found a small block had been cut out so someone could stash a tiny bag of white powder inside. Sighing and quietly lamenting the ruination of a perfectly good book, he turned it over to the desk officer.

He finished his task, then returned to Typo in his office. The man looked up.

"Something wrong?" he wondered. "You got a damaged book?"

"I'm done," Rifun reported, handing over three books with minor damage.

Typo leaned back in his chair, expression oddly amused yet disapproving. "You're new here, ain't you?"

"Yes, sir."

The man grinned and shook his head. "Don't fucking 'sir' me. I'm too old for that shit. How long you down for?"

"Sixty-three, parole in twenty-one."

"Well, let me give you a little advice. Punctuality is good, and good work can get you some perks. But there ain't no point in trying to hurry up and finish your work as fast as you possibly can. You ain't got no home to go back to, no wife to kiss or kids to see. There's only the fence outside. You understand me?" He rocked a little in his chair. "Of course, you also probably the first assistant I had in a while who could read and count effectively."

"All the colleges here don't teach anyone anything?" Rifun questioned.

Typo laughed. "Sure they do. But then those students get uppity about it. They'd rather spend their time reading the books, not putting them away, and they want to work jobs that are more 'constructive' and 'meaningful' and have something to do with whatever it is they studying." He waved a hand. "I don't blame 'em, though. Not really. I got no chance of getting out of here 'cept in a pine box. If they can get out of here, power to 'em."

"Then why are you here? In the library?"

The librarian laughed again. "Library's a popular spot for drug smuggling. I know you come across at least a few books, got pages cut out for drugs. Little shits come in here looking for books for their GED or whatever bullshit they claim, get a book, cut the pages for their drugs, return the book. If their buyer gets here fast enough, they can get the drugs before I get around to putting the book away. Even better if they get assigned to be the book boy."

"Why not a regular drug deal?"

"Harder to get caught. Once a book comes back, sits on that cart, can pass through any number of hands. Harder to prove whose drugs they was, can't prove who they was going to. I did that for a while. Long while. But then, I guess I got curious. Started reading the books before cutting out the pages. Started to enjoy reading. Eventually stopped dealing drugs and got more into the books. Next thing you know, I'm the head librarian."

Rifun nodded. Then, "Is it normal to give a life story upon first meeting someone here? Why tell me?"

"Not really, no. But you're a new ear for old stories, and the first one in a while to stand there and listen without making some bullshit excuse about where you got to go. And I looked at your arms. They fucked, but they clean. Your eyes and nose and lips, too. You ain't a user, and you too fast to be a dealer." Typo nodded. "First day and I like you. Long as you want to work in the library, I'll put you to work." He slid a few more books across the desk. "These came in while you were out. Put 'em away then get yourself got. Should be about suppertime, I think."

Rifun took the books, examined them there in the office, then left to put them away.

Unlike lunch, where he had been one of the last in line, Rifun was one of the first to dinner. Again he got lucky in that he chose an undisputed table, but he was very near the area where a couple of gangs were eyeing each other from their respective tables. He made a mental note of who was on which side and any identifying tattoos or scars. One gang seemed to favor a symbol that was like a spiral within a starburst. The other had some variation of a human skull but with bull's horns.

After dinner—which had an officer overseeing the return of food trays and all utensils—was, essentially, free time. A fair number of men made for the baseball field. Others headed to the recreational building. Rifun followed them, if only to better familiarize himself with the building and its "amenities." He found himself observing the various activities in the gymnasium: lifting weights, boxing, basketball, volleyball, even dodgeball. He made his way into the weights area, which was fenced off in order to contain any fifty pound frisbees, and helped himself to a bench press. He could feel eyes on him and tried not to react.

"You new here, peanut?" someone finally asked, walking up to him.

Rifun placed the bar back on the hold and sat up. "Excuse me?"

"You're new here, peanut." The man was a skinny Hispanic with tattoos on his face and hands. "You don't know the rules."

"And I presume you are about to inform me of them."

"It's our turn to use the weights, peanut. You see us?" He gestured around to the others. They were about fifteen in number, all Hispanic, most of them skinny and shorter than Rifun. Most had face and hand tattoos, though he couldn't say which symbol identified the gang. "We're Pinto Gang. You're not. We only give peanuts one warning, so here it is. Now get out."

"I'm guessing this is a closed-membership gang," Rifun said, knowing he was pressing his luck.

"You want to join up with the niggers, they're here tomorrow. Skinheads, day after that. Now get out."

There was no reason Rifun couldn't have beaten them all. He only needed to Band himself, make it so he was moving on a faster plane of Time than the rest of them, and then freely pulverize them. But he judged it in his best interest to not pick fights on his first day. He glanced over the gang, dipped his head graciously, and bowed out of the weights area.

"Stay out of our way, peanut, if you know what's good for you," the lead man warned to his back.

There was the prison violence Rifun had been waiting for. He was almost relieved. For a moment he had been worried that prison might actually be a semi-pleasant place to be.

He elected to head back to his block a little early, take a shower, and maybe get into his bunk before his new cellmate got back.

As expected, the showers were in an open layout, although there were paper-thin accordion screens at about waist height that could be utilized for some modicum of public decency; only about a third of the patrons utilized these screens, most of them scared eighteen to twenty year old kids. The toilets were the same way.

Afterwards, Rifun returned to his cell and sat down. Immediately he considered that maybe he should have grabbed a book from the library to read. He'd no sooner thought this than movement caught his eye and he looked up to see another man entering the cell.

He was a big guy, probably six-foot-six, two hundred seventy pounds, white with brown hair, wearing glasses. Rifun had a vague recollection that he had glimpsed this man heading off with the group intent on the baseball field. The sweat on his shirt and general body odor indicated that he had been doing some kind of physical activity anyway.

"Hey, new cellie!" The man's voice was far too loud for the size of the room. "Call me Bacon! Or Frank, if you want. I don't care!"

"Rifun," Rifun introduced.

"Where you coming from? Don't think I've seen you around."

"New here."

"Yeah?" Frank held out a hand. "Gimme your papers, lemme see."

Rifun didn't really want to, but it might be better than having a conversation with a loudspeaker. He opened up his tub and handed the papers. Frank took them in his massive hands.

"Shit, man, you got mercy," Frank observed with a whistle. "Good for you. Let me guess, your girl was going to leave you or you were going to leave her, the argument got heated, you took off with your kid, she called the cops, they caught up to you, there was a little misunderstanding, gun went off, officer gets hurt, trial goes to shit because she's crying on the stand like the bitch she is."

Rifun raised a brow. "Not even close."

Frank mirrored his expression. "No?"

"No."

Frank handed the papers back. "I don't believe you. If there's a kid, there's a woman."

"Wasn't my kid." Although there was a woman involved. "Not your business."

Frank shrugged casually and put his hands up. "I get it. You're new, still salty, still trying to find your place, figure out what to do with yourself for the next two dimes. You don't want to tell, that's cool. Give it a nickel and it won't matter. You're stuck here."

Rifun knew that in his head of course, but it wasn't until the next day when he was put to work in laundry did it really start to sink in. If Julianna came after him, he was dead. The end. But until that happened, he was stuck.

Lunch, doing some work at the library, a little free time before and after dinner, then lights out. Next morning, breakfast, working in laundry, lunch, working in the library, dinner, then the support group he'd been assigned to.

There were nine of them in the group plus the group leader who was also an inmate but had successfully completed some training course and now worked under the social workers.

To Rifun's surprise, another one of the group members had also effectively been a POW and had experienced torture. He'd been captured by insurgents in Iraq and tortured for information about a nearby military base. His captivity had only lasted two weeks before the U.S. Army blew the hell out of the compound where he'd been held, but the scars were still very evident, including a missing nose and ear.

The group was currently in the middle of a "processing unit" on self-reflection, what they saw when they looked in the mirror compared to what everyone else saw. The group homework, per se, that they had to complete before the next session in three days was to actually look in a mirror and contemplate what they felt was missing from the reflection. What did they expect to see that wasn't showing up?

Rifun had never given it much thought, but the idea was in his mind that evening as he took a shower before bed. He'd spent plenty of time in front of a mirror in the years following his ordeal, staring at the scars that mangled his body. He'd had his Akari abilities back then, and he had used an ability called Disguise—which was manipulating the DNA of an organism—and tried to change things, to either make it go away, cover it up, or just see what he might have looked like if he had inherited more French genes from his rapist biological father or more Betsileo genes from his Malagasy mother.

Disguises could be made permanent, though it was a very lengthy and painful process. Mostly, though, they were just tricks of the eye that resolved themselves after a few hours as the body dissolved it through natural processes. The body knew the DNA it was supposed to have, saw that something had changed, and slowly worked to correct it.

As he stood there shaving with a dull, single blade razor, he decided that he didn't know what he expected to see in the mirror. When he was a child and young man, being beaten by his stepfather or scrutinized by his countrymen, he supposed he expected to see his European genes. When he'd spent years praying desperately for the ancestors to cure him of his genetic taint, he'd expected to see his Betsileo genes. After being freed from French torture, he'd expected to see catastrophically mutilating scars. None of those things had ever manifested.

He finished up what he was slowly establishing as his routine, then returned to his bunk. Frank wandered in after a few minutes, greeting Rifun and everyone within three blocks, then ambled away to shower off the baseball practice.

"You should join us!" Frank declared when he returned, still shaking his head and flinging water droplets everywhere. "You're a fit guy, I bet you could hit a homer no problem!"

"I don't have the eyesight for it," Rifun replied.

"Hm." Frank frowned. "By the time you got glasses—wait time is eight months to a year, depending on how much they like you—it'd be next season. Well, maybe try out then!"

Rifun didn't bother correcting him. Glasses would be his excuse for this year, and blindness the next. He still didn't know what he was going to do when that happened.

Maybe Julianna was waiting for him to go completely blind before coming after him. Just let his body deteriorate as much as possible on its own, spend her time and resources elsewhere, and then pick him off as an afterthought. He swung his legs up into bed, unsettled by the thought.

He was still disturbed by the thought the following morning, and it plagued him for several days. The good and bad news was that his chores afforded him plenty of quiet time to think. Standing in the library one afternoon, a week after being released from the Fishbowl, he found himself staring at a page in a book, but not really reading. At the moment, he was saddened by the thought that these little ink marks on the page would one day be lost to him.

Would he dare risk the brain surgery the doctor had mentioned? He recalled numerous opportunities when he could have theoretically healed himself using the Akari, or had another Akari-bearer heal him. He'd always put it off. Too busy, too risky, too busy, too risky. Sure, the Akari could do medical wonders as it reshaped Matter, but the brain was a very delicate thing. Maybe if he'd just done it, he wouldn't be in this predicament. At this point, he should salvage what he could; there was no reason he could think of that it couldn't progress into other parts of his brain once it was finished with his eyesight. At least if he halted the progression here, he could still see to go about his daily life and write letters to Lalao. He wouldn't be playing baseball, but it would be far and away the better chance of surviving prison. And if Julianna did send someone after him, eyesight would be a good thing to have.

Rifun continued pushing his book cart up and down the rows, replacing books. He would have to see about that surgery. The only trajectory he was on right now was downward. The operating table posed no greater risk to him than waiting for Julianna or her hitmen to come for him.

He finished his work and found himself with a couple hours before dinner. In spite of his courage to undergo said surgery, he did not go to the clinic or the hospital to the discuss the situation. He would think about it for a few more days, maybe ask around and see how skilled the surgeons actually were here.

Instead, he headed out of the library down the hall to the gym. The Hispanic gangs had the weights area again. He'd discovered that one black gang was tolerant of his presence because he was from Africa while the rest were murderously insulted. White gangs were more mixed, and he had to catch the right one at the right time to be let in. Some were utterly appalled by his being a "mudshark" and refused him entry, while others thought it was only right that his biological French father had raped his nigger mother and spread good genes into that pool and let him into the area. According to some more neutral parties, it was uncommon for one gang or another to not have claim over the weights area at any given time, and even rarer that whoever was in the area didn't actually care who or what he was. If he wanted guaranteed access, he would probably have to join a gang, a prospect he refused to entertain.

In the end, he elected to head to the basketball court. One half of the court was involved in a pickup game while the other was occupied by those who just wanted to idle away their time.

"Mind if I join?" Rifun inquired. There were four men bouncing balls around and occasionally shooting.

"By all means," one said, vaguely indicating the bin of basketballs.

Dinner was unremarkable except for some side glances from a few of the gangs. Rifun had chosen a seat farther away to distance himself from any accidental affiliation, but he could feel their eyes. What would happen if the black gangs found out he sometimes worked out with the white gangs, and if the white gangs found out he sometimes worked out with the black gangs? They weren't going to get along, and he had a suspicion that he was going to get caught in the middle.

He stabbed at his macaroni and cheese. Why couldn't he have inherited more Malagasy genes? Even if it was just the ones for darker skin and hair, at least that might resolve some of the confusion and let him be able to choose a side. "Too light to be Malgache," his French captors had remarked on more than one occasion. "Too dark to be French."

He finished his meal and decided to head back to his block for an early shower; maybe he'd get a little peace and quiet for a bit and not have to listen to Frank right away.

The showers were empty when he arrived, and he breathed a sigh of relief. He undressed, picked a shower, and turned on the water. He didn't bother with the privacy screen; it wasn't as though anyone here didn't know what a cock or an ass looked like.

He was just finished rinsing his waist-length hair when he heard movement behind him. He didn't think much of it until he felt the water stop, despite the faucet still running. He knew the feel of an Akari Band; it was much lighter than a regular Time Band, easier to manipulate. He was moving on a faster plane of Time than the rest of the complex. Then he heard the voice.

"Faharoa."

Faharoa. His title when he led the Cult of the Akari, later called the First Order of the Akari. And the voice belonged to none other than Drinjin uh Ersik, one of his top generals.

Drinjin uh Ersik hailed from the planet Ardo. The Ardans were big and beefy, humanoid in that he had two arms and two legs, but weighing two or three times a human of the same height and general bulk, although they tended to be much larger.

With him was Torbak Martin, a Bardin from the planet Bari, and also one of Rifun's top generals once upon a time. He was shorter than Rifun, almost human in his general shape, but with a face that looked like he had an unfortunate run-in with a rock slide. His skin was a nearly luminescent green, almost yellow, and entirely unflattering.

Rifun faced them, dauntless.

"Well," he said. "At least she does me the honor of sending you."

And that was the last thing he remembered.

Date	Location
March 13, 2016	Cellblock F, Showers

Incident Type	Responding Officer
Violence - Great Bodily Harm	Potter, K.

Inmates Involved	Officers Involved	Staff Involved
981436	Potter, K.	Renard, M.
948221	Waterson, W.	Witkowski, L.
934328	Mitchell, D.	Arins, F.
	Nimms, E.	

Report

At 1856, Officer Potter (desk officer, Cellblock F) was alerted by inmate 948221 that there was a medical emergency in the showers. Officer Potter responded to the area to find inmate 934328 giving CPR to 981436. 981436 was initially reported to have been deceased as he had been badly beaten and, when found by inmate 934328, had no pulse and was not breathing.

Officer Potter radioed for backup and for an emergency medical response from the hospital. He directed first incoming officer to grab the AED from the office.

At 1901, Officers Waterson, Mitchell, and Nimms arrived to clear the scene and prepare for arrival of medical personnel. By this time, Officer Potter had removed 981436 from the shower area and was continuing CPR on rotation with 934328 and 948221. Incoming officers cleared the inmates from the area and took up CPR rotation. Officer Waterson retrieved the AED from the office.

At 1902, Doctor Renard, Nurse Witkowski, and Nurse Arins arrived on scene with a medical bag and gurney. Officers Potter, Waterson, Mitchell, and Nimms were continuing to give CPR to no noticeable effect. A monitor was attached to 981436 (note: difficult due to skin abnormalities) and Nurse Arins started an IV. 981436 was still not breathing; Officer Potter expressed a concern that because of facial trauma, including a broken jaw, 981436 did not have a patent airway. The broken jaw prevented the use of a cervical collar, but a pillow was used to stabilize the neck. A backboard was also utilized.

At 1915, after further CPR efforts and corrective shocks from the monitor, 981436 experienced spontaneous return of function. 981436 immediately went into seizure. Doctor Renard, Nurse Witkowski, and Nurse Arins continued their work while directing Officers Potter, Waterson, Mitchell, and Nimms to place 981436 on the backboard on the gurney.

At 1919, 981436 was removed from Cellblock F and taken to the hospital for treatment.

***

The building was immediately locked down so an investigation could be conducted. Officer Waterson and Officer Potter led a crime scene investigation looking for physical evidence while Officer Nimms and Captain Mann reviewed camera footage.

No physical evidence was found in the showers, and no conclusive evidence was able to be pulled from cameras. Footage shows 981436 entering the showers at 1830 in no apparent distress. The footage continues normally until 1854 when he suddenly appears on the ground in the state in which he was found only a few minutes later. Based on preliminary investigation and available evidence, crime scene investigators and hospital personnel estimate that such gross wounds would have taken at least two to five minutes to be inflicted depending on the number of assailants. Officer Potter denies seeing anyone enter Cellblock F between the time 981436 entered and when 948221 and 934328 entered and subsequently discovered the scene.

Lockdown was released at 0315 on March 14, 2016 with no suspects in custody. The investigation remains open. 981436 is reportedly still in surgery.

Reporting Officer
Nimms, E.

Date of Incident	Date Reporting
March 13, 2016	March 14, 2016

Location

General Population - Cellblock F - Showers

Report

At 1857 on March 13, 2016, Officer Potter reported a potentially deceased inmate in the showers in Cellblock F of the general population barracks. CPR was reported to be in progress. Doctor Renard, Nurse Witkowski, and Nurse Arins responded to the call.

At 1902, Renard, Witkowski, and Arins arrived on scene to find Officers Potter, Waterson, Mitchell, and Nimms giving CPR to the pt. They had attempted to attach an AED, however, extensive scarring and skin abnormalities made it difficult for the pads to stick. It was reported that when the pt was found, he was not breathing and did not have a pulse.

A monitor was attached to the pt where it was confirmed that he did not have a pulse. Dr. Renard made the decision to engage manual override on the monitor.

The pt had obviously suffered extensive facial trauma including a broken jaw, which made it impossible to use a C-collar or intubate normally. Dr. Renard inserted a tracheotomy. After suctioning the pt's airway, he attached O2 at 3 L. Nurse Witkowski utilized a pillow to stabilize the neck in lieu of a C-collar. Nurse Arins started an IV in the left arm. Officers continued rotating on CPR.

At 1912, Dr. Renard directed Nurse Witkowski to deliver .5 mg of epinephrine.

At 1915, Dr. Renard delivered a manual shock to the pt to no effect. After another CPR rotation, he delivered a second manual shock. Pt experienced ROSC and immediately went into seizure. Pt has known occipital epilepsy. Pt's heart stopped again and Doctor Renard delivered another 0.5 mg of epinephrine. After another rotation of CPR, his heart started again as did another seizure. The decision was made to quickly load the patient on a backboard onto the gurney and take him to the hospital.

Vitals 1

HR: 232 bpm
BP: 80/43
O2: 3 L/min
Temp: N/A
Time: 1919
PA: FA

Vitals 2

HR: 189 bpm
BP: 65/30
O2: 3 L/min
Temp: N/A
Time: 1933
PA: FA

Vitals 3

HR: 58 bpm
BP: 110/75
O2: 2 L/min
Temp: 35.2C
Time: 1641 (3/14)
PA: FA

Field Drugs

Epinepherine
0.5mg 1912
Epinepherine
0.5mg 1915
Ativan 2mg 1925

At 1925, patient arrived at the hospital. He continued to experience seizures and cardiac arrest. Dr. Snyder administered 2 mg of Ativan to stop the seizures.

At 1931, pt was admitted into emergency surgery for extensive head and brain trauma. It was determined that he was most likely attacked either with fists or a large blunt object. There were multiple skull fractures and extensive swelling in the brain in all lobes. Pt also suffered fractures to his spine at the C4, T2, T5, T6, T7, T14, and L1. Pt's pelvis was also fractured in multiple places. Pt suffered a compound fracture in both femurs and a punctured left lung. Examination also revealed eleven stab wounds to the chest and abdomen. Additional injuries include a fractured mandible, fractured orbitals, broken nose, nine broken ribs, five broken fingers, and damage to existing rods and screws in the lower right arm. An inch wide piece was also cut from the top of the pt's left ear. It may also be pertinent for investigators to note that the pt was reported as typically having waist-length hair, although most of it appeared to have been violently ripped out of the scalp. All remaining hair was shaved off in surgery to grant surgical access.

At 1640 on March 14, 2016, Dr. Snyder made the call to place the pt in a medically-induced coma for a minimum of four weeks in hopes that will allow the pt's brain to heal.

Reporting Physician
Arins F., PA

Three
Wake

He didn't think he was supposed to be alive, but he couldn't remember why he thought that. The pain felt right for the situation, but he wasn't sure why.

Opening his eyes to darkness, fear initially seized him. That's right. He was in Madagascar, in a prison near Tana. He had been one of the last holdouts, holed up in the university at Fianar with Radaoroson and Lehoaha. The French had been pressing on them for months, and finally, they broke. Scattered into the forests. He had been found and captured, ultimately sentenced to death. But torture was worse than death. How he longed for something so sweet as death! Even if he were condemned to be a moth, a lonely, forgotten soul, surely it would be better than the burning, the waterboarding, the electrocution, the flogging, the—

Something touch his eyelid, forced his eye open. He mentally recoiled although he was physically restrained. His chest tightened. They'd always left his face. They wanted him to look in the mirror and pretend it never happened. Apparently they'd tired of that thought, and now they were going to gouge out his eyes. He waited for a hot metal poker, heart pounding madly, but none came. He dared not relax, however, as something touched his other eye, forced it open.

The first thing that started to poke holes in his fear was a mechanical beeping that he was suddenly aware of. It didn't sound like a radio noise, or like the occasional tick and pop from the battery that powered the electrocution torture. The second thing that mixed confusion with his fear were the voices, one coming from right before him, whoever was touching his eyes. They weren't speaking French. He didn't know what language they were speaking, but it wasn't French.

No hot metal poker came for his eyes, but his relief over that was still overpowered by the dread he felt at the restraints.

More voices, more words he didn't understand. Then there was more noise and the voices stopped. He didn't know. He didn't understand. He couldn't see! Why couldn't he see? He was fairly certain that when he'd gone to sleep—or whatever he'd been doing—he had been able to see. What had changed?

He wanted to move. Couldn't. Almost didn't dare as he felt himself moving involuntarily, as if someone were picking him up and spinning him around. Nausea bubbled up in his brain and his stomach. He closed his eyes as if it might help, but it didn't. Then the spinning stopped and he was leaning back, his head lower than his heart. After a moment, whoever was controlling all of this put him back to rights, or lying down anyway.

He figured he must have slept on and off, though he could not say for how long. Fitful unconsciousness was occasionally punctuated by someone touching his face or other odd areas of his body. He still waited for the burns, the knives, something, but the worst that happened was a tap on the bottom of a few of his toes. What was the doctor looking for?

Doctor? How did he know that was a doctor?

There were more voices, still a language he did not recognize.

Then, a language he did recognize.

"Vous m'entendez?"

He knew the language. Could almost place it. But he found he couldn't quite run over the words in his head. He needed to hear them again.

"Monsieur?"

French. That was it. He knew it was French.

"Monsieur," the voice repeated. *"Vous m'entendez?"*

He blinked. He knew it was French. Or he thought it was. It certainly sounded familiar. This person was asking...asking...

He wanted to know if he could hear him.

More voices, a language he didn't know.

"Vous. Me. Entendez."

He could, yes. Now, how did he go about letting him know? He moved his tongue inside his mouth. He swallowed. He heard more voices, but he couldn't give up yet.

"Mm," he managed, a hum of the lips. Yes, that was right. That sounded better.

"Vous m'entendez?" the voice asked again. The accent was not Malagasy French, but neither was it Parisian French.

"Mm," he repeated.

"Comment vous appelez-vous?"

What? Why change it? What was he saying now? He was fairly certain it was still French. He remembered *vous* at least. *Comment...* His name. This person was asking his name.

No. He couldn't answer. He knew how that went. If he gave his legal name, he would be punished for a bastard. If he gave his true name, he would be punished for a liar.

Problem was, he couldn't actually recall either right now.

"Comment vous appelez-vous?" the person repeated. After a moment, *"Vous m'entendez?"*

"Mm," he replied.

They went back and forth for some time, the French speaker interrupted occasionally by someone else speaking the new language. Then, after a while, both strangers left.

He wanted to think about what just happened, the words that had been spoken. But somehow, he couldn't remember what had been said. He knew it had been French, but what had the person said? It was like turning over an empty box, expecting something to fall out, knowing there should be something there. He knew it was French, but what did that even mean?

Rifun did not sleep well that night, but his first thought upon waking was that he remembered his name. Of course, how could he have forgotten it? His second thought was wondering why his head felt both heavy and yet lighter than air. He couldn't tell if he was lying down or standing up or hanging upside down, as his brain seemed to think he was in all three positions at once.

Voices again. One a strange language, the other French.

"Bonjour," the French speaker greeted. He knew it was a greeting of some form.

"Mm," Rifun replied.

"Vous m'entendez."

"Mm."

"Comment vous appelez-vous?"

"Mm...ooh," Rifun stumbled, finally opening his mouth. Yes, he could make more sounds, though there was some pain in his face from doing so. Now if only he could figure out what to say. If only there were something in the box he could use.

"Ah, non. Comment vous appelez-vous?" Each word, every sound, was said deliberately.

"Mm...mm...moo....oom. Moo...oon." That was a good sound.

"Parlez-vous français?"

Rifun just blinked. More new words, more new sounds. This speaker was demanding more words, but Rifun wasn't sure he was storing the ones he was figuring out. The speaker wanted...to know if he could speak French. Of course he could.

"Mm...oo..." What was the next bit? "Oo..." There was more to it than that he knew. "Oo...ii..." That sounded right.

"Oui. Le mot est 'oui'."

"Oo...ii. Ooii. *Oui.*"

"Oui! Tiguidou. Et présentement, c'est le temps pour le déjeuner."

Rifun still could not keep up with how fast the person was talking, but then he was suddenly confronted with the taste of food in his mouth. Yet there was no food. What was this? What was going on? He felt something being pressed against his lips. Cautiously, he opened his mouth. The taste vanished but at the same time his nose was inundated with the smell of hot oatmeal.

He wasn't entirely sure which way was up, but he was able to eat and swallow. As soon as the food reached his stomach, he was overcome with a ravenous hunger. Somehow, he knew he hadn't been eating much lately. He finished the breakfast in its entirety, which was apparently big news to the doctors and signaled something very good.

After breakfast, he got a visitor. There was some dialogue in the strange language, but eventually the interpreter began to speak.

"Mr. Ndolo. My name is Jim Peters. I'm the chief administrator here, what you probably call the warden."

That was a lot of long words, and Rifun couldn't put them all together so quickly. Nor could he articulate this to the interpreter even as he continued speaking.

"Do you know what the hell happened to you in the showers?"

What happened? In the shower? As far as he knew, people bathed in the shower, washed body and hair. Was this man asking if he had cleaned himself lately? Were there repercussions if he hadn't? He didn't understand, but he could not communicate even that.

Eventually the man, the warden, left, saying more things to the interpreter and the doctors.

Gradually, over the course of the next week or so, Rifun got used to a routine and began to sort some things out as his memory pieced itself, imperfectly, back together.

He was in prison. He knew Julianna had attacked him. That attack had caused damage to all areas of his brain, though the extent and longevity of this damage was yet to be fully determined.

He had already been losing his sight on account of epilepsy. This attack merely accelerated that blindness in an unconventional way. But, as such, any brain damage relating to visual input could not be evaluated, for better or worse.

His sense of taste and sense of smell appear to have flip-flopped in his brain. He could not smell food when it was outside his mouth, but he could "taste" it to a high, if still limited, degree. Similarly, he could not taste food while it was in his mouth, but he could "smell" it.

He was reportedly once proficient enough in English as to be considered fluent—and he did basically remember learning English while in the army— but he had no knowledge of the language now. Nor the Irish, Welsh, or scattering of other European languages he had apparently professed. Malagasy remained well in tact, and French was slow to worm its way through his brain as he struggled to put words, grammar, and concepts together like a first-year French student.

He was frequently and often suddenly disoriented, being subjected to massive waves of vertigo even though he still was not physically moving on account of casts, braces, and other measures designed to keep his body immobile while it healed. This immobility also made it difficult or impossible to assess any physical deficits resulting from massive head trauma.

"Touchez votre nez avec votre main gauche."

It was a social worker who happened to be originally from Quebec who was acting as an interpreter.

Rifun sorted through the words until he could piece together what the doctor was asking. Touch his nose with his left hand. He knew what he had to do. He knew what it took. Somehow he just couldn't find the right muscles to get his hand to move. He could move his shoulder reasonably well, considering the back brace, but it was like there was a disconnect between his elbow and his hand. He could get some muscles in his hand to move, as for his fingers; he just didn't know how, and he certainly couldn't coordinate them.

"Si sa main droit?"

Right hand, then. He could feel that arm very well, if not for the cast, then certainly the rods and screws. Slowly he managed to bend his elbow and bring his hand up generally to his face.

"Bien. Relachez votre bras."

He let his arm down.

It was the best he could physically do until the casts and braces started coming off. The arm was easy enough, but the spine, the pelvis, the femurs, those were a little different. They needed a little more time.

In the meantime, another doctor started to visit. He was some kind of cognitive speech specialist. He only knew English, but he was confident that he could still apply the same techniques to help Rifun essentially re-learn his French and get through it a little faster. And maybe he could tease out a little English as well.

Four days into this speech therapy, he got yet another visitor.

"All right, Mr. Ndolo, I'm told that you're starting to speak and remember," the interpreter interlocuted. "Now then, what do you remember about your attack?"

"Who are you?" Rifun wondered.

"I'm the warden. Jim Peters. We spoke a couple weeks ago."

He recalled being asked about the attack, but he didn't remember the warden.

"What do you remember?" the man repeated.

Rifun knew he couldn't tell the warden about Julianna. It would take too long to explain. And he certainly couldn't explain the existence or presence of alien species, even if he couldn't recall the names of those species or the individuals. As for the incident itself, he truly had no memory of it.

"I showered," he said slowly, picking out his words. "I was alone. I turned around—"

"And whom did you see?" the warden pressed.

"I don't know. I don't remember. Truly I don't. I'm sorry."

A nearby doctor said something to the warden, and the interpreter also jumped in. After a moment of unintelligible conversation, the interpreter began interpreting.

"We're coming to suspect that he has difficulty remembering people who don't speak either Malagasy or French. Even though Cam is here to interpret, and he does certainly hear your voice, he can't make those connections right away between your voice and you as a person, someone to remember. It takes repetitive interactions in order for him to remember you."

"Because I'm speaking English."

"Yes. Part of his ability to commit people to memory is somehow filtered through what language they speak, which makes sense given his, well, previous linguistic abilities. He categorizes people based on what language he has to use when talking to them. Since English seems to be out the door for the moment, he's not making those memories and commitments the way he used to."

This explanation did not please the warden, but at least it was an explanation, one Rifun contemplated that night after lights out.

His memory was altered, some pieces missing entirely. His brain had been injured and rewired in ways he didn't like. He was still stuck in these infernal casts. He had some notion of something called a Band, and it related to Time in some fashion. It was something helpful, something he could use to help himself heal, even in a limited sense. He could reflect on past events, past people, and he could recognize those people and events, knew that he had been there participating, but it felt fragmented, disconnected. There was something he couldn't quite grasp.

He knew of a place called the Wheel of Time. He had head knowledge that it was the hub of the Time industry and it was located at the place where all black holes converge. He knew about the buying and selling of Time, whole lives stripped from the dead to be given to those who could afford it, who wanted to extend their own lives. He knew for a fact that he had, at one time, brought an army to bear against that place and taken it over successfully. He knew for a fact that he had later been deposed. But it was the difference between reading an encyclopedia article and actually visiting a place, the true, physical experience. He couldn't engage himself in the memories, bring himself to feel joyous triumph over the victory, anger or despair over the ensuing defeat. He couldn't muster up any sort of fear or worry on account of the fighting. It was all removed from him, which caused all manner of frustration in the present moment. He wanted to know. He wanted to feel. He wanted to remember.

Staring into his blind darkness, feeling the air from the hospital ventilation system, Rifun tried to bring anything to mind, some image or visual. There was nothing. It was as though he had been born blind and never had the privilege to glimpse anything and so form a mental picture. But he knew that wasn't true. Probably just another side effect of all the new intrusions into his brain, to say nothing of the seizures.

Despite the doctors' best efforts at removing all foreign matter from his brain and intracranial cavity, as well as the surgery to contain his seizures, he was still having seizures. He knew they had been bad before, but being restrained while his body desired to tear itself apart was somehow even worse, and he was too grateful for the reprieve of sleep, even if it was dreamless.

The following morning, he had another visitor, one who was not a doctor and whom he had not requested. It was one of the chaplain understudies, a civilian contractor.

"Hello, Rifun," he greeted, speaking through the interpreter. "How are you feeling this week?"

"Have we met?" Rifun wondered.

"My name is Jeremy Long. I've been by almost weekly since your accident. The first time I visited after you were brought out of a coma, you couldn't talk at all. The second and third time, you still weren't really talking well. Last week was the first time we could converse but we didn't get through much more than introductions before you started to not feel well."

He might have remembered? A little bit?

"Chaplain understudy," Rifun stated, thinking slowly. "Aren't the chaplains Christian?"

"Usually, yes. I am. But I am Navajo and incorporate some of my ancestral beliefs and practices, too."

"Navajo."

"Yes."

There was something he wanted to ask regarding that, but he couldn't quite think of what. It had to do with Time, but that was equally out of reach right now.

"I understand that you declared yourself as a pagan animist," the chaplain went on, unfazed, "but I still thought it important to let you know that someone was still on your side as it were, praying for you and your recovery."

"Oh. Thank you." He didn't know what to make of that, but then the man was moving on to a different topic. Rifun struggled to keep track of the conversation.

"The doctors say you're doing well. Your body is healing; they expect you should start losing some of these heavier casts soon. What do you think?"

"I think I would like to walk again."

The man laughed. "I can understand that."

"You're Navajo."

"That's right, straight from the desert of Arizona."

Rifun didn't know where that was, didn't know if he'd ever known that information. "Why are you here?"

"Oh, well, I started my degree at home. Then I kind of fell out of favor with my family and the local tribe, so I started looking for opportunities to escape as it were, and I found this. Still going to school and working under the chaplain."

"What color are your eyes?" He didn't know why, but that seemed like an important question to ask.

"Um, brown. Why?"

"Do you know anyone with gold eyes?"

Rifun couldn't bring either of those colors to mind, but he knew that one was important, when it came to eye color.

"Can't say that I do. Should I?"

"I don't know. Seems like something...a critic would say."

The understudy and the chaplain murmured back and forth a moment, tones puzzled.

"Critic?" the interpreter inquired, speaking as himself. "Is that the word you want? Is there a Malagasy slang term I'm not familiar with?"

"I don't know," Rifun admitted. "It has to do with him. Or, his people. Or, someone..." He huffed in frustration. "I don't remember."

Someone new entered the room. Rifun recognized the voice, but it wasn't until the interpreter said that it was the speech therapist was he able to put the two together.

Was that really how he had done it? Was that how he'd remembered people when he met them? Was it really based on their language? Or was there more to it but it had all been stripped away? Somewhere, in the recesses of his mind, locked behind thickets of impenetrable damage, he knew there was supposed to be a way he could find out for himself. He'd had conversations about it before, regarding his seizures. He had the feeling of a wall, that whatever this was that he couldn't remember, he was very resistant to it.

And now, the best he could do was a speech doctor.

"Listen, my time here is limited," the interpreter said abruptly. Rifun wasn't sure who had spoken. "Chaplain's got me on kind of a short leash. Do you mind if I pray over you before I go?"

Rifun had never been fond of Christians or Christianity. Catholics and Jesuits had beaten him in school, to say nothing of the national occupation. But before he could answer one way or the other, Jeremy was already speaking, the interpreter faithfully interpreting. Then the understudy departed, not even waiting for a thank you.

Thus began his session with the speech doctor. The man seemed very confident that all of Rifun's knowledge remained in tact—linguistically speaking—he just needed to be able to access it. When it came to such extensive brain damage, time was of the essence. Everything was very malleable right now, new connections being made in order to compensate for what had been lost. Now was the time to exert heavy influence over that healing.

The majority of the session was spent working out his French. He was given objects and asked to identify them, describe them. He was asked to repeat certain sounds or verbal patterns. He didn't know how much it was helping. He felt ridiculous. Then he was given what he thought was a great amount of information at one time and then asked questions about it. He would think about it later and slowly realize that the "great amount of information" usually wasn't more than four or five sentences in a row. He should be able to handle that, shouldn't he? He knew he'd done it before. He must have, if he'd led armies into battle. Why couldn't he do it now?

"I think what would really help," the doctor said through the interpreter, "like learning a new language from scratch, is simply...usage. Lucky for you, you have a conversation partner right here."

The interpreter did his duty, then said something to the doctor. They exchanged some words Rifun did not understand.

"Let's move on to English," the interpreter told him finally, translating the doctor's words. "Do you remember the word for 'Bonjour'?"

It sounded as good a place as any to start, Rifun thought. It was always good to be friendly and polite when speaking to other people in a foreign language. The way the interpreter said it, though, made it sound like they'd had this discussion before. Had they told him that word before?

"I'll give you a hint," the interpreter jumped in, speaking of his own volition. "You might say something very similar when you answer the phone."

Well, that didn't help at all.

The doctor sighed.

"*'Allo,'*" the interpreter said. "And the English word is 'Hello.'"

Allo. Hello. Rifun was made to repeat both words multiple times, speaking to both the interpreter and the doctor, being sure to enunciate the various sounds.

"Do you remember the word for *'S'il vous plait'*?" the interpreter asked, his tone suggesting wavering hope.

"Rather," Rifun blurted. He didn't know where the word came from or what it meant. He wasn't sure it was the word they were looking for, but maybe he would get lucky.

"No, but good guess. The word is 'Please.'"

Again, he was made to repeat the word several times and enunciate the various sounds. He did this for more useful words like "Yes," "No," "Goodbye," and "Help."

"Your pronunciation is improving, in both French and English," the doctor informed him. "We just need to figure out a way to get the English words to stick. I think that once that ball gets rolling, it will start to really come back to you. And that would make things much easier on everyone."

Himself most of all, Rifun thought. If he could just figure out what the doctors were saying, what the warden was saying, what the chaplain was saying, what the interpreter was saying, things would be a lot easier. If he could handle more than one or two sentences of information at a time, that would make things easier. If he could just heal his brain back to the way it was supposed to be, before he'd been injured in the first place with that damn pickax, things would be much, much easier.

He had a notion that such healing was possible, in theory. He just hadn't been confident enough either in himself or anyone else to do it. Was it their ability, or their motives? He had a feeling that it had been both, depending on the person. Some he knew were capable, but he didn't trust them not to kill him out of spite. Others he knew were loyal, but he also knew they lacked the ability. And he had been either unable or unwilling to try it himself.

There was more to it than that, but he found himself wondering how much might be different if he had gone through with it. Given the state of things now, it couldn't have been any worse. It had already killed him, and he was in worse shape now than he had ever been. If he could figure out what piece of the puzzle he was missing, whether it was a person or an ability or something else he could not recall, he might just decide to go through with it next time he had the chance.

Despite the confidence from the chaplain understudy and the doctors, Rifun was not able to get the heavy casts and braces off until late the following week. His pelvis was still fragile so he couldn't walk, but he could sit up and had limited mobility in his back and neck. His first time sitting up, he was immediately light-headed and felt as though he'd been flipped upside down. It was nearly an hour before his head righted itself enough that he could try again. This time, although he felt inexplicably tall, as if he could reach up and touch the ceiling and was, if he had his sight, looking far down upon everyone else in the room, he at least felt upright. A minute later, that feeling of being either very tall or else hovering over everyone else also faded.

To put it simply, his back hurt, and he wasn't sure if it was from the injuries or disuse. He needed every muscle in his back and abdomen just to keep himself upright, but it was hard. It hurt. He hurt. But he was not permitted a reprieve until the doctors got their notes.

"Hold both arms out front," they ordered, still speaking through Cameron the interpreter.

Other than losing almost half his body weight and doing basically nothing for a period of several months, Rifun had no trouble with this in his right arm. His left was a slightly different story. He could move the shoulder and get his arm basically up, and he could move his hand at the wrist, but there was still a kind of disconnect between his elbow and his wrist. When he went to use his right arm to position it manually, it was almost as if he couldn't locate his arm, despite knowing where it was supposed to have been. Finally he had to start at his shoulder and work his way down to find his uncooperative arm. From there he could use his right hand to put his left arm in the proper position, and it would stay there, but he could not make it go there on its own. He had similar problems with his left pinkie and ring fingers.

"How does that work?" he wondered.

"Well, everyone knows about the work the spinal cord does," one doctor answered. "What's going on here is your muscles are physically functioning, you just don't have voluntary control over them. Now, this could be from the cranial nerves in the frontal lobe of your brain, or it could be hemispatial neglect in your temporal lobe. If it's the cranial nerves, there is little we can do. It's almost like severing the spinal cord, but only to that particular part of your body. If it stems from the temporal lobe, it may be possible to retrain yourself to be able to move your arm voluntarily; you just won't be aware of it moving. Or it could be some strange combination of both."

There was a long pause as the doctors gave Rifun time to mull this over. So either his brain couldn't control his body, or his brain wasn't aware of his body. He didn't know what to make of it. Even if he were able to keep up with everything they were saying as they said it, he wouldn't know what to think. He'd never heard of something like this. This wasn't torture, but it didn't feel much better.

"Arms out to the side," was the next command.

His right arm was no problem, except for a shooting pain in his back. His left arm, the shoulder and upper arm were fine. He could feel that it was out straight as requested. But when he moved his wrist, he found that his elbow had bent and lowered in the maneuver and he couldn't figure out how to get it back up straight. It was like he couldn't find the right muscles. Again he reached over and straightened his arm. His wrist said that it stayed where he put it. Then, with his arms straight out on either side, a nurse listened to his heart and lungs and said everything sounded good.

"Now then—you can put your arms down—can you curl your toes?"

Rifun lowered his arms. He felt his upper left arm against his chest, and he felt his chest against his upper arm. He even felt his lower arm, but only through his chest. He felt around for his lower left arm and pulled it tight to himself. Eventually he could feel pressure on the skin, but the amount of sensation that he'd lost was a bit unsettling.

"Can you curl your toes?" the doctor repeated.

He was able to do so strongly in both feet. When it came to rolling his feet and ankles, his left foot was strong, but his right was weak. He had more control over it than he did his lower left arm, but there was still a notable deficit.

"All right, last one. And if it hurts too much, in your hips, stop. All right? This one is important; if it is too painful in the hips, do *not* push yourself. Understand?"

"I understand," Rifun told him.

"Are you able to bend your knees? You don't have to bring them all the way up, just a little bit, just enough to get some movement."

The resounding answer to that was, no. He could not get his knees to bend. The doctor could bend them and set them, as Rifun's feet let him know, and his legs would stay, just like his arm would stay if positioned, but he himself could not voluntarily bend his legs.

There was some conversation among the doctors. While they were talking, Rifun curled his toes and rolled his ankles. He moved his arm and positioned his elbow. Maybe it just had to do with how immobile he had been. If he could get some blood flowing, start regaining some strength, maybe he could get some function back in his limbs. He tried to bend and reach forward to position his knees, but his hips quickly let him know that was still a very bad idea. Finally he leaned back and tried to relax.

"Okay, so here's the thing," one of the doctors began. "Once your pelvis is free of all casts and braces and we determine that you're generally good to go, you're going to be moved to acute medical segregation."

Rifun had a notion that he was supposed to be there, but at some point he had been glad not to go there. "What if I can't walk?"

"Good news is, the building is one hundred percent wheelchair accessible. But you don't need to be in the hospital that much longer. Sometimes we can get a physical therapist in, if there is a tremendous need, but anything like that, you're going to have to do on your own. If you want to try to retrain yourself to walk, it's going to have to be your initiative, your discipline, your time. The other good news, most in medical segregation aren't on the chore rotation, or it's in very limited capacity, so you're going to have lots of time to yourself."

He didn't know how he felt about that. He couldn't walk, had limited use of one arm, missing fingers on the other, couldn't see, still dealt with seizures even if infrequently. This wasn't torture. It was worse.

After the doctors and nurses all left, Rifun spent a fair amount of time doing all the exercises he had just done as well as a few new ones he invented himself. Arms up in front, out to the side, bring one hand over to touch his shoulder. Right side, no problems. Left side... He couldn't figure out how to get it done. It was like his muscles were just gone. He also didn't like not being able to coordinate his other arm to be able to find it without having to start from his hand or shoulder first.

He brought his left arm down, tried to get his hand to grip the siderail on the bed. Thumb, index, and middle fingers, all perfectly responsive. Ring and pinkie fingers, had to be positioned. He did this several times. Get the blood flowing, get some strength back.

Next were his legs and feet. He started with his toes, well and functional. Then his ankles. Left ankle was fine. Right ankle was somewhat less responsive, but he forced it to move around and around, up and down, side to side. Get the blood flowing, get some strength back.

As for his knees, there was nothing. And he couldn't reach forward to manually position them. He laid back, his brain suddenly confused about which position he was in and which one he was looking for and how to get there. He relaxed as much as he could when he felt his back hit the mattress, but his brain seemed to think he was still leaning forward. Then the sensation passed and he was lying down again.

It was another week and a half before the last mechanical restriction on his hips was removed. Rifun sat up and leaned forward as much as he dared. He was sore and stiff and there was plenty of residual pain all over his body. But at least he could stretch and move again.

His left hip was almost as useless as his left knee. His right hip had only the barest of response when he tried to move it voluntarily.

"Do you want to try—?" the doctor began.

Frustrated, Rifun forced his hips to twist, dragging nearly-useless limbs along with it, then pushed his feet over the edge of the bed. He felt his foot strike something soft and thought he heard Cameron clear his throat. He was able to use his left shoulder and hand to position his left arm on one side of him, then got his right arm on the other side, used his hips to scoot forward as much as he could, and simply sat on the edge of the bed.

"All right," the doctor stated. "And how are you feeling? Any pain?"

"Of course there is," Rifun told him. "Mostly I'm stiff."

"That's understandable. Now then, if we could—"

Cameron cut off his interpretation as the doctor started into some other line of thought, most likely protests as Rifun scooted forward until the toes of his right foot were touching the ground. Ignoring the doctor and happy that he was able to shrug him off his right side, Rifun forced his left hip forward so that his left toes were also touching the ground. With the barest strength in only one arm, he pushed himself forward.

For just a moment's breath, he was standing. Unfortunately, he was not able to move his feet under him correctly in order to balance his weight, and he promptly pitched forward. He got his good arm out to catch him and got his deficient arm out to try and do something. He felt hands grab on either side of him, preventing him from slamming into the wall. There was some grunting, some words, and the hands, which likely belonged to the doctor and the interpreter, managed to get him back upright for a couple of seconds, then back to sitting on the edge of the bed.

"I admire your determination," the doctor told him, "but it might be a tad early to try anything freestyle."

Instead, he was given a walker and allowed to use it only to try and stand up; walking would come later, and likely on his own time in medical segregation.

Rifun was able to position his feet in such a way that he could balance his weight correctly over his legs, but it wasn't what he would consider standing. Nevertheless, it was better than anything he had done over the last month or so, and it was a starting point for him to plan out his self-motivated rehabilitation.

He pushed the walker out a couple inches and leaned forward. Then he used his toes to inch his feet across the floor, mildly helped along by a deficient right femur and his hips.

"All right, wise guy, that's enough out of you," the doctor said.

Someone new spoke in the doorway of the room. No, not someone new. He knew that voice. It took a minute, but he recognized the warden.

"Looks like he's scootin' right along," the warden observed, Cameron interpreting.

"Well, he's upright anyway," the doctor told him. "I'm doubtful of his ability to get back up on his own should he fall."

"That's true of more than half the old heads in medical segregation, and a few in genpop. Is there anything he really needs constant medical surveillance for anymore?"

The doctor hesitated. Then, "No, I don't believe so."

"Keep him for the rest of the day, finish up whatever tests you need to do, notes you need to jot down. Ndolo, you roll up in the morning."

Everyone gave the affirmative in their own way.

"Do you remember anything more about what happened?" Peters asked again. "Cameras are useless. For whatever reason, we just can't pull anything from them. And no one else heard or saw anything. If you want anything to happen, you have to tell us."

Rifun was not unfamiliar with the "snitches get stitches" mantra, although he had never feared it. But he still couldn't tell anyone anything about Julianna or the aliens who had attacked him. Even though it was the truth, it sounded insane and would, at best, just get written off as part of his brain damage. At this point, for all he knew, maybe it was.

"I'm sorry," he answered finally. "I don't remember."

The warden sighed. "All right, if you say so. Be ready to roll up first thing in the morning. I'll have the lieutenant take you to breakfast, then over to medical segregation."

And at eight o'clock sharp the next morning, that was exactly what happened. An officer who introduced himself as Lieutenant Oswald arrived in Rifun's room with a change of clothes. Once Rifun was dressed, he was helped off the bed and safely into a wheelchair. Oswald handed him something which felt like a plastic tub, then began pushing him briskly down the hospital hallway. Rifun felt over the tub. Apparently he had been given this on his first day out of intake and it had important things inside, important documents and such.

Then they burst through heavy metal doors and Rifun took in a huge breath of fresh air. It was warm enough, but there was a cool tinge underneath, like the end of spring or beginning of autumn.

The man pushing his wheelchair made a comment, probably about the weather, but the interpreter was not around. Rifun did not necessarily expect that he would follow him around constantly, but it would make things more difficult.

Another set of heavy doors and they were in a large room where lots of people were congregating. Any one conversation wasn't especially loud, but there were multiple conversations going on. Rifun could follow none of it and instead focused on the food in the vicinity. He swallowed several times as he tasted a whole palate of food.

The cafeteria, he realized as his wheelchair was parked at a table. Breakfast. Of course. Would he have to be brought here every day? Or would breakfast be served to him in medical segregation?

He heard something being set on the table in front of him. He tentatively reached out and felt the plastic tray, found the utensils. The man pushing his wheelchair spoke to him, maybe tried to explain things, what the food was, where it was. Rifun did not understand him, could not picture what the tray was supposed to look like. He picked up a utensil, a fork, and gingerly probed around the tray. He leaned forward, hoping that the smells activating his sense of taste might be able to tell him what food was where.

Scrambled eggs, fruit, buttered toast, nothing that was going to spill. Even the drink had a lid, though he did not know what the drink was. Water, maybe.

He straightened and looked up, unsure where the man pushing his wheelchair had gone. *"Merci."* (Thank you.)

"De rien," came the reply behind him. (No problem.)

"Parlez-vous français?" (You speak French?)

"Non, pas du tout. Je...etudie au lycée. Il y a des années." (No, not at all. I...study in high school. It was years ago.)

Rifun nodded and turned his attention back to his meal.

Several people came to his table. Whether they were trying to talk to him or the officer he did not know. Whatever the case, they exchanged a few words with the officer, then departed.

"Ils vous appellent Prison Jesus, *Jésus de Prison, ou PJ,"* the officer informed him. (They're calling you Prison Jesus, Jésus de Prison, or PJ.)

"Jésus de Prison?" Rifun echoed.

"Vous mourez, vous retournez." (You die, you return.)

Rifun thought about this for a moment. Then, *"C'est stupide."* He took a bite of eggs.

Oswald laughed.

When Rifun was finished, Oswald returned his tray and utensils, then grabbed the wheelchair and pushed him outside, swiftly heading for medical segregation.

The first thing that hit Rifun upon entering was the smell, which regrettably manifested itself as taste. It was old people and medication and sterility and stale air and death. It was worse than the hospital, and Rifun immediately recoiled.

"Je ne veux pas du tout être ici," he told Oswald. (I don't want to be here at all.)

Oswald sighed, but it was in such a way that Rifun thought he was silently agreeing. *"Si vous pouvez vous promener, vous pouvez partir."* (If you can walk, you can leave.)

Then the lieutenant turned his attention to someone else. They exchanged words. Rifun had a notion that a slip of paper was being handed over to someone, another officer, sitting at a desk. A few more words were exchanged, and then they were off again. Down a corridor to an elevator, up to another floor, down another corridor, turn right, down another corridor a short distance, and he was introduced to his new cell. It was roomier than the last, if only because it had to be wheelchair accessible. Oswald took Rifun's hands and helped him orient himself to the location of the bed as well as all safety bars on the walls.

"Merci, monsieur," Rifun said as the officer turned to leave. *"Mais...pourquoi vous m'aidez? Je ne pense pas que c'est seulement parce qu'il est votre travail."* (Thank you, sir. But...why help me? I don't think it's only because it's your job.")

He could hear Oswald shift his stance. *"Mon frère a travaillé ici. Il s'a blessé. Sa tête. Il a continuelement besoin d'aide."* (My brother worked here. He was injured. His head. He needs continual help.)

Rifun nodded. *"Merci beaucoup."*

"De rien."

And the lieutenant departed.

If you can walk, you can leave.

With the taste of old people and medication still in his mouth, Rifun leaned over and grabbed one of the safety bars.

Peters: Good morning, everyone. Thank you for being on this conference call.

Bartlett: At least you finally returned my calls.

Renard: What is this about, specifically?

Peters: If everyone would first like to introduce themselves for the official transcript? My name is Jim Peters, administrator of Mt. Olive Correctional Complex.

Bartlett: Kevin Bartlett, lawyer of Rifun Ndolo.

Renard: Matt Renard, head doctor at the hospital in Mt. Olive.

Piper: Rick Piper, head chaplain at Mt. Olive.

Zitha: Josina Zitha, international lawyer working on behalf of the Senate of Madagascar.

Oswald: Remy Oswald, lieutenant corrections officer at Mt. Olive.

Bartlett: Lieutenant? You don't have a captain?

Peters: I'll explain in a moment. Mr. Bartlett, Miss Zitha, why don't you explain the legal situation so we all know what we're dealing with?

Bartlett: All right. So, at the start of Ndolo's trial, because he's a foreign national, we were legally required to give him the option to contact his government or nearest embassy. He waived that right, signed off on the paperwork and everything. Now, regardless of whether he did or didn't want to make contact, a copy of that paperwork still has to get filed with his government, to let them know that one of their people is in trouble. Well apparently, that paperwork was not actually released until March of this year. Miss Zitha didn't get the paperwork until April of this year. And when she did, she started digging and called me.

Oswald: Forgive me, but, that doesn't sound like much more than a sterling case of government efficiency.

Zitha: First of all, international law not only requires that the home country be notified, but they must have a chance to respond, to send help or not. And when I started digging through the transcripts and other particulars of his trial, I discovered multiple irregularities. Some were minor, and some were alarming, especially in light of some recent events here in Madagascar which I believe are related.

Renard: And what events are those?

Bartlett: My client was regrettably sucked into a horrendous terrorist organization which he tried to flee. It seems that they weren't ready to let him leave. And as they say, snitches get stitches.

Zitha: Back in March, there was a massive string of attacks in the rural area west of the city of Fianarantsoa, in the south of Madagascar, and several smaller attacks in other areas. Farms were destroyed, livestock slaughtered, crops burned, homes burned to the ground or ransacked. Over one hundred and seventy people were massacred, from the oldest man to the smallest babe. In all of my investigation, I've found no surviving relatives.

Oswald: My sympathies, but what does that have to do with us?

Zitha: They were all related to Mr. Ndolo. Whoever it was massacred his entire family.

Piper: Good Lord...

Oswald: [censored]

Renard: [censored]

Piper: Oh, dear Jesus, watch over them...

Bartlett: I understand prison is a little more secure, but gangs still find a way in.

Peters: Unfortunately, Mr. Bartlett, they did.

Bartlett: What do you mean?

Peters: Ndolo was found deceased in the showers back in March. March 13, to be exact.

Bartlett: WHAT—?!

[muted]

Peters: Another inmate found him, started CPR, and got help. He was able to be revived.

[unmuted]

Bartlett: Damn it, man, it's September now. Is he all right?

Renard: He suffered extensive brain damage which has resulted in total blindness as well as speech and comprehension impairments. He has issues with equilibrium, and corporeal spatial orientation, proprioception. We took the opportunity to perform the surgery necessary to stop the progression of his seizures, although they do still occur. He can't walk and has limited use of his left arm. He can't speak English anymore; that got wiped out with exception of a handful of random words. Even his French was questionable for a while, though that has been pretty well cleared up with some therapy and talking to a staff member who can speak French. His Malagasy seemed to be in tact, but we are somewhat lacking in those interpreters.

Bartlett: Does he remember what happened?

Renard: No, unfortunately.

Bartlett: Does he know who he is, where he is, why he's there? Has he been rendered an idiot?

Oswald: It doesn't seem so, no. I can't say my French is great, but I can read people. He knows his name, where he's from, remembers his military service, remembers his trial, knows why he's in prison. He is very much present in the moment, whatever he's doing, and he can recall the events of the day. Overall he remembers a lot of facts, but how well he connects those facts to himself as his life, I can't say.

Renard: He is also exhibiting a very unique memory deficit which may contribute to that. He doesn't remember people who don't speak Malagasy or French. At least French, but we're assuming Malagasy as well. It took him, on average, four days longer, assuming that person visited daily, to recognize someone who only spoke English compared to someone who spoke French.

Bartlett: So you're saying he might not remember that I'm his lawyer?

Renard: He might have a physical memory of you from his trial, but he probably won't recognize you by voice alone, no.

Oswald: So, bringing this back around, what's the...what are we looking at here? Are we looking at INTERPOL, CIA, what? I mean, Ndolo is out of the hospital now. And even so, he was quite the celebrity for a while, and we still don't know who did it. They could try again. Are you sure about this whole family thing? If so, he might be the only target. If not...

Zitha: I will be flying to the United States in a couple of weeks to speak to you all personally, as well as other government and military officials. Yes, I was very thorough in tracking down all of the victims. They are all blood relatives of Mr. Ndolo as well as their married and extended families. For the time being, we do believe that he is the only target. But more than that, I will also be working with Mr. Bartlett to get his convictions overturned based on the irregularities that I have discovered from his trial, though that is not necessarily your concern.

Peters: What do you suggest we do in the meantime? He can't look after himself.

Zitha: I wish I had answers for you, or even a suggestion. There was some mention of the terrorist group In Jezik early on, but no one has officially claimed responsibility for the attacks. You know your facility the best and which precautions may be most effective.

Peters: Hm.

Zitha: However, if I may make one request, specifically of the chaplain.

Piper: Of course, anything.

Zitha: Let me be the one to tell him.

Piper: [sigh] It goes against my nature, but I can respect that you will understand cultural sensitivities better than I.

Zitha: Thank you.

Bartlett: Doc, what's his prognosis? Is he going to be helpless forever or you think there's hope?

Renard: He certainly has the determination. That is not the issue. All that really remains to be seen is whether his body will cooperate.

Bartlett: Hmph.

Peters: Is there anything you need from us, Mr. Bartlett, Miss Zitha?

Bartlett: I'd like a copy of whatever medical records he's got. For my own curiosity and it might help me in some of these appeals.

Peters: Miss Zitha?

Zitha: Only his incarceration records. The rest I can get from Mr. Bartlett or the local courts.

Oswald: I'll see to that, sir.

Peters: Thank you, lieutenant. Is there anything anyone else needs?

Bartlett: Another cup of coffee.

Zitha: A good night's sleep.

Oswald: A vacation.

Peters: Very funny. All right, thanks, everyone.

Call time: 9:31

Four
Forward

Rifun lay on his stomach on his bed. He got his right hand under his right shoulder in position. He got his upper left arm into basic position, then used his left hand to finger-crawl his hand into its position under his left shoulder. After a few anxious breaths, he pushed up. He managed to get his right thigh to respond enough to get his hips in the air and take the pressure off his lower back. Then he let himself down. And up, concentrating on his lower left arm and right thigh. And down. Again and again. Ten bad pushups was about all he was good for, but it was enough for the moment.

He lay on his side, breathing hard and in some moderate pain. Couldn't stop now. If he could walk, he could leave.

He scooted to the edge of the bed and reached for his wheelchair, found it. The good news was that he could finagle himself to and from his bed and wheelchair, and the toilet, too. All things considered, he was pretty independent compared to others in this particular population.

Rifun got his chair turned around and facing the wall where the safety bar was. He held onto the safety bar with his right hand to orient himself. He lifted his left arm at the shoulder. At the same time, he flexed his wrist to get it in position to grab the bar. As soon as one finger brushed the cool metal, he turned his hand and grabbed on. He held on more tightly than necessary, trying to engage all of his arm muscles. He still couldn't feel his lower left arm, but he was fairly certain that he was making progress in being able to move it.

Then he pushed back a few inches, released the bar, and leaned forward to engage the brakes on the chair. And repeat. Right hand on the bar for orientation, lift the left arm. Turn the wrist. Intentionally do not move the left shoulder. Think about engaging the rest of the arm, from the elbow to the wrist. Flex the wrist, try to engage it from the bottom up.

81

Without seeing or feeling his arm, it was impossible to say just how much movement he got, but he was fully aware that one moment his fingers were not touching the bar and the next moment they were just brushing the metal. He turned his wrist again and grabbed the bar.

Rifun slid his feet off the rests and managed to use his hips to scoot forward until his feet touched the ground. He did not wear shoes while doing these exercises; he still needed his toes. He'd been able to increase the movement in his right foot just a little bit, but he took whatever he could get. Between his foot and his hip, he was able to get one leg in a good starting position. He still didn't have conscious use of his left thigh or calf and the best he could do was flex his ankle and use his toes to scoot his foot around where it might work the best.

Taking another breath, Rifun pulled himself up, putting most of his weight on his right side until he was more confident in his balance. So there. He was standing. Gingerly, he loosened his grip on the bar. He felt himself wobble, but he willed himself to stay upright and not reach for his crutch until absolutely necessary.

He was able to free stand for almost a full second, but that was fine. It was fine. It was great considering he had almost no idea what was happening between his hips and his ankles.

He scooted his right foot out a little, about half a step, using his toes and flexing his ankle in something resembling a stepping motion though his foot never actually fully left the ground. Then he reached down the bar with his right hand. Then he slid his left hand along the bar. Then he used his left foot, toes and ankle, to get his left leg down toward his right. He released the bar and managed to free stand for another almost-second. He considered his plight and shifted his feet. Then he released again. One full second, almost two. Even better.

He repeated his maneuvers down to one end of the bar near the door, then started moving the opposite way. Moving left was considerably slower.

As he was doing this, he was struck by a wave of vertigo and his world turned sideways and twisted. His left hand missed the bar and he was unable to correct himself fast enough to avoid falling, although his right-hand grip did manage to save him somewhat.

He couldn't say whether he sat or lay on the ground as his spatial perception was momentarily erased from existence. When he did come back to himself, he wasn't really doing either. Instead he lay half-cocked against the wall, chest pressed against the wall, feet lying on the floor.

Groaning, he rolled onto his back and sat up, head dizzy but at least in the right spatial position. Well, unless someone was watching the cameras, no one had seen that. He turned himself so his right side was against the wall. With a sigh, he reached up, grabbed the bar, and started pulling. He was nowhere near as strong as he used to be, but he was strong enough that he could hold himself while he got his right foot into position. As his foot got into position, he was able to get his thigh to respond. Then he reached for the bar with his left hand, got it, and, with painstaking effort, stood up. Well, he was vertical, anyway, still heavily dependent on the bar as he got his feet situated beneath him.

Unwilling to quit, he continued to make his way down the bar to the left. At the other end of the bar was the wall and a walker. He got himself situated again so he could stand for a second or two, then grabbed the walker and got it set up.

He forced his ankles to flex with each step, shifted his weight back and forth, trying to imitate a natural gait. He got to the door of his cell and paused to listen. Nothing out of the ordinary that he could tell, no one nearby.

Slowly he made his way out into the hall and turned, sticking close to the wall and the safety bars. He passed by several other cells. The residents spoke to him. He still did not understand them, but he managed his own greeting and a side wave as he shuffled by. Then he was at the next corner. He couldn't have gone more than thirty feet and he was tired.

But, he thought as he got himself turned around, it was better than how he'd started out when he first arrived. He hadn't been able to do much of anything: a single pushup, grab the bar without extreme effort, never mind stand and walk. Or shuffle anyway.

He returned to his cell, put the walker back against the wall, and grabbed the safety bar. Then he maneuvered himself back down the wall to his wheelchair and sat in a heap. After a moment, he unlocked the brakes, turned himself around, and got back in bed where he did five more pushups. Only after that did he get on his back and try to relax. It was almost lunchtime. He'd get something to eat, rest a bit, then do it all again before dinner. After dinner, he'd take a shower, and, if he continued to survive that ordeal, return to his cell for maybe a few more repetitions of simply using the bar to stand up. If he could get a good standing balance, then it might be easier to get his hips and feet to coordinate in order to walk, and maybe he could get the rest of his legs to function properly.

He could hope. He didn't know what for, really, other than he didn't want to end up like all the other patrons of this place. At least being beaten in a fight was a noble way to go. At one point, the doctors had mentioned he'd had defensive wounds, suggesting he'd at least tried to put up a fight. Rotting in a wheelchair at the mercy of an overworked nurse's aid was not on his list of ways he wanted to die.

He heard movement down the hall. A little early for the nurses to come and start gathering people for lunch, but then, who knew what else they had going on? Better to be too early than too late. Huffing a sigh, Rifun sat up and reached for his wheelchair. He could get around fairly well on his own, but he wasn't going to be the last one to lunch. An inmate was not someone to mess with when it came to chow time, and that didn't change just because he got old or sick. Even without being able to see or understand them, Rifun knew these guys could be brutal.

Two sets of footsteps came down the hall and stopped at his cell.

"Hello," Cam the interpreter greeted.

"Cam? Not Oswald?" Rifun wondered.

"You have a couple of visitors." It took a second, but he recognized the warden's voice underneath Cam's interpretation.

"It's not the weekend, though."

"Well, lawyers make their own rules."

Rifun did not have the time or ability to ask questions as someone stepped behind him and began pushing him. Out of his cell, down the hall, to the elevator, to the ground floor, and out the door into the chilly autumn air.

"Does this have to do with being attacked?" he inquired.

"Somewhat, but not in the way you might think," Peters replied. "I'll just let them explain."

84

Them. Last he remembered, he only had one lawyer. But that lawyer had an intern. Maybe he had a new intern.

Something dawned on him then, when he thought about the intern. The intern had been wearing a disguise. He'd had a personal goal of getting him, Rifun, convicted. But there was something else. Julianna had infiltrated the court, too. And there were others involved. A bailiff wore a disguise, too, but he was friendly. He had been on Rifun's side, trying to figure out which court personnel belonged to Julianna. What was the bailiff's name? His real name, the man under the Disguise.

Disguise. Not just a disguise, but a Disguise. It was like peering through a foggy window. He knew the reference, knew the connection. He just couldn't make it happen. It wasn't quite Time, but something very close. More powerful than Time alone. He had some memory of the Akari, but it remained just as disconnected from everything else. A rote fact, like something he had read about long ago but since forgotten.

They crossed the complex and entered another building. This building was warm and didn't taste like stale old people and medication. Rather, it tasted like dirt and sweat with a hint of blood. He did not bother trying to keep track of where they were going, just let himself be taken.

Finally they slowed and Peters opened a door. Rifun was pushed inside and immediately assaulted by a boisterous voice. The warden answered this person and got him calmed down, at least until Rifun was seated at a table. This room tasted more like dirt and metal polish.

The boisterous man spoke again, and Cam, who had pulled up a chair on his right, interpreted.

"You remember me, Ndolo? Kevin? Your lawyer?"

Rifun blinked. "I know I had a lawyer. I think his name was Kevin, but I don't fully remember."

"Well I am. How are you? What happened?"

"Better than I was a few months ago. I can almost stand on my own, can sort of walk. Unfortunately, I still don't remember what happened."

"Hm. Well, damn. Anyway, I'm not the only one here to talk to you. I'll just let her do the talking there."

"Good morning, Mr. Ndolo."

It was a female voice, but more to the point, she was speaking Malagasy. A cascade of emotion and memory poured through his brain. Memories that he had only glimpsed the surface of since waking in the hospital sprang to life.

"Are you all right?" the woman asked.

He blinked back to the present. "Yes, yes, I'm fine. Continue."

"My name is Josina Zitha," she went on. "I am here—"

"You speak with an accent," he cut in. "Where are you from? What people?"

She hesitated just a second before answering, "I am actually from Xai-Xai, Mozambique. My father was Tswa, and my mother was Malagasy, Sakalava to be specific."

The Sakalava lived in the west of Madagascar, one of the côtier people. One of the more prominent peoples, the Sakalava held their own kingdom before the Merina took over. And because of the Merina, the côtiers and the highlanders, which included the Betsileo, did not always like to associate with one another.

"You say 'was,'" Rifun observed. "Are they no longer alive?"

"Regrettably no."

"I'm sorry to hear that. But what are you doing here?"

"I'm working on behalf of the Madagascan Senate, investigating your trial as well as some recent events."

"How did you manage that?"

She cleared her throat. "A few handy personal connections, and, well, let's just say it makes me a very convenient scapegoat in the event something goes wrong."

Rifun hummed a reluctant acknowledgment. "I understand. Highlanders and côtiers."

"Full-bloods and half-bloods."

He grunted. "What do you need from me? I don't know how much they told you, but my memory isn't all that great right now. If my lawyer is here, he can answer your questions better." He shifted position. "What do you mean you're investigating my trial?"

He could tell she was trying to keep her explanation short and simple, whether because she was trying to explain to a layperson or because she was trying to be mindful of his present shortcomings, he did not know. He could also tell that he was missing a lot of details because of how simple she made it, and he hated himself for it.

As she explained it, he recalled some memories of his trial, distant though they remained. Julianna had moles on the inside, influencing his trial. He supposed it only made sense that she would have her moles withhold some paperwork and prevent him from being able to contact his government, even if it was only basic formality to let them know of his troubles.

There were other aspects of the trial she was investigating, too. He didn't understand what they were or their significance, and he couldn't convince himself it was solely because of his faulty brain; he just wasn't well-versed in the nuances of the American judiciary. That was the whole point of lawyers. But he did understand when she said that, if she and his lawyer were successful, they might be able to get his convictions overturned.

"So I go back to jail and wait for a new trial," he said.

Josina turned her attention elsewhere and began speaking English. A man with an annoying, nasally voice replied. Then she began to translate.

"Not necessarily. Calhoun got ousted in the election, and the new district attorney isn't willing to try your case again."

"Calhoun?" Rifun wondered.

"The prosecutor at your trial. He's no longer in his position. And the new DA isn't willing to take you back to trial."

Rifun blinked. "I'm not ungrateful, just confused. What's changed?"

"Biggest thing, his two star witnesses are gone."

"Gone? They left the area?"

"You could say that."

Rifun sifted through broken memories of his trial, but without a visual reference or the ability to understand what anyone was saying, it was little more than unreliable surface knowledge of events.

"What do you mean? I don't remember, I can't put things together."

"Legally, I can't tell you what happened to them because they are, as of this moment, still considered your victims and you can't have knowledge of their status or whereabouts. Just know that they're gone, and without them, the new prosecutor doesn't believe he has a case against you. That means if we can get these convictions overturned—even if we have to go all the way to the West Virginia Supreme Court or the Supreme Court of the United States—you walk out of here a free man and can go home. I'll even call up Calhoun and get him to buy you a plane ticket home just like he promised."

Rifun did not remember that promise, but figured that was a minor thing. Instead he asked, "How long will this take?"

"Depends on how far we need to go. There's a process that needs to be followed. We're already working on appeals. If the appeals court sides with us, you could be out of here in three months, six months, a year, all depends on how fast we can get on the calendar and the protocols for bringing in Miss Zitha and international law. And there are different avenues we can try for this; one failure does not mean all is lost. But, if the appellate courts reject our claim, we may have to go to the Supreme Court, and that could take a significant amount of time. So, don't start packing your bags, but I believe there is a reasonable amount of hope to be had."

"Why would irregularities in the trial result in an overturned conviction? What about the jury?"

"Well, you weren't there, but we had a hell of a time with jury selection. Lots of lawyers, members of the Bar, it was a real circus. That precedent is still being reviewed and argued and appealed and rewritten; it's not actually codified law or regulation yet. If we can jump on that and even get that overturned, we bust open a massive avenue for us on the basis of a tainted jury. And that's just one example."

Rifun nodded slowly. Memories of things he experienced was sketchy enough; trying to piece things together that he didn't experience was even worse. He would think about it later.

He turned his attention back to Josina. "You said something about other recent events."

Rifun might not have been able to see, but he was able to perceive a definite shift in the atmosphere around the room, especially around Josina as she sighed. "Yes. There were some disturbing events taking place at home at the same time that you were beaten here. The government believes they are connected and would very much like some answers. You may be the only one who can provide them."

"I'm sorry it's come to that if that's the case. What's happened?"

She hesitated again, then, "I am very sorry to have to tell you this, but...your entire family and extended family is dead."

Rifun heard the words. He understood them very well. It was still a moment before they filtered through his damaged brain. "What?"

"At the same time you were being beaten to death here, everyone in your family was being murdered. Not just in and around Fianarantsoa, but Mahitsy and Antananarivo as well."

He shook his head. "I don't...understand." He went on before she could speak. "Faliarivo. He ran the farm with his wife and children. Last I remember, he had five children—"

"All dead. Faliarivo, his wife, his children, their spouses, their children, his siblings and their families. They comprised almost a quarter of the village, though you probably knew that. The crops were burned to ash, the cattle and all livestock slaughtered. The house was utterly ransacked. Even the family tombs have been desecrated. This was an intentional, murderous rampage, not merely a random act of violence."

Rifun could feel his chest tighten. His lungs would not cooperate and his heart started to race. He felt tears start to run down his cheeks unbidden.

"Relatives in Mahitsy suffered the same fate," Josina went on.

"Lalao?" Rifun asked, his words choking in his throat. He got his right hand up to hold his head. He whispered, "Please not Lalao."

"I'm so sorry."

"Her sons?"

"And their wives and children. Everyone from the oldest elder to the youngest babe who hadn't even left the house yet," she confirmed somberly. "By the time all the dead were counted, almost two hundred people had been massacred. For a while, no motive could be found, but when I received word of your trial and started going through the files, I started some digging of my own and determined that you were the most likely link to most or all of the killing. And, honestly, you are the only survivor, if just barely."

Rifun was barely listening at this point. He had basically melted onto the table, trying to comprehend it all.

It was all gone. They were all gone. Every family member he knew, every family member he didn't know. But most of all, Lalao had been taken from him.

In a sudden snap of rage, he sat up and beat his fist into the table. Several things happened as his fist met metal. The skin over his knuckles broke and started bleeding. Searing pain beyond this minor abrasion shot from his fist, up his arm, straight into his spine. He made an involuntary cry of anguish which was tempered by a wash of vertigo that almost took him sideways. Someone else in the room barked at him, but it was the click of a gun safety that got him to force himself straight and put his hands up. Rather, his right hand went up, and he did the best he could with his left.

There were a few words exchanged around the room. After a moment, Cameron let him know he could relax.

Rifun dropped his arms, then melted a second time onto the table, weeping. As he did so, he did something else. He Banded. He didn't know how he knew how to do it, barely remembered what it was beyond factual knowledge, but he knew he did it. He was in a Fast Band, moving on a faster plane of Time than everyone else, stretching out this moment into hours so he could weep in peace.

After a while, he relaxed and let the Band drop. He did not move for a long moment. Then, finally, he sat up.

Josina was the first to speak. "I'm—"

"Were they given proper funerals?" he asked, wiping his eyes.

"From what I understand from the village presidents, the allegations of witchcraft are quite strong. Shamans were brought in to cleanse the bodies before any funeral arrangements, but because of the nature of the attacks and the desecration of the tombs, the national government prohibited burial pending investigation. To my knowledge, they still have not been buried, though that could have changed."

He sniffed, fatigue creeping into his bones. "What's happened to the farm? Faliarivo's farm?"

"It was also cleansed, but no one dares to go near it for fear of vengeful spirits," Josina explained. "Legally, however, you are the sole heir to all of the properties as the last surviving family member."

His nebulous grief and fatigue was momentarily punctured by a pinprick of confusion. "Can I inherit since I'm in prison abroad?"

"I'm looking into that as well. American law says no, but I don't believe that such laws can affect you as a foreign national, and we take inheritance a little more seriously." Her tone turned teasing, in a tired sort of way, an attempt at comfort perhaps. "You might be a highlander, but I would hate to see you lose out on this inheritance."

He sniffed hard and wiped his eyes. "Thank you."

He heard a shuffling of papers and some other movement. "In order to do any work on any of this, however, I need some information from you."

Truthfully, Rifun didn't feel like doing much of anything, even answering questions. His thoughts were more fixed on Lalao. He'd only just gotten a letter that she'd written him back in March before the attack. He'd been contemplating off and on how he was going to reply. First he needed someone to write for him. Then he needed someone who understood French and could properly transcribe what he was saying. None of that mattered now, it seemed. "What do you need?"

"First, in the matter of your inheritance, I need to verify who you are. I understand you were born during communism, and, assuming your mother didn't hide you entirely, many records from that time have been lost. I obtained a photocopy of your birth certificate, including your comment about the misprint, but when I went looking, I couldn't find anything. Now, this isn't entirely surprising; many people don't even have that much, but every little bit helps. I also got photocopies of your passport and visa, but there seemed to be some complications with them.

"In the matter of investigating the attack, do you have any idea who would hate you or your entire family so much that they would do such a thing? Whether witchcraft was involved or not, a massacre of this scale is unheard of outside of war, and to target a single family is unprecedented."

Rifun hummed a sigh. He knew exactly what had happened. Maybe not minute details, but he knew the game. Julianna had tried to murder him. Even been successful, for a few minutes. But that wasn't enough. She wanted to ensure that he and his entire family were erased. From history, from the gene pool, from reality itself. As long as there was a single living family member, he could honor the ancestors and pass on heritage and wisdom. If there were no living family members, they would all just fade away, powerless among the spirits.

He remembered the time he had asked her to aid in a little charade he'd had going, asked her to pretend to be his daughter. He knew that she wasn't fond of it, knew she'd resented him for it. If he hadn't asked her to do such a thing, would she have spared them? Had he unwittingly condemned his entire family to death because of his own fear?

If the investigation continued, he had an idea of how it would go. Josina may or may not be able to find enough solid proof of his identity, enough to put forward to claim his inheritance. Depending on how the courts were feeling and how much they demanded in bribes, his odds of actually getting his family's farm went from bad to worse to nonexistent. Similarly, he could give her vague names and notions, the government may or may not investigate, but they certainly wouldn't find anything.

He was the last surviving member of his family, the last Andilan. His ancestors were counting on him to avenge their deaths and carry on the name and line. There was only one good way he could see to do that.

"How bad do you want to catch these people?" he asked Josina.

"It's one of the few things all of the politicians can agree on," she replied diplomatically. "It's probably the one issue the president, the prime minister, the senate, and the assembly can agree on."

He shook his head slowly. "No. I mean, how bad do you want to catch them?"

It was a moment before she answered, "I would like it very much." Her tone had a sincerity to it that Rifun guessed she had some personal motivation.

"Then you're going to need to understand some things."

"I'm listening."

He Banded, just the two of them. All of the extraneous sounds in the room —heavy breathing, a shoe squeaking on the floor, the rub of fabric as someone tried to discreetly scratch an itch—suddenly ceased. There was only a mild gasp from Josina.

"I know this looks like witchcraft," Rifun said. "When I first learned of it,

I considered it as divining the spirits."

"What...what did you do to them?"

"Not to them. To us. This is a Fast Band. We are moving on a faster plane of Time. We can spend hours talking, but they won't notice any of it because, to them, it will only be a moment. It's one of the more efficient ways to have a private conversation."

Josina was quiet for a long time. Rifun could hear her rapid breathing and nervous shuffle of papers. After a few minutes, she stood up and walked around the room, stopping occasionally to try to talk to one of the others in the room to no avail. Finally she sat down, but was still silent for a few more minutes.

"What is this?" she asked, tone stern. "What trick is this?"

Rifun shook his head. "It's not a trick."

"If you can do this, why are you even here? How were you beaten to death?"

"Because the ones who murdered me and my family can do this as well. Honestly, they can do a lot worse."

Josina sighed in frustration. "There were a few passing mentions, early on in the investigation, about possible involvement from In Jezik. A couple years ago, when In Jezik was active in the world, there were many reports of odd phenomena during military encounters, but it was all attributed to stress and mental health on the part of the soldiers. In your trial, while In Jezik wasn't mentioned, there are a few details that could point to them. Were you involved with In Jezik?"

"It's a long story, but you might say that I'm the reason In Jezik exists, and it's not because we were allies."

Making another frustrated sound, she stood again and made several laps of the room. She approached him a couple times but the best he could do was lean away from her. Maybe she wanted to ask a question, maybe she wanted to hit him, he didn't know, and he wasn't keen to find out the hard way. But then she left him and made another lap of the room, occasionally murmuring under her breath. He could not hear what she was saying specifically, but he knew it wasn't Malagasy or French. He decided to break up the tension with a few distracting questions.

"How did you come to work for the Senate?" he inquired.

She stopped muttering to herself, but it was a second before she answered, "Some handy connections. My father held some influence in his life, and my mother was *ampanzaka* among the Sakalava. It helped to get the job, but I know I'm still a scapegoat."

"What influence does a Mozambican have in Madagascar?"

She made her way back toward the table. "He was a businessman, specialized in imports and exports. Sometimes he would cut deals."

Rifun nodded. "I see."

Her chair scooted across the floor. There were some more noises, and then she sat down.

"Fine," she stated. "Let's just pretend that..." She trailed off, her tone suggesting she didn't even know what she wanted to say. Finally she said, "Tell me what you want, I'll figure out the rest, I suppose."

He shifted in his seat. "The date on my birth certificate is not a typo. I was born March 13, 1897. My mother, Lalao, was raped by a French soldier during the Menalamba Rebellion. Now, it is true that my stepfather hated me, beat me, treated me like a slave. When I was sixteen, I ran away from home to Tana to join the VVS, the original VVS. Shortly thereafter—not because of me, whatever you might find—our operation was outed. I was arrested and sentenced to hard labor. In 1923, just days before we were pardoned, I got in a fight with another inmate and he put a pickax in my skull, rendering me blind."

He heard her scratching out a few notes.

"The first name you'll want to look up is Alexander LaPouir. Last I knew, he was living in France working as a botanist. Don't mention my name. Just ask about his time in Madagascar. He was one of the guards while in prison, and he saw the fight, was ultimately the one who rescued me, as odd as that may sound. He is the one who introduced me to Time."

"This makes no sense," Josina murmured, half to herself.

"If you want, ask a shaman to commune with the spirits and see if you might communicate with Lalao, the old woman living in Fianarantsoa who had three sons. She was my cousin, named for my mother. She knew who and what I am." His sudden irritation faded quickly as he sighed and wiped his eyes quickly, more tears beginning to form. "I loved her."

"I'm sorry," Josina said softly. "So, what does it mean, this 'Time'?"

"Time...is an industry." He frowned as his more tangible memories gave way to things that were, for the time being, still just rote book knowledge. "When a person is dying, a Time Agent called a Harvester takes the time that they have left—the hours, days, weeks, months, maybe even years—and stores it in something called a Time Capsule. The capsule is sold to Merchants who purify it and resell it. Consuming a Time Capsule grants a person all of the hours, days, weeks, whatever that came from the person who was dying."

"Now that does sound like witchcraft."

Rifun half-shrugged. "It's an industry, no different than buying or selling physical goods, as far as anyone who is involved is concerned. But, as with any economy, there are thieves, called Runners. It is the job of Time Agents called Timekeepers to apprehend these thieves. Monsieur LaPouir was a Timekeeper, and he taught me as a Timekeeper also."

He could hear Josina shift in her seat. "So...pretending that everything you've said is absolutely true, it is possible that whoever attacked you and your family was a very large and dangerous band of thieves looking to steal the time from your family. Because you're a Timekeeper."

Rifun chuckled and shook his head. "Oh, it is much worse than that, I assure you."

She sighed. "How so?" Her tone was mildly disbelieving.

"The Time industry would like to think itself the sole proprietor of universal physics, but it's not. There is more out there than just Time. There is the Akari as well, and it encompasses Time, Matter, and Energy. The two primary factions of Akari-bearers were the Akarin and the Cult of the Akari. I didn't really know about the Akari; the Time industry teaches that it is a myth for the overzealous. At the time, I was busy with World War II."

"World War II?"

"Yes. I fought in the Battle of Antsrinana Bay, took a round to the shoulder, shattered my collarbone. After the war, as you may know, was the Uprising. All of us who had fought in World War II were discharged without so much as a 'thank you.' I went south to Fianarantsoa where my family's farm had been commandeered by the French and run into ruin. Infuriated, I joined the resistance, led many campaigns all over the south."

"And why didn't your Time abilities help the people to win the war?" Josina's tone was a tad accusatory.

"We were poorly armed. Some had spears, few had guns in working order. Most had farm equipment or only their bare hands. I might be able to help my own men, but I can do nothing for anyone else in other places. And we were not the only ones who knew how guerrilla warfare works."

"Hm." She either didn't believe him or wasn't impressed.

"After we lost the war, I was captured again, imprisoned again, this time sentenced to death. But before the French could carry out that sentence, they spent ten years torturing me."

"And you didn't try to escape?"

"I wasn't going to leave my people. I was still known as the Bastard of the VVS, and a leader does not abandon his followers."

"Hm. Go on."

"When the French relented and freed the prisoners and granted Madagascar its independence, I left. I couldn't bear to stand in the wreckage of what was once my beloved homeland. I fled to Europe, spent some time in France and the UK, went to school, tried to put it all behind me."

"And where do these Runners or other agents come in?" Josina questioned.

"I heard a rumor about the Akari, that it could heal Matter. I thought maybe I could use it to heal my body, be rid of the scars the French had left behind. I was approached by one of the leaders of the Cult of the Akari. She was an Englishwoman by the name of Julianna Brown. She agreed to teach me the Akari, but I had to do her one favor."

"And what was that?"

"She wanted me to kill one of the other leaders, a man called Cassius, real name Kokumbo. He was originally Yoruba, taken as a slave back in the seventeenth century. He was volatile and violent, a danger to himself, others, the entire operation."

"Is he the one who tried to kill you?"

Rifun laughed. "Which time?" He grew serious again. "Make no mistake, he was a mad dog and he was eventually put down—not by me—but that was only one problem solved." He hummed a sigh. "I did learn the Akari, as promised. I learned how to wield Time, Matter, and Energy. But Julianna had other plans, plans I did not agree with. She turned against me, tried to have me killed once, failed, although I was gifted with these beautiful seizures. Then I was stripped of my Akari abilities and left to rot. Not long after, I surrendered to police. She got wind of it and sent several moles into the courtroom to try and influence things. She also tried to have me killed while in jail, failed again. I suppose she was upset enough over her failures that she decided to forego subtlety and just ensure that I died."

Josina scratched out some more notes. "When you say she sent moles to influence your trial, what do you mean?"

"I don't know the specifics," Rifun admitted, "and I can't say quite why. It might be that I never really knew, or it might just be locked away because I remember far less about events and conversations that were primarily or exclusively English. I admit, there is a lot more to this story. I also admit that I am withholding some for the time being so that you can do some preliminary investigation. There's no reason to overwhelm you with everything if you don't believe even the basics."

She scribbled some more, making a sound that was both suspicious and understanding. "So, just for my own knowledge, I suppose, trying to make sense of things, I'm assuming, then, that you consumed some of these Time Capsules and that's why you are allegedly over one hundred years old yet look no older than thirty?"

He shook his head. "No. A Timekeeper's use of Time will grant him extended life naturally, no Time Capsules needed. Even Harvesters may skim some for themselves when they take Time from the dying. The Akari also grants extended life and reasonably good health."

"Is the Akari, perhaps, an extension of or maybe another name for the *razana*, the life force of the ancestors?" Josina inquired thoughtfully.

"It very well could be. That was how I chose to see it, as I believed that I was divining with the ancestors. But, as I said, that is information that I do not believe you are entitled to just yet. If you talk to Monsieur LaPouir, you can verify at least a few things."

97

"And why don't you want me to mention your name?"

"Because I fully believe that Julianna thinks she finally succeeded in killing me. I don't want it to get out that I'm still alive. Obviously I was unsuccessful in deterring her before; I'm practically helpless now."

"How closely do you think she's monitoring things? If we go to the higher courts, if you do manage to inherit one or more properties, do you think she will still be looking for you?"

Again Rifun half-shrugged. "The best I can do is hope not. Given that it has been several months now, I'm hoping that she has more important things to worry about than the fate of a dead man. As long as I do not draw attention to myself, maybe you can overturn my convictions, get me back to my family farm, and I can just live peacefully for once."

He dropped the Band, then, to avoid any more questions. If she didn't believe him on the basics, she wasn't going to believe him on the details. As far as she was concerned, this was all entirely confined to Earth. She didn't need to know that there was more out there.

Life in the room resumed. Someone was breathing heavily. Someone was scuffing a shoe on the floor. Someone was scratching an itch. Josina coughed and cleared her throat, perhaps to cover up the surprise of returning to Base Time where everyone else in the room was blissfully unaware of the conversation they'd just had. Not that it would have mattered, seeing how no one spoke Malagasy, but if there was any hope of getting any justice for his family, she needed to know. And maybe it would save her life, too.

"Don't pack up just yet," he told her before too many seconds passed. "You just asked me a question and I haven't answered yet. You can't leave now."

She cleared her throat again, said something to someone else, maybe asked for a glass of water. Then she turned her attention back to him. "Fair enough."

"Unfortunately, I don't remember the original question."

"You said that I needed to understand some things, and I told you that I was listening."

He nodded. "Well, they can't understand us anyway. But what I can tell you, and what may be easier for you while you're here...Walter and Tommen

Forbes were Timekeepers, too. Walter was a Captain, overseeing Region Four, District Four, which is the eastern United States. Tommen was an Apprentice, but also an Akari-bearer. I understand that my lawyer can't tell me about them, but if he discloses their whereabouts with you, you can follow up with them and ask them more realistic questions about the trial itself and the incidents which prompted the many charges brought against me. It may be pertinent to know that Walter's real name is Owain Fforidd. It would not surprise me if he elected to use that name in a new life."

Now she made a more thoughtful sound as she shuffled papers and packed up her things, perhaps eager to leave. "I see. Well, it has been an interesting conversation to say the least. If I have any more questions, I will be sure to let you know."

Before he could reply in kind, she was speaking to others in the room. The next thing Rifun knew, someone came up behind him and he was being wheeled out of the room, though not so brusquely as before. Cameron the interpreter still followed on his left.

"Is there anywhere you'd like to make a quick stop before heading back to your cell? Commissary, maybe?"

Rifun understood the words through Cameron, but he recognized the voice as belonging to Jeremy, the chaplain understudy.

"No," he answered simply.

"Is there anything you need, any way we can help you mourn for your family?"

Rifun let out a breath. Then, "I think a spear might be out of the question, but a *lamba* would be nice."

Cameron relayed the message, then followed up with his own to Rifun. "I'm sorry, I don't know what a 'lamba' is."

"It's a cloth, about so big—" He stretched his right arm out as wide as he could and, with some determined effort, got his left arm partially straightened and cooperative. "The women wear them in many bright colors, but for men it tends to be blue, green, and brown. It is no bad thing if it is another color. They may be solid or patterned; generally the more intricate the pattern or design, the greater social or economic status it represents. There aren't usually fringes, but they might be added for personal taste."

"We'll see what we can do," Jeremy promised. "Anything else?"

Rifun shook his head. "No. There is little that can be done here."

He was taken to the cafeteria first just in time to grab the last bag of leftovers from the lunch line.

"No fasting for you, eh?" Cameron asked.

Rifun again shook his head. "If the prison wants an excuse for a feast, I can direct them in what and how to prepare a Betsileo funeral feast."

"And what does that entail?" Jeremy inquired.

He listed off the dishes and how to prepare them, as well as some of the more minute details he knew the prison could accommodate if they so chose. He didn't think it was likely.

"I mean, it is a request for a cultural and religious accommodation," Cameron stated. "And it would provide some benefits to the complex as a whole. The food service college could get in some special practice, and it would be good for overall morale."

"We'll see what we can do," Jeremy repeated.

Then they returned to the nursing home, back to the taste of old people and medication, back to his cell with his walker and the safety bars. Jeremy and Cameron both expressed their condolences for his loss, then left him alone.

As soon as Rifun judged them gone, he positioned himself near the bed and scrambled over onto the mattress. His chest and throat were tight and he had to force himself to breathe.

They were gone. They were all gone. Slaughtered like cattle because of him. Gone, his family's farm, his *nenibe*'s farm, ruined. Not merely in the hands of occupiers, but tainted by death and vengeful spirits, the future uncertain. A farm with hundreds of years of family history, a pillar of the community, leveled.

And Lalao. His beloved Lalao. He remembered her laugh, her tease. He'd loved her as a woman when she was young and beautiful. He'd loved her as an elder when she was old and wise. He should have stayed with her all those years ago, been a loyal husband. She'd waited for him, all those years ago, and he had let her down. She'd trusted him, believed that he could slay the dragon, and he had gotten her killed.

No. Julianna had done this. Because she was a witch, a true witch who took the essence of the *razana*, the Akari, and used it for such heinous destruction. She could not be allowed to continue. She could not be allowed to live.

Rifun wiped his face and sat up. He got his legs over the edge of the bed, then reached and pushed his wheelchair away. Taking a few deliberate breaths and summoning whatever strength he had anywhere in his body, he forced himself upright. For just a second, he was able to get his feet in proper position to stand, almost managed to take a step. Then he fell forward, his right hand confidently catching the safety bar, his left hand hitting the bar but unable to react quickly enough to grab on.

Eventually he got himself righted and standing, the same position he always started in. With Lalao's laugh echoing in his ears, he began shuffling down to his walker.

Rifun knew he wasn't coming back to wakefulness. For one, the air was pleasantly warm with a kind of smoky ambiance. Two, he was lying on a soft, woven mat near what he assumed was a campfire. Three, someone was beating out a drum rhythm, albeit softly, murmuring words he did not understand.

If this was a dream, it was the most vivid one he'd had in months, since losing his ability to see dreams. Even considering when he did have normal dreams, this was extremely lucid, almost like... a dream-walk. He knew that term. He remembered he had done it before, but he couldn't quite capture what that meant.

He sat up, his dream body no stronger than his waking body, to his vast disappointment.

At the same time he was thinking this, the drumbeat and the singer stopped.

"The desire to be whole comes as much from the soul as the body," the singer told him in Malagasy.

"Who are you?" Rifun inquired.

"You know who I am, if only by association and vague memories you still do not intimately grasp."

"I remember people who speak Malagasy. Surely I must know you."

He heard some movement and then footsteps which slowly drew closer to him. Rifun felt his heart begin to race as he wondered about this man's intentions. "Oh, no. You see, I do not speak Malagasy. This is the work of the Author, facilitating this communication in anticipation of the commencement of your healing. Your true healing."

"I don't understand."

The man stopped in front of him, probably knelt or squatted down. "Do you want to be healed, Rivotra Andilan?"

"How do you know my name?"

"Do you want to be healed of the curse of Rifun Ndolo? Do you want to be healed of the pain and the suffering and the deep-rooted self-loathing that has led you down this path of destruction even to the point of death?"

Rifun blinked. "I don't even know who you are. How can you promise such things?"

"My name is Anagalasgi. You murdered my nephew, Sabelu."

As soon as he said it, the memory hit Rifun like a ten-ton boulder. He'd known this factually, of course, but only now was his body inundated with the memory of using his gun to hit Sabelu in the back to incapacitate him.

Then he used a bow to shoot six arrows into him and pin him to the ground to die as a human sacrifice.

He gasped in sudden agony and leaned forward, hand on his chest as it pounded wildly, throwing itself against his ribcage. Anagalisgi knelt and put a hand gently on his shoulder, pushing him back to a sitting position. Rifun's heart still beat rapidly and he could barely breathe. Finally he managed, "Are you the one who sent them to kill me?"

"No," Anagalisgi said gently.

"Why would you want to help me?"

"Because it is the will of the Author that I should at least try. Sabelu served his purpose, he served the Author."

"I tried doing that once. I thought I was doing that," Rifun said pitifully. "It turned me into a murderer and a terrorist."

"That was Rifun Ndolo, foolish, naive, easily blinded to spiritual matters despite believing he had mastery over them. The Author made you to be Rivotra Andilan. So tell me, Rivotra. Do you want to be rid of Rifun Ndolo and serve the Author—for real this time—and fix the terrible things he has done?"

Rifun swallowed anxiously, but there was something else. Something deep inside his chest, beyond the tight lungs, the racing heart. Deep within his soul, he felt movement. His anxiety was two-fold. Rifun Ndolo, afraid that he would be cast out. Rivotra Andilan, desperate to be rid of him. And he, that nascent soul holding them both together, had a choice to make.

"Right now, your body out there is contorting in horrendous pain," Anagalisgi went on. "Julianna may not know you're alive, but the Shadows do, and they are trying everything they can to stop you. You have been given chance after chance, and you know that. Even in death, you were given another chance. But time has run out, Rivotra. You need to make a choice. Now."

"Yes!" Rivotra gasped, finding some air to fill his lungs. "Yes!"

The tightness in his chest released, but not before he contorted in a semi-seizure there on the ground. There was a horrendous shrieking noise he could not identify, echoing in an apparently small space. Then everything was quiet and he was left lying on the ground, weeping.

After a moment, Anagalisgi put a hand on his shoulder again. Rivotra opened his eyes, maybe expecting to see, still finding only blindness.

"Healing takes time," Anagalisgi told him, as if sensing his thoughts. "Making the choice to be healed is only the first step."

Rivotra heaved a massive sigh. "He's going to come back and try again."

"He will. But not today. And not here."

"What's the next step, then?"

Anagalisgi shifted position, sitting down on the ground and getting comfortable. "All these years, all of the hurt and suffering, and you've just been piling it away, pretending it made you stronger, pretending it was a good thing. Good things may be learned from suffering, but that does not make such suffering inherently good. Layers and layers of callous, of ignorance. In order to begin healing, we must rip off all of those layers and dig down to the root of the problem."

Even as he spoke, Rivotra felt tremendous anguish ten times worse than anything he had ever felt rip his body apart. He felt every scar reopen: the head and stab wounds where he had been beaten to death just months earlier; the stab wound where he had been poisoned years ago; the crippling, twisting scars from years of burning and electrocution and flogging many decades ago; his shoulder where a bullet had shattered his collarbone; his head wound where the pickax buried itself in his brain; the bruises and broken bones from his stepfather's abuse. All of it assailed him at once. He could not move, could not breathe. Even once the pain subsided, it was replaced only by such fatigue that he eventually lost all sensation in his body.

"Now," Anagalisgi said. "Now we can work on your healing."

Five
A Feast of Questions

Rivotra forced himself down another hall, keeping his walker and his feet constantly moving, taking his attention off the pain with the sounds of "Tsireko" and "Sery Hazolahy." If he was grateful for anything, it was that his voice remained in tact, even if the neighboring inmates thought he sounded like a dying cow.

He had to sing. It was the only thing he could do to honor the ancestors. Jeremy and Cameron had procured a *lamba* for him to wear, though he still could not dance. The best he could do was push himself to walk. Since returning from the meeting with Josina two weeks ago, it was basically all he did aside from eating and sleeping. Once the trays were returned and his time was his own, he was up and walking, singing the entire time and annoying the neighbors.

He could stand up and sit down now without much issue. He still had only limited awareness in his right thigh and maybe a ghost of awareness in the rest of his legs—he couldn't be sure if it was real or just wishful thinking—but he had managed to train himself how to stand and balance even without being conscious of his limbs.

Walking was an entirely different beast, and the biggest issue was arguably patience. His first step was just building strength in his legs. While he certainly felt stronger even after just a few weeks, it didn't seem to be doing all that much for him as far as the nuances of walking. His better bet came from trying to exploit the motion and control he had. He could lean on his weak left leg, take weight off his right leg enough that he could use that tiny bit of conscious control of his thigh to sort of lift his leg, enough that he was able to flex his foot and ankle and take something that resembled a natural step. Then he shifted his weight to his right leg, flexed his left foot and ankle, and more or less threw his left leg forward, just trying to help his weak side keep up with his strong side, "strong" being a relative term.

Being so mobile also presented a new revelation: his larger spatial orientation was terribly defective. He could walk up and down the hall outside his cell just fine, but the farther he got, the fuzzier his mental map became. He would turn the corner and somehow start to lose the sense of what he'd just done, spatially, and where he was in relation to his cell. He knew generally where he was in the building, knew generally where he was in the prison complex as a whole, but when it came to specific directions, he just didn't know.

He told himself that it was only because he couldn't see. Humans were very visual when it came to such orientation, after all. And yet, as he reached another hallway junction, he questioned whether this was the one he wanted. Would this take him back to his cell? Or would it take him farther away? Where was he, exactly? He didn't know, he couldn't see to try and orient himself with any visual landmarks, and the acoustics of the building, in addition to his singing, did not allow for easy aural navigation either.

Frustrated, he picked a direction and committed, continuing to sing to distract himself. Lean, raise, flex, almost step, balance. Lean, shift, flex, shuffle step, balance. Repeat. Just keep moving. He had to keep moving, build strength, maybe gain some physical control, worry about precise coordination later.

After a while, singing became hard. He was thirsty, his throat was raw after two weeks. He took a break from that and instead turned his thoughts to other things to distract him.

He hadn't spoken to Anagalisgi again since that first night. Initially he'd wondered if it had been nothing more than a dream on account of an episode of *status epilepticus*. Then he considered a few things: first, there were no dreams with seizures, not normally, and certainly nothing so vivid; second, he had regained the depth of a very significant memory; third, he had felt the movement of the spirits. Worse, he had felt the movement of spirits within himself.

Rifun Ndolo had done some terrible things. The darkness that had been placed within him at birth had seized control. And yet, he couldn't play the victim completely. He had been very aware on multiple occasions where he'd had the chance to walk away. His *nenibe* had offered it to him. Lalao had offered it to him. But Rifun had weaseled his way back to the forefront, using serpentine reasoning about slaying demons and dragons when, in reality, he had been advancing their cause all along.

But then, contemplating this, he was faced with another dilemma. The family shaman had divined his future, divined that he had a choice apart from fixed fate. Considering that such a choice had clearly favored Rifun Ndolo—a path of stars and monsters, kingship and treachery, compared to dying young and without children as a withering branch—did that mean that the evil spirits had spoken through the shaman in order to give Rifun the advantage? Had the shaman lied about his perceived choice and destiny? Or had it been orchestrated beyond even all of that in order to intentionally bring him to this place, and his perceived choice had never been a choice to begin with? Fate was fixed after all. Had his perception of being able to step outside of such mortal restrictions been an illusion the entire time?

It was humiliating in a way he was grateful he did not have to articulate to anyone here. He could just shuffle and limp along, mulling over his thoughts and problems. He couldn't understand them and they couldn't understand him. While frustrating on many occasions, it served its purpose, too.

"Ndolo!"

He completed his step, balanced, and paused, quietly flinching. He had begun requesting specifically that he wished to be addressed by his real name, Rivotra Andilan. Some respected his request, others ignored it. In the case of Lieutenant Oswald who was speaking to him now, the man simply stated that he would address inmates by their legal names. He didn't do preferred names (with exception of shortening of a name, such as Matt or John) and he didn't do nicknames. If Rivotra legally changed his name, Oswald would change how he addressed him.

"*Vous allez plus rapide,*" Oswald observed, coming up on Rivotra's left side. "*Je pense que vous devenez mieux aussi.*" (You're going faster. I think you're becoming better, too.)

"*Je ne me sens pas mieux,*" Rivotra lamented. (I don't feel better.)

"Well, here's a chair. It's time for lunch."

"I don't want a chair. I want to walk. I have to walk. I have to get better."

"And I have better things to do today, and I think you want to eat lunch while it's hot. This was all your idea."

Rivotra hesitated, then shifted his balance and felt for the wheelchair behind him. He sat down and let Oswald do whatever it was he was doing. After a moment of indeterminate sounds, he was moving.

Now that he was traveling at a normal speed, it really didn't feel like he'd gotten very far in all his shuffling. Down a hall, around the corner, down another hall, and there was the elevator. It took them only a few seconds pushing him in the wheelchair, but it had taken forever with his walker. Rivotra told himself that he had simply ended up where he was by going a different route, a longer route, one that probably would have gotten him lost on account of his disorientation. There was no way he had spent so much time trying to walk less than thirty yards.

The elevator dinged and they were moving again. Oswald exchanged words with someone else but did not stop or slow except to get through the main doors. A chill wind blasted Rivotra in the face, but he gratefully breathed in the fresh air. The air inside the medical segregation building only got more stuffy, more stale, and worse tasting with each passing day as it was slowly sealed off in order to try and conserve as much heat as possible. If nothing else, Rivotra had made it his goal to be able to walk just so he might have a chance at moving back to the genpop barracks. Granted, sweat, body odor, cigarette smoke, and the occasional tinge of fresh blood from a recent stabbing wasn't his idea of refreshing potpourri, but at least he wouldn't be marinating in it all day.

"I can't lie, I still can't believe warden approved this," Oswald commented. "Giving you a special cloth for personal mourning, that's great. Organizing a huge dinner like this? The warden must be bored."

"Maybe he wants to try something new," Rivotra suggested.

Oswald barked a laugh. "Peters is the warden because he likes things strict and predictable. We can know what day it is in what he brings for lunch. Tuna sandwich is Monday. Pizza is Tuesday. Ham and cheese is Wednesday. Salad is Thursday. Spaghetti or lasagna is Friday. If he works the weekend, mac and cheese is Saturday, fish sticks are Sunday."

"Sounds terrible."

"I agree. But I still can't believe he approved this."

They reached the cafeteria and entered. Immediately Rivotra could taste all of the dishes, and he was surprisingly not disappointed.

Someone called out something, but he didn't understand what was being said. He judged it nonthreatening, given the lieutenant's lack of reaction.

"The tables have all been moved to line the walls, center of the room is open," Oswald reported. "Lunch line is obviously the same. Basically it's the layout, chow, and after meal activity that's changed."

Rivotra tilted his head back toward Oswald. "You're trying too hard to make English syntax work, I think."

"Fuck you." That French had certainly been perfected. His tone was more annoyed than anything. He continued pushing Rivotra. "I studied French in high school years ago, only started looking at it again a few weeks ago. All for you, by the way. You're welcome." He sighed. "Eventually you're either going to remember English or you're going to have to learn it again."

"I would prefer to simply remember. It took months, even years, to learn the first time, and that was with a functioning brain."

"Let's hope."

"And I highly doubt you did it out of the goodness of your heart. More likely you and Cameron are trading shifts. He has the advantage of a native language, but, in his absence, you are the next most qualified individual."

"Fuck off."

"Did you learn that in high school?"

Oswald did not reply. A moment later, they reached the lunch line. Rice, vegetables, beef, spices, coconut, and more, all of it hot and fresh. This was a welcome change for Rivotra in the sense that it was actually hot and fresh. Medical segregation typically got their food delivered, and by the time it reached him, it was cold. He couldn't taste cold food because it didn't typically have much of a smell. Even when he did put it in his mouth, it still didn't have much of a smell to enjoy.

Was there any way to get those wires uncrossed?

Normally, lunchtime was a single tray with limited options. Oswald informed him, per the lunch person and approved by the warden, inmates were permitted two trays today.

Oswald also informed him that many inmates were thanking him for the event—Rivotra couldn't decide just how serious the man was being, given his limited French—and seemed to think he was just the coolest thing to happen to the place for a while. Between coming back from the dead and now multiplying the food at lunchtime, he really was Prison Jesus.

"Now if only I could heal myself," Rivotra mused.

"If only."

Oswald parked Rivotra at a table, then wandered off to do his own thing, whether that was take up a nearby security post or duck out to do something else for a little while.

In spite of this event allegedly being made to resemble a Malagasy funeral, Rivotra wasn't sure what to do. He knew what was normally supposed to happen, but this was hardly a normal occasion. Someone was supposed to start them off with a prayer, and then they would eat. Once most everyone had eaten, there would be more songs and dancing. Among his people, the dead were removed from the tombs and also given seats at the table, complete with plates of food. After everyone had eaten, they would take the dead bodies, lift them above their heads, and parade them, singing and dancing, back to the place that person had once called home. There the living family would show the ancestor around the house, telling them all about the family, what was going on with everyone, and ask for help and blessings. Then, still singing and dancing, the bodies would be returned to the tombs, wrapped in new linens, and laid to rest again.

Without all of that, this was little more than a fine lunch comprised of what he would consider comfort food as well as whatever had been planned for afterwards. Rivotra had been told there would be dancing. His idea of dancing and these inmates' idea of dancing were likely two very different things.

He shouldn't be offended, he told himself. It was amazing he had gotten this at all. As Oswald said, a particular cloth for personal mourning was one thing. Upending the schedule of the entire complex in order to accommodate the desires of one foreign national, that was something completely different. Even if the warden were particularly sympathetic to Rivotra's loss, this was still a very big deal.

Taking a breath and hoping that these inmates didn't carry out the threats that his medically-impaired neighbors probably threatened every morning and afternoon, Rivotra opened his mouth and started a prayer song. His sphere of influence was limited on account of the throng of people and general din of conversation. There were some complaints, one threat, evidenced through tone, but also a couple lazy rebuttals. No one hit him, beat him, or even touched him, although he did note that someone did come into his personal space, and it wasn't because they were trying to defend him from someone else. He kept his song short and sweet, hoping he maintained an air of confidence throughout the entire thing. He didn't want anyone to get the idea that he had been intimidated into stopping early.

To cover up any lingering anxiety, he started in on his food. Whoever was in his personal space moved away without saying a word. He breathed a small sigh of relief.

Rivotra couldn't say that the food was as good or better than his mother or *nenibe* or Lalao. The culinary students knew how to follow a recipe and cook with flair, but they didn't understand what the food was or how it was actually supposed to taste. It wasn't bad. There was no question that it was very good. But it was still an Americanized version of his food. He didn't know how thrilled he was about the prospect of a second helping except he didn't want to pass up a second helping.

Someone stood across from him at the table; he could feel them. They said something to him. Judging by the tone, he guessed it was mildly approving in some fashion. Maybe they were thanking him for the occasions. Maybe they were complimenting him on the menu. Maybe they were complimenting his *lamba*. Maybe they were saying how glad they were that he survived his attack. He didn't know for sure, but he tried to convey some manner of acknowledgment, if not gratitude. He didn't know what else to do.

He finished the food on his tray, listening to the hum of the room as everyone else turned from talking to eating. There was still yelling, shouting, some rough-sounding replies, and some talking with mouths full, but the overall atmosphere of the room was that of a regular cafeteria. A moment later, Cameron walked up beside him.

"Want to go back for seconds?" the social worker asked.

113

Rivotra nodded and gathered up his things. Had to make sure that everything he took he gave back, even if he was just getting it back again. Cameron returned him to his spot but did not leave right away, instead crouching or kneeling beside him.

"I understand that now may not be the best time, but I don't know that I will be sticking around for the entire thing, and I wanted to make sure you got all the details."

"Details about what?" Rivotra inquired.

"First of all, after lunch, the lawyer from Madagascar is going to meet with you again."

Rivotra shrugged. "All right."

"Second of all, starting tomorrow, you will be attending English classes in the morning after breakfast. This was arranged by myself and Andrew, who is your actual assigned social worker. Whether it's learning or remembering, we need to get you caught back up with everyone else. Lieutenant and I aren't your babysitters. You're doing really well on trying to walk again. If you can walk, you can most likely leave medical segregation. But we're not going to follow you around to translate whatever it is your work crew leader is telling you. Understand?"

"I understand."

"I'll get your slip ready for you while you're meeting with the lawyer; just give it to the instructor when he comes by in the morning."

Rivotra nodded and the man backed off.

He wouldn't say he didn't want to get his English back, or at least know enough to make sense of what people around him were generally saying. And yet, he had this fear that, if he hadn't gotten back any of his English by now, apart from a handful of random words and repeated phrases, then maybe he wasn't going to be able to learn. He might pick up basic niceties or things repeated over and over and over again, like a trained dog, but what if he couldn't get his complex thoughts to cooperate? What if that part of his brain was truly dead? What if he was physically incapable of learning?

The majority of the inmates went back for seconds. Those who didn't got up and started milling about in the center of the room, as if they knew what was about to happen. Rivotra found himself a little offended by the thought.

114

This was supposed to be his idea, an honorary funeral for his dead family, and yet these imbeciles knew more about what was going on with this event than he did. He should be the one leading this, not them. Sure, maybe they didn't speak Malagasy, but still.

It occurred to him then that whatever good intentions had gone into this, assuming there had been good intentions and this wasn't an intentional slap in the face, this was nothing more than a hollow facsimile, a mockery, of a Malagasy funeral. The songs could not be sung because they were not in Malagasy. The dances could not be performed because they could not appreciate the steps and the comradery. The dead could not be honored because they were not here to witness. This was a grand display of nothing for the amusement of those gathered.

As Oswald had said, the warden must have been bored. Or maybe it was some sort of appeasement for Josina, playing nice while the international lawyer was close enough to pitch a fit.

Rivotra felt his heart sink and his suspicions confirm as the first voice rang out. Everyone in the room quieted except for a small group in the middle. A few began some kind of rhythmic performance while another started talking. Rivotra didn't know if he was talking or singing, and there were other noises he could name but not picture in the way he expected. A shoe or a palm slapping the floor, a single clap, a rapid succession of stomps and squeaks on the linoleum.

Then another group came up as if to challenge them. They had their own rhythm keepers, their own singer, and Rivotra supposed the last one was a dancer. Was this what Rivotra had once heard called a "rap battle"? And why would he know that phrase out of all the possible English words and phrases he could know? He didn't like it, the phrase or this thing that he was now ascribing to it.

He tried to consider the layout of the room, where the doors were, and where he was in relation to them. But he just couldn't do it. His detailed spatial orientation was too scattered after being taken back and forth through the line a few times, moved to and from the table. He just wasn't sure.

The two "rap battle" groups went back and forth several times before the crowd at large apparently decided a winner. There was hooting and hollering and some unsavory-like comments as well, but no violence yet. There was some interlude chaos, and then two more groups took to the floor.

Rivotra felt a cold breeze brush the back of his head. There. Behind him. Unlocking the wheelchair brakes, he slowly inched himself back. No one seemed to care that he noticed; all attention was focused on whatever the hell these idiots in the center were babbling about. Rivotra didn't know the words specifically, but there were a couple that registered as being quite unsavory.

One wheel hit a new type of flooring, the rug that laid in front of the doors. Rivotra turned his wheelchair and eased his way toward the door. With no one around to help, this was going to require some coordination he probably didn't have. The doors were too heavy to just ram open, so the best he could try was to lean forward, force his left arm to cooperate and maneuver the handle, and then, once he felt the door give, use his right arm to force himself over the threshold as a wedge. From there, it was just inch by inch until he was on the gentle decline away from the door to the outside.

The horrendous sounds passing as music cut out as soon as the door clicked shut, and Rivotra breathed a sigh of relief. He closed his eyes and said a prayer, begging for forgiveness for allowing such a blasphemous display to have been convened. Better for there to have been no funeral at all than whatever that had been.

Now then, to return to medical segregation. He didn't want to, but it seemed like the most logical option at the moment. Briefly he considered getting out of his wheelchair and using it as a walker to hobble back to the building. It would further his goal and buy him more time out in the fresh air.

He was just getting situated to push himself to a standing position when he heard approaching footsteps. He counted at least four sets, but there could have been more. He settled back into his chair and waited as the newcomers surrounded him. He might not have been able to see their expressions or posture, but he could feel the tension in the air tighten considerably.

One of them, in front and just to the right, said something. The tone wasn't a threat, but given the underlying smirk, this wasn't a friendly welfare check.

"I'm sorry, I don't understand," Rivotra replied, trying to get his bearings as much as he could with the rest of his senses. He could probably Band and try to shuffle his way back toward his building, but he wasn't entirely sure which way it was. To the left was the best he knew, but were there any other directions, any quick jaunts? He couldn't remember.

Another man spoke up then, his tone much the same way. Rivotra could hear all of the men take another step closer.

Suddenly he felt someone tugging on his *lamba* to the left. It hung loosely over his shoulders and tied about his chest so it did not come off, but it was a very unwelcome sensation. Now he did Band, enough that he was able to quickly reach over and take the fabric out of the person's hand.

Then two people touched it, one on either side. A second later, someone grabbed the front where it was tied. This person said something, now less smirking and more threatening.

But, the thing about this person being so close was that he was close. Banding again, just enough to give himself a little advantage and try to make a point, Rivotra reached up, grabbed the person's shirt, and cracked his head into his assailant's nose, hearing a satisfying crunch as cartilage separated from bone. Pain exploded in his own head, but it wasn't so bad that his ingrained training couldn't override it for the moment and tell him to put it away for later and focus on surviving this encounter.

He didn't need to know English to know that the words that came from the man's mouth were profane in nature. Unfortunately, while he was enjoying a moment of smug satisfaction, he was unprepared for the sudden blow to his left cheek. About halfway through the strike, as more pain spider webbed from his eye socket to his jaw, some kind of Reflexive Band finally kicked in and he was able to skirt the rest of the blow.

Before anyone could do anything more, there was a shout and then another. Rivotra's attackers backed up several steps, shouting more profanity, maybe trying to run. Unsure what to do, he just stayed where he was, hands readily visible. His right was up where it was supposed to be, and his left eventually followed.

He heard a commotion, more words, more profanity, but no one bothered him for the time being. After a couple of minutes, he dared to put his hands down. About thirty seconds later, he heard Oswald's voice.

"You all right?"

"Fine," Rivotra replied, wincing at the pain in his cheek which set off the pain in his head.

"What happened?"

"I came out here. After a few minutes, they followed. They surrounded me, said some things, tried to take my *lamba*. One of them punched me."

"One also had a bloody nose, and I know his friends didn't do it."

"I'm in a wheelchair, a sitting target, what do you want me to do?"

Oswald sighed. "I'm going to pretend I didn't hear that, if only because I know exactly how that's going to go in court. Yes, they attacked a man in a wheelchair. The man in the wheelchair goes free. Obvious outcome, but more paperwork for me." He sighed again. Then, "This party is kind of for you, you know."

Rivotra shook his head. "Blasphemy. I never should have suggested it."

The lieutenant muttered something to himself. "If the warden asks, you loved it."

"But—"

"If the warden asks, you loved it. It was great. We should do things like this again in the future. Understand?"

Rivotra sighed. He knew where this was going. "And I just got overwhelmed by the wonderful display of thoughtfulness and understanding; that's why I left early."

"You don't need to put that much butter on him. Just say you liked it." Beat. "Well, you have a meeting with your lawyer from Madagascar. Might as well get you to that."

Rivotra did not argue, and the lieutenant whisked him away in another direction. A few minutes later, he was back in a small room sitting at a table, waiting for Josina. Only Oswald was present for security. Rivotra briefly wondered if it was just Cameron who was tired of acting as interpreter; the lieutenant didn't seem to mind since it meant he got a relatively easy assignment. If defending a man in a wheelchair from thugs could be considered easy.

The door opened again and Rivotra heard the light, beautiful footsteps of Josina Zitha. He unlocked his chair, scooted back a couple inches, relocked, then used the table to get to his feet.

"Oh," Josina said. "You seem to be doing better."

Cautiously putting his weight on his left arm to hold him up, he held out his right hand. "Since we were unable to be properly introduced last time."

She took his hand and he noted that her pinkie and ring fingers didn't feel quite right, nor did her skin. Actually, her skin felt kind of like his skin, twisted and scarred. Maybe it was just him, getting his sensory input mixed up again. Then they sat down.

"I'm relearning how to walk," he went on. "I'm just not fast enough for these guys."

"Or to escape a blow to the face," she observed, her tone a question.

"Ah, a few people didn't like that I tried to leave the party early."

"Yes, I was given lunch when I arrived, told that there was some Malagasy feast being held." Now her tone was one of utter disbelief. "Are you sure you're in prison?"

Rivotra chuckled. "I was beaten to death within forty days of my stay and just now suffered corporeal punishment for trying to leave a party early. Yes, I am in prison, I assure you. Now, how is your investigation into getting me out?"

"Certainly more colorful since our last discussion," she replied formally. "I was able to track down Monsieur LaPouir in the sense that he's been missing since last year around December 1st."

"What?"

"Mhm. He just vanished, right out of his home as far as anyone can tell."

Rivotra let out a breath and lowered his head into his hand, rubbing his forehead which was still aching. "Shit."

"Are you able to do that thing again? That...Band, I think you called it?"

He straightened. "Of course." He Banded the two of them, effectively excluding Oswald from the conversation even more and ensuring that it could not be recorded by the cameras in the room. "There we are."

Josina cleared her throat. "I decided to track down another lead, Walter Forbes, though you were correct in your assessment that he is going by Owain Fforidd these days."

"And?"

He could hear her shift position in her seat. "I am obligated to adhere to relevant local law which states I cannot tell you anything about him or his whereabouts. However, I believe I can tell you what he told me about you."

"I told you to keep my name out of this."

"You said you wanted to ensure that no one knew you were alive. I approached him under the premise that you were murdered in prison and the government of Madagascar is conducting an investigation. As one of your victims, I wanted to find out if he might have had any information or maybe anything to do with it."

He thought it over a minute. Then, "Well, between Owain and Tommen, I'm sure that information will disseminate quickly."

Josina went on, "I told him that the name Julianna Brown had come up during the investigation, and I wanted to know if he knew anything about her involvement with you. I also inquired whether In Jezik had come up during his investigations or during the trial that he was aware of."

Rivotra managed to finagle his arms into something resembling a folded posture. "I admit, I would have loved to have been there. What did he say?"

"He told me that In Jezik was new within the last year and you had never mentioned it. You claimed to have been part of the Cult of the Akari. Julianna was not at the warehouse nor did she come up in the investigation." She made a noise like she was debating something. "He did let slip that there was some animosity between you and her. He refused to elaborate until I inquired if the Time industry had anything to do with it."

"What did he say to that?"

"He got a little suspicious, so I decided to bring up Monsieur LaPouir's disappearance, see if I could get him to acknowledge the connection. But he didn't necessarily connect LaPouir to you—although he knew of the connection supposedly. Rather, he mentioned that LaPouir had been working on the cure or antidote for the poisons that In Jezik was known for. Then I asked if he thought maybe In Jezik had kidnapped or killed him because of that."

"In Jezik doesn't exist like it used to," Rivotra said, shrugging.

"Maybe not, but he had a different theory. He said that earlier this year—March 13th, in fact—his granddaughter was assassinated with a poison very similar to—"

Rivotra put his hand up. "Wait, wait, wait, wait, wait. Did you just say what I thought you said? Say that again."

Josina's tone softened. "His granddaughter was assassinated on March 13th, the same day that—"

"That fucking bitch," Rivotra hissed. "Absolute fucking bitch." He shook his head, feeling it pound harder.

After a moment, she continued. "His theory was that LaPouir had been kidnapped and was perhaps being forced to develop new toxins, not for In Jezik, but against them. And Julianna just happened to use his granddaughter for a test run."

He leaned back in his chair. "Fucking cunt. Who would stoop so low, honestly? Entire families, helpless babies... She's the psychopath here, not me." He shook his head again. "I don't doubt that she's behind LaPouir's disappearance, but I doubt she press-ganged him into developing such toxins. LaPouir isn't that smart, I'm sorry. He's a botanist, not a chemist. Maybe he'd grow toxic flowers, but he wouldn't be the one refining them."

"He mentioned the Borelians in tandem with In Jezik," she went on. "When I inquired whether that was a family name, perhaps who is or was overseeing the terrorist group, he got suspicious again. He asked what I really wanted, basically tried to interrogate me. I told him that I was a lawyer working for the Madagascan Senate investigating several strange deaths including yours, and his name had come up on several occasions in different capacities, including being linked to this mysterious Time industry and possibly In Jezik."

"Leave it to a lawyer to say everything and nothing," Rivotra mused.

"He gave me some more names to investigate for disappearances: Paul Haunstein—"

"Shit."

"—Miach, Micaiah, and Kayla Durvin—"

"Wait, what?"

"—Nathan Wilde—"

"Please no."

"—and possibly Godwin Lore."

"Damn it."

Rivotra could only slump in his seat.

Julianna was cleaning house. Absolutely cleaning house. With fire.

"He wasn't sure on the last, Mr. Lore. Mr. Fforidd did not seem to hold him in high esteem and said he wasn't sure of his normal movements, so he might not actually be missing."

Rivotra shook his head. "If Nathan is gone, so is Godwin. And the Miaramila, too, most likely." He shifted in his seat. "But Godwin is hard to track down. How was Julianna able to get to him but not Owain?" He went on before she could speak. "Killing his granddaughter. And, obviously, Tommen's daughter. She isn't going to kill them, not directly. She's going to torture them over years instead." He shifted again. "I guarantee she's got eyes on them. Which means you may have just entered her radar. Which means it may be only a matter of time before she figures out what you're up to and that I'm alive."

"But if I'm investigating your death...?"

"And yet you're going to spend significant time with my lawyer and go to court to argue to overturn the conviction of a dead man?" Rivotra put his face in his hand. "Shit. I shouldn't have sent you to him."

"You couldn't have known."

"No, but I should have suspected. Julianna wouldn't have had any issues convincing her generals to come after me. Taking the time and effort to massacre almost two hundred people? That would have been more difficult, unless it was part of a bigger campaign to be executed at the same time."

"Then you do know who attacked you," Josina stated.

Rivotra sighed and straightened. "Yes, I do. But there is no way I could reasonably explain it. We're in a Band now, we were in a Band then. I'd be willing to bet that it was a few days before you took up my directions because you were trying to convince yourself of what you experienced first-hand. Now explain it second- or third-hand and try not to sound crazy."

"Fair enough. And maybe it also has something to do with the possibility that her generals are not human?"

"Wow, and she still came back to talk to me."

"Owain took me to the Wheel of Time. He told me—"

"Owain's not an Akari-bearer; he shouldn't be able to get through the

122

shields. You might know them as the Safe Earth Defense System. Whatever the news pundits claim, it has nothing to do with improving phone signal and protecting the planet from small asteroids. It was put in place to stop an invasion by the Borelians. But it also stopped the use of Time portals."

"He said he'd only recently begun learning the Akari, said that most Time abilities could translate over pretty well and that the Akari was not affected by the shields. He told me that if I was serious about pursuing the investigation, then I deserved to know what I was really up against. He said that if I could handle it, he wished me all the luck in the world and would help any way he could. But if I couldn't handle it, then to just walk away. Say I hit all the dead ends, everyone checked out, whatever my superiors would believe in order to kill the investigation. He would Suppress me so I couldn't use any Time abilities, and it was up to me to keep my mouth shut."

"Yet here you are," Rivotra stated.

"Here I am."

"Going to the Wheel of Time, that's more than enough exposure for most people to unlock nascent Time abilities, usually Banding."

"He told me that, too. He also showed me how to keep it in check so I didn't accidentally Band when I didn't consciously want to."

Rivotra leaned back again. "I'm impressed. So you do believe me."

"It's hard not to when you witness the gathering of hundreds of aliens from across the universe. I still don't know I'm not crazy or that it wasn't some kind of awful trick, but it is opening up many more possibilities and dangers in this investigation."

"Oh, you have no idea. Is he your Master, then?"

"I had him show me how to keep the Bands in check, but I told him I would have to think about it first."

Rivotra nodded. "Did Tommen tell you anything? I know, I can't know his whereabouts, but did he say anything in regards to this?"

"He wasn't there."

"Hm. Father and son must have parted ways, then. Good for him, becoming his own man." He shifted position again. "So, you have a bunch of new information. What's next? I have to assume that Julianna will track me down through you eventually, so my goal is the same as it has been for a while, get walking again and see what I can do from there."

"Your lawyer Mr. Bartlett is continuing to handle things here in regards to filing motions and other paperwork. We will remain in contact, and I will return when it comes time to argue before a judge. In the meantime, I am returning home to continue that investigation."

"Have you been able to determine anything about the land inheritance?"

"Not yet. That will be one of my first priorities when I return."

"When you do, know that...going forward, I want to rid myself of Rifun Ndolo. He has been nothing but a curse. I wish to finally and permanently take my name as Rivotra Andilan as it should have been from the beginning. At this point, I am the last Andilan."

"I make no guarantees, but I will see what I can do," she promised.

He dropped the Band. "One more question. Maybe a few more. You seem oddly calm about all of this. Considering the prevalence of witchcraft among our people, considering we are not inundated with millions of bizarre ideas perpetuated by media every single day like the Westerners, what is it that you are drawing on? For me it was twisted spirituality, ideology."

For a moment, he was afraid she wouldn't answer. Then, "I told you my father was a businessman, successful in imports and exports. Well, some thought him too successful. Others didn't like his political leanings. Still others thought he was not 'Muslim enough' because he encouraged his daughters to go to school and become literate and successful."

"You're Muslim, then?"

"No, not anymore."

"But someone killed him because he was everything they couldn't be?"

"Someone, or multiple someones, tried to kill all of us. They succeeded at killing my mother, all of my sisters, and most of my brothers. I was hospitalized with my father and two remaining brothers. When I was released, for my safety, my father sent me to live with my mother's family in Madagascar. A few months later, he and my brothers were shot and killed when they were leaving for Maputo on business."

"I'm sorry to hear that," Rivotra told her sincerely.

"No one was ever held accountable, not even questioned," Josina went on, voice cold. "Any time I go back and look into the matter, I have never been able to get answers, only death threats." She hummed a sigh. "I will find out who did this to you and your family, and I will make sure they are held accountable. And if they are holed up in some fortress across the universe, thinking that their mystical, witchy abilities will protect them, I will happily let them know that they are wrong."

He nodded. "Thank you." He cleared his throat. "If I may ask, how old were you?"

"Ten, the second-youngest daughter of five and third-youngest of twelve children of my parents."

"I'm sorry."

"Twenty years gone. Still I search. I will not give up so easily for you."

Their meeting ended shortly after that. Josina wished him luck and said she would visit again when she returned to the United States next. He said he looked forward to the visit. Then she departed, and Rivotra was left with Oswald for company as the lieutenant wheeled him back across the complex toward the correct building.

"Is she pretty?" Rivotra asked.

"Who?" the lieutenant wondered. "The lawyer?"

"Well I'm not asking about your sister."

Oswald made an exasperated sound. Then, "Well, she's not bad looking. Real dark skin, has her hair short, basically shaved, nice body. Tall as you, though, which is weird in my opinion; I don't like really tall women. She has some big scars on her right side, though, face, neck, and hand."

Rivotra blinked. "Really?"

"Yeah. Looks like scars you would see on a wounded soldier, like fire and..." He trailed off, apparently unable to come up with the word. "Pieces of metal."

"Shrapnel. Like a bomb?"

"Yeah, I guess."

A ten year old victim of a bomb blast, Rivotra thought. And it explained why her hand had felt weird in the handshake. It wasn't him this time, it was her. Actually she was probably lucky to still have all her fingers. She must have been one of the farthest from the blast, or perhaps shielded by her mother or an older sibling.

He kind of felt sorry that she was leaving. Yes, she was going home to do her job, but it was so far away. He wanted to talk to her again, keep talking to her. He wanted to talk about home with someone who would understand. He wanted to explain more about Time and the Akari and show her things. He didn't know how since his abilities were a bit lacking right now, but still. Walter might try to arrange for a mentor for her, but he was right here. If he was able to be set free and return home, he could train her just fine. Maybe he could call her.

No, he told himself. He couldn't get attached. She was doing her job. This was exactly what she was expected to do. Maybe learning Time and Timekeeping was a bit of a stretch, but she was utilizing all available resources and digging to get to the bottom of this mystery. She was trying to help her client. She was the lawyer, and he was the client.

All the same, he did like talking to her.

Oswald returned him to his cell, mildly wished him a good day, and left. Immediately, Rivotra got to his feet. His first thought to grab his walker and keep up his strength routine was briefly interrupted by immense gratitude that he was able to stand and pee like a man again. Then he grabbed his walker and started his strength and shuffling routine.

If anyone found Josina's conversation with Owain at all suspicious, it wouldn't take but a few days to track down his lawyer and, ultimately, him.

Another thought occurred to him. She was very calm about all of this. Most people, especially if they were older than twenty and came from a very superstitious culture, would not be so calm after learning about the existence of Time, the Time industry, and the Wheel of Time with its many alien species. And it seemed to be very convenient that she would have a history that was so similar to what he was just now experiencing. What if Julianna already knew he'd survived? What if Josina was an Order agent? What if Josina was Julianna herself?

But why? Why would Julianna go through so much hassle to try and trick him? She had sent out a massive assault on hundreds, maybe even thousands of people, including regular civilians, slaughtered them like cattle. He had been directly involved, dead for at least a few minutes. If Julianna wanted him gone, she was clearly very tired of drawn-out games and would make sure he was gone. Whether Josina was real or a Disguise, she could murder him in one of these interviews and slip away without ever worrying about how much security was installed in this facility.

Or what if Josina wasn't that calm, but she knew she couldn't afford to show weakness or uncertainty in this place? She admitted it took several days for her to get up the courage to pursue such a line of thought and investigation. And, Rivotra reflected, Owain probably would have been one of the best people to explain it to her as he had been in his forties when first introduced to Time. If anyone could make it palatable to those over twenty, it would be him.

Neither explanation really satisfied him, she wasn't going to be around for a while to ask, and he didn't really have any means of conducting his own investigation. The best he could do was just shuffle along with his walker, trying to get his dead limbs to cooperate, and mulling over endless thoughts that were only likely to become more outlandish and possibly paranoid as time went on.

Julianna had pushed his trial through quickly so as not to waste time, just skip to the end when everyone could hear his verdict and rub salt in that wound. Without any more moles, how long was this appeal going to take? Months? Years? Rivotra had a vague notion that there were multiple appellate arenas in the American judiciary, so while his lawyer might not have been worried about losing the first appeal, Rivotra was looking at time. If Julianna suspected he was alive, he wanted to not be in prison when she came for him. Maybe his absence would be enough, who knew?

He tried to push such thoughts aside and focus on his walking. Whether he was in prison or at home, he was useless in a fight right now. He could barely fend off a few petty thugs. He needed to get himself back together.

A wave of vertigo almost took him off his feet. Actually, according to his head, he was nearly upside down, perhaps in some odd contortion given that he knew his feet were still on the ground. He gripped his walker as tight as he could, focused on the knowledge that he was still upright. He was upright, he was walking, he just couldn't convince his brain of that fact.

Gritting his teeth, he forced one foot forward. He didn't try to walk necessarily, just wanted to keep moving. Had to keep moving. And, after a few seconds, the vertigo subsided and his head went back up on his shoulders where it should have been, where it always was. Letting out a breath, he tried not to break stride as he resumed his walking motion.

If Julianna doesn't already know I'm here, she's going to find out eventually. And at that point, I'm dead all over again.

He didn't think he would be coming back a second time.

Every wound he had ever sustained had been reopened. Every cut bled freely, every brand sizzled, and every so often he would turn his head and cough up a bit of water.

Rivotra lay on his back by the fire in Anagalisgi's cave. The mat beneath him tasted of hair and the plants used for dyeing. He had arrived in this place completely naked and in some excruciating pain, and Anagalisgi had made no effort to change that. Instead, he'd instructed Rivotra to lie in such a position and simply wait.

He could hear the man rummaging around amid what he assumed to be clay jars. Neither one of them said a word. Anagalisgi seemed to be very confident in whatever was about to happen, and Rivotra was, admittedly, too afraid to ask what that was. Then the rummaging stopped and he heard Anagalisgi's footsteps return. The man still said nothing as he knelt beside Rivotra, plopping down a cloth with some small items inside. Rivotra could not identify what the things were made of, although he knew they were not metal. Wood or bone, perhaps.

"Tell me about your mother," Anagalisgi said calmly. "I don't mean her name or what she looked like. Tell me about her. What did she like to do?"

"She enjoyed weaving and sewing," Rivotra answered, unsure how detailed he was supposed to be and wary of what this discussion might be intended to distract him from. "She loved making *lambas* for every occasion or no occasion at all. Sometimes she was able to sell them and bring in some more money."

"Mhm. And how did she relate to your father?"

"My stepfather? She tolerated him enough to give him eight more children and died in the process."

"Do you think that maybe she loved your stepfather?"

"If she did, I don't understand why."

Rivotra had more to say but was startled by a sharp poke into the skin of his chest. He flinched and hissed in pain, but Anagalisgi put a hand on him to keep him down. Another poke, and Rivotra concluded that the man was stitching up his wounds. But why? This was a dream. These wounds had not existed before; could he not make them go away just as easily?

"Why don't you understand?" Anagalisgi asked.

"He was a horrible person. How can you love someone who beats your child and treats them so poorly?"

"Do you blame your mother, then, for your treatment?"

Rivotra hesitated.

"What did you do?" Anagalisgi went on.

"Eventually I ran away. I joined the VVS."

"Why?"

"Try to prove myself."

"To whom or what?"

"Everyone. Everyone who thought less of me because I was a half-French bastard." Rivotra flinched again as Anagalisgi continued to thread the needle through his skin. He noted, somewhere in the back of his mind, that there was no actual thread attached, or it didn't feel like there was. Yet the skin closed up as expected.

"And were they impressed?"

"No. They hated me even more."

"And you sought to prove yourself once more, ultimately giving control over to Rifun."

"Yes."

"Mm," Anagalisgi hummed, sticking him again. "What did you think about your shaman's prophecy? Stars and monsters, kingship and treachery, a destiny walked upon the edge of a knife."

"I thought it sounded more promising than dying young with no family and withering on the vine."

"And now?"

"Now I wonder if it wasn't the Shadows speaking all along, pushing me in the direction they wanted me to go to advance their agenda. Maybe I would have been just fine if I had stayed." Rivotra turned his head and spit up some water. Then, "Did I ever really have a choice, or was it all just an illusion? Was I always destined to walk the path I did?"

"Some people call me a prophet," Anagalisgi mused, tugging on a fine thread. "Where they get confused is what they think prophecy is. Prophecy isn't telling you what you're going to do. It's telling you what you've already done. The Whites jump in and out of time as they wish. Yawi has the ability to jump back in time and visit with Sabelu. He can walk ahead and see Sabelu's descendants for many generations. The Shadows do not have this same ability. For them, there is only the now and what they believe is the future, as blind as any common mortal. The Whites are proactive, the Shadows reactive."

"I don't understand what that has to do with me."

"Rivotra has a path to walk. He has always been walking this path. In two hundred pages, there you are, still walking that path. But the Shadows, not knowing what is coming in two hundred pages, do everything that can to try and steer him off course."

"And Rivotra was pushed aside in favor of Rifun and his foolish ambitions. But why?"

"To accomplish the Author's purpose. Nothing more. Nothing less."

"And when I was dying and you asked if I wanted to be rid of his curse?" Rivotra wondered.

"Rifun's time was done. He served his purpose, according to the Author, though he may have denied and done everything he could to oppose it. But no one is forced to serve. Once Rifun was gone, you had to make the choice to continue, to serve."

"What if, in ten years, I decide I don't want to?"

"Then Rivotra, this beautiful creation of the Author, will again be supplanted for the will of another angry Shadow."

"And what if that Shadow gets me killed permanently next time? What if I don't have a chance to talk to you and decide to undo everything I've done?"

Anagalisgi stuck him again. "What indeed?" Another stick. "Few people are so overtly involved in such spiritual matters. For most, it is day-by-day, hour-by-hour, with far more mundane decisions to make. Yet the premise remains the same. Your decisions these days are rather mundane, compared to some you've made. Perhaps now is a good time to consider yourself before anyone else."

Six
Higher Power

What a time to remember how to walk, Rivotra silently grumbled, making his way through the wind and snow toward the chapel. The snow wasn't more than an inch or two deep, but it was still quite miserable.

With one hand on Oswald's arm and the other hand gripping his cane, Rivotra hobbled along the snow-covered pathway. His right leg was almost normal now, midway through February. He had good balance, good form, good motion overall, even though he still couldn't actually feel his knee or lower leg. His thigh had improved somewhat, but there was still something off that he couldn't quite articulate in any language. His left leg was, well, usable. He had only the ghost of sensation in both parts, but it was enough for him to try and exploit. He'd moved past throwing his hip and shuffling his foot to get it to move, but he still lacked repeated, sturdy, natural motion.

He could walk fine with his walker, but his spatial orientation was still too disorganized for that to be prudent in the cold weather. No one might have cared, except Oswald happened to be in the building at the time and Rivotra managed to flag him down for help.

As much as Rivotra was grateful to be walking and no longer dependent on the wheelchair, there were times when he still considered its use. Oswald would have much preferred it, he knew.

They reached the chapel and ducked inside, grateful to be out of the wind. Rivotra could not suppress a brief shiver.

The chapel wasn't anything fancy; it couldn't be when anything and everything could potentially be a weapon. Even the cross was rumored to be bolted to the wall just in case. Services were held on Sunday mornings, Sunday evenings, and Wednesday evenings, for inmates with a busy schedule. Today happened to be a Tuesday, and the main chapel area was empty.

Oswald led the way to the front of the room and through a side door, then stopped short.

"Oh!" a man gasped. "Hello, lieutenant. Can I help you?"

In the last few months of near-daily tutelage, Rivotra had recovered a bit of English. It felt more like learning from scratch rather than finding something he'd lost. He had to think about most things being said even if they were spoken slowly and enunciated well, and he sometimes struggled to put sounds together. The good news was, he could generally make his needs known, and he could better remember people he spoke to.

So it was that he could not well follow what Oswald was telling this man, presumably the head chaplain, beyond a few common, frequent words that his brain involuntarily latched onto. The chaplain replied, most of his words just as incomprehensible. They were probably just fine, really, but he also spoke too fast for Rivotra to follow.

Then they were moving again. The whole exchange lasted less than five seconds, yet Rivotra was still mulling over a handful of scattered words. "Where," "he," "office," and "your." He knew all of these words, there was nothing special about them, but he was also fascinated by them for some odd reason.

And again they stopped, turning to the left into a room.

"Lieutenant," Jeremy greeted. "Mr. Andilan."

"I...need..." Rivotra got the jump on the conversation before Oswald, but now he staggered through his words. "...talk...to you."

Jeremy cleared his throat. "Should we ask Cameron to come here?"

Rivotra felt Oswald shrug and heard him reply. Jeremy said something back.

Oswald took Rivotra's hand from his arm and guided it to a chair. Rivotra thanked the lieutenant and made it into the seat without incident, leaning his cane against the understudy's desk. He heard the door behind him squeak, but it did not close, and footsteps walked away down the hall.

"Slow," Rivotra said. "Please."

"I understand," Jeremy said calmly. "It's good you're able to learn."

Rivotra nodded. "I am happy to speak. Cameron is happy I can speak."

The understudy laughed. Then, "How can I help you?"

"Who..." No, that wasn't right. "How..." That wasn't it either. "What..." Yes, that was it. "What you do know..." He sighed. "You are...N...Na..." He almost knew the word. It was right there.

"Navajo?" Jeremy offered.

"Yes."

"Yes, I am."

"What...you do know...about...the Krydik?"

He could hear Jeremy shifting position in his chair, something bulky like a winter jacket crinkling with every movement. "What do I know about the Krydik?"

"Yes."

"Hm...that is a big question. With a lot of big and strange words."

Rivotra sighed. "I...thinked so."

"Why do you want to know? Or maybe, why do you want to know now? Why not wait until you learn more words?"

"I learn too slow. I need...information."

"About stories?"

"About the Krydik."

Jeremy made an odd sound, one Rivotra decided to classify as being in the neighborhood between hesitation and uncertainty.

"The Navajo call the Krydik the coward people, the people who ran away. Even when the Krydik fight, they always lose."

"Where live the Krydik?"

The understudy did not answer for a long minute, and Rivotra could feel the scrutiny.

"It is said the Krydik live among the stars," he answered evasively.

"Among the stars," Rivotra echoed, trying to put the words together. "On Hl...Hl...Hol...Holhi."

"They call their reservation Hlohi, yes."

Rivotra shifted in his seat. "You do tell Julianna I am alive?"

Jeremy hummed, the tone bored. "Who? I don't know who that is." He paused, and Rivotra could feel an uncomfortable tension. "But I do know that you killed Sabelu a couple years ago. When it happened, the Krydik sent word near and far about who you were and what you'd done."

Rivotra swallowed. "You say nothing?"

"Not my people. Not my problem." The chaplain understudy shifted position again, his tone relaxing. "And not my place. I believe in forgiveness, even if forgiveness is not easy."

"But you know. About everything."

"I don't know the details, only the stories."

"You come here...with intention...for me?"

"Actually, no. I say only that it must be ordained by God."

Rivotra nodded absently, both surprised by the admission and also immensely frustrated that the conversation couldn't be more productive. "What news...you hear...out of Holhi?"

Jeremy sighed again, himself sounding frustrated by the stunted communication. Or maybe because this was not the conversation he expected to have today. Then, "You tell me why you killed Sabelu. I tell you what I know."

The only way to do that was with fractured English because there was no way he could ask for anyone to interpret a murder confession.

"I lived in...not God," Rivotra began, mentally kicking himself and greatly regretting his decision to try and push this through too soon. "Not God. Soul. Mother, father, grandmother, grandfather. Dead are strong. Good and bad souls. Good and bad...speak to souls. Speaker to speak to souls."

Briefly he wondered if this wasn't some kind of self-indulgence on Jeremy's part, whether the chaplain understudy enjoyed watching him squirm in such humiliation.

"Telled to me to be speaker to souls," Rivotra went on. "I see souls. My mother. And more. Tell me to kill dark souls. Not men. Souls in men. I go out, I go..." He made a following motion with his hands until the word came to him. "After. I go after dark souls in men. I meet Cassius and Julianna. Julianna tells me dark soul in Cassius. I have to kill dark soul. Kill man do no good, dark soul escape.

"I go after Cassius. Go after dark soul. I do not know...how...to kill. I try...bring soul...close. Walter and Tommen...not good. Not die, but not good. Cassius and dark soul go away."

There was so much more to this. He just didn't have the words, damn it!

"I find Cassius. He is mad. I try to kill dark soul. Cassius died, dark soul go away. I also run. I talk to good souls, I think, ask for help. They tell me Sabelu. Tell me where to find. I go after Sabelu. Souls tell me he is also speaker to souls, but bad souls. He is together with bad souls. I kill souls but I also kill man to stop dark souls. I do a..." He didn't know the word and nothing was coming to him. "I do a thing and I wait for him. He walks into my...thing. I think he is weak now."

Rivotra let out a breath. Since talking to Anagalisgi, he remembered that hillside confrontation. He remembered the ritual he had performed. He remembered watching Sabelu as he made his way directly into the sacred circle. And he remembered how calm Sabelu had been.

"Sabelu speak to me. He asks if I know...why I am here. There. If I want to know why I am there." Rivotra shook his head. "He do not help him. He do not...try. To fight. He stays. He waits. I kill him. One and five." He wished he could see Jeremy's expression, wondered if Oswald was listening to this. Too late now. "After, I do not know. I think bad. I...question. I ask. But good souls tell me I do good. I do not know."

"And what do you think now?" Jeremy wondered, tone neutral.

"The dark souls, they...do not help me. I go to bad places, I do bad things. For the dark souls. I think they are good souls, but they are not. I know they are not. But Julianna has dark soul. I am not with the dark souls now, and the dark souls kill me."

"Hm." Jeremy shifted position and there was a minor sound on the desk, as if he were now leaning on his elbows on the top. "With bad English, it is hard to tell, I understand. But I can also see that you are s—" He caught himself before using a big word. "You are good. You want to do good even if you do not have everything. You do not have many words, but you have enough."

"Thank you."

"I have heard news from the Krydik," the understudy went on. "You wanted to help. You wanted to bring together. I do not know the full story. You helped the dark souls, the evil spirits, for a time. But in the end, you wanted what they did not, and they left you. Then they tried to kill you. But Julianna wants what they want, so they use her. She attacks the Krydik."

"She wants to kill..." Rivotra searched for the word. "This person. And that person. And that person. Me. And Sabelu. And Tommen Forbes. And Walter Forbes. We have books. Good books. She does not like that. She wants to have only book. Krydik have books. Sabelu talked to good souls, knew the good books. I killed him. Julianna killed me. She killed others. What news from the Krydik? She kill them...before? In March?"

Jeremy hummed a sigh and said something Rivotra did not catch. Then, "I do not know where story stops and news begins. The Krydik...are small. Their land, not big. Hidden here. They say they are from the stars, that Hlohi is not here. They say Krydik are not from here, that Krydik are many people. Is it good, or is it story? The Krydik are good. They have been here. But where is Hlohi? How does Julianna attack?"

"Holhi is in the stars. Ground and sky."

"Another planet?"

It took a minute for Rivotra to put the words together. He didn't fully grasp the second one, but it sounded familiar enough that he said yes. "Nathan and Andrew take the Krydik—not the Krydik, before the Krydik—to Holhi. They run."

"The people who ran."

"Yes. Krydik run to another planet."

"If I believe you, if Hlohi were a planet, how does Julianna attack?"

"She goes to Holhi." What was being lost in translation here? "Like Nathan and Andrew take Krydik to Holhi."

"How?"

"A door. In the air."

Now Jeremy's sigh was skewed toward disbelief. Rivotra started to speak, but the understudy cut him off. "I know. I hear the stories. I do not have a better answer." He sighed again. "All right. Why do you want news from Hlohi? Why do you need information?"

"I want to know...if Julianna...is...doing good...in her want. I want to know...if...my people...not Malagasy, other people...if my people...do help." He sighed. There was so much more he wanted to say. Most of it he didn't have the words, and the rest could easily be misconstrued as threats. Some of them actually were.

Jeremy said something, then quickly corrected himself. "You want news...from soon."

"Yes."

"I do not have new news. I have old news, before March."

"You ask?"

The understudy hummed and cleared his throat and shifted position. Rivotra wondered if there were some prison security protocol he might be breaking, or whether there was some tribal tension he was stirring up. Finally, "I can try."

"Thank you." A new thought came to Rivotra. "Do you know Anagalisgi?"

"No, I do not know him. Him? Her?"

"He is...brother of father of Sabelu. No. Brother of father of mother of Sabelu."

"I understand. He is good? Good to know? Important?"

Rivotra figured he was already pushing his luck with his attempt at explaining doors in the air; there was no way he was going to be able to describe meeting with a three hundred year old doom prophet in his dreams. Instead he settled for, "Yes. Good. And important."

"I will remember that when I ask."

"Thank you."

More seat shifting. "And how are you? You still wear your *lamba*. How long do you wear it?"

"Many months," was the best Rivotra could answer. "Many months on all dead."

"Some people say you sing every day."

"Many people dead. I sing every day for every dead. Walk because I cannot...dance."

"Why don't you come here? Why don't you sing here?" When Rivotra hesitated, he added, "If you know the souls before were bad, why not sing to good souls?"

"Dark souls can see as good souls. Does not make good souls not good."

"Yes. And here we sing to good spirits, the Holy Spirit. You can come here and sing, too."

Rivotra shook his head. "No. I stay where I am."

Jeremy said something Rivotra did not understand, but it was no stretch of the imagination that it was something along the lines of, "If you change your mind..." Then he asked, "Have you heard news from home?"

Rivotra shifted in his seat. "No."

"Is that good or bad?"

He shrugged. "I do not know. Madagascar..." How was he supposed to explain the complexities of foreign customs, foreign government, and corruption using only the most rudimentary of words? The majority of English words might have Latin roots, but it was always the important ones that seemed to differ. *"Il y a beaucoup de corruption."*

"Corruption," Jeremy repeated. "I know that word. And 'beaucoup' is 'a lot.'"

"A lot of corruption, yes."

"Is your lawyer helping you? Is Miss Zitha helping you?"

"I think. I do not know. I do not hear of her."

The understudy said several incomprehensible things. Rivotra again latched onto a few odd words he did know and puzzled over a few that sounded similar to French words, but he was loathe to automatically assume they meant the same thing.

After a minute of silence, the understudy cleared his throat. "Do you want to say more?"

Even he knew it was a polite way of asking if he needed anything else because otherwise he was just taking up space. He understood. Rivotra chuckled humorlessly. "Yes, but I have no words. I learn more and speak the words after."

There really was so much more that he wanted to say, wanted to ask, wanted to know. There just wasn't any good way to go about it at the moment. And he wasn't too keen on going back outside in the cold and snow. The little space heater he heard humming in the room was doing wonders at making him perhaps a little too comfortable.

Jeremy called for an officer at one of the chapel doors. Then Rivotra thanked him, stood, cautiously took the officer's arm, and began hobbling away. This officer did not speak French, but he wasn't in much of a talking mood. He'd muddled through this conversation, probably lost half of what Jeremy had said while being unable to relay more than half of the story he needed to tell to make him understand.

Jeremy probably thought Rivotra was asking for information about folktales or historical events or, perhaps, some tiny tribe that meant nothing in the larger scheme of things. He didn't realize that Rivotra was looking for real news about a real people who really lived on another planet and were under very real attack from Julianna. All because the Krydik had a Book, an Authored Book, one that detailed their lives and history as ordained by the Author. He, Rivotra, had three Books. Miach and MacEoghan had Books. Aklaq White Bear had a Book. According to Josina, they were all missing, likely dead. Owain and Tommen also had Authored Books, although Julianna seemed to be toying with them first.

Julianna, meanwhile, didn't have an Authored Book. She hated them. It was why she'd pushed her husband Richard to write his journals, to try and supplant the power of the Books. But those journals had not detailed use of the true Akari, only the Shadows' bastardized version of it.

It wasn't so much that Julianna hated the Books, Rivotra reflected, working hard to steady himself in the wind. Her problem was that the Books focused on "other" people. "Lesser" people. The Krydik—who had been only Cherokee at the time—had been the first recipients. Then there was him and Cassius, both African. Miach and MacEoghan were Irish. Aklaq was Inuit. Owain and Tommen were Welsh. All of them "less than" compared to her pure English blood. If there were a Book about her, she would be more than happy to beat everyone over the head with it. Yet the Books seemed to be about everyone but her, and she couldn't stand it.

She was going to kill everyone who had an Authored Book, then write her own, Rivotra knew. And he had taken the ramshackle Cult of the Akari, turned it into the First Order of the Akari, and propelled it all the way to a position where she might have a shot at doing just that. He couldn't let that happen, he thought as he and the officer ducked into the medical segregation building, grateful to be out of the wind. He had been given a chance to make things right. He had built the First Order, and he was going to dismantle it brick by brick. Just as soon as he could bloody walk.

Once inside the building, the officer let him go. Rivotra thanked him and turned his attention inward. He was still anxious about his spatial orientation, but he had at least learned to navigate between his cell and the front door. If nothing else, he could count his staggered steps and get fairly close to his desired destination, even if it was just the elevator.

At some point, one of the social workers had decided to make up a braille label for his cell. There was a sticky label attached to the door and the wall beside to denote who currently resided there. Rivotra had tried, with only moderate success, to learn braille, or his name and number in braille, and, after a few unwelcome mishaps, it certainly helped to clear up any lingering confusion. Every so often, some sneaky bastard would come by and peel the labels off, but there was enough leftover residue underneath to feel regardless.

He'd just sat down on the bed when the announcement came for lunch. The announcement always came early, seeing how the majority of residents needed assistance to get to the private cafeteria in the building. Rivotra groaned, stood again, and slowly made his way down to the main floor, then to the cafeteria. Three steps in, turn right, his was the first table he came to, just to make things easy. There he sat and listened to the nurses and a couple officers as they shuttled elderly inmates into the room.

There were a few minutes of general conversation. Then, across the room, there was a whistle. This was followed just half a breath later by a series of more cat-calling whistles. That meant that either there was a female food service instructor in the kitchen with the inmates, or a female nurse delivering the noonday medication. Cameron had explained once that it was illegal to discriminate based on sex, that they could not use such a reason to deny any female applicant employment, nor could they advise any of the outside contractors to not send competent female workers. The social worker had also explained that they did this anyway, in both scenarios. But, due to various reasons, many of them having to do with being short-staffed and having a high turnover rate, sometimes things just couldn't be helped.

Indeed, as one of the food service inmates came around with his cart of lunch trays—"meals on wheels" Rivotra had heard it called in the nursing home—there was a female nurse handing out medication and an extra cranky officer accompanying both of them and getting after the inmates for rowdy behavior. Other than himself and maybe a few others, Rivotra didn't know what the officer expected any of the old heads to do. They were incapable of caring for themselves; most used walkers or wheelchairs to get around—and that badly—and had required assistance just to get to lunch. He was no longer the one in the worst shape, as sorry as his condition was. What this officer was waiting for, he did not know, nor did he want to ask.

"981436," Rivotra reported when they got to him. A number in exchange for a takeout meal.

Five others sat at the table with him. Cameron had once told him that all of them were blind or very nearly so. The reasoning behind putting them together was to minimize the chance of a table mate stealing food off each other's trays. And, with as immobile as everyone generally was, it was unlikely that someone from a neighboring table was going to steal anything either.

Didn't matter much to Rivotra. On the one hand, it wasn't a lot of food to begin with, just enough to meet the caloric requirements set forth by the state so no one was technically at risk of starving to death. Plus, old heads just didn't eat a lot, which made things easier on the cooks over in the main cafeteria. On the other hand, because of Rivotra's use of Time, his metabolism slowed down to the point where it almost stopped. He was more at risk of gaining weight, even on such paltry rations. Now that he was several months removed from his hospital stay and working rigorously on his rehabilitation, this tiny meal consisting of a tuna sandwich, macaroni and cheese, broccoli, and grape juice was just right for him.

"So, what do you boys think?" one of his table mates wondered. His tone might have been conspiratorial, but between smoker's lung, emphysema, lung cancer, throat cancer, and being almost deaf in addition to almost blind, half the room heard the squelching radio static that was his question.

"About what?" another table mate asked. He was the opposite, having gone quieter and quieter the more his vision and hearing deteriorated.

"The woman? Was she cute?"

Someone from another table responded in the emphatic affirmative to the delight of several others.

The man to Rivotra's left, called Skipper, elbowed him in the ribs, causing him to flinch. "What do you think is a beautiful woman, huh, PJ?" He said more, perhaps making suggestions that Rivotra wasn't sure he wanted to hear.

He mentally sighed and decided to humor the old man. "Malagasy, first."

"Mal-what?"

"Malagasy, from Madagascar."

"Oh, yeah, yeah, yeah, that's where you're from, ain't it? Yeah, be nice to have a girl from back home. But, when I was in the army in Nam..."

Sometimes, Rivotra was almost glad for his lack of comprehension; it spared him from having to listen to the same old war stories a dozen times. He'd originally thought such a phenomenon was unique to his people, or poor peoples in general, trying to cope with poverty by remembering a time when things were grand and heroic and maybe a little mythological. He'd heard a little bit of this when he lived in France, and he then suspected that it came from peoples whose nations had seen war, real war in their backyards. As it turned out, not so. No, even these Americans who had never had to defeat a foreign army in their own land were prone to the same exaggeration as every other soldier and civilian.

That was fine, he thought, fishing for the last of his mac and cheese. What did these old heads have to look forward to, anyway? Another day of whiling away their time in a wheelchair, whistling at pretty nurses, grateful to be able to feed themselves even as they needed help to wipe their asses. Let them have their stories.

"911342!" an officer bellowed.

"Here!" someone chortled.

"924031!"

Mail call. In genpop, the mail was delivered in the morning at count. If an inmate was where he was supposed to be, he got his mail. Here, it was wordlessly delivered by hand by an accompanying social worker.

"981436!"

Rivotra reacted more out of instinct as he raised his hand, but he was more surprised than anything. He didn't get mail. No one knew to write to him. What was this?

The envelope was stuffed under his tray and the social worker ambled off. It was one of the first jobs for a new social worker, Rivotra knew. It was a way to get the social workers close to the inmates without having to talk to them just yet, something that many green workers apparently struggled with. It wasn't the talking necessarily or the desire to help, it was the ingrained and only slightly exaggerated cultural fear that they were going to be shanked or beaten up or taken hostage their first day on the job.

Rivotra touched the envelope, felt it. All of the mail was heavily scrutinized before it ever got to its intended recipient, so the chances of it being dangerous were only slightly higher than the average mail customer on the outside. Junk mail like political ads or credit card offers was filtered out. Ideally, only mail of substance actually got through.

Could be from his lawyer, he figured, feeling that there was some thickness to the papers inside. Maybe it was just a formal update on the appeal process; guaranteed if the appeal had gone through and his conviction overturned, he wouldn't be sitting at this lunch table. Or, maybe it was from Josina, some progress on his inheritance back home. Did he dare allow himself some kind of hope? Hope could kill a man in prison, but so could the absence of hope.

Didn't matter anyway, given that he couldn't actually read the letter. And if he had someone read it to him, would he even be able to understand?

Rivotra finished off his lunch and managed to get the attention of the social worker who had acted as the delivery boy.

"I need to speak to Cameron," Rivotra told him in his best English.

The social worker began babbling, probably reciting some protocol about filing a request, making an appointment, and so on. After a couple sentences, the mail officer stepped in and cut him off. The two conversed for a few minutes before the social worker finally agreed, saying something Rivotra still didn't catch.

The food service inmates came around to collect trays. Once a tray was cleared, the restaurant patrons were free to leave. Rivotra grabbed his cane and his letter and made his way out the door. He deliberately retraced his steps back to his cell where he decided he would wait for Cameron. After about ten minutes, he wondered if the man would show up that day at all, or if his time might be better served continuing his exercise regimen. Well, he could do his pushups and other exercises in his cell just fine; he just wouldn't wander off.

It was several hours before Cameron showed up.

"Busy day in the office?" Rivotra wondered, sitting on the edge of his bed after yet another set of pushups. He reached for the letter and handed it over. "You might understand why I needed some assistance."

He knew the envelope had already been opened by those in the post office. Now Cameron fished out the papers and unfolded them.

"Who is it from, anyway? My lawyer?"

"The envelope is from his office," Cameron informed him, "but there are two different things here. One is from him, the other has a letterhead from the Senate of Madagascar."

"She must have sent it to him first so he could get it to me."

"That would be my guess. Any preference on which to read first?"

Rivotra shrugged. "Read his. I imagine it is simply an update on the appeals case."

"All right. I'll skip the formalities and give you the good bits." Cameron cleared his throat, perhaps running the translation through his head first. Then, "Because of the international aspect of this case, the appeal has taken longer than expected. However, the date for the oral arguments is set for June 30th. You do not need to do anything. After the arguments, it could be several weeks or even over a month before the judge delivers his ruling. If he rules in our favor, you are a free man and can walk out of prison immediately. If he does not rule in our favor, there are still avenues of appeal we can utilize."

Rivotra nodded. "About what I expected. Still, June feels very far off."

"It's not unusual," the social worker told him. "Appeals can take years." He shuffled the papers around. "And this is the one from Madagascar. The good news is, it's in French."

"Most official business is," Rivotra explained. "Easier on the international scene, easier at home. Malagasy has multiple home dialects, but French is French."

"Are you sure? Because there are a few words I don't recognize, or don't make sense in context."

"How about you read and I'll interpret for myself? I never said we didn't bastardize French, too, to some degree, we were just more uniform about it."

Cameron grunted and started to read the letter. "Another notice about the oral arguments. She will be in the United States a couple weeks before so she and your lawyer can prepare and rehearse in person. She plans to meet with you at least once, if not twice, in order to go over any last details that could be helpful. Most likely she will leave the day after the arguments. If the ruling is favorable, she will return immediately to collect you and take you home. Otherwise, she will continue working on your case from home."

There was some more shuffling of papers. Then, "As for the matter of your inheritance, due to the heinous nature of the crimes committed and the ongoing international investigation, the federal government, the Senate, has elected to seize control of all of the properties for the time being. She will continue to make your case as long as she can, but your best bet would be to make the appeals yourself, in person."

Rivotra sighed and let his head drop into his hands. He knew exactly how that would go, and that wasn't even considering his current situation.

"And as for your name change request," Cameron went on, his tone growing more and more doubtful, "the last she heard was that the request was 'pending' and she could get no more information on any kind of holdup."

Again, not something that boded well for him.

"Sorry, man," Cameron offered.

Rivotra shook his head still in his hands. "It's not your fault." He lifted his head. "Anything else?"

"No. Like I said, formalities."

Rivotra thanked him and he left.

Nothing but bad news today, it seemed. He grabbed his cane, turned it over in his hands. Wordlessly, he swung it hard into the floor. It struck the peeling linoleum with a loud crack! When he lifted the cane to inspect it, he found the start of a crack running right up the shaft. His own fault entirely, but just another mark against the day.

He stood, tested his cane. It appeared to hold his weight without issue, so he started out on a walk. It was all he could do. All he could do. He couldn't go home to make an appearance on his own behalf. He couldn't hope to write any kind of letter to persuade them. Even if they did suddenly reverse their decision and decide to grant him the properties, there was nothing he could do about it. He couldn't do anything with them, couldn't clean them up, couldn't live there. The most he might be able to do was sell some of the properties to pay for others to go in and clean up the farm, as if to prepare for his arrival, but even that wouldn't amount to much. For one, he'd need some kind of estate executive, and without family, there was no one he could trust. Furthermore, everyone was still worried about vengeful spirits. Cleaning fees would be high for anyone he could find, and if the fear wore off too much, it could invite lesser bandits to rob the place of whatever might be left. Dangerous bandits didn't care one way or the other, but a little bit of fear could keep at least some of the amateurs away.

He walked up and down the hall in front of his cell. Back and forth until the announcement came for dinner. By then, he still had no good answers. The only thing he did have was some jerking pain in his back that had been his nearly constant companion since the hospital.

It was February now and the hearing was in June, the verdict unlikely to be rendered for another month. It would be six months, minimum, before he could even entertain such notions as his inheritance. In that time, the government could easily pass off the properties to various loyal members and he would have no real recourse. Sure, he could legally dispute it in a court of law, but he was predetermined to lose. When a judge had to decide between a lowly half-breed peasant who just got out of prison, or a government official who could tell the president to yank that judge's job the next day, it didn't take a genius to know how that judge was going to rule.

Rivotra had discovered an odd phenomenon among American prisoners. While no one really wanted to be in prison, there was a certain urgency about needing to get out. Their wife was going to leave them, they were going to lose their home, they were going to miss a kid's wedding. There was a desperation about them that the world was going to end if they didn't get out right now to address that problem.

He had never quite experienced that before, and he saw a similar attitude among those with heavy gang affiliations. Although they were on the inside and couldn't do much, there was a network out there that they trusted to take care of things and do it well. For the gangs, that was usually drugs and murder. For Rivotra, he'd trusted his family to take care of the farm and each other. He could endure his own season of suffering knowing that everything outside was taken care of.

He no longer had that, and now he was beginning to understand that former desperation. The world might not end, but his would. If he lost the family farm, it was gone for good. There were no other family members to rely on who might be able to bribe or persuade judges or officials. There wouldn't even be anywhere for him to go whenever he did make it home because his entire family was gone, every last one of them. That farm was his last hope to cling to.

His heart raced as he made his way down to the cafeteria. He wanted to just leave this place, but he couldn't. Time portals couldn't get through the planetary shields and his Akari abilities were still gone. He was stuck here like everyone else. And even so, what did he think he was going to do, anyway? He couldn't see, could barely walk. He could help himself reasonably well here, but on his own?

His first inclination was to make an offering and pray to the ancestors, but he wasn't sure how he felt about that anymore. Evil spirits were as likely to answer him as good spirits, and he didn't know if he was strong enough to tell the difference anymore. Did he dare ask the Author about it? She had given him this second chance at life, could have very easily left him dead in the showers last year. But how did he know that she didn't intend for him to sit here for twenty years first, to truly think about what he'd done?

He got on the elevator with an officer pushing an eighty-two year old inmate in a wheelchair. The man was one of the oldest inmates in the prison, two hundred ninety year sentence for the premeditated rape and murder of his wife and her unborn child, her mother, her four sisters, and some friends who were unlucky enough to be at the same baby shower. Apparently, the baby wasn't his and he got a little mad. Now, almost sixty years later, this man could barely get up in the morning, didn't have the coordination to feed or bathe himself, could barely speak. If he'd been a dog, the kind thing to do would be to put him down.

Then the doors opened and Rivotra staggered out down to the cafeteria where he took his customary place.

The northeast place was for the elders and honored guests, he mused. The southwest was for slaves and those of dishonorable repute. If he were to go home today, which place would be his? Technically, he was the elder of the family now. Assuming he had children at some point—a very distant possibility, but not one he was willing to write off—they would take their places along the north while his wife's family would sit along the east. At the same time, imprisonment wasn't exactly what one would call honorable. Even if his sentence got overturned, the fact remained that he had still gotten involved with a terrorist group that had ultimately resulted in the massacre of hundreds of people, his own family. That would not go unnoticed or be forgotten easily.

"You get bad news at lunch, PJ?" Skipper asked, perhaps noticing something in his face or posture.

"It wasn't good news," Rivotra replied.

"What was it? Wife leave you? Kids being little shits?"

Rivotra took a breath, then just shook his head wordlessly. He didn't have the heart or words to explain it, and he wasn't keen on his problems becoming the topic of endless gossip among a bunch of cackling old roosters. Bad enough he could hear about all the problems at four other tables.

Dinner was a soft meatloaf, a plain salad with the scarcest amount of dressing, a cold dinner roll, and a small dollop of chocolate pudding. Rivotra ate because he was expected to, not because he was all that hungry. He tolerated this American sustenance they called food, but now he found that he had a true craving for rice. The Betsileo were considered the best rice growers in Madagascar. His family had been growing rice for generations. Now he was deprived. Wheat was the grain of choice in the United States while rice was relegated to the back of the cupboard. They had it occasionally, cheesy rice, taco rice, rice and beans, rice and vegetables, but nowhere near the volume he was accustomed to.

If he had to sum it up, he wanted to go home. He really wanted to go home. Looking back, even when he'd spent ten years in prison being tortured, he had never felt so strongly about getting out. Maybe because he had already been in his home country, maybe because he'd still considered himself a freedom fighter suffering with his fellows, maybe because he'd believed that things would be taken care of in the end. Whatever it was, he had none of that now. He was far away across the ocean, he wasn't fighting for anything but his life and ability to walk, and there was no one he could trust to keep things running. He was alone, his family farm abandoned.

He yearned to pray, to exhort the spirits, to beg for mercy for himself and his farm. Would the spirits listen? Would the good spirits listen? Or was his life all he was permitted?

Conversation went on around him, but he did not pay attention, did not respond if anyone spoke to him. He had to get out. Had to get home. As soon as he was finished with dinner and allowed to leave the cafeteria, he was going to return to his cell and he was going to pray. It was the only thing he had left that he could do.

A working inmate came around to collect trays, laughing and joking with the old heads as he did so. Rivotra waited quietly, if impatiently, for his turn. He did not respond to the younger man's attempts at humor, didn't understand half of what he was saying anyway. Then, as soon as his tray was cleared and he was given permission to leave, he grabbed his cane and stood.

"Where you going so fast?" one of his table mates chuckled.

"Sprat got bad news," Skipper told him, and, by extent, every table around them.

They didn't even know what that bad news was and already it was making rounds. No doubt they would badger him about it for at least a few days or weeks.

He shrugged it off as best he could as he made his way out of the cafeteria to the elevator, then out of the elevator and down to his cell, briefly feeling for the braille sticker and relieved when he found it. From there, he just hobbled over to his bed, dropped his cane, and lay down on the thin mattress.

All he could do was pray and hope that the spirits were able and willing to bestow a drop of mercy into his bleak, dry desert.

Rivotra again found himself in Anagalisgi's cave. He woke up here about twice a month or so and would spend the night under the poke and prod of the man's bone needle, going over his every wound and stitching it up. Some wounds were obvious, like the many wars he had witnessed and fought in. Others were so small he had never really noticed them before or considered them wounds, like having to consign himself to a Merina nationalist group. At the time, the Malagasy were the Malagasy, united against the French. But when push came to shove, the Merina still largely considered themselves superior to all other peoples, and they harbored a special loathing for the Betsileo who had been the only ones to resist the Merina kingdom in the days before French occupation.

"Something is bothering you," Anagalisgi observed as he knelt down to thread his needle and begin his work. "Tell me about it."

Whatever reservations he'd managed to keep while around his fellow inmates, they evaporated instantly and Rivotra poured out everything from the letters, his assumptions, his fears, and his sudden, wretched desperation to get home before his family farm was lost forever.

"If I lose my family farm, I don't know what I'm going to do," he finished, not even flinching as Anagalisgi's needle punctured skin. "Anything could happen in six months."

"Mm," the Native man mused. "Yes, it is certainly ripe for possibilities."

"Is there anything you can do? You have the ear of the good spirits, the Whites. You talk to the Author. There must be some way to…"

There was silence for a long time. Rivotra felt the heat of the fire in front of him, felt Anagalisgi and his needle, felt the soft hair of the mat he sat on. He could taste the comforting earthiness of the cave and the sweet wood burning in the fire.

"Tell me about your family farm," Anagalisgi said finally.

"My family owned it since before French occupation. Family legend says the land was gifted to our Andilan ancestor for his role in defeating the Vazimba. At first, it was a small hut, a few cows, a bit of rice. Over the generations, the family built it up into a very big house, large herds of cattle, vast *tanimbary*, vanilla, grapes when the French came. There were also goats and chickens. Ducks were taken out every day to eat the snails in the *tanimbary* and protect the rice. In hard times, whether it was drought or family problems or financial hardships, it was often our farm that supplied the community and got them through. The Betsileo prize family and community. It is our duty to help others."

"Yes, you have said that before. And what would you do if you were able to go back and reclaim the farm? Assuming you could do anything."

"I would plant the fields again, tend the cows in the pasture, restore the farm or at least keep it from falling into ruin."

"Surely having many hundreds of cattle and many acres of rice is too great a job for one man?"

Rivotra sighed but could not deny the point. "Maybe so, but I can't let it go to waste."

"Do you think a new owner—one of these government officials—would let it go to waste? After all, the value is in exactly what you just described, using it for cattle and rice and everything else. Why would a government official want to squander that? Surely he would hire hands from the village or surrounding villages to do the work. Then he is keeping the value and providing jobs. And over time, surely it would pass to his children. In a couple generations, his family would be well-established."

"Is that what you tell yourself when you think about the wrongs done to your people?" Rivotra asked hotly. "My family was taken from me. I can't do anything about that, however much I wish I could. This farm is all I have left. I am all that the family farm has. And it is likely to be taken from me, too, just because of bureaucracy and corruption."

If Anagalisgi was affected by his statement, he did not say so. Instead he asked, "Why the farm? Why not any of the other properties you stand to inherit?"

"I have no desire to live in the city. Even pretending I could return to Mahitsy, I do not wish to live among those who hated me. The people now may not remember, but I do."

"What about any of the smaller farms around your grandmother's farm, the ones owned by aunts, uncles, cousins?"

"Because then I would have to wake up every day and look upon my grandmother's farm and remember and know that there is nothing that I can do, that it is gone. Hundreds of years of Andilans, gone, the chain finally broken. I left that farm—foolishly, I know—believing that I was going out to restore order, fix injustice, and make things right. Perhaps losing my family and the farm would be entirely deserved. But I can't give up without some kind of fight. Josina says she is still working on my behalf legally, though her word means little. The only thing I can do where I am is pray. So I am praying, Anagalisgi, I am begging. I need to go home. I need to save my family's farm."

"The farm is fine, Rivotra," Anagalisgi said. "There is nothing to save it from. What you want is to save yourself."

"Is that wrong? Rivotra fought for me when I was still running around as Rifun Ndolo. I owe Rivotra that entire life that I once denied him. Part of that life was living on that farm. Even if I do die young and without children—in which case the farm will go to some government bureaucrat anyway—I must die on that farm and be buried with my family in the tombs." He took a measured breath and flinched as he finally felt the needle. "Please, Anagalisgi. I don't know what to do."

Seven
The Old Rut

Morning count in the nursing home was far less traumatic than in genpop. The lights came on and the officers came around to make sure everyone was still in their cell and breathing, no need to come to attention at the window. Rivotra had basically learned to sleep through morning count and instead wait for the breakfast announcement.

So it was quite surprising when, one day, the first day of April if his groggy brain could compute correctly, the door slid open and an officer was yapping at him to get up and roll up. Rivotra startled awake, trying to make sense of everything going on, but the officer was already gone.

Roll up. That meant pack his stuff because he was moving. But where? And why?

Rivotra really didn't have anything to pack, just his cane and his tub with his papers, his *lamba*, and a few odd miscellany he'd somehow acquired. As he sat and waited for the officer to return, he went over in his head all the possibilities.

He wouldn't be told to roll up if he was going to court or being punished, so that was a relief. Administrative segregation was unlikely seeing how he couldn't read; his English was better than it was a month ago as something had evidently unlocked, though it didn't help his eyesight any; his spatial orientation was only just passable in his opinion; and he wasn't working, in class, or pushing hard for extra good behavior time before parole. Would they really send him back to genpop? It was true that he was walking—still needed a cane, but he was physically walking again—but he wouldn't consider himself able and ready to defend himself if needed.

If you can walk, you can leave, they'd told him. At the time, it had sounded quite promising, a small light at the end of the tunnel. Now, suddenly faced with that prospect, he wasn't so sure.

He shook his head, silently scolding himself. And what did he expect to do when he made it home? He was going to be on his own dealing with much rougher terrain. He couldn't even be sure that the neighbors would help him much on account of his own dishonor and the circumstances surrounding his family's death. If he couldn't find his way around here—a contained, industrial complex—he was not going to survive the highlands, and his family's farm would either rot or go to a bureaucrat.

That wasn't to say that his heart didn't jump a little when the officer returned and told him to move it.

Hobbling out of the cell, cane in one hand, tub in the other, Rivotra felt a slip of paper touching his cane hand. He paused and adjusted his grip so the paper formed to his palm around the cane.

"Gen pop," the officer told him. "Neighborhood E, House 11A."

So they were sending him back to genpop. He could walk, so he was leaving.

"I keep my cane?" Rivotra wondered.

"Yes. Now move."

The officer's tone said he disapproved of Rivotra being able to keep his cane, but there were too many weapons available in any given location to be able to raise an issue over something he needed to walk. Probably in their eyes, they either put him back in genpop and got him back to work, or they left him in the nursing home until he could walk without a cane, which might not happen for a long time, if ever. He was young, he was somewhat fit, and even if he was blind, he could work.

The officer escorted him as far as the front door of the nursing home, gave him general directions back to the genpop building, then departed. Apparently his escort service had also been revoked.

Time to find out just how good his sense of direction was. A year after his death, he was walking and talking, so the prognosis couldn't be all bad.

His first direction was "to the right," and he hated that it took him a second to remember exactly which way that was. He blamed his faulty English, but even when he got it situated into French and Malagasy, it took longer than he was comfortable with to turn in the correct direction.

The next direction was, "straight ahead, third building on the right."

Rivotra navigated his way to the right edge of the walkway and kept his cane just scraping the edge of the pavement and tapping dirt. Assuming there were no other walkways leading to other places, he should be able to count out the paths leading to the buildings.

The first time he had gone blind, he had the assistance of Mina and her family, and Monsieur LaPouir, at least until he started regaining his ability to see through blindsight. This was probably the first time he had truly been left to fend for himself, and it was arguably the worst possible environment. At the same time, if he could make it here, he could make it anywhere.

He found the path leading to the first building. So far, so good.

In the cool morning air, he could hear any and all activity going on in the complex. He heard a door shut, a small group of men talking and laughing, probably heading to get some coffee before breakfast. He startled and paused as something sounded near his head. Reflecting, it had been a small bird suddenly darting through the area, getting close enough to him that he could hear its wingbeats. Letting out a breath, he continued on.

For a second time, his cane hit pavement instead of dirt. Building number two. Other than the sudden bird surprise, nothing had happened. He was making his way, out on his own. He didn't walk quite as fast as he used to, but he had something resembling a natural gait and he just kept moving forward. As long as he didn't let his uncertainty become obvious, he shouldn't have too many extra problems.

Path number three. Keeping his cane still on the right edge, he followed the pavement as far as he could before he was able to dredge up some latent knowledge that he had to move more to the middle of the path. It wasn't too far... His cane hit something solid before him. Trying not to drop anything, he shuffled around his cane and paper and reached for the door. Blessedly, he had no issues. He found the handle, it wasn't locked, and no one was waiting on either side for him to figure out what he was doing.

Then he was in. He had made it to the genpop barracks. Well, he had made it somewhere anyway.

"You lost?" someone asked. It came from his left. He prayed silently that it was the desk officer who had spoken. Gingerly, he turned that direction and let his cane lead the way, pausing when he felt the dull metallic thud of it hitting what he hoped was the desk. He leaned the cane against the desk and held out the slip of paper. The slip disappeared and he took his cane back.

The desk officer invoked the name of Jesus, but Rivotra had a suspicion from his tone that it was not referring to his nickname, and it was hardly reverent in context.

"Too fit for the nursing home," the officer mused, "but still blind and crippled." He cursed again. "None of my business, I guess." Now a huge sigh. "All right. Here's what you do. You turn and walk forward about a hundred yards—"

"If someone can help me, that might be more easy," Rivotra suggested. "When I am there, I can learn."

"Shut the fuck up and don't interrupt me." Nevertheless, the officer called for someone. From name alone, he was unable to discern if it was officer or inmate. Then, "Neighborhood E, House 11A."

"Cool," the person said. Inmate, then. "Isn't this PJ? Yeah, he be diggin' wit Copper."

"He's blind. Get him down there. Says he's fine after that."

"You got it, C.O." The inmate turned his attention to Rivotra. "What up, PJ?"

"Where am I going?" Rivotra asked as evenly as he could.

"Yeah, sure, come wi' me."

He put his hand on Rivotra's arm, but Rivotra pulled his arm away, saying, "I can follow."

"Suit ye'self."

The whole way down to the new neighborhood, his escort told him all about the neighborhood and its various residents. From what he could gather, in between long bouts of explanation lost on him due to an overabundance of slang, Neighborhood E seemed to be the one with the fewest gang problems. Most residents were those with good time, but maybe not good enough to get moved to admin. Decent guys, he was told, good family men, just made some stupid decisions and landed here. If he needed help, almost half the guys would probably be willing to help for a small fee. The other half would be willing to help for a slightly larger fee. Depended what he was looking for.

Walking into his new Neighborhood, Rivotra knew a moment of tragic anxiety, not because he was brand new, couldn't see, and needed a cane to walk, but because of an irrational fear of being attacked.

"I told you to stop bringing men home with you, Lightfoot," someone to their right said, the tone obviously teasing. It helped to break Rivotra of his trance and turn his attention to the conversation.

"You know me, C.O., I'm a lover. And this one's even got papers."

As soon as he said it, it occurred to Rivotra that he hadn't gotten a slip from the desk officer at the entrance. Clearly he'd given it to his escort, Lightfoot, to give to this officer.

"This is Prison Jesus, isn't it?" the officer wondered. "Well, PJ, I hope you learned your lesson about picking fights."

"I'm the one who died," Rivotra defended himself.

"Yeah, well, don't go dying in my showers. This is a good neighborhood here, not a lot of trouble. Troublemakers tend to get kicked out."

"Petey here is kind of the HOA's bitch," Lightfoot commented nonchalantly. "Everything got to be just so, whatever the HOA rules say."

"Fuck you, Lightfoot. Show him to his new house. Give me lip, I'll make you take him to breakfast, too."

Lightfoot just laughed as he walked away. Rivotra followed him to a ground level cell. Lightfoot banged on the door and earned a curse in reply.

"PJ, this is Copper," Lightfoot introduced. "Copper, PJ."

"Go away, Lightfoot," the man in the top bunk grumbled. "It's too early."

"Coffee's on, man. That's where I was heading before I got redirected."

"Then redirect yourself again and get out."

Lightfoot laughed again and meandered away. Rivotra entered the cell, located the bottom bunk, slid his tub under the bed, and sat down on the mattress. Up above, he heard a groan and a sigh and a shuffle of position.

"You're the one who was killed in the showers last year?" the man, Copper, inquired.

"That's what they tell me," Rivotra replied.

"I wasn't here yet, so I've only heard stories. You look good for a dead man."

"They tell me that, too. I don't know. I'm blind."

"Yeah? Shit. What's your name? Your real name, not this prison shit."

"Rivotra."

"Nice to meet you, Rivotra. I'm Vin." He cleared his throat. "Sorry. Shake hands?"

Rivotra reached up and eventually found the man's hand for an awkward vertical handshake.

"Where you from?" Vin went on. "Got an accent I can't place."

"Madagascar."

"Mad—" The man cut himself off. "Wait a minute. I know you. You were the one who kidnapped Tommen and shot Walt at the warehouse, weren't you?"

"You use their names, which means—"

"I knew them. Fucking hell, I worked with Walt."

As soon as the words were out of his mouth, Rivotra could hear him cut himself off and scramble and stutter his way to something like a distracting line of thought.

"Is that why they call you Copper?" Rivotra asked. "You were a police officer?"

Vin stopped his stammering and sighed. "Yeah."

"What are you doing here?"

"Shot a suspect who was surrendering. Honestly, I almost hit Walt in the process."

"No, I mean, what are you doing here? How are you not already dead?"

"Oh, I will be, eventually. Minimum security wasn't enough to make the prosecutor happy, sent me to a medium-security facility. Then the warden got a hair up his ass, said a dirty cop ought to be punished to the fullest extent of the law, pulled some strings, got me sent here a couple months ago. It's been a back and forth debate over whether to send me to solitary for my own protection, but nothing's happened yet."

"How long?"

"Two to nine."

"That's not bad."

"You were murdered within a week, or so I heard."

Rivotra shrugged. "There is that. But I knew some bad people, worse people than you'll ever know."

"I don't feel so bad, then. They killed you once, they'll try again. Maybe you'll be a bigger target than me."

"Maybe."

There was some noise and a thump as Vin got down to the ground. He said nothing and left the cell. Rivotra did not say or do anything. He didn't have any more slips of paper, so, other than breakfast, he wasn't sure what he was expected to do, what chores he had been given.

About thirty seconds later, there were footsteps.

"You need help getting to breakfast?" It was Vin and his words didn't sound enthused.

Rivotra was not inclined to breakfast, but he did need help getting around and getting a feel for things. He grabbed his cane, stood, and lightly touched Vin's arm. More and more inmates were moving around which made it more difficult to distinguish Vin's footsteps.

"I think they put us together for a reason," Vin growled. "They put me with the man who tried to kill my partner. Do I avenge my partner and brand myself a dirty cop forever, in addition to tacking another twenty-plus years onto my sentence? Or do I not?"

"What is there to avenge?" Rivotra wondered. "He's fine."

"But he might not have been." Vin scoffed. "They did this to me on purpose, I know it."

It certainly wasn't impossible, Rivotra knew. And it could easily go both ways. Would he, Rivotra, try to bully this man into giving up information about Owain and Tommen, try to perhaps coordinate some kind of communication or way to "finish the job" as it were? Or would he not?

If he had any such inclinations, he had better means than this former cop. Even Josina would likely be a better avenue of information and coordination. But, fortunately for everyone involved, he had no such inclinations. In fact, he was glad Owain was alive. He was glad the Author had chosen to provide a means of saving him. Rifun had done some awful things. Rivotra was going to try and make them right, but bringing back the dead was not something he was capable of. Having his victims alive made it easier on everyone.

Vin did not say two words to him the entire walk to the cafeteria, and Rivotra could feel the hatred. In a way, it was unsettling because there was a chance the man would act on his wrath. On the other hand, it was almost amusing. He had died last year. He had faced down two of his top generals, the best of the best of the army he had once led. True, he'd lost, but the fact that it had taken both of them to kill him was a small badge of pride. With any luck, he'd gotten in at least a couple good blows, maybe some scars for them to remember him by.

Of course, in the present moment, he wasn't sure how he'd feel about a fight with some average thugs. He could Band, yes, but physicality was a little more painful than it used to be.

"All right, we're here," Vin announced. "I helped you here, but you're not sitting with me. And I've got laundry duty."

"I don't know what I have," Rivotra said. "I didn't get that notice."

"Not my problem."

As soon as they were in the building, Vin jerked his arm free and abandoned him. Rivotra managed to follow the direction of his footsteps and landed a couple people behind him in line.

"Copper don't like associatin' with the likes of us," the man behind him said. "We used to be the ones he'd lock up. We're beneath him."

"His reckoning is coming, don't worry," someone else commented, keeping his voice low. "For as much as the fuzz don't like dirty cops, they still defend their own. Goes for turnkeys, too. He knows that. But he'll be alone someday."

Did the man take an officer into the showers with him? Or was there some new policy in place over his incident? Rivotra doubted it. His incident was only sensational because he'd come back, but he was neither the first nor the last to be caught alone somewhere and murdered. He elected not to say anything about it and instead concentrate on making it through breakfast without making a fool of himself.

Today boasted a fine collection of toast or biscuits, fruit, oatmeal, cereal, eggs, and either two small sausage links or two strips of bacon. And no, they couldn't be mixed and matched, to the chagrin of basically everyone.

Rivotra got his tray of food and made it to a table without incident. He even managed to pick a table and seat without starting any fights. Now he just had to be able to do this every single morning for the foreseeable future.

He started into his food and listened to the conversations going on around him, grateful that they were more exciting than having proper bowel movements, taking certain medications, and war stories forty or more years old.

Only a few minutes into breakfast, Rivotra noted the approach of two people to the table.

"We ain't doin' nothin', C.O.," someone said.

"981436," someone, likely an officer, said behind Rivotra.

Rivotra turned in that general direction and felt a piece of paper touch his hand. Then a third man spoke, his overall tone and demeanor suggesting he was a social worker.

"We didn't get these to you in time earlier, and I apologize. These are your chore slips. First one, in the morning, so right after you're done here, you'll report to the admin building. Second one, in the afternoon, you're in laundry. Do you know where those are?"

Rivotra shook his head. "No, and I am afraid that my sense of direction is a little off."

"Well, when you leave here, turn to the left, to the west, and just keep going."

"It's a start but still not very helpful."

In the time it took the social worker to try and explain things, Rivotra had finished his breakfast and suggested the man take him there. It was less about having the escort itself and more about getting the man to stop talking; he just wasn't helping, and the more he tried to correct himself and give better directions, the worse it got and the more confused Rivotra became.

"He can find his own way," the accompanying officer hissed under his breath. "We're not a babysitting service."

"All things considered," Rivotra said, "with the nature of prison, I think you are."

Likely only because the social worker was standing right there did the officer not actually do anything. The worst he could manage at the moment was, "Shut the fuck up."

"Okay, so we're going to go this way," the social worker began.

"Don't speak," Rivotra told him. "Let me think on the directions."

First, out the north door, and then a left turn. If he had gone out the south door, it would be a right turn. North left, south right. North, left, and then they continued straight for a fair distance. He did not note any extra walkways branching off. When he did find one with his cane, it was apparently the one he needed. So, out the left door—no. Out the front door— the main door—the north door. Out the north door, to the left, and it was the first walkway to his right. Then straight again, and they entered the building. Well that was easy enough. He might just be able to remember that.

"All yours, Jimmy," the social worker said. To Rivotra, "Give him the paper."

Rivotra had two papers and didn't know which was which, so he just handed both of them to the desk officer, Jimmy, who glanced at them and handed one back which Rivotra put in his breast pocket.

"All right, Andrew, I got him," Jimmy sighed.

"Good luck," the social worker told Rivotra, then wandered off, his bad-tampered companion in tow.

"Why am I here?" Rivotra inquired of the desk officer.

"Janitorial duty. Sweep, mop, vacuum, that sort of thing." There was a shrug in his tone. "You able to follow or do I need to take you to the prom, too?"

"It's quiet; I can follow footsteps. Don't go too fast."

"Come on, then."

Like the rest of the complex, everything was block and concrete. This building, however, was nice enough to warrant peeling linoleum on the floor and a very fresh coat of paint.

"How do I clean dirt I can't see?" Rivotra wondered, following the officer down a short hall and making a right turn.

Jimmy laughed. "Some inmates can't clean dirt they can see. At least you have an excuse."

"So, the admin inmates don't clean this building?"

"Sometimes. A lot of the time, though, they're a little too high and mighty about their extra good behavior jobs and privileges, trying to kiss every ass they can to win parole recommendations."

"What kind of extra good behavior jobs you are talking about?"

"Filing paperwork, working for the social workers here, working for the lawyers in the courthouse, working for the chaplains, working for the colleges. The intake secretaries, they're all admin privilege. Anything that gives them access to paperwork, to the outside world, especially the computer work. But you got to have a lot of years of spot-free record, and the smallest thing can get it taken away. So if you have any hope or any ideas of wanting to be admin, just keep that in mind before you start any more fights."

Why did everyone seem to blame him for the fight? Was it just because they'd never found his killers? He'd never made any threats of vengeance that he could recall, at least not against them specifically. Or in a language that anyone here could understand. Yes, he did want Julianna to pay for slaughtering his family, but there was nothing he was going to do about it here, except, perhaps, get himself back into something resembling fighting shape.

The officer stopped and directed Rivotra to a room on the right. There was no linoleum, only concrete, and just by the taste he knew this was a janitorial closet.

"Mop, bucket, broom, vacuum," Jimmy stated. "It's not a big room; you won't get lost. Something to note, since you can't see. All of the cleaners here are natural, eco-friendly, bio-friendly shit. You can drink this stuff and it won't kill you. Won't kill anyone else, either. So if you get some crazy idea in your head, or if someone else asks, no one's getting poisoned by any of this."

"Isn't that stuff expensive?" Rivotra inquired.

"Yeah, but so are healthcare costs and a murder investigation. Besides, they smell nice. Nice break from the stink of sweat and concrete. Typically it's one cap of cleaner to one bucket of water. Can you do math?"

"Yes."

"Then you won't have trouble. Any questions?"

"How much do I clean?"

"If it's inside and there's a floor, clean it. I recommend vacuuming first. Then sweep the halls, finish with a mop. When you think you're done, let me know and we'll see. You do good, you get to go to lunch."

With that, Jimmy left Rivotra to his own devices, standing there in a small cleaning closet, trying to process the man's words. He was struggling to understand the situation as much as the language, and it was a minute or two before he was able to put a name to it all. In English, they called it "the rut" or "the grind." He was back in "the grind." For the last year, his life had revolved around restoring his mind and body, and a number of exceptions and accommodations had been made for him. From the prison's viewpoint, some of it may have been ethically or legally required, but the rest was just trying to put a broken piece of machinery back together. If he could walk, he could leave the nursing home. But he was still in prison. He still had a role to play. He still had chores to do.

And that was all, he figured, taking his cane and leaving the room with the intent of trying to spatially map the building and orient himself. There was a lot of ongoing drama in his life: his family, his name, his inheritance, this upcoming hearing for his appeal, his talks with Josina and introducing her to Time, his one talk with Jeremy about the Krydik to which the understudy had yet to respond, his irregular chats with Anagalisgi in his dreams. But that was all "outside." That was beyond his daily reach. He had no one to oversee, no one to command. Here, on the "inside," he was the one being commanded. He'd had only a small taste of the grind before his murder, but now, here he was, right back at it, as if nothing had happened. The cog had been fixed and put back in the machine.

"And where are you going?" Jimmy asked from some distance away.

"I can't see," Rivotra told him. "I have to know the building, know the floor."

"Well make it quick."

He could Band, he supposed. Take his own sweet time trying to learn the building. Then, if his head would let him, he could keep Banding and hold it throughout the entirety of his work. Let Jimmy turn around and suddenly find the entire floor pristinely swept and mopped.

Actually, Rivotra thought, that might not be a horrible idea. Maybe he wouldn't Band quite that strongly, just enough to give him an edge so he wasn't limping along behind a broom until dinner. Then maybe he could get in a little extra time at the gym—assuming whoever was controlling the cage let him in. He could do his walking exercises here, then do some extra strength training, all before lunch. Well, maybe he would give it a day or two, until he knew his job a little better and could more confidently walk himself from one building to another.

He was not confident in his map of the building, but he did find his way back to the janitorial closet eventually. There he surrendered his cane and grabbed a vacuum. The beast was bulky and heavy, and he wasn't sure how much he liked that it rolled so well. But he just told himself that he needed to make free walking his next goal.

Being Saturday, many of the social workers were not in their offices. Those who were working were currently supervising visiting hours. This made it easy for Rivotra to vacuum the offices without disturbing people, having to endure some kind of well-meaning conversation, or potentially humiliating himself in front of a social worker. He could understand the concept of rehabilitation, but these people took a nauseating interest in the lives of the inmates.

From vacuuming the offices, he moved to sweeping the halls using a massive shop broom. Again, he could not put his full weight on the broom because it was designed to move. He had to keep himself upright. The mop was a little sturdier, but he forced himself not to lean on it. By the time he was done, however, he was ready for his cane.

He made his way back to Jimmy.

"All done?" the officer wondered, as if he hadn't been watching Rivotra sweep and mop this area.

"You tell me," Rivotra replied.

Jimmy got up from his chair and started down the hall in long strides. Rivotra wasn't sure how thorough of an inspection this was going to be, but he wasn't going to be able to keep up that kind of pace.

"Not the best job I've ever seen," Jimmy said, returning just as quickly, "but pretty damn good for a blind fucker. Better than some assholes who come through here. All right, get yourself to lunch."

Rivotra just nodded, turned, and headed back in the direction of the door.

Straight out from the door to the main path. He'd come from the right...or the left...He'd turned right to get onto this path, which meant turning left now. But how far was he supposed to go? Were there any paths between here and there? He'd turned left which meant turning right again, but at what point?

If nothing else, he could just follow his taste buds. The wind was blowing just right that every time the door opened, he could taste lunch. Vegetable soup, he thought. If they were lucky, there might even be chunks of beef in it, though how real the beef was, or what cut, was often a matter of some debate, or it had been in the nursing home.

He made it to the cafeteria, got in line, got his food, and found a seat, all without issue.

The next step, then, was figuring out where laundry was. He knew he had been there once last time in genpop, but he couldn't think of how to get there. The Fishbowl and the nursing home had laundry delivered, which wasn't helping him any. Well, now might be time to make some friends.

"Where is laundry?" he asked of his table mates.

"Shitheads get you the wrong size boxers?" one asked, his tone only half-teasing.

"Fucking Jerky is in there this month," another one grumbled. "That asshole will—"

"I just need to know where it is," Rivotra cut in.

"What, DJ didn't give you the deluxe tour out of Fishbowl?" a third man chuckled humorlessly. "It's in genpop. Instead of going straight to the neighborhoods, take a right and follow the smell of detergent."

"And when you see Jerky, punch him for me," the second man said. "And let him know I'll do it myself later."

At least laundry was in the genpop building. For the foreseeable future, then, Rivotra only had to care about the genpop building, the cafeteria, and the admin building. That much he could probably handle.

He finished his lunch and headed out. Straight out, then a slight right, then straight? Right? No. He tried to remember the path he had taken this morning with Vin. No, that was right. He was right. Because they had gone left, and the opposite was right.

He made his way to a building at least. Whether it was the correct one remained to be seen. He really didn't feel like asking the desk officer either.

He was tired of feeling helpless, except he kind of was.

Instead of going forward, he turned to the right and kept going. No one said anything, and no one shouted at him to watch out for a wall. After a minute of his cautious hobbling, he got the taste of detergent. So he was right. That was a good sign. Unfortunately, just like janitor duty in the admin building, he was going to have to spend several hours tasting soap. He didn't care how eco- and bio-friendly it was, or the fact that it allegedly couldn't kill him; it tasted absolutely sour.

There was a desk officer in this area, like the rest of them. This officer was presently reading a newspaper and Rivotra couldn't be sure he even glanced at the slip of paper.

"Morning's washing and drying, afternoon's folding," the officer told him. "Get to it."

"Um...where?" Rivotra asked.

Now the officer moved, a mass rustling of papers. Then, "Shit, man. All right. You go out, there's bins of dry laundry next to the tables. Just start picking and folding, put them in piles. Shirts, pants, boxers, socks, whatever. When you've got a good stack, there's more bins along the wall. Put them in there."

"Sir, I can't see."

"Fucking hell." The officer growled something. Then, "Shack!"

"Yeah, C.O.?" a man asked, walking up.

"Blind fucker. Show him how it's done."

And with that, the officer went back to his newspaper.

"Yes, sir," the inmate, Shack, said, though his tone was not entirely enthusiastic. Then, "You really blind or you just enjoy pissing off the officers?"

"I promise, there are better ways to annoy an officer than faking a disability," Rivotra told him.

"All right, come here, I'll show you how it's done. Or, you know, whatever."

The concept of folding laundry was not difficult; he just needed to know where he had to be, where the unfolded laundry was coming from, and where to put the laundry when it was done. After that, he was happy to work quietly.

Back in the rut, he reflected again. Just doing a job, whiling away his time. So many things going on in the "outside" world, but all that mattered on the "inside" was him and his laundry.

He again considered the desperation that some men felt, that heart-wrenching yearning to get out and do something, stop something, see someone, before the world otherwise inevitably ended. He again felt a hint of that desperation. The hearing for his appeal was in two, almost three, months. His family farm sat in the hands of bureaucrats and corrupt government officials. There were intergalactic enemies who could make easy work of him if they ever learned he was still alive.

And here he was, folding laundry. Folding clothes that had been worn a thousand times and would be worn a thousand times more before being retired as little more than leftover lint.

Because visiting days were Saturday and Sunday, laundry day, where the inmates got their clothes for the week, was on Friday. Everything here, then, was exchanged clothing that had been worn last week. That would make up the entirety of laundry for the weekend, Shack told him. Monday and Tuesday were for washing towels and linens. Wednesday and Thursday was for catch up and everything else, including "special laundry."

"Is there an illegal meaning I don't understand?" Rivotra wondered.

"Well, there definitely could be. But there's some legit stuff, too. You make a little money, you can get yourself some real clothes. Commissary's got nice wool socks for winter, cotton boxers that are nicer on the boys. You make enough money and maybe toss in some extra favors, might even get yourself a real pair of jeans."

"Jeans?"

"Sure. They can only be worn if you have visitors or if you go to church or whatever, but it's a nice change from this government-issued shit."

"How much do jeans cost?"

"Officially, they say fifty dollars. But that's only if you want a pair of jeans. You want a pair that fits nice, gonna be extra. What kind of extra depends on who's working."

"I don't do drugs and I'm not gay."

"Well, depending on how fast you think you're gonna get that fifty dollars, you *are* working laundry right now. You might offer them well-fitted clothes in return, set a good set of clothes aside Thursday night with their name on them so they can get them Friday and look nice for their mamas on Saturday. That sort of thing. Be a little entrepreneurial."

Rivotra had only just gotten back in the rut. He didn't have anything to his name. He wasn't even sure how prison money and commissary worked.

But, all things considered, he probably wasn't going to be getting a pair of jeans any time soon because he was pretty sure he didn't have any money. If he had to hazard a guess, it wasn't about having real money in some kind of bank account, but it worked on some kind of in-prison credit system that could be added to or subtracted from as his behavior dictated. Maybe the admin inmates who worked in the courthouse got "paid" from the accounts of inmates who got in trouble, but that was only a guess.

Laundry was uneventful and the lot of them meandered their way to dinner just in time to see—or in his case, hear—a heated argument right at the tipping point of a real fight. If Rivotra was understanding them correctly, picking out what little English remained between heavy prison slang and what he believed was Spanish, the problem here was two-fold. First, the baked beans were allegedly cold, so that was apparently the server's fault. But the gang or group that the server was with jumped in to defend their man, and then there was some dredging up of another offense that Rivotra was unable to quite understand.

The argument did eventually come to blows. By the time things got sorted out, with not a few guys being dragged off to the Hole, it was almost closing time at the buffet. And by then, the baked beans were, unfortunately, definitely cold. Rivotra ate them anyway, then headed back to genpop for the night.

Another big difference between the nursing home and genpop was that the showers in the nursing home were supervised, if not assisted, and even so, there were still plenty of falls. Now, suddenly, Rivotra was faced with the possibility of being alone in the showers again. He didn't mind such an illusion of privacy, cameras notwithstanding, but as he walked in, even hearing that there were at least half a dozen others in there, he felt his heart jump into his throat.

He couldn't not bathe, and he really wasn't any more or less safe here than anywhere else in the complex. His enemies still had use of Time and the Akari. They could, as they did before, walk in, murder him, walk out, and no one would ever know. These guys in here would just turn around and find him dead. Again. And he didn't think he'd be coming back a second time.

"You ain't gonna die on us again, are you, PJ?" someone asked as he turned on the water.

"That was never my plan the first time," he informed them.

That earned some laughter and a few jabs that went over his head.

What hair that hadn't been ripped out in the attack had been shaved off for the benefit of the surgeons. Now, a year later, his hair had grown back out to about his shoulders. This he washed using the standard issue shampoo/body wash that was handed out every week when they got their laundry. It was their job to keep track of their own soap. If they lost it or used it all up before the next issue, that was their problem. Rivotra happened to know that some guys intentionally skipped a shower (or two or three) every week in order to save up the soaps, pour one small bottle of leftovers into another, and sell it to those who did happen to lose theirs or use it all up before the next week. They were supposed to turn in the empty bottles in order to receive the new ones, but that rule was only scarcely enforced.

Rivotra didn't know if he would trust secondhand soap, not from this place. Allegedly there was a similar market for toothpaste, and he did not want to consider how that came about or what the men were actually stuffing back in the tubes.

If anything major happened and there was a mass raid in a neighborhood, soap and toothpaste were one of the first things confiscated, just in case they were stuffed with drugs. Then, unless someone had managed to hide something really well or wanted to spring for something a little nicer from commissary, they were pretty much out of luck until the next week.

He rinsed, toweled himself dry, dressed, and left the showers, all without dying. Then he made his way back to the main area where many of the guys were milling around before being forced back into their little private cubes for the night. Rivotra found his cell and sat down on his mattress, unable to suppress a sound that was somewhere between a sigh and a groan.

"So, you found your way after all," Vin said sarcastically from the top bunk.

"Sorry, your hit didn't pan out," Rivotra told him.

"Who needs to hire a hit when you're more likely to do yourself in? Seizures, blindness, multiple traumatic brain injuries, it's a wonder you can do anything."

"You should see the sorry sods in the nursing home."

And that was as far as their conversation went. A moment later, Rivotra heard the sound of paper, as a page turning in a book. He couldn't say he didn't understand why Vin might not like him, but he couldn't be blind to his own predicament. Or maybe that was just it. Vin knew he was the biggest target in the prison and now he had found perhaps the only person in genpop who was currently weaker than him to try and bully.

Outside, the desk officer started yelling at the men. Time for bed, princesses, go get your beauty sleep. There were some sarcastic replies, but, eventually, everyone got where they needed to be and things started to quiet down. After a time, Rivotra heard Vin close his book, shift and shuffle overhead, then go quiet.

Sighing, Rivotra also lay down. There was nothing worth staying up for. Everything that mattered was going on "outside." Meanwhile, he was still here on the "inside" where he could do nothing. All that awaited him for the foreseeable future was a morning of vacuuming, sweeping, and mopping floors; and an afternoon of folding laundry.

The rut.

Jeremy: Jeremy Long speaking.

Netami: Why are you looking into my brother's death?

Jeremy: Sorry, who is this?

Netami: Netami, of the Krydik.

Jeremy: Oh. Hello, Netami. I was hoping to finally talk to someone.

Netami: Why are the Navajo interested in Sabelu's death?

Jeremy: Because it was the only way I figured I was going to get through to you. The Krydik aren't known for picking up the phone and having a civil conversation.

Netami: Few Terran tribes want to talk to us and fewer are worth talking to. What do you want? We have plenty of problems without prank social calls being one of them.

Jeremy: How did your brother die?

[pause]

Netami: He was shot in the back on a mountainside. One bullet to bring him down and five arrows to pin him there.

Jeremy: Why did he die?

Netami: Because it's hard to get good help in the wilderness for those kinds of injuries.

Jeremy: No, I mean, why? If my understanding is correct, he could have run. But he willingly went to his death. Why?

[pause]

Netami: How much do you know about us?

Jeremy: Stories only. You're the coward people, the people who ran. Even when you do fight, you only lose.

Netami: What do you know about Sabelu?

Jeremy: I heard he was a priest.

Netami: Priest, prophet, yes, it runs in the family, along with a certain vein of only being able to see evil.

Jeremy: But...?

Netami: Sabelu had an unusual ability to know people. He could look at a man and know that man better than the man knew himself. He could look at someone and know their hopes, dreams, fears, thoughts, emotions, their past, present, and future. With perfect accuracy.

Jeremy: Sounds like a good reason to kill him. So he knew about his death in advance.

Netami: He couldn't see himself. He was his only blind spot, and that's also why he chose to live a more solitary life. It quieted the noise in his head.

Jeremy: So this ability wasn't voluntary.

Netami: By no means. He had a very troubled childhood.

Jeremy: Then he didn't know about his death.

Netami: He did, but only by looking at it through the eyes of others. He would look at my future and see me mourning his body. He said that such a thing was the only thing in the world that ever truly frightened him.

Jeremy: I can imagine.

Netami: No, I don't think you can.

Jeremy: Maybe. So again I ask, why would he voluntarily go to his death? If he could see it, if he had such advance notice, why do it anyway? Surely you must have asked him that question.

Netami: Many times, yes.

Jeremy: And?

Netami: He said that it was his time. He said that it was going to buy time for us, for others, that the time was needed in order to make changes and prepare for an even greater battle. [sigh] And war.

Jeremy: A war that I suspect you are currently fighting.

Netami: We are, yes.

Jeremy: Hm. [incomprehensible]

Netami: Again I ask, why are you interested?

Jeremy: Do you know who killed your brother?

Netami: We do.

Jeremy: Have you ever considered going after him?

Netami: Our mother sorely wanted to. I wanted to. We even had the chance, but we couldn't take it.

Jeremy: Couldn't?

Netami: At the time, that same man was our best hope for staving off an attack that could have wiped us out.

Jeremy: How so? [pause] I know that you call your reservation Hlohi. But there are no wars going on here. I've also heard that you live among the stars on a planet called Hlohi. Yet you're talking on the phone to me right now. Netami, make it make sense. Who are you, where are you, what is going on?

Netami: Tell me why you want to know about Sabelu's death and our war.

Jeremy: [sigh]

Netami: We have too many enemies at our door to entertain another potential one on the phone. If you can't tell me, then—

Jeremy: Can I trust you not to say anything? At least right away? It's...technically, it could be considered a breach of privacy.

Netami: Depends on the information, and that's the best you're going to get.

Jeremy: I'm a chaplain understudy at Mt. Olive Correctional Complex in West Virginia, and Rivotra Andilan—or you probably know him as Rifun Ndolo—is one of our inmates.

Netami: Hm. So this has nothing to do with you. That dog is looking for his pack, is that it?

Jeremy: I'm trying to judge his story, judge his change of heart, justify his spiritual stance, but I feel like I only have half a story.

Netami: What do you mean?

Jeremy: He was talking about...how he killed Sabelu. He believed he was working for good, but he was suspicious of how Sabelu died. And he's been considering that maybe he was wrong. Some of the things he said...weren't making sense.

Netami: What things?

Jeremy: His English wasn't very good at the time—

Netami: Well, that's a dead giveaway right there. He's playing you. His English is fine.

Jeremy: He was murdered last year, then brought back. But he's sustained extensive brain injuries. He's learned to walk again and he's recovered some of his English, but he is far from recovered. I wanted to get your side of the story as it were.

Netami: When was he attacked? Specifically?

Jeremy: Mid-March.

Netami: Did he name his attacker?

Jeremy: Not really. I don't know if it was the bad English or if he was hesitant on account of...whatever this is. But, if it helps, at the same time, his entire family in Madagascar was murdered, almost two hundred people.

Netami: And that's not the worst of it.

Jeremy: What are you talking about?

Netami: What is your end goal here, chaplain? Are you looking to save his soul?

Jeremy: It'd be nice, but first I have to understand what exactly he's been dealing with. Most people have some spiritual troubles, but he seems to have gotten in much deeper than anyone I've ever encountered.

Netami: Let me bring this up to my people. I'm afraid the answer is not so simple as you might hope.

Jeremy: Shit.

Netami: Don't worry, we won't send a raiding party to kill him. Yet. We'll see what my mother thinks, since judgment still falls to her in my brother's death.

Jeremy: Shit.

Netami: And next time you talk to him, let him know that the Miaramila fought valiantly.

Jeremy: I assume he'll understand what that means?

Netami: He should, if he isn't completely brain dead. Good day, chaplain.

Eight
Visitation

There were very few times in prison that an inmate had the opportunity to say "No" and refuse to do something. One of those times was for visitations. It broke no staff member's heart to have to tell an outsider that they couldn't come in. No inmate ever had to twist an officer's arm to not be taken to the visiting area for an hour.

With exception of lawyers who were specifically representing an inmate, all outsiders had to make visiting arrangements at least two weeks in advance. Then, every Friday morning, inmates were notified of their visit requests and permitted to say they did or did not want to meet with that person. Once they accepted the request, a visit time was officially scheduled.

Rivotra never expected to have any civilian visitors. He'd barely expected to have a visit from his lawyer or Josina, but lawyers were not bound by the same advance notice rules, and Rivotra could not deny that visit unless he wanted his lawyer to stop working for him. So when his number was called that first Friday after returning to genpop as part of the weekly rundown of visitation notices, he was quite thoroughly surprised.

Like almost everything in prison, notes were written on little slips of paper and given to the appropriate authority. The officer with the visitation slips handed him his slip, then moved on.

"Can you read this?" Rivotra asked of Vin up top.

"I'm sure I can," the former cop stated.

"Will you?"

The man sighed dramatically and snatched the slip of paper. "981436, Visitor Request. Expected date: April 22, 2017. Visitor name: Natalie Wolf. Relation: Friend. Accept or Reject."

"Natalie Wolf, you said?" Rivotra questioned.

"Yup." Vin waved the slip in front of him and he snatched it back.

Natalie Wolf, known as Netami among the Krydik, was Sabelu's older sister. There was only one way she could know where he was and how to legally get in to see him.

If he rejected her request, would she come in by illegal means, kill him anyway? Was this perhaps some kind of curious investigation, maybe a little reconnaissance to see what he was capable of, see how many warriors she would have to send to take him out?

Rivotra left his cell and made for the desk officer. He still had his cane, but his daily cleaning routine in the admin building was helping him get back upright and free-walk short, familiar distances.

"Got your visitor slip?" the officer wondered.

"Mark 'Accept' for me, please," Rivotra told him.

The officer made some kind of mark, then pushed a pen into Rivotra's hand and guided him where to make a scribble that said he was authorizing the visit.

"I would also like to request a meeting with Jeremy Long, the chaplain understudy," Rivotra said, releasing the pen.

"It's Friday. Sunday isn't soon enough?"

Rivotra hesitated. He didn't want to go to church, but it would be faster than trying to file paperwork through the proper channels. Typically, the only people who did file paperwork to see the chaplains were those in the Hole, supermax, or the bedridden in the nursing home or the hospital. The rest just went to church.

But then, he could be waiting a while to talk to Jeremy if that were the case. While there were truly noble souls who believed themselves saved and forgiven and went to church out of true reverence, most of those who went to church did it for something to do or to talk to the chaplains to try and broker deals with them. Go to church ten Sundays in a row, get some kind of recommendation with the warden or the parole board.

"Got to know by lunchtime, so you might as well decide now," the desk officer prompted.

Church in prison was less friendly to the whims of the Holy Spirit; here, an inmate had to get permission and schedule his time in the pew. The officers had to know what kind of security detail they were going to need.

Rivotra sighed. "All right, fine. Better than paperwork and another day of sweeping and mopping."

The officer made a sound somewhere between a scoff and a laugh. "Ain't that the truth?"

With that taken care of, Rivotra left the desk and proceeded to go about his daily routine. He could walk through the buildings with only light reliance on his cane, but he was less confident outside, even on the pavement. Most of it had to do with inconsistent temperature, wind, and uneven ground. For all his progress, he still couldn't really feel his legs. His right thigh had some feeling, but his lower leg was still a ghost, as was his left leg. Everything he did was just forced repetition, building new muscle memory based only on input from his feet and hips, exploiting the light sensation in his right thigh and trying to force that sensation and movement on all of the other muscles. The same went for his lower left arm as he grabbed his cleaning supplies. All of it forced muscle movement, bridging the gap between his elbow and wrist. His left pinkie and ring finger were the only appendages that hadn't improved much since the first day, probably because there was nothing on the other side to force them to move and develop fine motor control.

He thought about this as he forced those fingers to bend around and grip the broom and mop. When he was finished, he intentionally put his cane in his left hand, forming his fingers around it. He only had eight fingers; he couldn't afford to lose any more.

After lunch was laundry. On Friday, that meant clothing exchange. It was a madhouse. Rivotra was spared the wrath of the inmates demanding certain sizes or cleaner rags, but he couldn't say he was spared the worst of the chaos. He had to deal with sorting the incoming clothes. Sometimes that included finding drugs or paraphernalia in the shirts and pants pockets, or literal shit in the boxers from an inmate who either didn't want to care for himself or just wanted to cause trouble for whatever reason. These he tossed in a separate bin to soak and wash separately.

With working the afternoon laundry, Rivotra had already exchanged his clothes the previous evening. Once the worst of the madness subsided as the lunchtime ended and people made their way to their afternoon work, he wondered if he shouldn't wash his clothes again in the shower that night. He couldn't really put off the exchange until after the insanity because there was little to choose from. Those who were too late to the party or unwilling to fight ended up with clothes that were too big or too small.

Once everything was sorted and all discovered drugs either turned in or squirreled away, it was well into dinner. Rivotra ate quickly, then returned to genpop for a shower, electing to indeed give his clothes a quick rinse if nothing else. He was not the only one with this idea as several men tried to scrub out questionable stains before visitation days.

Natalie Wolf. Netami. The only daughter of Ola Achukma and Nendawagan, older sister of Sabelu, and good friend of Aklaq White Bear. This meeting was not going to go well, Rivotra knew, whatever the reason for it. As he puzzled over the possible reasons half the night and through the next day, one thing was certain: Netami wasn't coming for a social call.

Sunday morning after breakfast, Rivotra and all those approved to go to church were rounded up and taken to the chapel. Despite going to a Christian service, Rivotra couldn't help but feel like a sacrifice being marched into the pen before the slaughter.

If there was any rhyme or reason to the seating arrangement, he did not know it. He made his way to the wall and found the back pew, but he also found someone else sitting in the coveted back corner seat. Not wanting to be sandwiched in the middle, he kept moving forward. The next pew was also occupied on the end, but the third one proved empty in that spot. He did not know how many rows there were, but he had a sneaking suspicion that he was closer to the front than he wanted to be.

As soon as he heard the piano, dozens of unhappy memories from his childhood floated to the surface. Between the Catholics and the Jesuits, the Christians had made his life Hell. Speak French. Speak proper French. Read only the Bible. Pray only to the saints. Be glad for the righteous instruction. Even if they had been entirely correct in their spiritual assessments, they had been sorely lacking in their delivery.

Rivotra did not sing, though he knew some of the songs, or the tunes anyway. He did not open a Bible yet he knew well the verses the chaplain preached. By the time it was over, Rivotra almost didn't want to talk to

Jeremy anymore. Only because his life was potentially in danger did he stick around. It ended up being Jeremy who approached him, sitting in the pew in front of him.

"Well, it's good to see you here," the understudy said, his voice all smiles. "Is there something—?"

"Who did you call?" Rivotra demanded.

"I'm sorry?"

"I got a visitation request from Netami. Who did you call?"

Jeremy made a strangled sort of sound. "Ah, perhaps we should talk elsewhere."

The understudy flagged down the chaplain and said he was taking Rivotra down to his office for some materials and private prayer. The chaplain wished him well and said he would see him at lunch. Then Jeremy and Rivotra headed down to Jeremy's office.

"At least your English has improved," Jeremy commented, taking a seat.

"Is Netami coming here to kill me?" Rivotra asked hotly. "Is she being more polite about it than the other two?"

The Navajo man sighed. "After our last conversation, I reached out to the Krydik. They aren't the most social, and it took a little while. I was trying to understand their point of view, get their side of the story, and maybe dig up more about your perspective of the good and bad spirits. Again, with your English as bad as it was, as vague as it was, I didn't know quite what I was looking for or how I'd know if I found it."

"And?"

"I don't know what to believe."

"Don't give me that."

"What do you want me to say? Suddenly I'm perfectly okay with colony worlds and alien wars? I won't lie. I've done peyote. I've done a few wild things. None of that compares to what Netami showed me, and yet, it's the only logical conclusion I can come up with."

"You take peyote to speak to your spirits and ancestors, yet suddenly you doubt the larger universe," Rivotra stated.

Jeremy made a frustrated sound. "You know, I can almost accept a Native American colony planet, a place where our peoples can live the ancestral ways. I can even accept their seeing-fruit, which is a kind of peyote derivative, and the Whites and Shadows. Alien worlds and the aliens who inhabit them? A bit far for me." He shifted in his seat. "She also showed me the Authored Books."

"And?" Rivotra prompted.

"The Krydik are skeptical of them. The ones that aren't their own, they don't care much about but hold in safekeeping anyway."

"But what do you think about them?"

"Biographies written by God? I don't know." He made an exasperated sound. "Rivotra, I investigated this because I wanted to understand your spiritual mindset, what drove you to kill Sabelu, regret it, and now seek to explore spiritual righteousness. You came to me hoping I would have news of an intergalactic holy war because one of the factions involved tried to kill you and is going after all the others. These are hardly the same motivations."

"Rifun started this," Rivotra stated. "He did a lot of bad things. I want to make them right. I want to undo what he did. But I have to know. I have to understand the physical situation on the ground, who is where and doing what. I also have to understand the spiritual situation, to know that I am fighting for the right side, that I am doing good, real good this time."

He got a certain impression that the understudy was leaning over his desk, head in his hands, completely overwhelmed.

"What are Netami's intentions?" Rivotra asked. "Did she tell you?"

Jeremy let out an even breath. "My best guess, based on our conversations, is that she is assessing your physical and mental capacity for trial. She initially took the matter back to the Krydik, specifically her mother, Nendawagan, who still holds judgment rights over the death of her son. After that, she took me to Hlohi and showed me everything. She wanted me to understand the bigger picture of what Sabelu's death meant for the people, and what your involvement really signified."

Rivotra sighed and pinched the bridge of his nose. "I survived one assassination attempt only to die by justice. How fitting." He lowered his hand. "Do you believe in the death penalty, chaplain?"

"Oddly enough, I do think there are some circumstances where it is appropriate."

"Is this one of them? The murder of a holy priest?"

"I don't know."

"If God wanted me dead for my crimes, He wouldn't have had to bring me back from death last year."

"Believe me, that thought has occurred to me. But it is out of my hands."

Rivotra couldn't deny the point as he nodded. "It's only a polite formality anyway. Nendawagan can judge me at any time and ten Krydik warriors would jump to carry out her execution order. And they could do it far more savagely and thoroughly than what Drinjin uh Ersik and Torbak Martin did."

"Then you do remember who attacked you."

"Of course I do, but they're not here, and who is going to believe that a couple of aliens bent Time around us so they could beat me to death without anyone being any wiser?"

"Fair enough."

Rivotra shifted his position. "Did you make any other phone calls? Am I going to receive any more surprise visitation requests?"

Jeremy cleared his throat. "Those were the only calls I made. Anything else that comes along, I have no knowledge of."

"Hm. Well, the good news is, Julianna is unlikely to hear about this. As much as the Krydik could tell her that I'm alive and let her send someone to finish me off—and as satisfying as it would be to consider how she would punish her top two generals for their botched attempt—Nendawagan isn't going to give up her rights to justice. A mother scorned and all that. At the same time, Drinjin uh Ersik and Torbak Martin only beat me to death. I've seen what you people are capable of. I'm not sure it won't be worse."

"I'm not sure how to take that."

"Any way you want, it's true. They're living the old ways, as you said. It wasn't all dreamcatchers and peace pipes. You people were savage toward your enemies."

"Guess you'll find out in a couple weeks if they consider you an enemy."

"Why wouldn't they?"

"Well, as you said. If God had wanted you dead, He wouldn't have had to bring you back last year. And if you want to undo the things Rifun did, that means making amends to those he wronged. You're jumping straight to justice and execution. What if there is some manner of forgiveness in the cards instead?"

"I'm happy I can sweep, mop, and do laundry. I'm not much of a slave."

"Even so, I wouldn't go straight to doom and gloom yet."

"Easy for you to say. You aren't sitting there with dozens of intergalactic entities who want you dead."

"No, but I'm still a chaplain in a maximum security prison who frequently has to tell very tough inmates that I won't put in a good word for them. And I don't have the advantage of being able to bend Time or whatever it is you people think you can do."

Well, there was that.

"Oh, and one more thing," Jeremy said. "She did want me to tell you that Godwin and the Miaramila fought valiantly. Whatever that means to you, I don't know and I didn't ask."

Rivotra blinked. Then he took a breath and said, "It means a lot of good men are dead."

It was a moment before the understudy said quietly, "I'm sorry."

Rivotra shook his head and left the office. He eventually made his way out of the chapel and back to the cafeteria for lunch.

If Netami knew about Godwin and the Miaramila, then either they had done something truly heroic, or they had been defending the Krydik. Considering how stubborn and reclusive the Krydik were, they must have been in dire straits to have to reach out to the Miaramila for help. Given the fate of the twins, Aklaq, LaPouir, and the rest, there did not seem to be any good option.

He mulled this over in the weeks leading up to the visitation. Jeremy seemed to think forgiveness could be an option. The more Rivotra thought about it, he decided that it was unlikely to be forgiveness and more like a grudging alliance. The Krydik had needed help from the Miaramila. At one time, Rifun had been a respected and intelligent military leader. There was no reason Rivotra could not accomplish something similar. They hated his history, but they needed to utilize it anyway, to save themselves. Slavery by a different name, he supposed. Nendawagan would reserve judgment until her people were safe, by his mind or hand, then execute him.

It was not a comforting thought as he rummaged through the clean laundry Thursday evening, hoping to find something that fit well and had as few stains as possible, though he could only take the others' word regarding the stains. He might have gone for the leftover rags the following night, the things that didn't fit well and looked terrible, in order to try and elicit some sympathy from Netami, but ultimately decided against it. He wasn't helpless, and he wasn't trying to run. Furthermore, he had to wear the clothes the rest of the week, and such poor clothes were a magnet for bullies.

The following day, Rivotra understood the anxiety the other inmates felt as they demanded the nicest clothes. One was trying to impress his wife, convince her not to file for divorce. Another was trying to ease his mother's fears, convince her that prison wasn't all that bad and he would be fine. One wanted to show off to his brother that he was losing weight and getting in shape. Although Rivotra did not have such familial fears, that his family members would be worried or offended or somehow impressed, he would admit to feeling some measure of self-consciousness. What was he expecting out of this visit? How did he want to convey his position, or disposition?

He found himself lying awake well into the night, listening to Vin's snores overhead and contemplating all possible events, good and bad, that could happen the next day. Worst case scenario, she cut his throat right then and there, then escaped back to Hlohi. He wasn't sure what he could envision for a best case scenario. Forgiveness was not hers to grant, and anything else he could not rightly expect from her. Any best case scenario for him already bordered on the miraculous or other divine intervention. He didn't know what he wanted out of this visit, except, maybe, to live.

How far had he fallen that his greatest wish was just to live? Such a thing sounded noble, the musings of a well-off man pretending to be humble, but for the destitute, it was, truly, life.

He figured he must have slept at some point because the next thing he knew, officers were yapping at them for morning count. This usually passed without incident, but every so often, someone decided to be difficult and cause a scene, prompting a forcible extraction and minor lockdown for the rest of them. During the week, this was merely annoying. Given that it was a visit day and the visitations started early, whoever it was could expect a visit from a roughhouse gang later. He'd probably end up with a black eye, broken nose, maybe a few broken fingers, just a little reminder to not ruin visit day for everyone else.

Rivotra's visit was not scheduled until one, so he still had to report to the admin building for his morning chores. Just over a week and then chores would rotate. Where would they put him next? Morning laundry and afternoon cleaning? Maybe cleaning a different building? He'd gotten good at it, and it had improved his balance and walking ability. Who could say for sure?

By this point, the desk officer no longer followed Rivotra around to inspect his work afterwards. Once he was done cleaning, he was free to leave. If he did decide to shirk his duties one day, someone would most certainly complain, and then he would be chastised for it the following day, probably given even more cleaning chores to do as punishment for a few days.

"What time is it?" Rivotra asked the officer on his way out.

"Eleven-fifty," the officer reported. "You got a visit today?"

"Yeah, at one."

"Better eat lunch quick, then. Oversight officers want you in the bullpen ten minutes before."

He already knew this, but he did not say so. Instead, he thanked the officer and left the building, using his cane to guide him to the cafeteria.

Only now did Rivotra realize that few or no sloppy foods were served on weekends. There were also no tomato dishes served on weekends, no spaghetti, no chili, nothing that could irrevocably stain clothes on the day of a visit. The turkey and cheese sandwiches were dry, but then, excessive condiment could drip and ruin everything. If Rivotra cared enough about his fluke visit to notice this, he could only imagine the stress of the other inmates who had regular visitors and were desperate to keep up appearances.

Visitations were held in another wing of the admin building, one Rivotra only cleaned during the week when there weren't dozens of people milling about for one reason or another. He knew how to navigate with a broom and mop, but now having to dodge people, he quickly became disoriented.

"First time?" someone asked, touching his arm.

"Yes," was the best he could manage.

"Come on. Bullpen's this way."

He did not refuse the invitation, but he could neither see his escort nor hear his footsteps. After a minute or two of still being alone and confused in a busy hallway, his escort returned, grabbed his arm, and started pulling him in a direction. Rivotra, unable to compensate for the sudden, unexpected movement, managed to save two steps, then stumbled and fell on the third. His escort cursed and hauled him to his feet.

"Give me one end of your cane," his escort grumbled, snatching up the end of the cane. "Come on."

This Rivotra could manage a little better. He was taken to a room where a dozen other men waited and shown to a chair. A TV was turned on to some sports channel. He did not know who his escort was, nor did he get a chance to thank him. In the end, he just sat quietly and waited to find out what happened next.

"974445!" an officer shouted from the door.

"That's me," another man said, standing, his chair grating obnoxiously on the floor.

And so it was. Just sit and wait for his number to be called. Was there something he was supposed to be doing? Or was it just about waiting and thinking about what he was going to say? He didn't know. He really didn't know. It wasn't like this was a family member with whom he could reminisce and joke and plan and everything else. This was someone who wanted him dead and whose family had every legal right to order that death.

"981436!"

Rivotra stood on unsteady legs, keeping his cane closer than he had in the last month.

"Fucking hell, Ndolo." It was Oswald. "Come here."

Rivotra took the lieutenant's arm and let himself be more properly escorted out of the room.

"I thought I got rid of you," Oswald complained lightly.

"I can speak English again, but I'm still crippled," Rivotra informed him.

"All right, fine. Well, since I know you can't see the signs, I'll just tell you. Visits are a maximum of one hour long, not a minute longer, though they can be cut short for any reason. Displays of affection are to be brief. No shouting, yelling, cursing, running, horseplay, or other unruly behavior. There is a playground outside if you have kids, but all time limit rules still apply. Don't smuggle drugs or make any illegal plans or you both get in trouble."

"I don't think you'll have to worry about any of that."

"Yeah, that's what they all say."

Oswald opened a door and the noise level doubled. It was a large room with probably a dozen tables set up. Rivotra heard talking, laughing, crying, from adults and children alike. Still he held on until Oswald came to a stop.

"Chair here," the lieutenant reported.

Rivotra found the chair easily enough, sat down, and thanked the officer who wandered off without a word.

"Well, well," a female voice said. "Rifun Ndolo."

"I am assuming that you are Netami?" Rivotra began.

"You look a little different than the last time I saw you, when we were on Tacaga, discussing what to do about the Borelians and their toxins."

"That was a few years ago. I might say something similar about you, but you might see that I am blind."

"That's what I heard. Blind, crippled, helpless, yet still able to fend off death itself."

"I had help." He shifted position. "The question is, are you here to finish the job?"

Netami made a sound between a grunt and a scoff. "I'm not an assassin like Julianna, although the thought did cross my mind. No, the right of judgment belongs to my mother. The right of execution belongs to my brother."

"And you're just here to figure out how tender the meat is."

"My brothers are busy fighting. My mother is busy with the council. I was the only one available."

Rivotra nodded. "I can appreciate that, given that I have been led to believe that you are in a rather precarious position."

"Well, that's one way of putting it." Netami huffed a sigh and he got the impression that she was leaning back in her seat, unimpressed. "Why are you really asking for information, Rifun? Are you concocting some godawful scheme again?"

"The only scheme I am concocting is how to undo every terrible thing I've done." He Banded the two of them so no one else could hear. "Your brother was a priest and prophet of the Whites, servant of the Author. And I murdered him. My blindness, my spiritual blindness, caused by Shadows and accepted by an empty, desperate soul, caused me to believe that I was doing the right thing, when in fact I was only advancing the Shadows' agenda. When I began to question it, question myself, it was already too late. The Shadows had their new pawn, and I set her up perfectly for a devastating takeover. Now, if that were the end of things, Julianna could have sent her minions to kill me, and that would have been the end. That would have been my end as dictated by the Author. But she brought me back, against all odds. I'm alive, and I'd like to make it Julianna's problem."

Netami laughed bitterly. "Too little, too late, don't you think?"

"Obviously not, because you're here," he told her. "If the situation were truly dire, you wouldn't care. You'd kill me yourself or even tell Julianna, maybe buy yourselves five seconds of breathing room while she comes back for me."

"First you say our position is precarious, then you say it's not that bad. You really don't know what's been happening, do you?"

"Staying out of Julianna's sight means I don't get much news. But I know Micah and Micaiah and Kayla are dead. Godwin and the Miaramila are dead."

"They wish they were dead," Netami cut in. "I'd kill them myself if I had the chance. Actually, I hope they are dead, because Borelian slavery is much worse."

Now Rivotra leaned back in his chair. "Fuck."

"Last March, the Order launched a massive attack against everyone who had an Authored Book. The twins and Kayla and Nathan, we're not entirely sure. They could be dead or in slavery. Probably dead, just to make sure they can't come back on some off chance. Godwin and the Miaramila helped to defend Hlohi. They were successful in repelling the attack, but at heavy cost. Survivors were captured and taken into slavery."

Rivotra took a slow breath. "I may have heard through some sources that Owain and Tommen Forbes also suffered a blow. The murder of an innocent child."

"There was that, yes. Then, three months later, Tommen killed himself."

Now he blinked and sat up. "What?"

"Mhm. Hung himself, or so Owain told us. He just...couldn't handle it anymore, everything he'd been through."

For a long moment, Rivotra could not speak. At least half of everything Tommen had experienced, Rifun had been directly responsible. He lowered his head and ran his hand through his hair. "Fuck. I...That's my fault, a good majority of it."

"You can break out of prison," Netami said nonchalantly. "Maybe win an appeal or get a pardon. Maybe some natural disaster will set you free, I don't know. The point is, the damage has been done, and it's not something you're going to be able to undo. My brother is dead, thanks to you. Tommen is dead, thanks to you. Your men, Godwin, the Miaramila, I hope they're dead, as a mercy. Nathan and Andrew, the Builders, gone. The twins and Kayla, gone. Julianna made it her goal to wipe out everyone with an Authored Book, and she is crossing names off that list very quickly. We're doing the best we can, but we can't hold out forever. All that leaves, then, is Owain and you, and you've already died once."

Rivotra was still trying to process everything, feeling very much like he had in the first few weeks of waking up in the hospital. Who was this person? What was she saying? Why couldn't he put it together in his mind? He could understand the facts of what she was saying, felt some deep and tragic emotion, but he almost couldn't understand just how they were related. Was he really responsible for this? Was he the direct or indirect cause of all of these deaths and horrors?

"Is Julianna seeking an alliance with the Borelians, then?" he found himself asking.

"We don't know. We don't have spies like Godwin did. What she's doing, why she's doing it, we're basically blind to all of it."

Again Rivotra ran his hand through his hair. "I can't believe that there is no hope, that you're just idling away your time until inevitable defeat."

"What you mean to say is, there has to be a reason you survived."

"I didn't 'survive' my attack, Netami. I was dead. I was not breathing, no pulse. I was brought back. And you're right, I can't accept that the Author brought me back just so I could sit in here for twenty to sixty years."

"Maybe, like Borelian slavery, there are fates worse than death," Netami suggested, her tone cheeky. "Maybe the Author wasn't ready to let you go before punishing you more."

"If that were the case, then I don't think your uncle would be the one visiting me at night."

"My—? Anagalisgi? He talks to you?"

"He does. He's the one who has been helping me so far. He isn't willing to give up."

Netami let out an even breath, but he could hear that she was mildly shaken, or maybe annoyed, by this turn of events. "Anagalisgi has appeared to us. He appeared to Tommen and Micaiah and Kayla and even to Owain. I don't believe you. Why would he appear to you?"

"He gave me a choice," Rivotra told her. "I could be rid of the curse of Rifun Ndolo and accept the life that the Author originally wrote for Rivotra Andilan—having to fix Rifun's choices first, of course, then returning to my own life—or I could die."

"So you're just trying to save yourself."

"Rifun would have made such a selfish decision. But in that darkness, Rivotra had a chance, a real chance, to be rid of Rifun, and to live and to make things right." He dropped the Band and life around them resumed. "I don't know what that looks like from here. As you said, I'm blind, I'm crippled. I can barely navigate my way out of a paper bag. But if I can do something, I will."

Netami sighed. "You know that trust is hard to come by as it is."

"I'm not asking for trust. I'm asking for a little faith and a little hope. The war isn't over yet."

Another humming sigh. Then, "Well, I have no real power here. Judgment belongs to my mother, punishment to my brothers. I will return to them and let them know of this conversation. It will be interesting to see how they react."

"Well, you know where I'll be."

As far as the officers were concerned, their conversation had lasted less than five minutes. Netami stood and left without so much as a, "See you next month."

"Damn," Oswald observed, meeting Rivotra as he stood. "Most men at least make it past the greetings before getting dumped by their date."

"She wasn't a date," Rivotra said.

"No?"

The lieutenant's tone was mildly taunting but Rivotra let it go. The officer took him out of the visitation room and got him pointed in the direction of the exit. From there, Rivotra was on his own. He still had an hour or two before having to report to laundry, but the last thing he wanted was to simply sit and be alone with his thoughts, mulling over the conversation he'd just had. Well, maybe he would see if he could get lucky in the weights area in the gym. Lunchtime and dinnertime were usually the best times for those not in gangs to try and get in a workout.

He got lucky that day, and he figured it had as much to do with the day as the time. Gang members had families, too, sometimes. In theory, gang members on the outside weren't allowed to visit with those on the inside, but that didn't mean they couldn't send their girlfriends or other non-criminal acquaintances to talk and pass on news and hit lists.

Most men fought over the bench press and other weight machines, but Rivotra made his way to the pull-up bar. He'd tried the weight bar once, didn't even put any weight on it. The new sensation and movement caused his left arm to fail and he'd dropped that end on his shoulder. Having no weight, it really didn't hurt, but he wasn't keen on it happening again when it did have weight. Or worse, if he had a seizure with a couple hundred pounds hanging over his chest. At least on the pull-up bar, he could still catch himself with his right arm if his left failed, and he could drop safely to the ground before a seizure hit.

Three pull-ups later, Rivotra started to feel an odd sensation. It didn't have to do with his arm, though he lowered himself for a moment just to be sure. It wasn't his seizure aura either. The sensation passed and he pulled himself up on the bar. As he was coming down, he felt the sensation again.

He paused, forcing himself to hold mid-stride while he tried to pinpoint the exact location.

It was almost like tightness in his chest and spiders crawling in his hair. Was this a hallucination? He couldn't recall anything like this before. He tried to swallow, but it was like his throat was paralyzed. Was it a stroke?

He dropped to the ground. As soon as he let go, his chest seized in horrendous fear. For a long moment, time seemed to slow through no will of his own. He knew every breath of a fly as he fell. Then, right as his toes touched the ground, he was able to identify it. As his heels touched down and he steadied himself so he didn't fall, he knew exactly what it was. He'd been expecting to die. He had known a moment of terrible fear, a phantom noose around his neck.

Tommen had hung himself. And Rivotra knew that he, as Rifun, bore at least half of that responsibility. Maybe he hadn't murdered Tommen's daughter, but he had dragged the kid through horror after horror, believing he was doing the right thing. Instead, all he'd done was make Julianna's work that much easier.

"You all right, man?" someone asked. "Pull a muscle?"

Rivotra blinked and straightened from where he was leaning against one of the bar supports. "What? No, I'm fine."

"Suit yourself."

Jumping had been the hardest thing to try and relearn. The amount of coordination and self-sustaining spontaneity required by leg muscles he couldn't consciously use was quite remarkable. Actually, he'd had to lower the bar so it was just within reach, then effectively bounce his way to being able to train his legs to jump. He wasn't going to be jumping rope any time soon, but he could get an inch off the ground to grab the bar.

The hanging sensation overshadowed him every time he went up or down, but he only worked harder, trying to shake it off. He hadn't murdered that child, and he had cut ties with Tommen long before. Tommen himself had said that he'd forgiven him. Right there in the courtroom, reading his victim impact statement in front of a room full of people, "I forgive you." And the kid had seemed genuine. He had even tried to help him, to the chagrin of many others.

If Rivotra was going to be honest, Tommen's forgiveness had played a small role in his questioning of his motives, in his acceptance of his current situation. Rifun had tried to coerce Tommen, as a chosen one of the Author, to do horrible things. Instead, Tommen, in his teenage rebellion and incessant and cynical skepticism, had slowly chipped away at Rifun's blind cockiness and self-assured righteousness. Now, Rivotra had a second chance to undo all of those horrible things.

So why not Tommen? Why wasn't he getting a second chance? Julianna had apparently taken everything from him, too, or near enough. At least Owain was still alive, which was more than Rivotra could say for himself. Tommen had a father. And now, Owain had lost everything. Again.

Rivotra dropped to the ground, grabbed a nearby hand towel to wipe his face and neck, then headed out to report to laundry as much as escape his thoughts.

But the thing about thoughts was that they could not be outrun easily, and folding laundry was not what one could consider to be mentally stimulating.

"You look like shit, man," Shack observed. "Visit day not go well?"

"No," Rivotra answered.

"Sucks, man."

"Learned that one of my victims killed himself last year. I actually cared about him."

"Sucks, man," someone else said.

"Friend of yours?" Shack wondered mildly.

"I wouldn't call him a friend, no."

"Well, then, don't be on about it. Sucks, man, but life do go on."

It was the polite way of telling him to stop talking about it. Prison wasn't therapy. If he wanted someone to cry with him, that's what the social workers were for. Not that Rivotra expected anyone to care or to want to listen, nor that he wanted to divulge in the first place. At the same time, what was he supposed to do with this information? Feel guilty? Well, he was certainly feeling guilty. But what was he supposed to do? He couldn't bring back the dead. And, maybe Netami was right, and he couldn't undo what he'd done, either. Maybe everything Rifun had done was as set in stone as anything could be. Rivotra knew that fate was fixed, but what about the past?

He made it through the rest of his day, working quietly, turning his thoughts over and over again, basically just waiting for sleep although he wasn't sure what would be solved by the arrival of morning.

"Do you still talk to Walter?" Rivotra asked of Vin after final count that night.

"Why? You're not supposed to talk to him," Vin replied sharply.

"Did you know his granddaughter died and his son committed suicide?"

There was a moment of silence, then rustling up top. Then, as if Vin were leaning over the edge of his bed, "How do you know that?"

"Visitor today told me. Wanted me to know so I could feel guilty about it and maybe kill myself." Rivotra wasn't sure just how true that was, but it was logical enough.

"I didn't know that," Vin admitted. "Last time I talked to Walt was right before I was transferred out of jail." More rustling. "Shit, maybe I ought to call or send a letter or something."

"He's moved on by now, and I'm obviously not finding out where he is."

"Maybe not, but I still have a few friends, though they might not admit it publicly." The man let out a breath and cursed softly. "Don't suppose you know what happened?"

"Granddaughter was murdered. Tommen hung himself."

Another curse. "That's bad. No, I didn't know." More rustling. "I'm really going to have to call or write." Pause. "Thanks for telling me."

"Walter was a good officer. He had a lot of good friends. He needs support."

With that, Rivotra rolled over and closed his eyes.

Rivotra sat by Anagalisgi's fire. He still had several open wounds that had not been touched, yet it seemed as though one that had already been sewn was now ripped open anew. It was on the back of his right shoulder, a deep gash from an embedded whip.

He heard Anagalisgi approach, kneel beside him. Heard the telltale signs of him picking a needle and preparing his thread. Before the needle could penetrate skin, however, Rivotra turned as if to look at the man.

"Did you know about Tommen?"

Anagalisgi paused, then let out a slow breath. "Yes. As a matter of fact, I tried to stop him."

"All the power of the Author, the Akari, and the Whites, and you couldn't do it?"

Even sitting right next to him, Rivotra could barely hear the soft, "No."

"What happened? What really happened?"

Anagalisgi touched Rivotra's shoulder. Rivotra flinched and twisted back into position, preparing for the sting of the needle. As Anagalisgi slid sharpened bone through broken skin, he spoke.

"Julianna Disguised herself as the pregnancy doctor. She used Matter to manipulate the DNA of the fetus, to give it problems and make it weak. After birth, it had to stay in the hospital. Then she Disguised herself as various doctors and nurses, and she used a derivative of Borelian toxins to very slowly kill the child. Tommen and Owain caught on, but she was prepared for that, too, and the child died. A few months later, Tommen's girlfriend left him, and he decided that he didn't want to live anymore. Julianna even told him that she wasn't going to kill him, just take away everything he ever loved and make his life a living Hell."

Rivotra raised his left hand to rub his face. "Shit. Was Josina right, then? Is Julianna using LaPouir to make this toxin derivative?"

"That I don't know."

Rivotra shook his head. "It's my fault he's dead. I kidnapped him, I exposed him to Cassius, I shot his father, I dragged him to war. Julianna may have pulled the trigger, but I gave her the gun."

"The Shadows did this," Anagalisgi told him, not unkindly. "Rifun the Shadow and all of his Shadow friends, they set this up. Your Shadows and her Shadows are fundamentally the same. Mortals are like toys in their hands; they might seem to be at odds, but it's all the same puppeteer. And Tommen made his choice."

"Why did I get a second chance and he didn't?"

"I was standing right there, Rivotra." There was sadness beyond tears in the man's voice. "I gave him that chance. All of the Whites were willing to fight for him, to rip apart every Shadow covering him. But for as much as his soul may have begged to be saved, he ultimately made the final decision. He let his soul die, and the Shadows took care of his body."

"Yes, I'm sure Owain sees it that way. And Netami and her family, regarding Sabelu."

At that, Anagalisgi chuckled. "Oh, I'm sure they'll have a few things to say about that."

"They're going to kill me, you know. The Krydik may not have liked Sabelu, but he was one of their own, and a priest at that. I murdered a priest, the savior of their people. They don't forgive things like that."

"You have no idea what's going to happen."

"What, you think there might be forgiveness in the cards, too? Anagalisgi, why should anyone forgive me? I may want to do good and make things right, but I still did some very bad things. It's like wearing a costume and doing horrendous things, then taking off that costume and telling everyone I'm sorry, it was all the fault of my persona. I was still the actor under that mask."

"But now that mask is removed and you are free to live as you are meant to live, as Rivotra, not Rifun," Anagalisgi said, sticking him again as he continued along the gash. "I didn't say it would be easy. I didn't say that everyone would forgive you. This is about healing, not making friends."

"Public execution isn't my idea of healing."

Anagalisgi laughed. "No, I think not. Don't forget, I've been where you are. Being executed was not my idea of helping my people, yet I was delivered at the last moment. And I had even less guidance than you; all I could do was trust the Whites to guide me, and they did."

Rivotra turned his head, almost getting stabbed in the chin in the process. "Do you know what they're going to do?"

"I do, and even they themselves haven't decided yet. First they're going to visit me and give me a piece of their minds."

"Because you talk to me?"

"Mhm."

"Were they so upset about you talking to Tommen?"

"No, but they also didn't understand the extent of our relationship, nor my attempt at guiding him. Of course, I can't imagine they would have been too upset over it anyway."

"Because Tommen wasn't a villain," Rivotra stated. "But I was. Yet we're all chosen ones of the Author. And if Julianna has chapters in my Books, if that makes her a chosen one as well, does that mean that you could visit her? Or that she could make the same choices that we all have? How does this work? Would it be right to kill her?"

"I can't answer all of that."

"Why not? You said it yourself, prophecy is merely telling us what we've already done. What has she done? What is she going to do in two hundred pages or the next Book? What am I going to do?"

Anagalisgi stuck him just a little harder than necessary on the next poke, Rivotra thought, but he stopped talking.

"You are not ready for any of that," the wise man told him sternly. "You are still wounded, both physically and spiritually. Things will happen as they will. Calm down, let yourself heal, and take things one at a time." He tugged on the string, cut it, and tied it off. The string and the gash both vanished and Rivotra rubbed skin that was the smoothest it had been in decades.

"It will be all right," Anagalisgi said, cutting off anything Rivotra tried to say. "For now, just go about your day."

Nine
Interested Parties

As it usually happens, April ended and was followed immediately by May. The comforting warmth of spring sharply gave way to heat and humidity which only got worse on rainy days. General chores also rotated, with a number of positions opening up on account of inmates getting ready for their various sports of choice. It was possible, then, to pick up extra shifts in more chores, and therefore make more money and rack up some extra good behavior time.

Rivotra stayed on cleaning duty in the morning, though his new assignment was the gymnasium, cleaning the floors and all of the equipment. This made it much easier for him to get in some almost private workout time in the morning when everyone was supposed to be doing one job or another. Doing a good job at keeping things clean and organized also helped him build some credit with all of the gangs so he had a better chance of using the equipment when they had control of the cage.

That kept him busy pretty much all morning. After lunch, he was assigned to assist the agricultural program. The program was run by one of the universities, designed to provide therapy through gardening, produce fresh food for the prison for most or all of the year, and give inmates the chance to earn a degree in agriculture and possibly get a job on a farm once they were released. Inmates enrolled in the program were on permanent farm chores, but they still needed help sometimes.

Rivotra was assigned to watering duty. Basically, he started out walking around the greenhouse with a garden hose and ensured that all of the plants were watered. One section was dedicated to seeds and seedlings, so those didn't get a lot of water; didn't want the seeds to drown and rot. Another section was dedicated to sprouts and those with their first leaves, so they got a little more water. The third section was comprised of plants that were a little bigger and almost ready to transplant. Those actually got less water in order to harden them. A fourth, smaller section contained plants that were either experimental or just needed a little more time inside before being transplanted, usually due to cold sensitivity.

But the agricultural program was not limited to just fruits and vegetables. They also had a rather large flock of chickens to take care of. It wasn't enough to give all one thousand inmates a fresh chicken dinner every night, but when butchering time came around in the fall—which was done outside the prison, for obvious reasons—there was a significant difference in the quality of meat for about a week or so. Year round, however, was a very large, very regular supply of eggs. Inmates who had done time in other prisons commented that other places had to use industrial, processed egg product; Mt. Olive was the only place that actually used real eggs.

So, once his time in the greenhouse was finished, he headed out to the chicken coop to deal with the chicken water. He took each waterer outside, dumped it, scrubbed it, then refilled it.

He'd never cared for chickens. They were stupid birds, as evidenced by their not even needing a head to survive, at least for a little while. He much preferred ducks. He'd enjoyed watching the ducks in the *tanimbary*, swimming in the deeper areas and sifting through the silt with their beaks to find and eat the pesky snails that would otherwise destroy the rice. And they were smart, too. In the morning, all he had to do was open up the duck pen and they'd run straight to the *tanimbary* to do their job. At night, they'd come running back to the safety of the pen, quacking all the way.

Unfortunately, he couldn't convince those in charge to get ducks. Too inefficient, they said, because of the water requirements and their lower egg production. It was also harder to butcher a duck, allegedly, because of the oils making it too difficult to pluck the feathers. Rivotra just heard excuses, but he was in no position to argue.

It was, perhaps, the first time he considered taking advantage of anything the prison claimed to offer by way of rehabilitation programs. His family's farm was far away, its status worryingly unknown to him, but this here was a farm that he could work on right now. Sure, it was tomatoes and chickens instead of rice and cattle, but it was something. And if he couldn't manage a farm here where everything was neat and controlled, he wasn't going to be able to do much at home.

He stuck around the farm after his assigned chores were finished, walking around, trying to get to know the area a little better, trying to orient himself to everything. He might ask about picking up some more chores here. He wasn't overly concerned about having money for commissary, and while he didn't need extra good behavior time for an impending parole hearing, he'd heard that it still looked good when appellate judges were considering his case.

A little over a month until the hearing, he mused. Then a few more weeks until the decision. Two months until he could be home free, legally speaking. He hadn't heard anything more from Netami or the Krydik, including Anagalisgi, so there was still that threat hanging over his head.

He left the farm, heading to the cafeteria for an early dinner. He might inquire about additional chores, but he wasn't going to start the full dog and pony circus when he could be out of here in under sixty days.

The only downside to working in the chicken coop was that, for as careful as he might be, he still ended up smelling like the chicken coop. There were plenty of complaints about it in the buffet line, and the only ones who would sit by him were the others who also worked in the chicken coop. They usually smelled worse because they were either cleaning the coop or feeding the chickens or trying to catch a chicken for one reason or another.

Every night, Rivotra would take his clothes into the shower with him to give them a rinse and a minor scrub. It certainly helped, but by Friday, he was more than happy to exchange those clothes for something fresh. He did not necessarily believe that the new clothes were any cleaner, but at least they didn't smell, or in his case, taste horrible. And, being blind, he could pretend that there weren't any questionable stains on them either.

Unlike the nursing home, mail in genpop was delivered in the morning. If an inmate cooperated for morning count, he got his mail. Again, Rivotra was surprised when he was told that he had mail, but he figured it was just a notice from his lawyer about the upcoming hearing. Nevertheless, he handed the mail to Vin and asked him to read it. Vin still didn't like Rivotra, but he could be bothered to help out a blind man sometimes.

The former cop opened up the envelope and Rivotra could hear him rifling through the papers.

"Out loud, please," Rivotra told him. "I can hear your voice, not your thoughts."

"Dude, you are fucked," Vin chuckled. "Your lawyer is so pissed."

"Do I get the benefit of knowing why?"

Only a month or so until the hearing, why would his lawyer be mad? What could he have found that would jeopardize everything at the last moment?

"I'm not going to read it word-for-word because legalese is boring," Vin told him. "Basically, he says that the Krydik Indians have decided to step in and lay a claim that you are responsible for the deaths of one of their members, and they want to take custody of you for trial on tribal grounds. Because of that, the hearing for your appeal has been pushed back to September while everyone has meetings with everyone else to try and figure out what is going on and how to work it in." Vin laughed again. "You are so fucked."

Rivotra was more confused than upset. Oh, he was annoyed that the hearing had been pushed back, but why were the Krydik making such a...legal scene out of all of this? Why not wait until after his appeal? Whether he was freed or not, it wasn't as though it would be difficult for them to swoop in and spirit him away to Hlohi for trial. Why the formal avenues?

"He also says that he and Miss...Zita? Zitta? Zitha?" Vin made an uncertain sound. "They're going to be coming to meet with you on May 16th to ask you some questions and figure out what the fuck is going on. A tribal lawyer is also going to be at the meeting." Vin waved the papers in front of Rivotra's face so he could grab them. His tone was still laughing. "You are fucked."

"Why do you say that? I'm just confused."

"Let me tell you, as a former cop, no one messes with tribal law. No white lawyer is going to represent you, and if they do, they're a scuzzball just looking to make a quick buck and won't do jack shit to help you."

All things considered, Rivotra wasn't sure any lawyer, scuzzball or otherwise, would be of any use anyway, not with this case.

Still, he just couldn't figure out why they were playing this so formally. What did they hope to gain? Were they just trying to make his life difficult? There were certainly better ways to go about it.

With the morning count finished and the mail delivered, everyone had a couple hours to themselves. Most rolled over and went back to sleep for a bit, a few slogged off to early chores such as cooking the day's meals, and a few got up to get some early coffee. Rivotra sat on his mattress for a few minutes thinking about it, then got up, grabbed his cane, and headed out.

He did not go to the cafeteria for coffee, although there was a certain appeal to it, given his odd sense of smell and taste. Instead, he headed to the gym to get a head start on his cleaning.

"You're early," the desk officer observed.

"Couldn't sleep," Rivotra told him. "Might as well make myself useful."

First he got in a private workout, then he started cleaning. This allowed him to finish a little earlier which meant he was able to visit commissary before lunch.

Commissary was not like a regular American store. A person didn't just walk in, browse casually, make his selection, then take it to the register. There were far too many thieves and drug dealers in prison to extend even that small amount of trust and normalcy to the population.

Instead, Rivotra walked into a small room with only a barred window and the clerk behind it.

"Well, well, look who it is," the clerk said. "Prison Jesus himself. Come to grace us with his presence."

"I don't know what you expect, but I don't do miracles," Rivotra told him.

Rivotra had a notion that this man was someone from one of the Hispanic gangs who sometimes let him work out with them in the cage, but he couldn't recall a name, or that they'd ever really interacted.

"Yeah, whatever," the man said. "What are you looking for? We have a fine selection of beef jerky. Or maybe you need some more socks, more comfortable rags for your bag?"

"Please, I'm not that old."

The clerk laughed.

"Looking for a pair of jeans," Rivotra told him. "Preferably, ones that fit."

"Ooh, now there's the premium. What you got for me for that?"

"As I said, I don't do miracles."

"They're only jeans, man. I ain't asking for a miracle. Maybe a little favor?"

"I already clean the gym equipment, and blind men can't smuggle well. What more do you want?"

"Nah, but sick men know how to cause a scene, cause a distraction." He lowered his voice. "You cause a little scene at lunch. You fucked up in the head, got epilepsy, right? Fake a seizure—or have one for real, even better—draw the attention of the fuzz, couple of my boys shank that little cop bitch you got for a cellie."

"Why ask me?"

"Cause you medical. My boys fake some shit, pick a fight, they get time in the Hole for drugs and fighting. But you? You're clean. Can't help that you fucked in the head."

Rivotra let out a breath. "Again, why ask me?"

Now the clerk chuckled, and it wasn't friendly. "Some dude or multiples dudes fucking killed you, and you still ain't snitchin' on 'em. You a cop killer, got a cop for a cellie, and not a fucking word. Means you can be trusted with anything. Can I trust you with this? Here, hold on."

He walked away, then returned a minute later and tossed something at Rivotra. It turned out to be a pair of jeans. "I'll even give you a little line of credit. Good jeans, gonna fit you real nice, really impress your lady. It'll be a few days before I can get my boys ready, but when you get the signal...you better do as you're fucking told. Cause if you don't, those jeans ain't gonna be the only thing I take off your body."

Rivotra folded the jeans and laid them over his arm.

"You understand me?" the clerk pressed.

"Very well," Rivotra said.

"Good. You do this, commissary is yours, whatever you want."

Rivotra left before the clerk could say anything more.

Despite being found not guilty for the deaths of the officers, Rivotra had still been labeled a cop killer. This made him rather popular among the inmates, helped to establish a more fearsome reputation that had apparently fed into his being revived from death and so created this Prison Jesus image. And yet, he'd never really harbored any ill will for the officers. He still didn't. But whatever illusory beef with police had helped to bolster his reputation was now being called out, and they wanted him to act on it.

Well, he would act on it, but it might not be in the way they expected.

First and foremost, he needed to know what was going on with his hearing and the Krydik. Thankfully, that meeting came before this desired shanking, so at least he would get one good use out of the jeans. He couldn't say just why he felt the need to wear the jeans specially for this meeting. Everyone knew who he was, what he'd done. He was already in prison; he wasn't fooling anyone.

Walking into the meeting with a bunch of lawyers with his new jeans—which, as promised, did fit very well—he felt very conspicuous.

"Well, you look better than you did six months ago," a man with a boisterous, nasally voice said as he took a seat.

"Mr. Ndolo," the warden cut in immediately, "you remember Kevin Bartlett and Josina Zitha?"

"Yes," Rivotra answered. He remembered Josina well, and he guessed that the man with the nasally voice was his lawyer, Kevin Bartlett.

"May I also introduce Diane Wolf, lawyer for the Krydik Indians."

Rivotra partially stood and held out a hand which was eventually taken. If they wanted to play formalities, he could play formalities, too. He knew, somehow, that Diane was really Nendawagan, Sabelu's mother.

"Mr. Ndolo," Bartlett began, tone already annoyed, "when we were talking about your trial, and I asked you if there was anything else I needed to know about, I wasn't talking about parking tickets. Where did all of this come from? And why wait until now to move against my client?"

"Ballistics," the new woman, Diane or Nendawagan, said. Rivotra heard papers slide across the metal table. "The ballistics report from his trial, the gun that was used to shoot Walter Forbes, is the same one that killed Saul Wolf."

"That doesn't mean he pulled the trigger. There are hundreds of miles between Charleston and where Mr. Wolf was killed."

"And the gun just mysteriously vanished from your client's possession, showed up hundreds of miles away in someone else's possession, killed Mr. Wolf, then made its way hundreds of miles back to Mr. Ndolo? Either he is the luckiest man alive, the unluckiest man alive, or else he did it. Or he ordered someone else to do it."

"Or it was never his gun to begin with; it belonged as property of the group."

Rivotra sighed and Banded himself and Nendawagan. "You know, for wanting to live in the old ways, you do seem to enjoy modern technology when it suits you." He shifted position. "Why are you going through all of this? Why the charade?"

Nendawagan huffed a sigh as if annoyed by his interruption. "Fastest way for me to conduct a trial."

"You could have waited until my hearing next month. Overturned or not might not matter much to you, but if it was, much easier to kidnap me to Hlohi."

"Or I can try you here, and if I find you guilty, I can just send my sons to carry out the punishment, much the same way Julianna did. Except she made the mistake of leaving your head."

Rivotra cleared his throat. "Yes, it would be more difficult to come back from that. But surely in the last few years, you must have already judged me guilty. This ballistics report is nonsense; the Books tell you far more. I might have expected this spat with Julianna to be of far more importance, given what your daughter told me about the Miaramila. Yet here you are."

Nendawagan did not answer for a long moment. Then, "The Books are not unclear. Rifun Ndolo is guilty. And yet...my father's brother maintains hope for Rivotra Andilan. I came because I wanted to see who was on trial."

"I see." Rivotra shifted uncomfortably.

"I know you murdered Sabelu in a ritual of human sacrifice," Nendawagan said quietly. "I know you sacrificed him to the Shadows."

Rivotra nodded, then paused. "I may have sacrificed him to the Shadows, for the Shadows, but I have a great suspicion that there was nothing for them to take and feed on."

"Do you have anything to say for yourself? Some kind of defense?"

"I have no defense," he told her. "It is not incorrect to say that a Shadow called Rifun Ndolo had seized me from a young age and effectively raised me in the path of Shadows, disguising it as any number of things which I believed good and righteous. But it is incorrect to say that I never had a choice in the matter. I did not have to kill him. No one held a knife to my throat or controlled my hands with strings. You know I doubted, but I did it anyway."

Again there was silence. Nendawagan stood, walked around the room a time or two, then sat down again. Still it was another minute before she spoke. "Netami told me that you wanted to undo everything you had done, or that Rifun had done. How do you plan to undo Sabelu's death?"

He made a strangled sort of sound. Then, "I can't undo death. Maybe the Author would bring him back, but by now, I doubt it."

"Exactly."

"What I can do is try to carry on his legacy and his mission. He worked to free your people and defeat the Shadows. I thought I was doing the same thing. I wasn't. But now that I see and understand what's going on, I can try again."

"A lofty goal for an epileptic blind man behind bars."

"I wasn't brought back for nothing."

"And what do you think of this?"

"I'm trying to decide." Rivotra notably flinched as he heard Josina speak. There was a laugh in her voice as she asked, "Do you regret showing me all of this Time business?"

Rivotra rubbed his face, trying to recover some composure. "I admit, I am unaccustomed to having to ask for help. I am not unaccustomed to people questioning my motives, although the two together, while understandable, is frustrating."

"For a lawyer, I like her," Nendawagan said. "She's thorough, not easily intimidated. She's managed to sleuth out quite a bit."

"So, how did you two meet? Was it just from this...?" Rivotra shifted position. "What is actually going on here?"

"I wasn't really aware of any of this until recently," Josina told him. "I was still working on your case, trying to find out more about Time, the Akari,

217

this hit list, and so on. Then your lawyer called me with news about the Krydik people and their charges. Somehow it came up about Hlohi; Mr. Bartlett said it was what they called their reservation. I recalled something about a human colony world by that name. I started talking to Netami, she told me about her contact with Jeremy Long and then her visit with you. Then I met with Nendawagan." Her tone didn't turn cold, but it was devoid of warmth. "You mentioned the work of the spirits. You might have also mentioned that you were deeply involved with dark spirits as well and this is far deeper retribution than a scorned woman." He opened his mouth, but she beat him to it. "I may not fully understand Time and the Akari and aliens and colony worlds, but I understand spirits and witchcraft."

"Spirits may influence a man to do this or that, but there is still a physical element to it," Rivotra said. "I know you understand spirits and witchcraft, but if you really wanted to help, you needed to understand the physical reality as well. Mortals can wield tremendous power. Whether it is part of the *razana* or not, I don't know anymore. But it is power, and these people are guided either by the Whites or the Shadows. This you know. But you did not know the faces of the physical people."

Josina sighed, and Rivotra imagined that the two women may have held their own private conference. He also guessed that Josina had been holding her own Band separately from him, and that was why he hadn't noticed her presence before.

"You're asking for a second chance," Nendawagan stated.

"Yes."

"A chance to actually do what you thought you had been doing this whole time."

"Yes."

"How do you know you'll do it? You've cheated death before, you've had doubts before, you've had outside influences and guidance pushing you to do this or that before. How do you know that the path you will walk now is that right path?"

"Because that path is no longer about serving myself and my goals. I wanted to heal myself. I wanted to liberate my people. I wanted success. I wanted to be the hero. I wanted to be the savior—"

"And now you want to be the savior of the universe and the Krydik by taking out Julianna, is that it? You want to show off that you can undo what you did?"

"I want to undo what I did because it is right. And I was wrong. I can't talk my way to that point. I can only do, or die trying."

Again there was a pause. Again he suspected the women were conversing privately. Then he felt Nendawagan gently pull out of his Band. He respectfully pulled it away from her, but before he dropped it from himself, he extended it to encompass Josina.

"I understand that everyone wants to make himself look good," she began immediately, "and that maybe you were trying to break me in slowly. But that was a lot of missing information I had to uncover by myself."

"In my defense, I can't call or visit any time I want," he said weakly. "And it wasn't as though you didn't know you were dealing with a criminal."

She sighed with some resignation.

"Before we resume this conversation, may I ask one thing?" he inquired.

There was a pause, then, "You may."

He cleared his throat awkwardly. "May I touch you?"

"I'm sorry?"

Rivotra squirmed a little. "I can't see you. My brain doesn't even let me picture you from what anyone else here tells me about you. I rely on sound and touch. May I touch you, so I can put a...feel to a voice?"

There was a long silence, and Rivotra could feel his skin burn with embarrassment. He swallowed nervously. He shouldn't have asked. The conversation was too heated for such gentle intimacy. He should have just kept his thoughts to himself. He did want to have an idea of what she looked-slash-felt like, but he would be remiss if he didn't admit to wanting just a little more. He wouldn't do it, of course, however much he knew he could get away with it, but there was that small desire. At least his desire couldn't show well, and it wasn't just the thickness of the jeans that would disguise it. The nerve injuries to his lower spine and hips had impaired—although thankfully not completely cut off—his more...passionate abilities.

"All right," Josina decided at last. "Only because I know the power you could use to do it regardless, but you're still polite enough to ask."

Her acceptance didn't actually reassure him, just made him feel more conspicuous. He stood when he heard her chair slide across the floor and gingerly held his hands out. A moment later, he felt her slender fingers.

"Just put my hands on your shoulders," he told her, still feeling ridiculous. She did so.

He could feel the tension and uncertainty as she stood there and waited for him to do something, anything. His fingers that he had full control over, he kept together in a straight line. The two fingers he hadn't quite managed to wrangle in, well, there wasn't much he could do.

Despite having been told that she was six feet tall, it still surprised him when she put his hands on her shoulders which were effectively parallel to his own. It was strange, but also a little exciting. He felt down her arms, down her sides, resisting every urge to touch her chest—although he would admit, if asked, that he may have Banded himself a second time so he could linger half a moment on at least the sides of her breasts, which were a lovely, shapely, less than obnoxiously robust round. He went down only to her hips, then back up to her shoulders.

He could feel the slightest deformation in her right side, a divot that existed in her right hip but not in her left, and something similar in her shoulders. When he touched the skin of her neck, he could feel the scarring from both haphazard wounds and surgical incisions. As he lightly touched her head and face, he noted both scarring of the skin and deformation of bone. Her ear was misshapen. Her jaw had been broken, her cheek, her nose, her eye socket. She'd suffered skull fractures, maybe even brain damage.

Rivotra felt an overwhelming urge to pull her close and hold her, to protect her from this mess that he had caused. He may have opened her eyes, but she wasn't ready to face the demons. And how could he ask her to face them at all when this was his problem? Why had he brought her into this? Hadn't she done enough for him, experienced enough in her own life?

He blinked, brought back to the present moment by Josina clearing her throat. He removed his hands which were still on either side of her face.

"Thank you," he mumbled, and returned to his seat.

"Am I what you expected?" she wondered, her tone difficult to discern as she also made her way back to her chair.

"One of the officers said you were tall."

"Is that all he said?"

"He mentioned the scarring."

"You still seemed surprised by it."

Rivotra shrugged. "It's not often I meet someone like me, who wears her scars with pride."

"I don't know if it's pride or just plain stubbornness," Josina admitted.

He leaned back in his chair. "So how does a Sakalava meet and marry a Mozambican?"

"Mozambican Tswa," she corrected him. "And Menambe Sakalava. My mother and her family happened to be in Tana at the same time as my father and some of his family. They met only briefly, but there was something about each one that the other liked. Grandparents on both sides suspected there was some political reasoning behind it, but I know there was love between them, too."

"Political?"

"Like I said, my father specialized in imports and exports. He facilitated a lot of merchandise coming out of Madagscar, directed it to wherever it needed to go in Africa or Asia, very rarely the Americas. And my mother's family was *ampanzaka*—"

"I'm sorry, I don't know what that means."

Josina scoffed teasingly. "You highlanders. It means that my family is considered nobility among the Sakalava, an offshoot of one of the old Menambe dynasties. It's more social than political, I assure you, but it doesn't go unnoticed. Having that trade connection was, for a while, very good for my mother's family and their village. And the Sakalava as a whole, if you were to believe my father."

"And you, apparently, if it got you a job with the Senate," Rivotra observed. "How did that come about?"

Now she sighed sadly. "I was not allowed to inherit from my father when he and the last of my brothers was murdered. Everything he had went to his brother who completely denounced my father and brothers and everything they had done."

"Because it wasn't 'Muslim enough.'"

"That, and for some of his less popular political views. Any good that my father had done for my mother's family was immediately cut off. And we were back to basically what my mother had grown up with: fish, farming, and family. And that was all I was ever going to get. Don't get me wrong, it's not a bad life. We never wanted for food, our social status did afford us some luxuries, my mother's family adored me and was always very supportive after what happened. But the most they could promise was that they would find a good husband for me."

"You wanted more," Rivotra stated.

"It wasn't that I yearned for city life or material possessions, although we had both in Xai-Xai. Mostly, I wanted justice. I couldn't just turn my back on my parents and siblings, throw my hands up, and say, 'That's life. I'll just have to try and do better.' I wanted to know who had killed them, and I wanted them to pay."

"How did you afford the schooling? Even for my family, that was still a fairly lofty goal. Not unattainable, but not everyone could do it."

"I finished my regular education at the village school at age twelve. I fished and farmed as expected for a few years. Then, in the early 2000's, when I was a teenager, tourism started to make its way to our part of the island. Westerners wanted to go out hiking in the jungles and take pictures of the animals. I started out by selling fish to them, local, freshly-caught fish that they would cook over fires on the beach. They would pay for, not only the fish, but for me to just sell them the fish. I learned very quickly about Western tipping. When I got a little older, I started to lead tours around the area, and I made even more tips. And the tips weren't just our worthless ariary, people gave me American dollars, Canadian and Australian dollars, British pounds, euros. It was pocket change to them, but it was my ticket to school. When I turned nineteen, I left home and traveled to the university in Fianar to pursue my law degree."

Rivotra nodded. "You're smart. You've done very well for yourself. What does your family think?"

"Some are happy for me. Others think I should go back to fish, farming, and family, find a nice husband and settle down. I admit, it does have its appeal. I'm not overly fond of the city and its noise and so many people. I just don't know that I could. I feel like I'd be turning my back on my parents."

"Maybe. But do you wonder what your parents would want for you? If you're thirty years old with no children... When would you marry? When would you have children? Or would you spend your whole life looking for their killers, maybe even get lucky enough to find and punish them, only to die alone yourself?"

"Is that how you feel about the murder of your family now?" She added quickly, "No. Stop. I'm sorry. That was inappropriate. It is still very soon after."

"I know who killed my family," Rivotra said. "And I know that it is primarily my fault. I would like to marry and have children, yes. But I know that there is a very real, very tangible threat out there—that I helped to create —that must be dealt with first."

"I understand."

He sighed. "And now, that means surrendering myself to the Krydik, too, I suppose."

He dropped the Band. Nendawagan said something to Bartlett that Rivotra didn't catch right away, but he didn't really care.

"So, what is the timeline of all of this?" he interrupted. "How does this play into the appeals hearing?"

"All tribal cases are automatically federal cases," Bartlett stated. "That's really the only hiccup. See, standard procedure is to appeal the verdict and kick it back to the lower court. Well, as I've said, the lower court is going to drop it immediately, but now the feds, that is, the Krydik, are butting in and asking to have a crack at you. It's all paperwork and nuanced legalese."

Rivotra didn't see how it made a difference. Excuses and buying time was all he heard. Maybe there was something to be said for Julianna's moles expediting his trial.

He turned his attention to Josina. "Any news from back home?"

"I told you that all of the properties had been seized by the government. Regrettably, due to issues with vagabonds and housing, or those are the reasons being given, the properties in Fianarantsoa proper—Lalao's home as well as those of her sons and their families—have been sold."

Rivotra let out a breath and settled his forehead in his hand on the table. "What about all of her stuff? What happened to her things and her papers and everything else?"

"Important documents were seized by the government or some of the banks, most likely disappeared by now. As for the rest of it, gone or sold. I'm sorry, I don't really know."

"And the rest of the properties?" he dared venture.

"Mahitsy has expressed interest in destroying the homes and hoping it puts any lingering vengeful spirits to rest, but no one is trying to actually lay claim to them. As for your family's farm and the surrounding farms, there has been some expressed interest in the smaller farms by other residents. For the larger farm, the residents have apparently discussed turning it into a tomb for the family, making the whole place like a memorial ground. But there have also been a few government officials who have talked about buying it as well."

"Where does the village president stand on the issue?"

"He is inclined to preserve the farm. But no one tells a federal official no."

Rivotra straightened, though his soul still slumped. "No, but they can make the official work for what he wants. Do you think you might be able to cause a little trouble until September?" He shrugged helplessly. "Maybe I'll be out of here. Maybe Nendawagan won't kill me. And maybe I'll be able to lay claim."

"I can certainly try."

While they had been discussing in Malagasy, Bartlett and Nendawagan had been having their own conversation. Neither one sounded satisfied, but their tones suggested that they didn't necessarily have to be here to continue it and try to come to some arrangement.

"Now then, before we leave," Bartlett said curtly, "is there anything else you'd like to tell me, Mr. Ndolo? Does anyone else want to lay claim to your head?"

"I certainly hope not," Rivotra answered.

"I'm being serious. I was all prepared to argue your case next month, and now this gets thrown at me. Is there anything else?"

"No. If there is, I am denying it entirely."

"Hm," Nendawagan commented.

"All right." The air was split by the screech of the man's chair across the floor. "Well, if something comes up, you'll get a letter from me."

Rivotra just nodded. To his right, he heard Nendawagan stand.

"We'll be in touch," she told him coolly.

"I look forward to it," he replied.

Slowly, he stood with the rest of them, shaking hands in turn.

"I will do my best to stall the officials from looking too hard at the farm," Josina promised in Malagasy, "but a few months is the best I will likely be able to do."

"I understand. And I thank you for doing that much."

The lawyers filed out of the room first. Then, Rivotra was permitted to leave to return to his cell where he changed out of his nice jeans and back into his regular pants. From there, he made his way to the farm where he got a late start on his watering chores. He might have expected to be alone the entire time, and he was quite surprised when he found two men in the chicken coop. Judging by their harried whispering, they weren't there for the chickens. He surprised them as much as they surprised him.

"Fuck, man, don't sneak up on us like that," one hissed.

"Am I interrupting?" Rivotra retorted.

"You in Neighborhood E, right?" the other said. "You're Copper's cellie."

"That's right." Did he want to admit to it?

"We got a tip that the Dirt's gonna do a random raid tonight. Any shit you got, you gotta hide, like, yesterday."

The Direct Intervention Response Team, also called the Dirt. Teams of four to six men who liked to kick down heavy steel doors, manhandle inmates out of bed, and rip everything apart looking for contraband and snacks. Raids might be in response to tips about contraband, or completely random. Or as random as it could be in an enclosed complex full of eyes and ears that didn't see or hear anything.

"You're sure they're doing it tonight?" Rivotra asked, an idea coming to mind.

"Sure as we can be, but do you wanna find out the hard way?"

225

Rivotra nodded thoughtfully. "What are you burying?"

"What's it matter to you?"

"Is one of these items a shiv or other sharp metal, perhaps?"

The first inmate laughed nervously. "You ain't fightin' the Dirt."

"It would never cross my mind. Answer the question."

"It could be," the second inmate said evasively. "Why?"

"Give it to me. I can make it disappear."

"Anyone can make anything disappear. How about making it reappear? I got contracts."

Rivotra changed his tone. "What contracts? You don't know anything about any contract. You don't even have a weapon to carry out a contract."

After a moment, the inmate chuckled conspiratorially, and pressed a piece of sharpened metal into Rivotra's open palm. "I like how you think. You do what you gotta do. Bring that back in a couple days."

"This one is going to disappear, but I'll bring you something better."

"This I gotta see," the first inmate said.

"Believe me, you don't."

Rivotra put the shiv in his pants pocket and went about his business, doing nothing else out of the ordinary that evening. He went to dinner, he went outside to take a walk in the fresh air, and he eventually returned to his neighborhood for his evening shower and routine.

He wasn't going to fake a seizure, and he wasn't keen on having a real one either. He had no desire to be a pawn, however cleanly he might be able to get away with his role. But he also couldn't justify trying to get overly involved and somehow take down those who wanted to maim or kill Vin. He couldn't see, which wasn't a problem for an active assailant, but he didn't know who his enemies were. He didn't know which gang this was, or who was involved in this scheme. And he wasn't going to get those answers without it getting around that he could be snitching.

His best bet would be to sidestep. It wouldn't make the problem go away, but it might buy Vin some time. Granted, it wasn't going to help his standing in the prison, but it would keep the man alive.

Rivotra finished another shower without dying and headed back to his cell. Once he was inside, he Banded so as to elude the camera. Then he pulled out the shiv, cut along the seam of Vin's mattress just an inch or two, using an existing small tear, and stuffed the shiv inside. He didn't push it deep, keeping it close to the hole. He'd thought about just putting it in Vin's tub, but that was too obvious, too easy to claim framing. Not that mattresses were any more clever, but it was pretty standard. If the Dirt did raid tonight, when they grabbed the mattress and flipped it, the shiv would hopefully fall out. Vin would be taken to the Hole for a bit, probably screaming obscenities the whole time. They'd check cameras, wouldn't be able to find anything on account of the Band, and Vin would be let go. He might not have much good behavior time left, but he also wouldn't have any official disciplinary action against him. And he would be alive.

Not that Rivotra didn't expect the gang to try again, perhaps very soon after Vin came back, but it would be a larger window of time for him, Rivotra, to figure out some other way of dealing with this.

With the shiv set, he dropped the Band and carried on, stretching a little before easing himself back on his mattress, any number of back pains making themselves well known. Vin made his way back eventually and hopped up onto his mattress without so much as a, "Honey, I'm home."

"How long did you say you were in for?" Rivotra inquired of his upstairs neighbor.

"Two to nine, why?" Vin wondered sourly.

"You can't have much time left."

"Ha! Depends on if you're looking at the two or the nine. If the parole board likes me, sure, I might be out early next year. If not, well, just one year after another in this shithole."

"What are you going to do when you get out? You got wife and kids?"

"Like I'm going to tell you."

"All right, that's fair."

Vin sighed. "I don't know. I got a few friends left. I'll probably crash on a couch for a while until I can get my life back together. I mean, two years isn't all that bad. Shouldn't be too hard to find a job, work as a grocery store clerk or something."

Well, he didn't have the greatest ambitions, but at least it was something. Rivotra didn't know if he was doing the right thing, but as the doors slammed shut and locked securely, there was only one way to find out. He rolled over several times, trying to find any semblance of comfort on his lumpy mattress, then closed his eyes and fell asleep.

Date of Search	Location(s) of Search
May 17, 2017	Cellblock E - All Cells and Showers

Search Type	Time Begun	Time Concluded
Random	0216	0256

Team Leaders	K9 Units
Copeland, N., Smith, J., Kline, J.	Pike, Rex, Mack

Contraband Located

5 x Drugs, Illicit, < 5g
2 x Drugs, Illicit, > 5g and < 20g
1 x Drugs, Illicit, > 20g and < 1kg
5 x Drug Paraphernalia
3 x Property Reported Stolen
4 x Tattoo Paraphernalia
2 x Weapons, Improvised, Bladed
1 x Weapons, Bladed

Inmates Arrested

Drug Paraphernalia
    911563, 974252, 966931
Drugs
    911563, 974252, 966931, 952333, 950123, 953121, 981455
Property Reported Stolen
    981455
Tattoo Paraphernalia
    921243, 933141, 967831
Weapons
    952333, 951011, 981436, 960154

Contact Reported

952333 attempted to use a bladed weapon on a K9 unit (Pike) and was subdued. Inmate suffered multiple bite wounds. K9 was not injured.

Injuries Reported

952333 suffered multiple bite wounds from K9.

No other injuries

Continued Notes / Report
Standard procedure

Reporting Officer
Copeland, N.

Ten
Two Step

He should have just put the shiv in Vin's tub.

At some point in the middle of the night, before the raid by the Dirt, Vin, who was apparently a very finicky sleeper, had shifted his mattress in such a way that the shiv fell out of his mattress and onto the floor. In the middle of a raid, no one was looking at cameras to see that it had fallen out of his mattress, and the whole situation turned into a massive he-said he-said argument, which resulted in both Vin and Rivotra being hauled out to the Hole at roughly three o'clock in the morning.

"Welcome to the Hole," an overly enthusiastic officer, probably one of the Dirt, greeted as they were herded into a small room. "Or the entrance to it, anyway. Some of you are loyal customers, others are brand new, so I'll give you all a quick rundown of what to expect.

"You will each get your own individual cube. As a perk of utilizing our escort service, you get to stay in your cube for three whole days."

"Does sucking my dick come part of your escort services, or that cost extra?" someone asked hotly.

"No, but I'll be happy to shove my boot up your ass for free." The officer answered the remark and returned to his speech without missing a beat. "There is to be no talking while in the Hole unless you are answering a question or command from an officer or one of the law admins when they make their rounds.

"Food will be provided three times a day. What goes in must come out. You will have a chance for a shower once a week, plus the day before or the day of your court appearance.

"The first three days are just a courtesy. After that, you will be put on the court schedule. We do not control when that is. You could be here three days, four, five, a week, maybe ten days or more. Depends on how busy they are. When you go to court, you will hear the charges and argue your case. There could be a ruling right away, or it might take a day or two. That is not up to us. If they decide to deliberate, you will be returned to your cube until they decide.

"Any further questions can be answered by those of the court when it is your turn. Until then, we'll show you to your rooms so you can get back to your beauty sleep."

Then the herd was moving again.

Absolutely no accommodation was given for Rivotra's blindness or physical limitations. He stumbled along with the rest, fell once, was dragged back to his feet, and shoved forward. He didn't know where he was, where he was going, his cane was gone, and he was overall just frustrated. Try to help a guy out and this happens. He should have just put the shiv in Vin's tub.

Then he was being pushed in a new direction. His general sense of personal space informed him that he was now in a very small room, and the slamming of a heavy steel door behind him only reinforced the point.

This cell was smaller than the one in his neighborhood, which he might have expected. It was also smaller than the one in the Fishbowl. Five and a half by five and a half and just a hair over six feet tall as the very top hairs of his head brushed the ceiling. When he sat on the even thinner mattress and tried to lie down, he couldn't stretch out comfortably; his legs were just bent.

His fatigue got him to sleep, but he woke up not much later and discovered he was stiff in places he didn't know could stiffen. Worse, because of his awkward position and the stiffness, trying to sit up and stand was like being thrown back to the first three months of his rehab. He couldn't find his legs, couldn't get his balance right away, and his head was not letting him know which way was up. He had to use his good arm to get his limbs sorted out, effectively stretch them by hand, and only then was he able to stand well.

Not that he could go anywhere since his available standing floor space was about two feet by two feet. The rest was either the bed or the toilet-sink unit. He could stretch his arms in front of him or behind him, bend over to stretch his back and knees, but that was all.

Rivotra had never considered himself to be claustrophobic, but perhaps that was because he'd never actually been forced into a very small and uncomfortable space. Thank the ancestors the French had never done this. Or had they? Could this be a new fear on account of his new head injuries? Was that even possible? He wasn't sure. He didn't like it either way. And it wasn't as though he could even close his eyes and pretend he was in a bigger room. He was already blind. This was simple awareness that he was in a very small room, and he wasn't going to be able to fool his senses that easily. Ancestors, what a time for his spatial orientation to suddenly work exactly how it was supposed to.

But there was absolutely nothing he could do. This was where he was going to stay for the next three days. Outside, down the hall somewhere, he could hear yelling and shouting. It wasn't going to change anything. Still he sat here. And it was only the beginning.

Wait. Yes. There was something he could do. A Slow Band. In the same way that he could take a single moment and stretch it out for hours or days, he could also take all three days and condense them into only a moment. He could do that easily, under normal circumstances. Here, he would still have to pay attention to meals and anyone who came by who needed his attention for some reason. But still, if he could make even just a few hours go by, it might save his sanity.

So he Banded, and the next thing he knew, there was a sound at the door. He dropped the Band just in time to hear some instructions on ensuring that whatever came in made its way back out. If he thought this was bad, there was worse punishment in store for those who broke the rules even in the Hole.

Rivotra ate quickly and returned his tray just as soon as he could. He heard the food service inmate collect it and move on. After another minute or two of waiting for something else to happen, he Banded again.

And again, the next thing to catch his attention was the arrival of the lunch tray. As he ate, he considered that he was going to basically eat nine meals in a row. Because of his slowed metabolism, he already wasn't hungry most days and didn't eat much when given a choice. Even working out only produced a marginal feeling of peckishness. Sleeping at night instead of

Banding might help some, but that was assuming he could sleep. Or should. He didn't know if he wanted to risk the debilitating stiffness again.

Maybe he could Band his stomach, speed up the digestive process a little. Given his options and abilities, it seemed like a reasonable course of action. So, once he sent the tray back, he sat back on the lumpy mattress and Fast Banded his stomach. He'd never done it before, though Pinpoint Banding was a simple enough process, except he was not prepared for the way it made his stomach feel. It was almost like the precursor to heartburn or vomit in spite of a lack of nausea in his head, but there was also a sudden stab of general indigestion and mild hunger.

He cut off the Band so his organs could figure themselves out. He nosed his foot around the floor until he found the toilet-sink, unsure exactly which way he was going to be approaching it in the next few minutes.

Trying to distract his thoughts, he instead turned to analysis. Was it just a bad idea to Band internal organs in such a way? He'd Band-healed injuries, but that dealt more with soft tissue damage, not necessarily the function of the organ itself. Should he have Banded his entire digestive tract rather than his stomach alone?

With no actual feeling of nausea in his head, those uncomfortable feelings slowly dissipated, leaving only the second option. The way Rivotra chose to look at it, it was a way to pass the time. He just wouldn't be repeating this experiment. Of course, that meant his only other real option, short of eating the next seven meals in rapid succession, was to not Band at all and instead take everything as it came.

Half an hour later, he was seriously considering another Slow Band. Maybe not so strong so that hours were turned into seconds, but just enough to pass the time. Maybe take an hour down to a few minutes.

Ten minutes later, with the hair on his arm standing straight up in fear over being in such a small box, Rivotra Banded.

He'd been in elevators before and never had a problem. Was that because he knew that it was just a short trip from here to there? Would it have been different if he had gotten stuck on an elevator for some reason? Was it because he'd always had the ability to conjure a portal and go anywhere at any time, regardless of physical location or limitations? Or was this something his injured brain cooked up on top of everything else that had gone wrong?

Dinner was later than normal, Rivotra thought, and it wasn't just because of his altered Banding. It really did feel later than seven or eight o'clock. One bite of dinner was enough to inform him why. It was later because these were leftovers. This was what the culinary inmates did with whatever was leftover from dinner, and probably breakfast and lunch, too, though he'd been too distracted by fear to notice. Whatever was left got scraped into takeout boxes and sent to those in the Hole. The macaroni and cheese was cold, the soup was cold, the roll was cold, and the drink was warm. Leftovers sent to the Hole, the dregs of the dregs of society.

He ate it anyway and dutifully returned the goods, including every tine on the fork. As he waited for his stuff to be picked up, not far away—perhaps three or four cells down, if he was judging distance correctly—there was a clamor and a commotion, some shouting and more shouting in response, including a variety of creative profanity. There was banging metal, more shouting, then, for a moment, quiet. A minute later, there was more shouting and then multiple sets of heavy footsteps stomping past Rivotra's door. Maybe someone didn't give back every tine.

Such constituted the evening's excitement. Rivotra's stuff was picked up, and he was left alone again for about an hour before final count for the night.

Then the question became, did he want to just Band his way to morning, or try to actually sleep? He wasn't tired in any sense of the word. As far as his body was concerned, he'd only been awake for a few hours.

He managed to lie down on the bed with his knees bent, but he knew this was not going to go well. He needed to be able to stretch out at some point; his knees and back demanded it.

The intake officer had greeted some of them as loyal customers. Rivotra had no doubt that some inmates were well familiar with the Hole. But how was this place not enough to deter at least a few of the lesser crimes that were committed? Were drugs really that important to some people? Or was the majority of the prison population five-foot-six or shorter? Were there even smaller cells so that shorter men could be punished in the same manner as the taller men?

Extreme discomfort combined with only being awake for a few hours anyway caused Rivotra to stiffly sit up and Slow Band his way to morning. Then, like most areas of the prison, if he showed up to count, he got breakfast.

He was also informed, since he was a new customer, he would not be receiving any mail while in the Hole. Even if it was from his lawyer, he would not be receiving any mail. The Hole was for internal affairs. Even if the president himself sent him a letter saying he was fully pardoned of his crimes, he still had to answer for the crimes of which he had been accused while incarcerated.

Rivotra wasn't worried, just ate his breakfast and returned his tray.

Day two. Or was it day one? Did they count intake day as part of that three days? Was it based on when intake happened? It had been three in the morning, so it made sense to him that they should count it as a full day.

The fear of it not counting as one of the three days caused Rivotra to Band his way speedily to lunch. Remembering that three days was only the minimum and it could still be a few days until he actually went to court pushed him to dinner. And what if they actually found him guilty of having a dangerous weapon?

He had some notion from a distant memory—distant, meaning, before his murder—that sport privileges were the first thing to be revoked. Well, he didn't participate in any sports. Wiping out good behavior time was next. He had some, but if his appeal amounted to nothing and Nendawagan ordered his execution, it wasn't much of a threat. He'd also heard of other punishments such as revoking college privileges, suspending gym and library time, heaping on extra chores, or all manner of odd jobs as the social workers or officers invented them. One inmate had to iron all of the officers' uniforms and shine all of their shoes as a punishment.

Was time in the Hole also a punishment? He couldn't see why not, other than possibly just needing the space. But how grave of an offense would that have to be? Being late back into the neighborhood at night was one thing. Doing or dealing drugs was so common that the Hole could be a neighborhood of its own if that were the case. Possessing a dangerous weapon? That was a serious offense.

Rivotra was willing to bend a few rules and ruffle a few feathers to try and save a man's life, if only because he considered it a minor debt to Owain. He couldn't say that he was willing to own up to this scheme and sign a full confession. And, on the bright side, if Vin got more time in the Hole, that was more time away from those who were looking to kill him.

Then the guilt came back to gnaw on him. This was his scheme, his fault. Vin was down for a two to nine. That was pennies, maybe even a nickel, compared to his dimes and quarters or possible execution. If Vin was nailed for this, he wasn't going to make parole, and that was only going to increase his chances of getting shanked.

But was that Rivotra's problem? He was trying to help the guy avoid a death for which he had been supposedly recruited to help with. But he wasn't Vin's bodyguard or babysitter. Rivotra just happened to know about this plan, but what if someone else tried something at some other time? Was Rivotra going to weep for the man? Probably not.

So then what the hell was he doing? He hadn't asked for this, being part of this scheme to kill a man during lunch. And he really could have just ignored the man in commissary, not played his part, and done his best to defend himself when the gang came to rip the jeans off his corpse. But then, Vin would probably be dead and he would be facing down an angry gang. Maybe he should have told Vin about the plan and let the man figure out for himself how he wanted to stay alive.

Rivotra Slow Banded his way, less strongly, to morning. Too many what ifs and what should have beens. Right now, he had to figure out what he was doing. Being sent to the Hole probably wasn't exactly a seal of approval on his appeal either.

In the four more days that he spent waiting, he couldn't come up with a satisfactory answer. Oh, he had some idea of what he might tell the officers and social workers, however it was that this worked, but it felt like too small of a blanket: no matter which way he pulled it and how much he tried to stretch it out, something was being uncomfortably exposed.

The notice came between lunch and dinner, an admin inmate who worked at the courthouse knocking on his door. "981436?"

"Last I checked," Rivotra said.

He could hear papers sliding through the door slot. Groaning, he stretched and reached and found an envelope.

"You're up tomorrow morning," the inmate informed him. "Need you to sign those papers and send them back."

"I'm blind, I can't see the papers to read or sign."

The inmate sighed, his tone bored. "These papers are not a confession or admission of guilt, it is simply an acknowledgment that you understand the charges against you and are agreeing to the arbitration of the panel of judges consisting of two officers, two social workers, one lawyer, and two law students."

Rivotra tipped the envelope so the papers slid out, and a pen tumbled to the ground. He used his foot to feel for the pen. "That doesn't help me know where to sign."

"Somewhere on the bottom. Honestly, it's like pulling teeth with most guys. They don't care as long as you do it."

Rivotra didn't like blindly signing legal paperwork. He probably could have pushed for some kind of disability accommodation, gotten someone to read the papers to him word-for-word. But that would have taken time, and he was more than ready to be out of here. He slipped the papers and pen back in the envelope and sent it back.

"Thanks, man," the inmate told him.

"Tomorrow morning what time?" Rivotra wondered.

"You're one of the first, so, maybe eight-thirty? Might get breakfast, might not."

Rivotra thanked the man and returned to the spot he had been sitting for the last few days. He had slept once, but it was not what he considered restful. The Banding was starting to really tire him, though, so he might try to sleep again tonight, hope for something better.

As promised, because his court date was the following day, he got a shower that night after dinner. He'd gotten one a few nights ago, too, because it was the weekly shower. If nothing else, it was a chance for him to stretch and get his legs moving again. He felt as though he'd relapsed several months in his balance and coordination, but he had no cane to lean on for support.

Warm water felt better than he thought it had a right to, and it relaxed him enough that he was almost able to get comfortable on the metal tray that passed as a bed. At the very least, he was able to sleep more than a couple hours at a time. At one point, he thought he might have dreamed about Anagalisgi's cave, the earthy cave, the warm fire, the comfortable woven mat, but he did not experience a full visit as he had in the past. If he'd had any hope of receiving some sort of guidance before his court appearance, he received nothing but the small comfort.

He felt rested when he woke, and not nearly as stiff. He didn't know what time it was, but since no one was screaming at him to get up, face the wall, and put his hands over his head, he figured it was still pretty early.

He jumped as a heavy hand banged on the door.

"On your knees, face the wall, hands on your head!" an officer barked.

There it was.

Rivotra managed to get in position half a breath before the door burst open. His hands were yanked down and cuffed, and he was made to stand and march out of the cell. He wanted to tell them they could have just asked nicely, but he had a suspicion that they wouldn't have a very nice reply to that. And, considering how many forceful extractions he'd had to listen to over the last few days, he could understand.

He was marched through the industrial Hole to a room that immediately hit him with the taste of four different chemical scents all trying to drive away some other terrible odor. The most he physically did was swallow, but he really wanted to gag.

He was taken to a chair and made to sit. A moment later, his cuffs were removed.

"981436," someone stated.

"Sir," Rivotra said.

"Charged with possession of an illegal weapon, improvised, bladed. How do you plead?"

"Not guilty."

"981436, on the morning of May 17th, the Dirt conducted a raid in your neighborhood. They discovered an improvised bladed weapon on the floor of your cell. Do you know anything about it?"

"No, sir."

"Do you know how it got there?"

"No, sir."

"Was it yours?"

"No, sir."

A pause. Then, "A review of the camera footage in your cell before the raid shows that it appears to have fallen out of your cellmate's mattress."

"Then it's not mine."

"Do you know how the weapon ended up in your cellmate's mattress?"

"Someone must have put it there."

"Do you know when?"

"No, sir."

"Do you know who?"

"No, sir."

"Did your cellmate ever talk about having or wanting a weapon?"

"No, sir."

"Did your cellmate ever mention a hit list or having enemies?"

Rivotra hesitated.

"981436?" someone prompted.

Rivotra let out a breath. "A few days before the raid, I was approached by someone who tried to recruit me into a plan to harm or, I believe, kill my cellmate because he's a former police officer."

"And who was this person?" someone else asked.

"I have no idea. We were in commissary and he did not identify himself."

"They wanted you to kill him, gave you the weapon."

"No, sir. He knew of my blindness, knew of my seizures, knew that I had not identified who attacked me over a year ago. He said that made me trustworthy. Said if I could fake a seizure or other medical episode at lunch, he and his friends would use the confusion to attack and kill my cellmate. Because of my medical history, he suggested I would get away clean."

"So who had the weapon?" the first man asked.

"I told my cellmate about the plan, tried to warn him."

"You had no intention of going through with this plan to be used as a distraction?" a third man inquired.

"That is correct."

"981436, medical history aside—and your apparent inability to identify these co-conspirators—do you have any idea why they might have approached you to help them?"

Rivotra let out a breath. "Because I was charged with the deaths of police officers at my trial. And convicted of attempted murder of a police officer."

"So you already have a reputation of hatred for the police."

"What other people think of me is their own business. They call me Prison Jesus, too, which is incredibly annoying. But I harbor no hatred for the police or any officers here."

"Where did the weapon come from?" the first man pressed.

"I don't know," Rivotra stated firmly. "Maybe he got it for himself for self-defense, because of this plan, because of my reputation, I don't know. We may be cellmates, but I wouldn't say we're friends."

There was one easy way they could rip open his story for the lie it was, and that was if they tried to get the footage from the cameras around the chicken coop where he'd found the two inmates burying their contraband. But, he happened to know that that camera was intentionally left dirty for that very reason and was covered in dust, feathers, and a bit of chicken poop.

The only other way this could go badly for him would be if they decided to choose Vin over him, and that seemed to be the more likely scenario. Given the choice between a terrorist and a policeman who made a mistake, Rivotra wouldn't blame them for picking Vin.

"Mr. Ndolo, what, if anything, did the man or his gang threaten to do to you if you tried to refuse to go along with this plan?" Just the fact that this new speaker was using his name instead of his number told Rivotra it was a social worker.

"Well, I had just bought a nice pair of jeans, so they were going to take those from me and then inflict unspeakable horrors upon me," Rivotra answered. "As if being murdered wasn't already the low point of my life."

"Did you feel safe after that? Were they watching you? Did they send reminders about what they were going to do?"

"I knew they kept an eye on me. They expected to give a cue at lunch one day and I would just follow along as they desired. As for feeling safe, I'm a disabled, epileptic, blind man in a maximum security prison. How safe would you feel? But to any follow-up concerns, no, I did not get a weapon for protection."

The room went quiet except for some scratching of pens on paper and the clicking of a computer keyboard. Rivotra waited for something to happen, and it was a minute before he heard a door open and someone new being escorted in. A second chair was placed a few feet to his right and Vin was plopped down beside him.

"960154," the first man greeted.

"Sir," Vin said stiffly.

"Charged with possession of an illegal weapon, improvised, bladed. How do you plead?"

"Not guilty."

"960154, on the morning of May 17th, the Dirt conducted a raid in your neighborhood. They discovered an improvised bladed weapon on the floor of your cell. Do you know anything about it?"

"No, sir."

"Do you know how it got there?"

"No, sir."

"Was it yours?"

"No, sir."

"A review of the camera footage in your cell before the raid shows that it appears to have fallen out of your mattress."

"I don't know how it got there, I swear to you."

"He says the same thing."

"Well then he's lying! He's trying to frame me because I was a cop!"

"Why frame you when he could have just harmed or killed you?" the second panelist asked.

"I don't know, ask him," Vin insisted.

"See, he told us a bit of an interesting story. He claims that he was approached by a gang, that they tried to recruit him in a plot to kill you at lunch. He says he warned you about the plan, suggested you take precautions." There was a pause, as if to give Vin time to rebut, but there was nothing. "Was this weapon your idea of a precaution?"

"No!"

"So how were you going to defend yourself against this gang?"

"I don't..."

Rivotra had never interacted with Vin before prison, but would admit to observing him on several occasions when he was spying on Owain. Vin was not the sharpest knife in the drawer. In fact, he had once been described as the spoon in an occupation that demanded knives. Vin could make accusations, he could insist and get emotional, but he wasn't one for thinking on his feet and he was no good at convincing lies. He didn't know that he could tell the panel that he, Rivotra, had never warned him about the plan. And that was just one way to try and edge Rivotra out of the spotlight.

"Have you been harmed before in this facility?" someone was asking.

"I've been pushed around a few times," Vin answered.

"Have you been threatened, in general or specifically relating to your time in law enforcement?"

"Countless times."

"So it would stand to reason that, eventually, someone would try something."

"I would imagine so."

"And the more notice the better."

"Yes."

"So you got notice of this plan to harm or even kill you, and you know that you can't take an entire gang by yourself without some kind of...backup, some kind of protection. So you got a little reinforcement."

"No!"

Another quiet moment with the soft sounds of pens and keyboards.

"Whose weapon was it?" the first man asked.

"Not mine," Rivotra and Vin answered simultaneously.

"And you can see why we have a problem."

Another pause, then someone new spoke. "Possession of a dangerous weapon is one of the more serious offenses in this facility. All privileges are revoked, all good behavior time wiped out, non-recommendations to the parole board, and some time in the Hole. 960154, I understand you are coming up for parole in the next year. 981436, your appellate hearing is coming up real quick and it sounds very promising. So, is there anything else either of you would like to say before we review this case and make our decision?"

Would they punish both of them? Rivotra hadn't even considered that, not seriously anyway. On the other hand, this wasn't like the outside courts. Out there, the bar was, allegedly, innocent until proven guilty. In here, it was guilty until proven innocent. The panel couldn't just ignore that a dangerous weapon had appeared in the cell. It had gotten there somehow. They were unwilling to let a guilty party go free, and they'd punish an innocent party to ensure the guilty party was punished, too.

He could speak up. He could admit to the weapon and trying to frame Vin to get him in the Hole and out of harm's way. The admission was even right there on the tip of his tongue. He just couldn't do it. Even if they were both punished, at least Vin would still be kept out of harm's way for a while—even if it was in the Hole—and Rivotra would consider all debts settled.

"All right," one of the panelists sighed. "Take them back. We'll have our decision before dinner."

Rivotra was taken back first, deposited into his tiny cell with hardly a word. Well, time to make friends with this tiny cell because he had a feeling that he was going to be here for a few more days.

He'd heard of other inmates being stuck in the Hole for a while. Two weeks, thirty days, sixty days, ninety days. Problem was, prison was so full of exaggeration it was impossible to tell what was true and what was someone trying to win the biggest badass award. He suspected that there were tiers of punishment, based on prior offenses, but however long his sentence was, he was going to be Banding through as much as he could.

Breakfast came around without ceremony, and Rivotra elected not to Band his way to lunch. He was going to take some time and prepare himself to actually hear the words, "You're staying in the Hole."

Once upon a time, Rivotra had locked Owain up in the black cells in the Wheel of Time, knowing it would psychologically scar the man. Well, now it was time for him to own up to it. With the claustrophobia creeping over his shoulders like spiders, he figured he was getting a glimpse of what Owain had endured. Considering the man had spent almost a year in the black cells and still gone on to recover his sanity and his life, Rivotra would admit he had a new respect for the man.

Lunch came by. Rivotra politely inquired about the time and what time his verdict might be. The working inmate just said he didn't know, and the accompanying officer told him to shut the fuck up. It was his turn when it was his turn.

Rivotra ate his lunch hurriedly and sent back the tray and utensils.

Again he did not Band. Whatever tranquility he'd managed to instill in himself over the morning ebbed as the afternoon wore on and vanished completely when he heard the approaching officer barking orders at him. On his knees, face the wall, hands on his head. The officer was no gentler this time than the last as Rivotra was cuffed, hauled to his feet, and unceremoniously marched to the courtroom.

This time, he and Vin were brought in at the same time, and they'd barely sat down and had their cuffs removed before someone on the panel was talking.

"981436 and 960154, both charged with possession of an improvised bladed weapon, first offense for both." There was some shuffling of papers. "Contrary to what you may think, this is not a unique case. Stashed weapons are nothing new. Framing is nothing new. Each one blaming the other is nothing new. Claims of self-defense are nothing new. Even murder plots are regrettably more common than we'd like to admit to.

"What makes this case interesting is you two. Prior law enforcement. Convicted cop killer who is, by your own words, blind, epileptic, and disabled, and now apparently trying to save the life of this cop. Either one of you have reason to hate each other, yet either one of you have valid safety concerns for yourselves."

Rivotra blinked, and he could feel Vin giving him a sideways glance.

"We can't prove one way or the other who did what, if anything, other than the weapon clearly came from the mattress of 960154.

"960154, we are hereby revoking all privileges—sports, recreation, commissary, college, et cetera—for the next thirty days and wiping all of your good behavior time thus far. You are also going to spend another five days in punitive segregation, and afterwards you will be placed on double chore rotation for ninety days, meaning you will have two sets of chores in the morning and in the afternoon. However, we will not make a non-recommendation against you to the parole board.

"981436, we cannot prove that you had anything to do with the weapon itself, but we cannot deny your involvement in a potential conspiracy. We are therefore revoking all of your privileges for thirty days and wiping all of your good behavior time. You will not be spending more time in punitive, however, you will also be on double chore rotation for thirty days. We will also not be making any non-recommendation against you in regards to your appeal."

With that, the case was settled. Vin sputtered nonsensical protests as he was taken back to the Hole, but Rivotra was permitted to leave. On his way out, he stopped at the intake desk where the officer handed him his extra chore slips, one for morning laundry and one for afternoon cleaning in the nursing home; his tub, which had been taken in the raid, mostly to protect it from theft and tampering while he was away; and another item he could not readily identify. It was long a slender like a cane, but it wasn't his cane.

"Powers That Be have decreed that you aren't allowed to have a regular cane anymore," the desk officer informed him. "You've demonstrated you can walk without one. But you need something, so the social workers got you a regular white cane."

"Oh." Rivotra was still examining the thing. It was collapsible so he could put it in his pocket when not in use, had a wrist strap so he couldn't drop and lose it easily, and the rubber tip protected anything he hit. "Thank you."

"Whatever, man. Get out of here."

"What time is it?"

"Not quite five o'clock. You drop your tub back in your house, might get lucky with an early dinner, then you head over to the nursing home, see if they need anything for a couple hours."

Apparently double chore rotation couldn't wait until the morning. "And where am I, exactly? How do I get back to genpop?"

The desk officer sighed, got up, and took Rivotra outside. From there he gave directions back to the genpop barracks and sent him on his way.

Rivotra intentionally took his time. He had no desire to return to the nursing home for any reason. Whoever had made that part of his punishment probably knew that. At the same time, he was just trying to work out the kinks in his neck, back, and legs. Sure, he could normally walk without a sturdy walking cane, but right about now as he hobbled along was when it would really come in handy. And he had gotten used to his cane. This regular white cane was so light and flimsy and the weight distribution and balance was funny.

He eventually reached the building and made his way to his neighborhood. This time of day, only a handful of inmates were actually in their neighborhoods or houses, trying to catch naps or read quietly before dinner.

"Well, well, look who it is," someone said from across the room as Rivotra made for his cell. "Prison Jesus, out of the tomb."

"Are you people ever going to stop calling me that?" Rivotra wondered.

"You were down a while; we were starting to worry. Where's your cellie? Copper?"

"I don't know."

"Yeah? What about you, you skate through?"

Rivotra still had no idea who was talking to him. "Double chore rotation for thirty days."

The man made a sound while a nearby eavesdropper whistled. "That's no fun, man. But it can make you a few bucks."

"Assuming Ramone lets him back into commissary," someone else added.

Rivotra found his cell, entered, slid his tub under his bunk and sat down for a second, grateful to have such a large cell and not unaware of how far he had fallen that he should be grateful for such a thing.

"That's right," the first man went on, ambling over to his porch, "Ramone's been waiting for you. Wants to chat."

"Yes, I'm sure that's what he wants," Rivotra retorted.

"I'm just sayin' is all I'm sayin'. Maybe you should have stayed in the Hole."

The man wandered off and Rivotra decided to make his exit to dinner.

Dinner was uneventful, but he knew without a doubt that Ramone and his friends who had planned to kill Vin were now perhaps reconsidering their target. It wasn't until he was about halfway between the cafeteria and the nursing home that they caught up to him. One tried to take his cane, but he managed to hold fast to it, and the man let go. He felt another man approach and get in his face.

"We had a deal, PJ."

"I don't control the Dirt," Rivotra informed him.

"You sure? Seems awfully convenient that you both disappear the day before we spring our trap. You snitch on us?"

"Are you in the Hole for conspiracy to commit murder?"

The man, presumably Ramone, tried to grab Rivotra by the shirt. Rivotra Banded to avoid the grab and took a step back.

"I'm not part of your gang. You can't order me around. And we made no deal."

Ramone stepped up again. "You think you're a big tough guy now? You can barely walk. I tried to be considerate of you, showed you a way that you could get off clean. What, you sucking that cop's cock at night? You defend him now?"

"I'm not defending anyone but myself."

Now the man made a sound that was somewhere between a scoff and a laugh. "Good. Because if you try to interfere, we'll kill you, too. I'll even do it myself."

"Prison Jesus forgives you."

Now Ramone tried to punch him, but Rivotra Banded to avoid that, too, saying, "Because you obviously know not what you do."

That only served to enrage the gangbanger further, but one or more of the others apparently spotted something unfavorable—perhaps they'd gotten the attention of a perimeter guard or another officer happened to be in the vicinity—and the group moved off. Rivotra let out a slow breath, then continued his trek to the nursing home.

Walking into the nursing home after even a short time away was profound, and Rivotra involuntarily gagged. Smelling would be bad enough, but the fact that his smell and taste had been swapped in his brain made it even worse. Old people, medication, and a subtle undertone of a full adult diaper.

"Welcome back," the desk officer greeted. "You look fine. Why you here?"

Rivotra handed him the chore slips and let the officer sort them out. One slip was pressed back into his hand.

"Double chore rotation, eh?" the officer mused, his tone turning positively smarmy. "All right, then. Well, you know where the nurse's room is?"

"Never had the pleasure," Rivotra told him.

The officer gave him directions. "See what chores the nurses got for you. But don't forget to keep an eye on the time so you make it back to your neighborhood before lights out."

Rivotra nodded sullenly and did his best to follow the officer's directions to the nurse's room. He had an idea of what they would have him doing, none of it pleasant. Dumping and scrubbing bedpans and urinals, taking out the biohazard bag full of dirty adult diapers, all of the chores reserved for inmates who needed a passive aggressive punishment. At least it was only thirty days. But it was still only day one.

Because of the late hour, his chores were limited, and he made it back to the barracks with a few minutes to spare. He spent a great amount of time in the shower, then returned to his cell for the night.

Regular chores were enough to keep a man busy and still allow a little time for recreation. Double chore rotation was designed to keep a man very busy with no time for recreation and very little time to even eat. Even if his privileges hadn't been revoked, he wouldn't have time to do anything. He got up for count and, once everyone was released, headed, not for early coffee, but his first round of chores. He was able to sneak in a very short workout at six o'clock in the morning, but soon had to get to his cleaning routine. The desk officers knew he was on double chore discipline with revoked privileges, and they frequently dropped in to see what he was up to.

He Banded to give himself an advantage and short breaks here and there, but there was no good way to make the punishment go by any faster. He might be able to move faster or slower, but Base Time was still Base Time, and everyone else was still bound to that plane of Time.

It wasn't bad to be busy, but it still surprised him when he got in for the night and found Vin back in his bed.

253

"What the fuck, man?" the former cop demanded.

"Sorry, is something not clean enough?" Rivotra asked, tone acidic.

"I know that thing wasn't mine. So either you did it, or someone else was trying to frame me."

Rivotra paused and listened for a moment. Then he lowered his voice. "I was trying to help you, you idiot! You were going to be killed the next day."

"And framing me, potentially fucking up my parole and having me sit here even longer was going to help how?" Vin challenged. "I can defend myself just fine."

"Against an entire gang?"

"You could have just told me."

Rivotra scoffed. "Even with the plan fully out there now, you still say you can handle them. You never would have believed me if I told you before. And if you had, even then you would have said you could handle it." He went on before Vin could speak. "I didn't have to do anything at all. I could have just not done anything, no warning, no distraction, and pretended to be perfectly ignorant of the whole thing." He sighed. "I can't even defend myself like I used to, never mind anyone else. I have to do what I can."

Vin hummed something like a sigh. "Well, it's not the weirdest apology I've ever heard."

"I'm not apologizing," Rivotra informed him.

"And why would you defend me anyway? You're a fucking cop killer, and you're the one coming to my defense."

"I consider it a favor for Walter, if nothing else." Rivotra sat down on his mattress. "And as I said before, I never held any ill will for Owain or the other officers." He sighed and rubbed his face. "No one was supposed to get hurt."

He could feel Vin's gaze boring into him. Then, "Why do you refer to him so familiarly? Captain Forbes, Officer Forbes, Forbes, fuzz, pig, asshat. I don't remember a lot about the case, but I remember there was some element of stalking to it. Not just targeting him and his son, but something more."

"The vast majority of that was Cassius."

"Yeah, whatever. Still, stop with the familiarity. You don't know Walt like I do."

"I know Owain better than you think." Rivotra lay down.

"What do you mean? I swear to God, if you're planning something against Walt, I will tell the officers, I will snitch. Kill me if you want, but I will not let you—"

"Please shut up," Rivotra sighed.

"No. Tell me."

Rivotra wished he could see exactly where Vin was. He imagined the man was peering over the edge of his bunk, somewhere near his head. "You talk a lot, you know that?"

"You know, I have an idea. Maybe I should frame you, get you sent back to the Hole for a while so you can't signal to your terrorist buddies to go after Walt. Is that what happened? They got upset that you got caught, so they tried to kill you and your family back home?"

If Rivotra were in better shape, he would have launched out of bed with a fury. These days, while he did have the fury, he couldn't be quite as spontaneous with his limbs.

He Banded both of them, then Banded himself again so he was still just a little faster. He got to his feet, situated himself, then grabbed Vin and dragged the man off his mattress. As the man came down, momentarily subjected to the forces of gravity, Rivotra's left arm faltered and they both almost went to the floor. Readjusting his stance and refusing to let go of Vin's shirt, Rivotra used every ounce of strength he had to lift and push the former cop against the wall and hold him there.

"You talk a lot, you know that?" Rivotra repeated, breathing hard, limbs shaking, sweat starting to snake down his forehead.

"Help!" Vin called.

"The less you know about something, the more you have to say about it. If only you knew."

Rivotra huffed a few breaths, then dragged Vin out of the cell. The man was still stunned and didn't put up much of a fight as he stumbled outside. It was only a few minutes before lights out, but Rivotra knew that everyone and everything would be frozen in place. Once in the middle of the room, Rivotra dropped Vin to the ground, then bent over to put his hands on his knees, using his remaining strength just to stay upright.

"If you knew the things I've seen...and done. If you knew...the things Owain Fforidd...has seen...and done."

"What is this, man?" Vin whimpered. He sounded like he'd moved off several feet. "You fuck up my dinner, too? You got something on your hands?"

"Being a cop didn't teach you anything," Rivotra said, straightening. "Prison isn't teaching you much either. Because you think you know. Maybe this will open your eyes a little."

"But...what...?"

Rivotra ignored the man, pushing him out of the Band, and limped his way back to his bunk. Once he was comfortably lying down, he dropped the Band. Activity outside the cell resumed. He counted off four seconds before Vin came scampering back and clambered into his bunk.

Night count was uneventful. Afterwards, it should have been the time when everyone rolled over and went to sleep. Instead, Vin rolled over to continue to talk.

"You know, I remember reading something online—obviously before all this shit—about some weird conspiracy theories about government experiments in time control."

Oh, good grief...

"I mean, everyone attributes that to going back and forth in time, you know, like *Back to the Future*, but what if it's not? Was that what that was? I mean, I got a kick out of it when I first read it—conspiracy theories are all over the place—but maybe...?"

Rivotra sighed. The spoon, constantly making its way into the knife block. He pinched the bridge of his nose. "What if I told you yes? What if I told you that Owain can do the same thing? What if there really was more to all of this than it initially appears?"

"I mean, that was pretty compelling."

Rivotra Banded, sat up, and felt around until he found Vin's head, upside down and peering at him just as he suspected. He grabbed the man's hair and dropped the Band.

"Ow ow ow ow ow ow..."

"Is everything a game to you? You want to play at being a cop? You end up here. You want to play at being a prisoner? You end up dead. If you can't take anything seriously, I have no reason to try and warn you of anything. No one has any reason to want to defend you or expect anything from you. Now you either take this threat against your life seriously, or you die. Because I can't help."

"Ow ow ow what about that time travel shit ow ow ow...?"

Rivotra let go of the man's head. "Party tricks to the idiots here." He lay back down. "Once you get into the serious stuff, then you start to realize what actually happened. To Owain, to me. To my family."

"I don't know." Vin retreated. "Maybe you're still just fucking with me. Frame me, fuck with me, soften me up. Maybe you're still going to try to kill me. I don't know. I just know I'll have plenty of time to think about it while I'm doing months of *double fucking chores!*"

Rivotra mentally rolled his eyes as Vin emphasized the last few words. Ignoring the man's lingering, grumbling comments, he turned over, and did his best to get to sleep.

Rivotra woke up in Anagalisgi's cave. Instead of lying or sitting there calmly and waiting for the man to approach and begin stitching up the remaining wounds, he immediately got to his feet and turned around. The cave was cozy, but it was still big enough that he found that he was not comfortable enough to just start walking.

"Sit down, Rivotra," Anagalisgi told him from somewhere in the cave.

Rivotra could hear him rummaging in his pots and cupboards, preparing his ointments, needles, and threads.

"I can't," Rivotra said. "I can't sit down. I can't..." He paced several feet in both directions in front of the fire. "Anagalisgi, I can't wait anymore. I'm going to lose my family farm. I'm either going to watch a man die or die myself trying to help him. That might not be so bad except he's an idiot. I have your people coming after me now. Julianna is still out there wreaking havoc. And I'm...cleaning and scrubbing bedpans and dealing with an idiot who can't take his situation seriously."

He could hear noises that were reminisce of the grinding of a mortar and pestle. "You're not ready, Rivotra."

"Ready for what? What do I need to be preparing for? I want to undo what I've done, but I'm going nowhere except to the hospital or the nursing home."

"And where do you want to go, exactly?" Anagalisgi never raised his voice, and his tone remained curious rather than accusatory. "Do you want to go home to your family's farm? Or do you want to go out for your revenge against Julianna?"

Rivotra blinked. "I can't have both? Be rid of her, then go home to live in peace?"

"Will being rid of her solve the problems of the universe?"

"Well...no. But I am responsible for getting her where she is. I am responsible for a lot of bad things. I have to make it right somehow."

"And if you were to be rid of her, by whatever means prove effective, and another takes her place, aren't you responsible for that person coming to power? Will you then seek to be rid of that person?" Anagalisgi let that hang there for a moment. "Of course, then everyone would know you're alive. You could also maybe try to get rid of the First Order entirely. But that's a lot more blood on your hands. You may seek justice against Julianna and her generals, but what about the layman who is simply confused and misguided?"

"That's what war is."

"And you're going to end that war?" Anagalisgi tapped on one of his pots. "Are you also going to end the threat from the Borelians? The Tacagans? Anyone else who doesn't like you, doesn't like humans, doesn't like this or that?"

Rivotra lifted a hand as if to try and illustrate a point, but he couldn't find the words. "I told Nendawagan that I was going to make things right. I want to undo what I've done, the chaos that was Rifun Ndolo."

"I know." The volume and tone suggested Anagalisgi had now turned to face him. "And I've had a talk with her about that."

"What does she—?"

"We're not talking about her. We're talking about you." He was now within normal conversational distance. "And you're still not ready."

Rivotra shifted his stance. "That's why you had my appeal pushed back."

"I didn't do anything. I've been here. And you've been there."

"Yes, but—"

"What do you want, Rivotra? What do you intend to do with yourself?"

He hesitated again and found himself making his way back to the mat where he sat quietly. A moment later, Anagalisgi knelt beside him, laying out the tools of his trade.

"I wish...Rifun Ndolo had never existed," Rivotra said finally. He barely noticed when Anagalisgi poked him with the needle, working on something on his side above his left hip. "Even if I would have died young with no family, it would have been better than what I've done."

"Are the Betsileo known for being warriors?" Anagalisgi asked.

"We held off the Merina. My name, Andilan, the Andilans were warriors."

"Andilan means warrior?"

"Well, no. It means isthmus. The Andilans forced the Vazimba onto an isthmus where they were swept away by the tide, thus ending the war between the Vezo and the Vazimba."

"And are the Betsileo known for being warriors?" Anagalisgi repeated.

Rivotra let out a breath and tilted his head down. "No, not really. We're considered the kind people, the family people, the rice people. Fianarantsoa is known for its art, culture, universities, churches, its acceptance of others." He looked back up. "Dying with no family as little better than *andevo*..." He shook his head.

"You were fully prepared to sit and wait and heal and be methodical about your life going forward," Anagalisgi stated calmly. "Then something happened."

"My family was murdered." Rivotra turned his head so he wouldn't disturb the man's work. "It always comes back to family. Not having a family. Leaving Lalao. The murder of everyone in my family."

"Which means what?"

"If I go after Julianna, she will kill me. And my family will be no more. Her goal delayed, but ultimately fulfilled."

"Or?"

"I am the last Andilan. I have to keep the family alive." Now he twisted. He could feel the needle in his side. "But families take years of care. Julianna —"

"Evil—" Anagalisgi corrected, gently touching his shoulders and turning him back in position. "—will still be there. And it will not be vanquished in a day."

"But I am still responsible for a lot of that evil. Just tell me something, Anagalisgi. If I hadn't joined the Cult—if I had joined the Akarin, or maybe if I had simply been healed of my scars and gone on my way—what would have happened? Would the Cult have still come to power? Would things be better? Worse? Would the Akarin still be in their fortress? Would the Time industry be the way it was before the Dispersal? Would my family be alive?"

"Was Julianna looking for you? Back in London?"

"Well, she showed up at my door."

"But was she looking for you?"

Rivotra let out a breath. "No. She just needed to be rid of Cassius." He twisted again. "So, if not me, it would have always been someone else."

"Who can say?" Anagalisgi's tone was a shrug even as he took Rivotra's shoulders, more firmly this time, and twisted him back in position. "What has been, has been. And what will be, will be."

"But you know me. You know I can't just sit still."

"You can," the man said, cutting the thread, "and you will. Because you must. And perhaps because this is the only way to make you sit. And listen."

Eleven
Defense

Double chore rotation got very old very fast. Rivotra was tired of it within a week. Tack on the threat of the gang who was still out to murder Vin—and possibly inflict some serious injuries on him as well—and Rivotra was paranoid and stressed out within just a few days of Vin's return.

Even after his normal chore rotation turned over and he was no longer on gym cleaning duty, Rivotra still went to the gym. He had to Band to do it, but he got in a full workout every morning. Manhandling Vin had only served to expose how weak he had really become; he needed to stop piddling around and being cautious. By this point, he was either healed or he wasn't, and he had to make the most of what he had.

He pushed himself as much as he could. He utilized every machine, added as much weight as he could stand and didn't stop until his arms or legs were shaking so bad he could fall over. From the machines, he headed to the mat for just as grueling pushups, situps, and every bit of calisthenics he could remember from the army. Half the time was spent just trying to get his limbs in position, but he figured there might be some value in expanding his general range of motion, too.

Once he was finished in the gym, he headed off to his first morning chore where he was back in laundry. Mornings in laundry were spent sorting dirty clothes, washing, soaking stubborn stains, and drying. And listening to the desk officer complain about whatever was in the daily newspaper. The topic did not matter, there was always something wrong. Rivotra could understand frustration over politics or world events, maybe even a little sports frustration, but when the man started genuinely griping about the food critic reviews of local restaurants and even the mundane, reader-submitted recipes, Rivotra decided the man was just a miserable human being who needed a serious career change.

"So, PJ," another inmate, called Spot, began, ambling up to him at a washer, "heard you got a little problem."

Rivotra felt over the knobs on the washer, twisted the second knob one way a certain number of clicks to a specific angle, the fourth knob the other way a certain number of clicks to a specific angle, then hit start. The machine roared to life in a torrent of rushing water. "I have a lot of problems. To which one are you referring?"

"Rumors be circulatin' about you and your cellie and the Pinto Gang." Well, at least that put a name to the voices and the constant feeling of being watched, though Rivotra couldn't say that he was familiar with this group at all beyond one that used to let him work out with them in the weights area. "Apparently there's supposed to be some shit jumpin' off soon 'tween you and them."

"News to my ears. What else do the rumors say?"

"Gonna be some shit 'tween the gang and your cellie, Copper. Pinto Gang's leader, Ramone, he wanna kill Copper."

"Lots of people want to kill him; he's a former cop. What makes this different?"

"'Cause he wanna do it in fron' a you, see what you do. Says if you try to interfere, he gonna make you suck Copper's dick while he fucks you up the ass, then he gonna kill you both."

Rivotra blinked. "That is...highly specific and...very disturbing." He moved on to the next machine and started loading clothes inside. "When is this supposed to happen?"

"Dunno. Just soon is all I know."

He closed the door on the washer and started feeling for more knobs. "And how did you hear about this?"

"Ramone been braggin' it up in the gym and in the store. Says he ought to sell tickets for people to get in line and fuck Copper, too, fuck the cop bloody before he kills him."

Rivotra hit start and the second washer roared to life. He turned toward Spot. "I know inmates harbor a special hatred for police officers among them, but that's a bit over-the-top, don't you think? What's his real problem with Copper?"

"Dunno," Spot said casually.

"And why are you telling me this?"

"Well, I try not to get too involved with the gangs, 'cept how to avoid 'em, 'specially when they're on a rampage like Ramone's bein' now. But if I don't want a cock in my ass, I don't think you want one in yours. I mean, maybe that's your thing, and I ain't judgin', but there's a limit on that stuff, you know?"

Rivotra nodded. "Thanks."

"No problem, man." Spot started to move off. "An' you dint hear it from me."

"Hear what?"

"'Zactly."

It was nice to have the warning, but it did nothing to help Rivotra's paranoia. He had no desire to witness or participate in any of this in any fashion. He had given Vin the warning, given him the harsh reality of things, and that was the most he could do. Except, it seemed, Ramone was now irrevocably linking them together. He couldn't not be involved now.

Fucking hell, who really put us together in the same cell? I might like to have a few words of my own here. At this point, Owain, you owe me.

From simple observation, Rivotra knew that "soon" in prison speak, in this context, typically encompassed a time period of not less than the next meal and not more than seventy-two hours. There were a lot of variables to consider in that time.

On the one hand, if Ramone was being so flamboyant about it around the gym, commissary, and probably a few other places, there was no way the officers didn't suspect something was up. It didn't even have to be a snitch, just being mildly attentive to the conversations going around at mealtime or during working hours. Even the foul-tempered desk officer here reading his newspaper, if he were even slightly concerned about the conversations going on in laundry, he might know about this alleged plan. If that were the case, considering most desk officers were more attentive than this guy, Rivotra knew he was looking at less than twenty-four hours before the shit jumped off. At best, it might be first thing in the morning before everyone was fully awake and alert, including the officers.

There was one upside that Rivotra could make use of. Ramone was intent on both him and Vin being present for this. Other than their shared cell, Rivotra and Vin only crossed paths at mealtime during the day, and even that was not guaranteed because of their double chores keeping them running all day. So either Ramone planned to drag them out of their chores in the middle of the day, hoped to get lucky at mealtime, or he was going to try and hit them in the evening.

Evening, Rivotra decided, likely right before the neighborhood locked up for the night. Everyone else would be distracted by sports talk or books or their general routines; the officers would be looking forward to getting everyone in so things would quiet down. Meanwhile, he and Vin would be racing to get back in time, some of the last ones out in the open. But if Ramone was bragging it up this much, he wouldn't do it in the dark.

As Rivotra had already accused the man, Vin talked a lot, and he was more than happy to complain as obnoxiously as possible about his extra chores that Rivotra had gotten him into. So Rivotra knew well what Vin was likely doing at any given time: kitchen chores and cleaning the genpop barracks in the morning, warehouse duty and laundry in the afternoon. There was no way he could get any word to Vin, but he also wasn't sure just what word he would want to send. He was an idiot, but he couldn't be completely oblivious to what was going on. If Rivotra heard about this plot, then surely Vin had heard by now also. At the very least, he had to suspect.

And what were they going to do? They couldn't snitch. Running away or sidestepping wasn't a long-term solution. Seeing how Ramone fully intended to kill Vin, there was no such thing as calmly accepting a beating. Stepping up and fighting appeared to be the only logical outcome. But to what end? Until officers intervened and everyone spent six months in the Hole? Until someone really was dead?

Rifun was the killer, Rivotra thought. He was trying to be better than that. But wasn't he looking to kill Julianna and her generals and dismantle the Order? Was defending one man somehow less noble just because it was less flashy and, perhaps, more risky? Was Vin worth it? If he hadn't been implicated, would he even care? Was it possible that Rivotra was just as selfish as Rifun? Or was this Rifun looking for a way to sneak back into his mind and convince him of some convoluted judgment and justification for whatever was about to happen?

Rivotra left his normal laundry chores for his added punishment of cleaning the chicken coop. Most of the chickens were out scratching in the yard by now, but a few remained. He shooed them out, collected any late eggs, then grabbed a rake and began scraping at the sawdust.

It was not unusual to find contraband buried in corners or stashed under the nest boxes. Most of the contraband was mechanical in nature, shivs and paraphernalia. Drug substances themselves were exceedingly rare since no one wanted the chickens to get into them. Rivotra had already found a suitable replacement for the shiv he'd taken and subsequently lost, and it had made its way back to the owner. As such, he also played dumb with some of the contraband he raked up now, spreading it out with the new sawdust and simply choosing to not acknowledge what he couldn't see.

As much as he might have wanted to help himself to another one of these shivs for the upcoming event, he refrained. He didn't need to have a good case of self-defense that would exonerate him of any liability for the fight itself, only to get in trouble again for having a weapon. Leniency might have been granted for a first offense, but he suspected that punishment for a second offense would be doubled. And he did not want to spend any more time than necessary cleaning the chicken coop or the nursing home.

Another thought occurred to him. What if Vin decided to try and frame him for something in this fight? What if he slipped a shiv in his mattress or did something else stupid to make him look bad? Would he be smart enough to do that? Could he pull that off in such a short time? Or would the man just take his chances and snitch to the officers? If he was going to die one way or another, might as well make one last plea for defense from those who were tangentially related to his former profession.

Rivotra took an even breath and let it out slowly. He couldn't be paranoid, but he couldn't be stupid about this either. He found his thoughts wandering to Godwin Lore. Godwin, called Win, had been a mercenary on and off for centuries before joining the Cult of the Akari. Eventually, Rivotra contracted him to act as a doppelganger in order to fool the Borelians when they had Rivotra under veritable house arrest. And although he'd led several campaigns in the quest to take down the Akarin fortress and the Borelian death temple in Ancrath, then later led the Miaramila and apparently did well to defend the Krydik against the Order, Win had always been more of a solitary mercenary than a soldier in a unit.

Somewhere, in the recesses of his mind, Rivotra recalled part of a conversation he'd had with Win. He'd asked the mercenary whether he preferred quiet or public hits.

"Quiet," he'd replied. "Those who go into mercenary work looking for fame, well, they find it, but only once. Twice if they're lucky. Thrice if they actually have some skill."

"And what about you?"

"Money's nice, but with Time, it doesn't matter much. I'm in it for the precision, the problem-solving aspect of it. The more precautions a target tries to take, the more fun it is for me."

"But you can Band and kill them in broad daylight."

"Yeah, but that's a last resort. It's the skill I'm proud of."

"What about interference? Bodyguards or bystanders?"

"Only if necessary. I'm fulfilling a promise, not butchering for fun."

"Isn't that kind of how mercenaries are portrayed?"

Win shrugged. "I don't concern myself with public opinion. If I do my job well, they don't know it's me, and they're just yelling at shadows on the wall anyway."

"Have you ever questioned a contract? What if you're working for a bad person and killing a good person?"

The mercenary hesitated. "A few of those have come up over the centuries. In my experience, mercenaries with too many rules tend to last about as long as those with no rules."

"Then you wouldn't kill the good person?"

"I didn't say that. I just typically want a better reason than, 'I don't like them.' I've refused a few contracts because of that. And there have been times where I will kill the target, and then I go back and kill the buyer for being an asshole. That's usually when I went dark."

"Have you ever been on the opposite side of things? Have you been contracted to protect someone and stop them from being killed?"

Win raised a brow. "You mean before you? I've gotten those, too, but usually only at the beginning of a new life. People tend not to trust career mercenaries to be loyal bodyguards."

"Aren't all bodyguards career mercenaries, though? They stop paying, you stop protecting."

"To be fair, sir, you're not exactly showering me with gold and platinum, and you want me to protect you from the most feared race in the universe."

"So then why are you here?"

The mercenary shifted position. "I'm not a superstitious man, haven't cared for religion in a few hundred years, but there's something here that's right. I need to be here." He shrugged again. "And it's a little more exciting than taking out business executives or low-level government officials."

"Well, it's going to get a lot more exciting before the end. Maybe you'll be ready for a little vacation where a business executive is the most dangerous thing you have to worry about."

Rivotra had always been grateful for Win's loyalty, even if he hadn't fully understood it. Had he simply been a useful pawn of the Author to direct Rivotra where he needed to go? Win hadn't been much of a threat to the Shadows, so he could have been used to weasel around Rifun's influence. Or was Rivotra simply trying to find some justification, some way to memorialize a good man who had vanished into death or Borelian slavery? Was he responsible for the mercenary's death as well, or was there enough time in between to say that it had been entirely Win's decision to help the Krydik?

Rivotra itched his forehead with the back of his hand. He needed to get out of here, but that wasn't happening until he dealt with this problem.

He finished up the chicken coop, dumping the dirty sawdust and spreading new, feeling the eyes of dozens of chickens waiting for their new bedding. That finished, he dropped off any remaining eggs he had found in odd places, then headed to lunch.

It wasn't three seconds into his first bite that he felt a hand grip his shoulder. Hot breath blew uncomfortably in his ear.

"Pin's on chicken duty in the afternoon, you know," Ramone hissed. "When we get done with your little cop bitch, we're going to chop him up and turn him into chicken food. Extra protein for strong chickens and good eggs, am I right?" He breathed a humorless chuckle, then turned serious again. "Interfere, and you'll join him."

He did not wait for a reply, just moved off. Rivotra returned to his meal without saying anything or giving any indication that something was amiss. He still suspected that this attack was going to come later in the evening. At the same time, it took a fair amount of time to chop up a body that small, assuming they didn't want anything to be found. Chickens would peck at a body regardless.

Or maybe it had been a simple exaggerated threat, try to scare him into not interfering.

Mercenaries for fame and fortune, Rivotra mused, taking a drink of water. *Usually once. Twice if they're lucky. Thrice if they have some skill. Once probably got them locked up here. Maybe they got lucky at some point before this. But they don't have the skills I do.*

He returned his lunch tray and utensils, then left the cafeteria.

Rivotra didn't know how far in advance the chore rotation was planned, but he was willing to bet that whoever was in charge was laughing his ass off in his office. Bad enough Rivotra had to clean the nursing home as part of his double chore punishment, but now it was his regular afternoon chore, too. For the moment, it meant he was spending from lunch until lights out, with only a small break for dinner, cleaning the nursing home. Even once his double chore punishment was finished, he would still be spending several hours a day for about another week or so cleaning the damn place.

July, August, September, he told himself. His chances of being put back on this chore were still fairly high, but maybe not that high? Maybe he should volunteer on the farm more. Even if he had to enroll in the school for just a couple months, he would take the chicken coop over this place every day of the week.

"Good afternoon to you," the head nurse, Isaac, greeted as Rivotra reported for duty.

"Your tone suggests you're about to tell me something I don't want to hear," Rivotra sighed.

"You ever meet Panzer? 911023?"

"Doesn't sound familiar."

"Well, he's developed a GI bleed. A rather explosive one. Not much to be done for it, I guess, but he'll be in the hospital for a little while. In the meantime, his cell needs a serious cleaning."

Rivotra rubbed his face. "Damn it."

Isaac pressed something into Rivotra's hand. It felt like a plastic bag. "Here's your suit. Gloves, suit, mask, the whole nine yards. Keep the shit off, but it's far from indestructible. I'll get a cart made up and then help you get into it."

"You were informed that the wires for smell and taste got crossed in my brain, right? I am going to taste that shit the entire time."

"Don't ingest it for real and you won't contract hepatitis," the nurse told him. "And the less you taste, the cleaner the room, right? You'll know you're done when you can only taste...ah, this one says lemon, but the new bottle is orange. So you'll be tasting citrus."

"I'll be tasting vomit before anything," Rivotra grumbled.

But there was nothing he could do about it. Isaac helped him gown up, gave him directions to the offending cell—telling him that the neighbors would likely let him know well in advance—and sent him on his way, pushing a cart of cleaning supplies.

He didn't even make it to the elevator before nursing home residents were telling him where to go.

"Just follow your nose!" he was told. "You may be blind, but your nose works just fine. You'll know where it is!"

Getting off on the appropriate floor, he immediately gagged and nearly vomited from the most foul smell he had ever tasted. He choked on his tongue and his throat closed up and he felt his lunch bubble up in his stomach. His vertigo made an appearance and he couldn't be sure if he doubled over, went upside down, or curled up on his side. Maybe all three.

Banding wasn't going to do anything, as it did not affect air so well. He was going to suffer through this like a normal person, and at this rate, it was going to take him all night. Maybe he would smell so bad by the end that Ramone and his gang wouldn't want to get within one hundred yards of him and that would be his ticket to surviving this encounter.

Ancestors, I hope not, he prayed silently, getting himself back in an upright position, leaning heavily on the cart as he finally emerged into the hallway.

"You know, I remember when my kids were babies," another inmate was saying, falling in beside him. "There was nowhere their shit couldn't reach. Whether it was coming out the front end or the back, it always made its way onto the floor, the walls, the damn ceiling! I didn't know kids could have projectile diarrhea, did you? And it splatters and gets into some weird places. You got to check around to make sure you got it all."

Rivotra was focusing more on not vomiting and did not reply.

He arrived at the offending cell to half a dozen remarks from the neighbors about hurrying up and getting it clean before they made a mess of their houses, too. Rivotra didn't blame them, but he did want them to stop talking. Stop talking about shit, vomit, and other bodily processes; just stop talking entirely. He was here, and he was certainly going to do his best to ensure no trace of the incident remained.

Top to bottom, he decided. He didn't know how widespread the offense truly was, but he was taking no chances. Scrub the ceiling first. And indeed, it was contaminated. He didn't know how, but there it was. Scrub the ceiling again, once the mass of material was gone. Scrub it a third time because he was blind and could have missed something. Scrub a fourth time just in case, and a fifth time for good measure.

Repeat for all four walls, taking extra time to scrub around the toilet-sink and polish the safety bars. He declared the mattress, pillow, and blanket beyond saving and stuffed those in their own biohazard bags. Then he took care to clean the metal tray as thoroughly as everything else. From there, he scrubbed the floor six times, every inch, nook, cranny, and cobwebbed corner.

By the time he was done, he was no longer tasting the partially-digested contents of the stomach mixed with bowel blood, and he was almost proud of himself for not vomiting even once, although he had come close a few times. There was still a chemical taste to the citrus cleaner, but he was in no position to complain. He wasn't sure he wanted to go to dinner, but he needed to get out of this place for at least a few minutes.

It took another half hour to dispose of the biohazard bags and everything else he could justify getting rid of. When he finally returned to Isaac in the nurse's room, it was almost six o'clock.

"You all right?" the nurse asked. He pressed a small paper cup into Rivotra's hand; Rivotra tasted ginger and carbonation. "You're white as a sheet."

"What, specifically, do you think I've been doing for the last four hours?" Rivotra asked him testily. "It wasn't a picnic."

"All right, all right. Drink that and go get dinner real quick. I'll go easy on you when you get back."

Rivotra upended the drink, tossed the cup in the trash, then grabbed his cane and headed out. He stopped once he was outside, deliberately sucking in lungfuls of fresh air. He stood there in the sunshine for several minutes, trying to clear his mouth and nose and reset his senses. Once he was satisfied he could no longer taste the GI bleed or the cleaner, he made his way back to the cafeteria.

The cafeteria was quite lively at the moment, and Rivotra noticed a certain frenetic energy that he knew as the precursor to something physical about to happen. The hair on the back of his neck stood up and he prepared for an attack, or even a direct challenge. Ramone or his gang, or both, were getting everyone riled up and ready for whatever shit was going to jump off. When nothing happened immediately, he got in line for food.

The officers could not be unaware of what was going on, he thought, wishing he could see them and read some expressions and body language. Even if they didn't know the specifics, they had to recognize the behavioral patterns. Ramone was advertising his intentions with everything but a literal megaphone; how did he actually expect to get away with this?

Or was it possible that he wasn't expecting to get away with it?

Rivotra got his food and found a seat at a table with a few other men.

"What's Ramone in for?" he asked.

"Murder," someone replied. "His girlfriend, her boyfriend who happened to be with a rival gang, their kid. Shot at the ambulance crew so they couldn't get to 'em to help."

"How long is he down?"

"Life without parole."

Rivotra nodded. "And I'd be willing to bet that Vin may have had something to do with his arrest."

"Dunno, man. Don't think it'd matter if he did. Copper's gonna cop."

"He snitch?"

"Don't need to," a second man said. "Everybody knows what's gonna happen, even the turnkeys."

"And they're not doing anything?" Rivotra questioned.

"Sometimes, you got to let it play out," the first man answered, his tone a shrug. "Can't keep them separate forever. Ramone's got a hard on for your cellie. Got to let it work itself out."

"You know that means that—"

Rivotra cut himself off. Someone was going to die. Ramone was looking to either get revenge or go down in a blaze of glory. He wanted the officers there. He wanted an audience.

Just like Cassius. Just like Rifun.

It wasn't just about Vin; Ramone and his gang were going to take out as many officers as possible. They were going to start a full-scale riot if they could.

Rivotra had to return to the nursing home after dinner, but Vin would be in the genpop building doing laundry for his double chore. If he was right, Ramone and his friends would be watching for both of them, waiting in their neighborhood or just outside if they wanted to try and get others involved. Each neighborhood had its desk officer and the two snipers up top. A lot of damage could be done before reinforcements arrived.

This wasn't just a petty feud between a couple inmates because one happened to be a former police officer. This was going to be the warehouse all over again, Rivotra thought, finishing his dinner. Ten officers dead or maimed because of him, because of Rifun. And because of Cassius. All of it orchestrated by the dragon.

Rivotra returned to the nursing home. As promised, Isaac gave him some light duty chores, sweeping and mopping and such.

So, now what? A petty fight was one thing, but this was something much bigger, much worse.

"What do you hear about the goings-on in genpop?" Rivotra inquired, pausing in his sweeping outside the nurse's station.

"Not much," Isaac replied. "We have a briefing between shifts, but it's basically just medical stuff, like Panzer's GI bleed. The officers would know more about anything else. Why?"

Rivotra did not answer, just nodded vaguely and returned to his sweeping. Didn't matter if it was an officer or a nurse, snitching was still snitching, and even the old heads would keep to that code. Even if the snitch was too little, too late, or even after the fact, a snitch was a snitch. Rivotra had kind of hoped to find someone who did have an idea who wasn't an officer.

So he was still on his own. And he wasn't sure what Vin was going to do. He might have expressed some bravado about facing down a small gang, but what was he going to do if a full-blown riot broke out, assuming he survived long enough to witness it?

Rivotra wasn't even sure he was going to be able to care about anyone but himself if things went sideways. His better bet would be to get a hold of the situation from the beginning and not let go for anything. He just didn't know how to do that. Right now, Ramone held all the cards.

Rifun held all the cards. He held Tommen at gunpoint to force the cooperation of Walter and the other officers. His expressed goal was the murder of Lily Guile, but his real goal had been to lure the dragon out of hiding and slay it instead. That hadn't gone as planned at all.

Rivotra balled up his right hand into a lopsided fist, then stretched it out, noting the absence of his index and middle fingers.

This wasn't going to be like that, he resolved. The Shadows were not in control here. He knew their game, and he wasn't going to let them win.

He finished his assigned chores and returned to the nurse's station.

"All right," Isaac said, "I know you had kind of a shitty day, all pun intended, so I'll let you off a little early. Don't get too excited about it, though; you're still doubled here for a couple more weeks."

"It's hard to forget," Rivotra told him.

"I'll bet."

Rivotra turned and started to leave, but Isaac called to him. He turned.

"Good luck, PJ," the nurse said.

Rivotra blinked. "What?"

"Good luck."

Rivotra paused a moment, then dipped his head once and carried on his way. Somehow, in that moment, his only real desire was to be able to sleep in his own bed that night. He didn't want to end up in the hospital, dreaded returning to the little cubes in the Hole, and he was certainly averse to dying. If he could make it through the evening and still go to sleep on his own thin mattress, then he figured he might be able to endure a couple more weeks of double chores in the nursing home.

He crossed the yard with increasing trepidation. Few inmates were out, but he could feel the stares of those who were. Maybe some of them were scouts, reporting his whereabouts to Ramone so the gang could coordinate their maneuvers and get into position. Maybe they were dragging Vin out of laundry, setting him up for his public humiliation and, if things went their way, execution.

A small group of inmates was loitering around the front entrance of the genpop building, a cloud of cigarette smoke inundating all who dared to enter or exit.

"They're waiting for you, PJ," one told him. "Got your cellie holed up in your house."

"How many?" Rivotra inquired, spitting once as if it might clear the acrid smoke taste.

"Ramone, four of his closest, half a dozen less obvious supporters."

"And the officers?"

"Aw, they know somethin's up," a second man said. "They just waitin' for the shit to jump off. They don't want to be responsible for escalatin' the situation."

Rivotra nodded and headed inside.

Well, that made things easy. At least he was less likely to get jumped on his way there. A minor thought crossed his mind that maybe he could just wait out the clock until the neighborhood closed down for the night. On the other hand, Rivotra had a feeling that Ramone was too hyped up to just let it go for another night. He wasn't leaving the neighborhood before starting something.

As Rivotra got closer to his neighborhood, he lifted his cane and started folding it up, all the links clicking out of place and folding neatly.

There were too many people in his neighborhood; he knew that even before he walked in the door.

"Prison Jesus!" someone called loudly.

Any general conversation evaporated and Rivotra could hear and feel organization slowly reassemble itself. Behind him near the door, he could hear shifting and grunting and the click of a safety being turned off. He calmly handed his white cane to the desk officer, then headed for the middle of the room, entirely confident that a circle was forming.

"PJ..." Ramone began.

"Ramone!" Rivotra barked. "I challenge you! And your stupid friends!"

Whatever speech, threat, or other intent Ramone had lined up, it was immediately cut off. Rivotra stopped walking and just waited. Fighting was certainly against prison rules, but there was still an unspoken code of conduct that sometimes overruled that. This was a formal challenge, two men fully agreeing to beat the shit out of each other in order to settle a dispute.

"A challenge?" Ramone said at last, his tone a mockery of humor and feigned ignorance. "You challenge me? What have I ever done to you?"

"Threatened to turn me into chicken food, for one," Rivotra retorted.

He could hear five sets of footsteps approach, but one got closer than the others. "You're really going to step in and defend this little cop bitch?" He turned his head and shouted, "You're really making friends now, Copper! You got blind, epileptic, disabled men coming to your defense!" That elicited a few chuckles. Ramone turned his attention back to Rivotra. "You know what that makes you, cop-killer? Makes you a traitor."

"I've been called a traitor my whole life," Rivotra informed him. "You and your friends want to face me one at a time, or all at once?"

Ramone laughed and backed up a few steps. Judging by some minor sounds, Rivotra guessed he removed his shirt. "I won't waste their time. And this shouldn't take long."

Rivotra let out a breath and Banded himself and Vin who was indeed being held hostage in the cell by some of Ramone's less ambitious gang members.

"Vin."

"Huh? What? What happened?"

"Don't worry about that. Right—"

"Is this more of that time travel shit? I knew it! I knew there was something fishy—!"

"Damn it, Vin, can you please focus?" Rivotra snapped.

"Oh, yeah, sorry. Hang on, let me just squeeze past these guys. Yeah, what do you need?"

"Just make sure no one tries to distract the officers or block their path."

"Uh...don't you want some help?"

Rivotra shook his head. "No, that won't be necessary. As I said, make sure the officers can do their job. How many are there?"

"Pete the desk officer, the snipers, two at the front door, two at the door to the bathrooms," Vin reported. "Seriously, man, like, what are you doing? What is this?"

"With any luck, the thing that will save your life. And, more importantly, mine."

With that, he pushed Vin out of the Band. He did not drop it entirely, but he eased back significantly, enough that he was back in the scene although he knew he was going to be strengthening it again very quickly.

He could hear and feel Ramone moving around him, but there was too much extraneous noise to pinpoint exactly where he was coming from. Rivotra got his answer soon enough as he felt a hand grasping for his hair. He brought his Band up, turned out of Ramone's grasp, and delivered a solid blow to the gangbanger's right cheek, dropping the Band and backing up several steps as he did so.

The circle of spectators erupted into uproarious cheering so that Rivotra could no longer hear Ramone's movements, nor his own thoughts. He could feel the circle shrink as everyone wanted to get the best view.

Ramone again came in from behind, this time going for a full chokehold. This time as Rivotra Banded, he ducked low and drove his elbow into the man's side, squarely into his floating rib. Then, taking advantage of Ramone's elongated stance—he was clearly shorter than Rivotra and had to stand up tall to try and grasp around his neck—Rivotra, unable to get his leg to work well enough, was forced to kneel and use his elbow again, driving the point down into the man's kneecap, feeling bone and tendon begin to separate and turn in several uncomfortable directions.

He finished off with a full push backwards, throwing himself back into his attacker while releasing his Band. Ramone shrieked in pain right in his ear. Rivotra flinched but still committed to the takedown, letting gravity drive his full weight on top of Ramone on the floor.

From there, Rivotra Banded so he could get to his feet, his nose bumping into a fist already in the air, clearly aiming for his face. He skirted this and drove his own fist square into the face of his new assailant, breaking jaw, teeth, and nose.

Once he was on his feet, he explored the circle and discovered that all four of Ramone's friends were in various stages of attack. The next one had both hands out, ready to grab and restrain, if his size was any indication of his role. Two more were still too far away to be in a position to strike. Rivotra eased off his Band, letting the first assailant feel his broken face, but also putting the reaching man in a better position to grab and attack. Once there, he brought the Band back, then approached the smallest of the attackers.

Despite his more rigorous workout routine, Rivotra still had some difficulty maneuvering the man into position so that he was the target of the reaching man. With that done, he stepped out of the way and again eased back on his Band.

Ramone was still on the ground, the punching man was making horrendous guttural noises, and the smallest attacker screamed as the reaching man latched onto him and delivered at least one blow before realizing it wasn't Rivotra in his hands.

There were several long seconds of confusion from both attackers and spectators. What had he just done? And how? Had he really done that? How fast could he move? How could he anticipate their attacks? Was he really blind or just playing at it?

Rivotra stood there, grateful for a chance to breathe and get his body back in order. Then he felt a shift in his head and a slight tremor in his hands. Was this just poor timing, or—?

It would have been incorrect to say everything went black, for he was obviously already blind. Rather, consciousness was ripped from him quite unceremoniously, and the next thing he knew, his head felt like concrete and his whole body ached. He tried to move and let out an involuntary groan.

He heard someone say something, but his brain was too slow to put the words together right away. Still groaning, he sat up.

"Rivotra? Can you hear me? You all right?" It was Vin.

Between Vin and how everything sounded and felt, at least he was back in his cell and not the hospital, the Hole, or dead. He rubbed his aching head, then his face. "What happened?"

"Little shit got in a cheap shot, flashed a light in your face, caused a seizure," Vin explained. "But that was about it before the officers decided to intervene. Ramone and his friends are going to the hospital, then they're going to the Hole, hopefully for a while. While they were fighting it out, I dragged you back in here out of the way. They haven't said anything about you, so maybe you're in the clear."

Rivotra let out a breath. He wanted to stand and stretch, wanted to lie down and go back to sleep. "That was a little less dramatic than I was expecting."

"No one else thinks so. No one can figure out how you did it! Blind, epileptic, disabled, and you kicked the shit out of, well, at least two gangbangers. Got another one to almost choke one of his friends, so maybe that's three." Vin chuckled. "Prison Jesus, turning tables in the temple."

"Motherfucker," Rivotra half-yawned. "I am never going to get rid of that, am I?"

"No, I don't think so." Vin's tone was a laugh.

Groaning again, Rivotra stood.

"It's lights out, man. C.O.'s gonna yell at us if we're chitchatting when we're supposed to be sleeping." Vin rustled around on his mattress, probably trying to get comfortable again.

"What do they care?" Rivotra grumbled, heading over to the toilet-sink unit to freshen up a little and clear the lingering fog from his brain.

He was just getting back in bed when the officer came around on his hourly check. When he'd moved on, Vin spoke again.

"But seriously, man, why did you do that? I mean, there's warning me about shit, and then there's going to bat for me. Why?"

"I wasn't lying. He did threaten to turn me into chicken food. You too."

"That's not what I mean."

"I already told you. I owe Owain a favor. Owed, now, I think."

More rustling from above. Then, "I think this time control shit is related somehow. And you're way too familiar with Walt. What happened?"

Rivotra rubbed his eyes. "Owain can do the same thing. We call it Banding. The basic principle is that you move faster or slower than Base Time around you."

"And that's how you beat the shit out of the guys out there. You could move faster, so you had time to figure out where they were and what they were doing."

"Yes."

"So, why are you here? Band yourself, climb the fence, you're free."

"Oh, I could, yes. But there is much more to it than that. For one, I have enemies. Those enemies can do everything I can do, and much more, much worse. They keep me imprisoned here as much as the officers."

"Are they the ones who killed you?"

"Yes."

More rustling. "I don't get it. This is just...it's too weird."

"Truth often is."

"And what's Walt got to do with it?"

"He was a Captain Timekeeper. His son Tommen was an Apprentice. I am a Warden Timekeeper, which is far above both. But there were other, darker entities at work as well. I thought I was doing the right thing. I thought I could lure that darkness into the open and destroy it. As it turns out, I was that darkness, and it was just using me to wreak terrible havoc and destruction."

Vin made a sound that was somewhere in the realm of dismissive. "Yeah, okay, I remember something about some religious theme here."

"You just watched a man bend Time, manipulate a fundamental aspect of reality, and you're still going to dismiss deeper spiritual or religious entities?"

"I mean, I believe in God and being a good person and stuff. You know, don't lie or cheat or steal, pretty common sense stuff. Anything else, I don't think we can really know."

Rivotra blinked. "Again, you just watched a man alter a fundamental part of the universe. What else do you want to know?"

"Well, I mean, if you can do all that, then why aren't things worse than they are? Like, if I could slow down time—or speed up, or whatever the fuck —and rob a bank, why wouldn't I? Or if I could just rob a grocery store, why suffer the high cost of food?"

"There are fewer Timekeepers in the world than you think. And some do exactly that, taking food or money or fuel. The Laws of Time only govern the use of Time as it relates to the buying and selling of it; they doesn't care how it's used on a daily basis."

"Buying and selling what?"

"Time Capsules. Taking Time from some people at the end of their lives and selling it to others."

More rustling, and Vin's tone turned dubious again. "Yeah, okay. I mean, I don't know too many people with epilepsy, but I feel like yours might have fucked up your head a little. Or maybe it was your head injuries from last year, I don't know."

"Maybe you should write to Owain and ask him about it," Rivotra suggested.

Vin hummed a sigh. "According to my contacts, he moved out of the area shortly after Tommen died. I don't know how to get a hold of him. No one does, apparently. Not that I'd tell you."

"No, I wouldn't expect so."

Rivotra yawned and rolled over. From the way he ached, he could only figure that Ramone's friends had gotten in at least a few good punches while he was down. Nothing hurt like it was truly broken, but his bones were probably bruised pretty good. Above him, there was more rustling.

"Listen, man, one more thing," Vin said. "Whatever your reasons, thanks for saving my bacon out there. I really wouldn't have been able to take on all those guys at once. And by the time the turnkeys got to me, I'd be dead. So...thank you."

"I'd say don't mention it," Rivotra said through gritted teeth, still trying to get comfortable, "except everyone already saw it. Just don't expect me to be your bodyguard."

"No, course not. But you were right about trying to play it tough. I've been doing that for a while now. I guess I—"

"Please don't get sentimental with me," Rivotra cut in. "You're welcome. That's all, and I think we can call it square."

"Yeah. We're square. We're cool. We're—"

"—going to sleep."

"Right, yeah. Good night."

"Vin."

"Hm?"

"You talk a lot. Shut the fuck up."

"Right. Sorry."

Rivotra just sighed. With any luck, his appeal would go through or Vin would make parole, because there were times when he wanted to strangle the man, too.

Rivotra came flying in awake in Anagalisgi's cave, heart racing, skin hot and sweaty. He sat up quickly, but everything was exactly as he expected it to be. The cave was comfortably warm, the fire crackling nicely, a wonderful taste alerting him to the presence of a stew over the fire.

"Welcome back," Anagalisgi greeted, sounding as though he were on the other side of the fire. "I hope you're hungry."

"What...?" Rivotra still couldn't figure out why he'd been so startled. "No needle and thread tonight? No stitching?"

"Wounds may be closed, but the body still requires nourishment in order to heal. As does the spirit."

A wooden bowl and spoon were pressed into his hands, and Rivotra felt his body relax. He let out a breath, then tipped the bowl up to sample the stew. Still very hot, chunky, but there remained a comfort in the broth that warmed his spirit as much as his belly. He gritted his teeth as he felt flesh tighten, tiny wounds closing on their own with no help from stitches. Then he picked up the spoon.

Neither of them said a word while they ate and for a short time afterwards. For this, Rivotra was grateful. But for as relaxed as he was, he still had questions.

"Did I do the right thing?" he asked finally. "Did I defend Vin, or just beat up some guys?"

"Either," Anagalisgi said. "Both. Or, perhaps, you let the Shadows know that you cannot be cowed by minor threats and twisted logic."

"Twisted logic," Rivotra echoed. "That apathy and pacifism are the only acceptable answers."

"They have their place, most certainly. But what were your actions compared to, even if in jest?"

"Jesus overturning the moneychangers' tables in the temple." Rivotra shook his head. "I hate that name they've given me. I don't know if I hate it because of my distaste for Christians, or if because even I am, on some level, offended by the obvious mockery of someone's religion."

Anagalisgi laughed.

"But how do I know when it's right to ignore something and when to take action?" Rivotra pressed. "That could have just as easily been the Shadows baiting me into a huge fight where I could have been seriously injured or killed, or faced disciplinary action, or any number of terrible outcomes."

The Native man stopped laughing. He cleared his throat and became serious. "I want you to do something. Reach up and touch your eyes."

"What?"

"You heard me. Reach up, yes, and touch your eyes."

Rivotra lifted his hands and cautiously brought them toward his face. He found his nose, his cheeks. He slid his fingers up to his eyes. He found his lower eyelid, and then...

In a maneuver that was painful and difficult even in this dream, Rivotra launched himself up and backwards, as if he could escape what he'd just discovered, or rather, not discovered. He had no eyes. His eye sockets were empty save for the tattered end of the optic nerve.

"The Shadows gave you eyes once," Anagalisgi stated. "They were cloudy and blind, only able to see the spiritual matters they wanted you to see. When they took their version of the Akari from you, it was necessary also to remove those dead eyes. Tawodi did that."

"Who?" Rivotra wondered, unsure if he wanted to know the answer.

"The White Hawk."

"The Shadows didn't take them back?"

"No. They would have left you with spiritually blind eyes, seeing only darkness and lies and confusion. In removing them, it gave the opportunity for growth, to see by way of something more than sight. As you do normally in the waking world."

Rivotra heard the tap of wooden utensils, some shuffling in the dirt, then footsteps as Anagalisgi approached. He took Rivotra's hand and pressed something into his palm. Just by feel and from the conversation, he knew they were eyes. He instinctively tried to recoil, but Anagalisgi held him fast by the wrist, keeping his hand over the eyes so they did not fall.

"You have done well to walk by faith. But now, it is time to return to you your spiritual sight. Real spiritual sight."

The man closed Rivotra's fingers around the eyes in his palm and took a step back. Swallowing nervously, Rivotra turned the eyes over in his hand, felt them. They were soft and squishy, as he might expect them to be. Carefully, he put one in each hand, lifted them up, and pressed them into his empty eye sockets.

He gagged as he felt the squishy marbles roll around in the sockets for a moment with each blink. Finally they settled in place, and when he lifted his hands to touch them, he knew a touch of pain and reflexively blinked.

"And?" Anagalisgi wondered.

"I don't feel any different," Rivotra stated. "And I...might have hoped to have regained my sight."

"I understand. The spirit may be strong, but we all must deal with our physical limitations."

"Do I have my Akari abilities back? Can I heal those physical limitations?"

"I thought you hated being called Prison Jesus?" Anagalisgi teased, returning to the fire. "No, you do not have your Akari abilities back, although that is not out of the realm of possibility. Right now, you must simply learn to use the gift of spiritual sight."

"Is it prophetic, then, like you?"

"No. It is simple discernment, good judgment when faced with difficult decisions. You may not know what will happen when you make a decision, but, if you learn to see well, you may make that decision confidently."

"I've made a lot of bad decisions confidently."

"Maybe so, but what do you expect to do?"

Rivotra let out a breath. "I don't know." He again touched his eyes, but with the safety of his eyelid between his finger and the actual orb. Still there. He lowered his hands. "Seeing how these eyes are not prophetic, I guess we're going to find out."

Twelve
Free Time

Vin was moved to the supermax a few days later for his own protection. Gathering up his tub of few worldly possessions, he expressed some hope about the situation, saying that maybe he could stay safe, stay out of trouble, and make parole in the spring. Rivotra could do no more than wish him well.

On the bright side, he had a house all to himself again. Between that and getting off double chore rotation and having all privileges reinstated a couple weeks later, he might have dared to hope things were looking up. He even went to a baseball game that first night he didn't have double chores though he couldn't actually watch the game. But then, the spectators were sometimes more entertaining than the players.

It was almost the last week of June and the lingering sunlight did its best to roast everyone as long as possible, the shiny bleachers doing their best to ensure even cooking on all sides. Rivotra used his sleeve to wipe sweat from his eyes. Baseball games in this prison were only three innings. This kept them from taking up too much time in general, and it prevented the spectators from getting bored and subsequently rowdy.

Knowing he wouldn't see much, Rivotra respectfully sat in the top row of bleachers at the corner, figuring out the ebb and flow of the game based on the shouts from those around him. He knew when someone hit well, when someone struck out, and when someone stole a base.

Rivotra startled as someone elbowed him in the ribs.

"If blacks is good at anything, it's stealin'." the man laughed, clapping slowly. "Two damn bases, almost three. Scottie's boys better wake up or they'll steal the whole damn game!"

"I'm not worried," Rivotra replied. "Whites have stolen plenty in their time, too."

Then the crowd was in an exuberant uproar; apparently someone hit a home run and sent three men over home plate. Down below on the ground near his corner seat, Rivotra heard an excited whoop and hard clapping.

"That's what I'm talking about!" It was Oswald. "Gimme something good! I wanna win today!"

"You guys take bets on the games?" Rivotra questioned.

"Eh, only sometimes. Why? A guy can't enjoy a baseball game?"

"Just seems like a breach of security to me."

"Nah. I mean, yeah, but nah. The bigger breach of security is when we play."

"You? The officers have a team?"

"Hell yeah. We practice off-site, though. End of the season, we come out and play a couple games. It's a hoot. Y'all try so hard to beat us, but we've whooped you guys for the last eight years straight."

"What happens if we win?" Rivotra wondered.

"Then we have to listen to it every damn day for at least the next year," Oswald told him. "And y'all get free seconds at chow the next day, but that's about it."

"What if you guys win?"

"Then everyone on the team gets eight hours of PTO. That's almost a free day off of work."

"You guys have other sports teams?"

"No. Everything else is considered too close contact. Football, basketball, obviously boxing. Bases notwithstanding, baseball keeps a good distance between us and you."

Rivotra nodded and turned his attention back to the game. He again found a stray thought floating through his mind, wondering if he really was in prison. Random bursts of violence aside, there were days when it just didn't feel like it. Maybe he was too accustomed to third-world prisons and torture that he automatically mentally disregarded the yelling, knowing that there were few teeth behind it. Maybe it would be different if he could see the officers and their guns, the razor wire and watch towers.

Then his thoughts floated back to his own predicament. He'd heard nothing from Josina about the farm, which could be good or bad. He'd heard nothing from Nendawagan or Netami, though he wasn't convinced that they'd judged him not guilty.

For the moment, everything was simply suspended. Unless something else dramatic happened, there was nothing to be done until September, maybe October, and it was only just about to turn into July.

From comments made by some of those in the vicinity, Rivotra determined that, unlike a regular baseball game—not that he had any experience—huge nets were set up between the stands and the field, preventing any stray balls from flying into the crowd. This wasn't so much to protect the spectators from a small meteor as it was to prevent the baseballs from being taken and used later in a less than sportsmanlike manner.

This did not stop several older inmates from occasionally mentioning how they once caught a ball when they went to a baseball game as a kid, nor did it dissuade some of the younger inmates from hoping that a ball would be tipped high enough that it would clear the nets and fall into the stands, even running down to the net itself any time there was a foul ball popped up especially high.

"You got anything like this where you're from?" Oswald asked below him.

"Stickball is universal, I think," Rivotra told him. "But my people prefer *savika*. You would compare it to rodeo."

"Rodeo, really?"

Rivotra nodded. "I rode *savika* a few times. Was gored once, and my mother put a stop to my going."

He did not mention that although *savika* was practiced by the Betsileo, he had been raised among the Merina near Tana, and the only time he'd actually done *savika* was the few occasions they'd gone to visit his *nenibe*. The last time he'd done it, he had been gored, and his mother had scolded him for being careless, in a loving, concerned, motherly way. He left home less than two years later and hadn't given *savika* much thought since, as far as being a competitor.

Well, he thought as the game ended, "Scottie's boys" losing at 8-6, he wasn't in much of a position to ride a cranky bull anymore. It wasn't just about the riding, trying to hold onto the hump of a zebu—there were no fancy saddles or gloves—it was also about jumping on the cow while it was running around the arena and then running away after being shaken off.

Maybe he ought to focus his efforts on something a little safer, like farming. That was his goal, and the prison afforded a unique opportunity to dust off his skills in that area before going home.

He let most of the crowd leave before making his way down from the bleachers. After a minute, he could feel someone fall in beside him.

"So were you the rodeo star or the clown?" Oswald wondered.

"I wasn't the best at it," Rivotra admitted. "Better than some. And what about you playing baseball? Are you the home run hitter or the mascot?"

Oswald laughed. "Shortstop usually, and a pretty good batter. I've gotten some homers in the last few years."

"I hope you're not trying to talk me into playing. You just said you can beat us well enough without having to handicap your opponents with a blind man."

"No, but I did watch the footage of you taking on five guys in a fight—and winning."

Rivotra nodded slowly. "Ah. So you're here to ascertain my capacity and capability for violence." He lightly tapped his escort's boot with his cane.

"Prison Jesus isn't just a celebrity among the peasants."

"No, he was quite popular with the Pharisees, too, though in a different way."

"And the Romans," Oswald commented.

Rivotra took an even breath. "Many have told me not to pin my hopes on my upcoming appeal, yet I find I can do little else, even if that means being taken from here directly to another courtroom."

"And what happens if your appeal is denied? Or if the Krydik find you guilty and send you back here anyway?"

The Krydik wouldn't send him to prison; he knew that much. Execution or exoneration, there was no middle ground. "I don't know. From what I understand, the first appeal is always the most likely, and anything after that is false hope and grasping at straws. If it fails, the best I suppose I can hope for is to survive twenty years."

Or some kind of far-fetched rescue, maybe. Regaining his Akari abilities so he could heal himself and break out on his own. But he knew that was more wishful thinking than a real plan of action.

"What do you think?" Rivotra wondered. "What's your opinion on appeals and parole?"

"That's a heady question," Oswald answered. "I can say that I've seen innocent men locked up, victims of a skewed judiciary tangled in red tape. I can say that I've seen monsters game the system and be granted parole when they have no business being outside this fence, or this side of the grave."

"And which do you think I am?"

"I don't know yet. You've been dead or disabled for the majority of your stay so far. Now that you seem to be settling into a normal routine, we'll see what you make of it."

"And so far?" Rivotra pressed, knowing they were getting close to the genpop building.

"Cop killer refuses to aid in killing a cop despite possibly being able to get away clean, defies a gang despite being highly vulnerable himself to retribution, even risks his own life to defend said cop," Oswald said thoughtfully. "At the same time, this blind, epileptic, disabled man not only publicly challenges the gang to a fight, but he fucking wins. I've seen former Marines in great shape in similar situations get their asses handed to them. Yet here you are. So am I to judge the actions, the outcomes, or the motives?"

"That sounds like your problem."

"You are my problem. And if you could keep your head down and stop being a problem, that would be awesome. Prison doesn't like sensationalism."

Rivotra felt his cane tap against the door and he paused, turning in the lieutenant's general direction. "You know, if you could get them to stop calling me Prison Jesus, that might help."

"Yeah? Then stop performing fucking miracles. Rome is getting annoyed."

"Caesar is annoyed? Or just the local centurion?"

He could feel Oswald's frustrated glare. "Either get inside, or I will make it so you have to clean the nursing home every day until your appeal."

Rivotra nodded once and ducked inside, heading for his neighborhood. The whole building was still abuzz with excitement over the game, and the neighborhood and the showers echoed with ribbing, laughter, and a few taunts between the teams. Rivotra could not add to the exuberance with his own observations, but he could enjoy the lightened mood.

The weekend passed uneventfully. Monday came around, just another day until the desk officer spoke up as Rivotra intended to head out for breakfast.

"Slip for you, PJ," the officer said. "After breakfast, you have to meet with your social worker."

The hall pass was pressed into his hand which he slipped into his breast pocket. He didn't think much of it. He had been informed that after a period in the Hole or after a punishment, the social workers would have a meeting to work through what had happened and ensure the inmate had learned (positively) from the experience.

So, after breakfast, Rivotra made his way to the admin building, showing his slip and being given directions to Andrew's office. When he believed he found the correct office, he knocked lightly on the door.

"Yes, Mr. Ndolo, please, come in, have a seat."

Rivotra was not actually all that familiar with his assigned social worker, and the ease and friendliness with which the man greeted him was slightly unnerving. Was he normally this way? Was he expected to be? Had Cameron and Oswald informed him of everything spoken of while he'd been restricted to French communication?

He made his way into the office, found the chair, and sat.

"You're looking a lot better today than you did a year ago," Andrew observed.

"That's what they tell me," Rivotra offered.

"All right, so, it seems like we're kind of back where we started. You didn't get much of an introduction to things before you were attacked, so some things you just had to learn as you went. And that includes how...prison justice and the courts and the Hole all work.

"The good news is that although it is listed as a disciplinary action on your record, it is considered a minor infraction, like a...like accidentally breaking the rules versus committing a serious crime. So when it comes to

294

your appeal or parole or anything of that nature, it won't be seen as anything really damning. You made a mistake."

"Is that what you really think, or is that something you have to say to try and keep my spirits up?" Rivotra wondered.

"No, it's true. Now, from a social work standpoint, my standpoint, it's a little more intensive. I have to consider the accusation and the punishment in conjunction with the fight that ensued and all of that in accordance with your work and what track we had you on before your attack."

Rivotra had spent plenty of time as a desk jockey in the army after his collarbone was shattered, and he knew the smell of corporate bullshit.

"Before, you were attending a support group for those with wartime PTSD. I'm reassigning you to that group. Right now it's meeting on Monday and Thursday evenings at seven."

He had no choice but to accept the slip that was handed to him.

"Now, all things considered, what you did fighting that gang...honestly, no one can really explain it, and I've seen the footage. By all accounts, I don't know that you should have been able to pull off that kind of physical feat. But even so, well, you did. And the way it manifested is...not good. Now, the support group should help, but having a physical outlet can be just as constructive. Since your privileges have been reinstated, you can get back into the weights area. And, although you're blind, I mean, like I said, you fought. And you won. Would you consider possibly becoming a boxer in the boxing league?"

Rivotra blinked, considered it for half a second, then shook his head. "I don't think my head could handle being beaten like that on a regular basis."

"All right, fair enough." Andrew's tone was a nod. "I just wanted to present it as an option. But, with that, I mean, it really needs to stop, the fighting."

Rivotra recoiled, confused and annoyed. "I was attacked in the showers and murdered, and I fought to defend someone in spite of numerous disabilities. Where does everyone get this idea that I'm going out and intentionally picking fights that are far above my skill level just for the fun of it?" He went on before the social worker could speak. "If you really want to know what I'd like to do, I'd like to pick up more chores on the farm. I wouldn't say I would enroll in the full program because I would still like to believe that my appeal is going to go through, but more chores I can do."

Andrew made a sound that was reminisce of thoughtfulness and being mildly impressed. "All right. I mean, your file says you have some experience that in regard, and you've done good work there on rotation. It's almost time for rotation again, so I can pull some strings to get you out there."

"Thank you."

"As for your appeal..." Andrew's tone turned neutral. "Sometimes they go through. Almost always, the retrial sends them straight back here anyway. I've seen that the Krydik tribe is gunning for you, too, and they might tack on a few years themselves. Far be it from me to dash your hopes, but I wouldn't roll up just yet. I will see about farm chores. I won't formally enroll you in the college program, although I will get that paperwork started. If things don't work out like you hope come September or October, then you'll have that waiting for you."

"You are a terrible motivational speaker," Rivotra told him, "but I appreciate the honesty."

"I avoid making promises I know I can't keep and getting your hopes up too high. I can't promise anything on the legal side of things, but I can offer resources to help you make the most of your time here and maybe help you become a better person."

Rivotra nodded. "Did you need anything else from me?"

He heard the scribble of pen on paper. "Nope. I'll get this sorted out for next rotation. Here's your slip to excuse being late to morning chores."

Rivotra pocketed the slip, stood, thanked the man, and left the office.

He wanted to believe that his appeal would go well and he wouldn't have to plan so far ahead. At the same time, if Nendawagan ordered his execution, did his appeal matter? And what was taking her so long? Was she waiting for the dramatic timing? Was it possible that she had forgiven him and so called off the bounty on his head? Or had Julianna gotten to them first and the Krydik were gone entirely? That might be a question for Jeremy to look into.

Rivotra reported for morning chores and went about his day with little excitement. After dinner, he dutifully reported to the veterans PTSD support group. It was led by the same guy as before, and many of the attendees had been in the group one year prior. Unlike before, however, everyone knew who he was as soon as he walked in the door.

"Come on, man," someone said, "got a seat for you right here." He slapped the seat of a chair loudly.

Rivotra followed the sound, found the chair, and sat down. He half-expected some kind of practical joke, but nothing happened that he was aware of. He made a quiet promise to do as Oswald suggested and keep his head down so maybe they'd stop calling him Prison Jesus and making a big deal out of him.

But just as easily as they had welcomed him on account of his fame, especially for his most recent fight, he also found himself being questioned. What had motivated him to issue the challenge? Had he felt depressed and maybe hoped to die? Had he experienced any flashbacks before or during the incident? Had he experienced something similar when in the army, when he was captured, or at any other point?

By the standard definition, Rivotra couldn't experience flashbacks because his brain was not capable of producing or interpreting visual input. He was not able to experience visual memories. That didn't mean that he couldn't hear or feel those memories. Such as, perhaps, the day he got a pickax put in his skull.

He had been on the chain gang and he had challenged another prisoner to a fight. That prisoner had friends who were more than happy to use the chains around their arms and legs to trip up Rivotra as he tried to fight, making him easy prey for the one man he had challenged. That man happened to be a Runner and could bend Time to a small degree, but, if Rivotra wanted to be honest, that was not the only advantage the man had. Even without Time, there was a good chance he could have still put that pickax in Rivotra's head; it just might have taken a couple minutes instead of a couple seconds.

Rivotra didn't mention Time at all in such recollection, but, he figured, it didn't matter much.

"Motherfucker," one man said, "how the fuck are you still alive?"

"You're not the only one asking that, believe me," Rivotra told him.

"That's what started your seizures, too, right?" the group leader asked.

Well, technically it had been exposure to Borelian toxins, but for the purposes of discussion, "Yes."

So this week's discussion had to do with being aware of flashbacks, identifying them, and learning how to stay grounded in the present moment. Rivotra wondered if his re-entry into the group just happened to coincide with this discussion topic, or if it might have been changed deliberately when the group leader got wind of his reassignment. Then he wondered how much that really mattered.

Was it possible that he had challenged the gang, somehow thinking that he was again facing his pickax attacker and his friends? Well, it wasn't impossible, he supposed. Was it possible he might have had latent suicidal ideations? Again, not impossible, but he wasn't going to try that until his appeals had been denied and the Krydik sentenced him to another hundred years here. Overall, he was fairly certain that the whole situation had still been a little out of his control and he just picked something that might have worked, if only to buy time.

After the group was finished, everyone made their way back to their respective neighborhoods. Rivotra showered and settled into bed as best he could, grateful to not have a roommate to contend with, though he knew that time would eventually come to a close. With any luck, he wouldn't have to deal with them for very long. He had to have some hope that things would work out well.

He made it to chore rotation at least. As the new schedule was announced and inmates given their slips, Rivotra learned that he had both morning and afternoon farm chores. This didn't bother him. Even if he was cleaning the chicken coop, he'd rather do that than clean the nursing home.

Unlike previous rotations, when he showed up to receive his morning assignment, which happened to be watering, he was also accompanied by one of the instructors from the agricultural college. He had a notion of the man leaning in the doorway while he turned on the water and made his way to the first area of the greenhouse.

"So, I hear you were a farmer back home," the instructor began conversationally.

"Of sorts," Rivotra replied. "I went into the army, but my family had a farm, yes."

"Plants or animals?"

"Both. Cattle, ducks, rice, vanilla, grapes."

"Yes, you said something once about replacing the chickens with ducks."

"Chickens are stupid birds," Rivotra maintained. "At least ducks are entertaining."

"Chickens can be entertaining, too," the instructor said lightly. "And in the interest of—"

"I know, I've heard. Efficiency, scale, cost, all those words. Be glad I'm not asking for cows, although a few good-sized steers could give everyone a nice steak for Christmas."

"Unfortunately, that's not happening either. How many cows did your family have?"

"Usually somewhere between two and three hundred, but there were also a dozen people living in the house."

The instructor whistled. "Did you pasture them?"

"Of course we did. Hay is an expensive commodity, already difficult to grow successfully in the clay, impossible if you can't harvest before the rainy season."

"And you still had rice and all the rest?"

Rivotra shrugged mildly. "The grapes were a personal luxury; it wasn't the primary business. The rest of it, though, yes, many fields, many acres."

"And you want to take the college courses...why? To show off?"

Now he paused and turned in the instructor's general direction. "I haven't signed up for anything officially. I still have some hope for my appeal." And who knew what the Krydik were going to do to him?

"All right, fair enough. I'll leave you to it, then."

The instructor departed, leaving Rivotra alone with his plants. He did his duty methodically. There were few seedlings and young plants this time of year except for a few experimental varieties. Summer and fall harvests were well grown, and late fall and winter harvests were not yet planted. He finished the greenhouse quickly and made his way to the chicken coop to clean and fill the waterers.

When everything was done, he returned to the office where a desk officer and an instructor were talking.

"Problem?" one of them inquired.

"No, I'm done," Rivotra told them.

"You've been here before and done good, we don't need to check up," the other, presumably the desk officer, said dismissively.

"Is there anything more I can do?"

"Some things require sight, and you're also not a student," the first man, the instructor, said, his tone an apology. "Not much we can have you do right now."

Rivotra frowned but nodded and left the farm. With the greenhouse almost barren, watering hadn't taken long at all, and it wasn't even lunchtime yet.

He headed to the gym, hoping to get in a workout, instead finding the Pinto Gang in the cage. Ramone evidently hadn't been released from the Hole yet, but it didn't make his friends any happier to see Rivotra.

"Well, well, look who it is," one said. "Prison Jesus himself."

Rivotra sighed and turned to leave, but before he could get more than a couple steps, he heard the door of the cage squeak and several men encircled him.

"No, no, no, no, no, you don't get to walk away." Rivotra noted that, although the group was uncomfortably close, no one dared lay a hand on him. "You got some explaining to do."

"Considering it's been over a week and you haven't figured it out for yourselves is very telling," Rivotra observed. "I will try to explain away your confusion, but I don't know that I can simplify it down that far."

Hot breath puffed against his cheek, blowing a few stray hairs so they tickled his eyes and nose. "You calling us stupid?"

"I'm going to give you two options, and you can tell Ramone when he's out of the Hole the same thing. First, you can leave me alone and we can all go our separate ways in peace. Or you can try something—anything—and end up more disabled than me. What's it going to be?"

Rivotra closed his eyes for good measure, just in case one of them did still have some kind of strobe light. Back at the cage, he could hear the clang of chainlink as more men pressed up against it, waiting to see what was going to happen. Around him, he could feel the tension, but also the uncertainty. They couldn't explain what he'd done the last time; how much did they want to risk this time without their fearless leader?

"We'll wait and see what Ramone thinks," the man with the hot breath decided at last. "Until then, stay out of our way. And our cage."

The group left and the door to the cage banged closed.

Well, so much for a workout before lunch, Rivotra mused. He made his way back to his neighborhood, if only for something to do. Entering his cell, he was surprised when his cane tapped against something relatively soft.

"Huh?" an unfamiliar voice wondered. "Oh, um, is this yours?"

"Who are you?" Rivotra asked.

"Um, Erik. I just got assigned here. Is the top yours? I got told—?"

"No, go ahead, take it." Rivotra sighed. "Damn it."

"Um...is something...?"

"I was enjoying a house to myself," Rivotra told him. "I knew it wouldn't last long, but all the same..."

"Oh."

"How old are you?"

"Nineteen."

"You're brand new here, aren't you? Fresh out of the Fishbowl?"

"Yes."

"What for?"

"Drugs, threatening someone with a gun. Turns out that someone was an undercover cop."

Rivotra nodded. "That'll do it. Well, since you're a newcomer, let's start with some house rules."

"Um...okay."

"You bring drugs in here, I will hurt you. You try to rope me into hiding, smuggling, or especially doing, I will hurt you more. Is anything unclear?"

"No, sir."

"Good. Oh, and one more thing. If you call me Prison Jesus, or PJ, you're going to find out quick that I don't do healing miracles."

"Oh. Okay. Um...so what should I call you?"

Rivotra sighed and reluctantly held out a hand. "Rivotra. Nice to meet you."

The hand that met his was skinny and limp. Once the awkward two seconds had passed, Rivotra Banded so he could pat the kid down. Five-foot-eight at the tallest, worryingly skinny with obvious ribs and bony shoulders. No drugs on him yet, but Rivotra knew that would change once he found his gang. If he had to take a guess, meth was his drug of choice. Wonderful.

He dropped the Band.

"So..." Erik began, "what's up with the cane? Is that one of those seeing eye dog canes? Are you, like, actually blind?"

"I am."

"Where's your dog?"

"I don't have a dog."

"Oh. I mean, I heard that they train dogs here, so I thought..."

"They train dogs to sit, stay, fetch, and do their business outside," Rivotra informed him. "They're not service dogs."

"Oh."

If this drug addicted teenager had any redeeming qualities, it was his apparent lack of vocabulary or will to exploit it. Rivotra was fine with that. As long as the drugs stayed in someone else's house, he could limp his way to his appeal.

He left the neighborhood before Erik could ask more questions, making his way to an early lunch. From there, he returned to the farm for afternoon chores. As expected, he was assigned to cleaning the chicken coop.

That was fine, he told himself as he grabbed a rake. Whether it was chickens here or ducks at home, someone was going to be cleaning the coop. Given that he would likely be the only one there, well, he would be the one doing the cleaning. And the Powers That Be weren't entirely wrong. Ducks did require water, and that water would necessarily make their coop wetter, dirtier, and smellier. Where the Powers That Be were wrong, or at least over-exaggerated, was how much water the ducks needed. They didn't need a whole ocean, just enough to wet their heads and preen their feathers.

It was still a losing battle. In addition to the ducks' less than industrial efficiency, the prison itself was situated on a hilltop in deciduous mountains, and they didn't have the same rainy season that could be found in the Madagascan jungle. Although flash floods were common in the area, it still wasn't enough. Even the more industrious inmates who worked in the utilities had tried to convince the Powers to invest in a rain collection system and got shut down.

Rivotra continued to rake and shovel, occasionally finding an egg or some kind of hidden paraphernalia. He couldn't get too invested in things. He had to hope that his appeal would turn out. Either that, or Nendawagan was going to execute him.

He wished he had some means of finding out how things were going on that front. He briefly considered asking Jeremy to look into it, but he didn't expect the Navajo man to get far. Assuming Nendawagan or Netami or anyone even spoke to him, they weren't likely to disclose the results of the trial. If Rivotra was alive, that was one indication. If he was found dead, that was another. And no one outside the Krydik—or perhaps outside of Nendawagan's inner circle—would know the verdict until the punishment was exacted or stayed.

But what if something had happened to the Krydik? What if Julianna really had gotten to them, wiped them out? What if the Krydik were just another target crossed off her list?

So what? he had to frustratingly admit. So what? What was he going to do about it? If he were going to do anything about anything, he would have done it by now. He would have left prison as soon as he arrived. He would have avenged his family. He would have claimed his inheritance. He would have changed his name. He would have healed his wounds. He would have done a lot of things. But he couldn't. Time was keeping him alive, but he still had no use of the Akari. He couldn't open portals. He couldn't heal. He couldn't, he couldn't, he couldn't. The most he could do, if he so chose, was Band to get this coop cleaned a little faster.

He didn't. There was no reason. Once again, that was all outside. And he was still inside. The only thing that mattered on the inside was the inside. As a lot of the lifers liked to say, he got nothin' comin' to him.

It was only just July. His appeal was in September. Could he hold out hope that long? Was it worth it? Did he want to entertain an idea of Josina helping him to break out? If she was learning the Akari from Owain, Nendawagan, Netami, or someone else, maybe she had learned how to open portals. Would she dare do something like that? Her job as a lawyer might be to help people, but there was a difference between representing someone in a court of law, and actually aiding a criminal escape.

He would set that idea aside until the results of the appeal came back. If he could do it the right way, then fewer feathers would be ruffled and he wouldn't risk the publicity of an international manhunt.

He finished cleaning the chicken coop and again found himself with some free time. With the weights area out of order, he elected to just take a walk around the complex. It was hot and humid despite the waning hours, but the sunlight and fresh air felt good. Smelled better than the chicken coop, too.

The evening was uneventful, and, heading in for the night, Rivotra calmly resigned himself to having a new roommate who was less than desirable. Of course, any hope he might have had of this teenager being a man of few words quickly dissolved once he got back in the house after his shower.

"What the fuck is all this?" Erik whined.

"What now?" Rivotra asked, sitting on his thin mattress and stowing his cane in his tub.

"Man, they put me back in school, got me going to rehab, want me to clean shit. What is this?" The kid sounded genuinely distressed.

"You would rather get beaten up and raped by a roaming prison gang?"

"I hate school. I left school for a reason. I was making good money selling drugs."

Rivotra just sighed, shook his head, and lay down. With any luck, only a couple months of this idiot. With better luck, this idiot would wind up in the Hole and he could get some peace and quiet. If the offense was bad enough, or repeated enough times, maybe this idiot would get transferred to a new neighborhood with more agreeable HOA rules and neighbors.

It was a rough first few days as Erik adjusted to prison life, and he did indeed end up in the Hole very quickly for drug-related offenses.

"Isn't that what the Fishbowl is for?" Rivotra asked of the neighborhood desk officer that evening. "Watch everyone, see what their tendencies are, see how prone they are to relapse?"

"Not my call, man," the officer replied, his tone a shrug. "Besides, we got open beds here. If other neighborhoods are full, they're not going to pack them in while there are open beds elsewhere, know what I mean?"

"But why put him in with me?"

"Dunno. Luck of the draw, I guess. Besides, you might be weird, but you ain't special."

Rivotra huffed a sigh and turned away. Only a couple months, only a couple months.

When Eric did return from the Hole a week or so later, he was quiet. Whether this was psychologically- or medically-induced, Rivotra did not know. He was just grateful to get another full night's sleep.

The following morning, the count officer came around, barking orders and numbers, handing out mail as the rats lined up in their cages.

"981436!" he snapped outside the cell.

With both Rivotra and Eric present, the officer took down whatever notes he needed, then handed over the envelope. After a moment of contemplation, Rivotra decided to pocket the envelope and wait until count was over and they were released for early morning activities. Then he approached the desk officer and held out the envelope.

"Can you read this, please?"

The envelope disappeared from his hand and there was some rustling of papers.

"Well," the officer began hesitantly, "I can tell you it's from a lawyer from the Senate of Madagascar, Josina Zitha. Otherwise, I'm afraid I don't read French. I mean, I took, like, one semester in college a few years ago, but I couldn't tell you what this says."

Rivotra nodded. "All right. Guess I'll have to find Cameron or Oswald."

The officer handed back the letter. "Oswald's got the day off, and Cam will be in at nine. I have a suspicion that he's the one who reads your mail and translates it, so he'll probably be expecting you."

"Yes, yes, to make sure I'm not conspiring with international terrorists, I know."

He left the office and elected to get his morning chores done early so he could meet with Cam afterwards before lunch.

305

Indeed, the social worker did seem to be expecting him.

"I'm guessing you want to know what was in that letter you got," he began.

"It would be helpful, I think," Rivotra said, taking a seat. "The fact that it was not accompanied by a letter from my state-side lawyer makes me believe that it refers only to my problems back home."

"It does, yes. Would you rather I read it word-for-word or give you the highlights?"

"Start with the forest, and I'll decide if I need to see the trees."

Rivotra heard a chair shift on the carpet. "All right. Well, I'll give you the good news first. Your name change officially went through back home. Rifun Ndolo has been stripped and your legal name is now Rivotra Felix Andilan."

Rivotra let out a huge breath and slumped back in his chair. He couldn't explain why it felt like such a big deal, but it did. It was huge. He was finally rid of the monster that was Rifun Ndolo, both spiritually and legally. He would never have to hear that name again in reference to his person. True, many people still knew him by that name, but it wouldn't matter anymore. There was no more sticking point to it.

"Congratulations," Cameron told him, although his enthusiasm was extremely muted.

"Good news," Rivotra mused. "What's the bad news?"

"The properties in Mahitsy, already held by the government, have been turned over to the village president. The homes are slated to be destroyed and the entire area effectively roped off as uninhabitable, cursed, off-limits, however you want to frame it."

The biggest loss there was only monetary, anything he might have been able to sell the properties for. But if they were being turned over just to be destroyed and sectioned off, that meant no one would be willing to buy them anyway. No harm, no foul, really. Annoying, but understandable.

Cameron made a strangled sort of sound. "As for the properties outside of Fianar, the smaller farms were sold at auction to various village residents."

Rivotra took an even breath, told himself it wasn't that bad. Again, monetary loss only. He could not physically live in all of the houses at once, and he was just going to sell them. Who was he going to sell them to?

Various village residents. And at least the properties had gone back to the village residents and not to a bunch of corrupt bureaucrats. Monetary loss only, he told himself.

"The large family farm," the French Canadian went on slowly, "was, however, sold to a government official."

Rivotra heard the man, but it was a long moment before he could actually process the words. It had always been his biggest fear, the Shadowy snake slithering around his mind and telling him that the worst would come to pass. But to hear it actually manifest as words and concepts and actions that were, very likely, already several weeks old, was shocking.

"What?" was the best he could manage.

"Mhm. In the letter, the lawyer mentions that the official who bought the property is sympathetic to your situation and, if things work out in the next few months or so, is willing to let you live there as a hired hand."

Hired hand. But not owner. Not family. His family farm was gone. Generations of Andilans, gone.

It was taken from the family before, he told himself, *maybe there's still hope.*

Taken by the French, removed from the French. You're not going to get that lucky with your own government.

"Did she mention who got it?" he asked, voice tight.

"She didn't list a name, no." Cameron's tone was sympathetic.

Then she probably didn't know. Maybe she wasn't told and only found out after the fact. Probably they didn't want her to know so she couldn't tell him until the back door deal was finished.

"Was there anything else?" Fatigue hit him suddenly, despite it being barely ten o'clock.

"She just mentions that she will be back in the United States in September to prepare for arguments before the appeals court. She'll meet with you at least once, twice if possible, to go over expectations and, I think, to have a little talk about what happened in this letter."

Rivotra nodded absently. "Yes. I would imagine so." He took another breath. "Anything else?"

"No. Sorry."

Rivotra stood and left the office without ceremony. Pure muscle memory got him out of the admin building. The sudden wash of heat on his face broke the worst of the trance and he paused, but he still couldn't formulate coherent thoughts. In any language.

His name was finally what it was supposed to be. What it should have been from his very first breath. Rivotra. The wind. Andilan. The isthmus. Last surviving son of a powerful warrior line. Homeless. Childless. Was it worth being the last one standing if there was nothing left to defend? If there was nothing to pass on to children he did not have?

Anagalisgi had told him not to seek out revenge. It would only destroy him and accomplish Julianna's goal far better than she herself could. But what was this? If Rivotra was supposed to return home and live quietly, well, he didn't have much of a home to return to.

He let out a breath and continued walking. If there was any silver lining, it was the sympathy of the new owner and this apparent willingness to let him return, even if only as a hired hand. Of course, it sounded like this offer was only good through his first appeal, maybe his second if it was soon enough. He should be grateful. It just wasn't coming to him.

He headed to the gym where the weights area was sparsely populated and those inside did not mind his presence. His first stop was the pullup bar. Easy, mindless, less danger if something happened because he wasn't paying attention. Taking a breath, he got his legs under him, forced them to cooperate, and managed the small jump up to the bar. Both shoulders protested, but his back appreciated the gravity-fed stretch.

He pulled himself up. And let down. And up and down, again and again and again, not bothering to count, just doing. His mind was empty of thought but filled with fog and fuzz. He didn't know what to think. He didn't know what to do. Didn't know what he could do. He wanted to believe that Josina was doing everything she could, that maybe her status as a Sakalava mixed-blood was causing her colleagues to put up artificial barriers. But whether she was or wasn't, what was he going to do about it?

He was still inside. Everything else was still outside.

He needed this appeal to go through. Wasn't sure he wanted it at all. Might have hoped for some kind of mercy from the Krydik. Wasn't sure he would have even cared about their order of execution. Maybe he should just be executed. Maybe the Andilan line should just end and let some new dynasty begin.

As he lowered himself from another pullup, he felt an eerie yet familiar sensation around his neck. He dropped to the ground, hoping it looked natural even as his heart raced and his mind, for a brief moment, waited for the noose to pull tight.

He had to keep fighting, but he didn't know why. He couldn't go back, wasn't sure he wanted to go forward. He felt as blind spiritually as he ever had physically. But hadn't Anagalisgi given him back his eyes? Wasn't he supposed to be endowed with some supernatural spiritual vision? Where was that? Where was this spiritual discernment that would let him discover the deeper meaning behind this turn of events? Where was his gift of prophecy to know what was going to happen on the next page, or in the next chapter, or the next book? Had he been mistaken? Had Anagalisgi been mistaken? The man might have the ear of the Author, but he was still human; he could be wrong sometimes.

But whatever the case, Rivotra was still inside. And everything else was still outside.

Another wound had reopened, this one the stab wound that should have killed him. After conquering the Akarin fortress, Rifun had gone down to parade the captive Akarin council in front of his men, when Aklaq White Bear broke through the crowd and pierced him with a poisoned blade. She'd been only centimeters from his heart, but severed his pulmonary artery. In additional to the physical wound, the poison on the blade, the Borelian toxin *urlo*, had reacted to his existing head wound and so caused his epilepsy.

Now that wound bled anew in Anagalisgi's cave. Rivotra sat with his knees draw up while the Native man worked on the exit side of the wound in his back.

"What good is going to come from this?" Rivotra asked. "That I get to be a servant in my own home?"

"Is it really necessary for you to be a leader?" Anagalisgi inquired. "Your family always treated any hired hands or volunteers very well. Why couldn't this official be the same way?"

"It's a slap in the face. Every day. I wake up, I am where I have always been, or wanted to be—"

"And you do the work that is expected of you. The difference is that you are not the one making the big decisions on finances or land management or estate management. If all you wanted to do was farm, well, that's all you'll be doing."

"But it has always been my family. Except for one time very briefly during the Second World War when it was occupied by the French, it has always been my family."

"And who is to say that it can't be your family again one day? Do you know who bought the property?"

Rivotra sighed. "No. The letter didn't say. But it doesn't matter. The laws of inheritance say it goes to the children, or whomever the owner wishes. It tends to be a very localized matter, my situation notwithstanding. Whoever the new owner is, he'll will it to his children, and then to their children, and so on. With land like that, and how much it must have cost him, there would be terrible fallout in his family if he were to will it to anyone else, even me, in the event you were going to try and argue that point."

"Are women barred from owning property?"

Now he shrugged. "Not barred, no, but it is uncommon, unless a husband dies very young. When my *dadabe* died, the estate could have gone to Nenibe or to the children. When it's all in the family, and the family gets along, ownership is a bit of a secondary matter."

"Mm."

Rivotra turned his head. "Do you know who bought the property, or is that not pertinent enough to know, or to tell me?"

"I do know." Anagalisgi tugged on the thread, then went to work tying off the back stitches. A moment later, Rivotra shifted position, sitting up straight so the medicine man could work on his front. "Regrettably, I am not permitted to tell you."

"What? Why not? Who is it? Someone I know?"

"I can't say."

"Then why bother telling you? Can you tell me later?"

Anagalisgi took an even breath. "I can't say that it isn't frustrating for me as well, but I trust the Author to know what she's doing. I encourage you to do the same. I can say that there is light at the end of the tunnel."

"Anagalisgi, that tunnel is likely to be the barrel of a gun, and the light is the flash from firing a bullet. At my head."

Now the man intentionally sighed. "You always were a dramatic actor."

Rivotra internally rolled his eyes. "I'm serious." He resisted the urge to shift position. "How are the Krydik doing? I expected to be beheaded by now."

Anagalisgi laughed. "Hardly."

"Then they haven't been taken out by the Order?"

"No, and it's not for want of trying, believe me."

Rivotra nodded slowly. So his trial had been suspended in favor of more pressing matters. He could respect that. He didn't like having it hanging over his head, but he could respect the circumstances.

"Clouds may block the sun, but they also bring much-needed rain," the Native man said sagely. "Consider this a time of relief and growth."

"Plants can't grow without roots, Anagalisgi. Mine just got ripped off."

"Or perhaps they have simply been exposed and you are being transplanted elsewhere. Somewhere with better soil. Perhaps your family used up everything there was on that land. Putting you there might have felt good, but maybe there would be nothing in that soil for you to grow. Maybe a little rest from the demands of your family is what is best for the land."

"It has lain untouched for over a year. How much more rest does it need?"

Anagalisgi did not reply, simply finished off the last few stitches and moved off. Rivotra felt the spot where the wound had been. Still mildly tender, but the agitated flesh was healing quickly and soon felt as normal as the rest of him.

Only in dreams did he feel normal, he reflected, and as much as his physical eyes were useless, his spiritual eyes felt doubly so. Cautiously, he reached up to feel his eye sockets, moderately surprised when he found eyeballs exactly where they were supposed to be.

"I've been given a tool but I don't know how to use it," he lamented aloud.

"It takes practice," Anagalisgi said, not unkindly. "I might recommend treating them like normal eyes, at least for now. If you can't see things that are far off, then turn your attention to things that are close by instead. You will reach the distant things in good time."

Rivotra was uncertain, but there was little he could do. Every bit of hope and control that he had been clinging to was slowly being taken away. Even now, he was unable to keep hold of the dream to ask Anagalisgi more questions. And soon enough, it was time for morning count.

Thirteen
Just Enough

Unlike his previous visit, Rivotra was now able to move fast enough to claim the back corner seat of the chapel. No one said anything to his face, but he knew the tense frustration of someone being outed from their usual spot, or at least the spot they wanted.

He stood and sat when ordered—or "invited" as the chaplain liked to say —but he still did not sing. Even if he thought he could—and his nursing home neighbors had frequently liked to remind him that he couldn't—he was not in the mood. He was not in any kind of mood to show joy or reverence to anything or anyone. Even if the song was more melancholy in nature, he still couldn't bring himself to think that any god could really empathize with the plight of mortals below. Kings could be sympathetic to the least of these in their kingdoms, they might be very benevolent rulers, they might experience the full range of emotions of any human being, but even they were still separated from their people. Why should a god of even greater power be any different?

Rivotra might have tried to take comfort in the ancestors, knowing that they had once experienced everything he had when they were alive, except he couldn't convince himself that those were the spirits that he would be praying to. The ancestors could bless and curse their descendants, true, but something about it felt off now. Something wasn't quite right.

It could just be him, he figured. He didn't know what to think anymore, didn't know what to believe. He wanted to believe Anagalisgi, wanted to believe that the nights spent in the cave stitching up old wounds were as literal as they were spiritual, that there would be some good to come from all of this. But for as much as Rivotra was being healed in the cave, his skin in the real world was still twisted and scarred. Was it all just wishful thinking, then? He had no doubts about Anagalisgi's existence or the dream-walks in the cave, but considering the plight of the Krydik, the deaths of Tommen, Micaiah, and others, and now his own issues, maybe the man wasn't as mystic or powerful as he was portrayed. Or as other people expected of him.

The service ended. The dozen or so men who came just for something different to do or to get out of morning chores left quickly, while others slowly meandered their way. Another dozen or so who were more reverent stuck around to talk amongst themselves for a few minutes. And still a few waited patiently to talk to the chaplain or one of his understudies. Rivotra remained where he was, leaning forward in his seat, unsure if he wanted to talk or not.

His decision was made for him as he heard the pew in front of him squeak under someone's weight. "Well, look who it is." It was Jeremy, still optimistic. "Welcome back."

Rivotra rubbed his eyes. "I don't know why I'm here."

Now the understudy's tone turned serious. "Something happen?"

He explained the letter he'd gotten a couple weeks prior. Then he bumbled his way through his spiritual ramblings to himself.

"I can only guess the Krydik have finally been wiped out," he stated. "There's no other reason they haven't come to collect their dues."

"They're not wiped out, that much I can say for sure," Jeremy informed him. "I've been talking to them off and on the last couple months."

"So what's the holdup? If they're going to execute me, they should do so. I've lost everything already, so it isn't as if they're robbing anyone of anything."

"They're also not going to execute you, at least, not before a formal trial. Netami mentioned that you are to be presented before her mother and the council for trial on Hlohi."

"Again, what's the holdup? They can kidnap me right out of my bed for that. They don't care what kind of chaos that would cause here."

Jeremy made a helpless sort of sound. "I don't know. I really don't. I don't intend to get too in-depth with anything, but you can't hardly ask them what time of day it is without wondering if that's part of their national security."

Rivotra shrugged lightly and nodded. "I can understand that, I suppose."

"I'm still trying to wrap my head around all this colony world business and the Akari and everything else. Seeing how I'm not willing to jump into their fight, they're not really willing to sit down and explain anything."

"What's to explain? In the beginning, God created the heavens and the earth, and he gave men the ability to fashion the heavens and earth as he so chose. And man chose poorly. But I'm guessing that you're not going to be using that for your college thesis."

"Ah, no. I've only got one year left, I don't need to screw it up now."

"Then you get promoted to full chaplain?"

"I could, if he decided to step down. More likely, though, I'll be returning home. There are some churches on the rez that are really struggling."

"And a college degree will make it better?" Rivotra wondered.

"It doesn't help when the kids know the stories better than the Sunday school teachers," Jeremy commented.

Rivotra nodded absently. "That might be a problem. Good problem for you. At least you'll get to go home to your people, your family."

"You might, too, if your appeal goes through."

"Yes, a hired hand in my own home."

Jeremy shifted in his seat. "Isn't that better than no home at all? Where would you live if this official weren't so sympathetic?"

Rivotra lifted a hand helplessly. "I don't...know. It won't be the same."

Now the understudy made a sound somewhere between a groan and a sigh. "It was never going to be the same anyway. Your family is gone. You were going to return to a house that, in the best of circumstances, was simply empty. Otherwise, it was going to be trashed because of bandits or wild animals, mossy and moldy and very dirty, and you were going to have to pick up the pieces of that broken life while still trying to rebuild yours. Now, you get to go to a home you know well, that is probably going to be cleaned up and functioning well, but this official, if I'm understanding this correctly, isn't going to know how things are supposed to be. He's from the city or from a different area, he doesn't know the house and land like you do. And unless this is a retirement home, he isn't even going to be there most of the time; he's still going to be doing government things. His name might be on the deed, but you're probably going to be running the show."

Rivotra bobbed his head uncertainly for a moment. Then, "When you put it that way, I guess it doesn't sound all bad. Still, it's hundreds of years of family history, just gone."

"I'm sorry," Jeremy said sincerely. "I can't help you with that."

Rivotra waved a hand. "No, I wouldn't expect you to. If Josina, another government official, couldn't do anything, you wouldn't have a chance."

"Maybe not, but I would have a prayer."

Rivotra sighed at the pun as Jeremy laughed. Then the understudy prayed for him and sent him on his way.

He headed to lunch, then to afternoon chores. In the heat of high summer, near the end of July, the chicken coop smelled bad, in spite of the daily cleaning and constant fresh sawdust. It didn't help when he found a rotten egg the hard way. Was it possible for chickens to lay rotten eggs? He was usually very thorough on account of his blindness, taking his time and doing some areas multiple times to ensure it was clean. Maybe someone had stolen an egg a while ago, let it go rotten, then put it back as a prank; that was not out of the realm of possibility, either.

It didn't make him feel any better about his day or his situation, say it that way. Still, he dutifully cleaned up the new mess and carried on. When he was finished, he was fairly confident that he did not smell like rotten egg, and no one made any comment about it at dinner, either to complain about the smell or take responsibility for the prank, if indeed that was what it had been.

After dinner, the majority of the men left the cafeteria and headed for the baseball diamond. The three-game tournament against the officers' team was less than six weeks away. Even though tonight was only a practice night, the inmates still had a huge interest in watching their team and making sure they had the best chance to win. On the part of the spectators, this usually amounted to a lot of yelling and calling hitters who missed, losers, and pitchers who couldn't strike out the hitters, pussies.

Rivotra sometimes went to the games, but he was not interested in the practices. Instead he first checked out the gym to see who was in the weights area. It proved to be inhospitable, so he returned to the barracks for an early shower. As he was rinsing his hair, he heard a voice.

"Hey! Yo! You! Good! You're here!" It was Erik. "Rivotra, I need help!"

"I'm naked, what more help do you need?" Rivotra retorted.

That confused the teenager for almost three full seconds before he apparently got the joke and laughed nervously. "Not that kind of help. Besides, your skin isn't what I would call top-notch boner material."

"Thanks a lot." Rivotra turned off the water, squeezed the excess water from his hair, and grabbed a towel.

"Yeah, sorry, man, it's just—"

"What—do—you—need?"

"Man, I got a math test tomorrow, and I don't know what I'm gonna do! I don't understand this!"

Rivotra toweled off and grabbed his clothes. "And this is your first test?"

"Well, yeah. But if I fail, I might not be able to go to the big baseball game everyone's been talking about!"

Ancestors forbid. Rivotra sighed and, having dressed, exited the showers. "All right, what's this big test of yours?"

"Adding and subtracting I get, that's fine. But then we got to do this big ol' times tables and shit with the multiplication and division. I think I got the times tables, but I don't know fractions."

For a moment, Rivotra knew an enormous burden of insult on behalf of every person with at least a third year education. Then he knew a similar burden of scorn for American public education. Fine, so the kid was a high school dropout, but how had he made it even that far? Did he at least know his letters and numbers?

They returned to the cell where Erik apparently had everything all spread out over both bunks.

"All right, what do you need help with?" Rivotra asked, forcing his voice to remain neutral. He might be annoyed that the kid was dumb, but he could give him credit that he was asking for help and genuinely seemed to want it.

"I don't know how to keep all these little symbols straight, for one. I mean, I know my pluses and minuses, but then I got these here that...why's there got to be a hundred different ways to say you want to multiply or divide something? Like this symbol here." Before Rivotra could remind Erik that he was blind, the kid was already stuttering an apology. "Yeah, no, sorry. This symbol here, it's like a line but it's slanted."

319

Rivotra discovered something interesting in that moment. Because he couldn't picture the symbol in his head, he actually didn't know what symbol was being discussed. He could do math just fine, but actually thinking about the numbers and symbols—and letters, when he took it further—he had no clue. Just how visual had his memory been? Was that normal for humans, or was he skewed too far to the visual side of things? Only when he managed to dredge up a math lecture from a century ago, and trace the described symbol on his palm, was he able to recall that this was, in fact, a division symbol.

"Okay," Erik said uncertainly, "but what about this one? It's like a box and there's like this curve in it—"

Reluctantly, Rivotra held out his hand. "Interesting aspect of my blindness. It's not in my eyes, it's in my brain. I can't see anything and I can't picture it in my head either. Trace it on my hand."

The kid did so. Rivotra then traced the same path, and memories of writing out that symbol hundreds of thousands of times informed him that this, too, was division.

It was a different kind of tutoring session, much slower than what it might have been if Rivotra could see. At the same time, the slower pace, having to trace the symbols and give them some thought seemed to help the hyperactive dropout. Rivotra even made him trace out the numbers, which also brought things down to a more manageable pace. After a couple hours, Erik had calmed down and seemed far more confident in his ability to do second year math. And, as it turned out the next day, he did very well on his test.

What started as a single instance of help quickly morphed into regular tutoring. About twice a week, Erik would corner Rivotra either in the cafeteria at dinner or in the showers, panicking over an upcoming test and begging for help. If he didn't have to be at his veterans support group, Rivotra would agree, and the two of them would spend at least a couple hours going over the material, tracing the numbers and symbols on Rivotra's hands, moving slowly and methodically until it clicked in Erik's mind.

"Man, thanks to you, I'm not failing my class, and I'll get to go to the game next week!" Erik gushed one night as they wrapped up. It was about ten minutes until lights out.

"You really like baseball that much?" Rivotra wondered.

"I mean, it's something normal to do in here, right? And...well, I don't really care about baseball, but it's one thing that I used to do with my dad when I was a kid."

"What happened to him?"

"He was a coal miner. There was an accident. That's all I know. After that, no more dad, no more baseball, no more money."

Rivotra nodded absently.

"What about your dad?" Erik wondered, putting his schoolwork in his tub and climbing up into his bunk.

"My biological father was a rapist. My stepfather beat me and treated me like a slave. Ran away from home when I was sixteen, joined the army."

"PTSD fucked you up, didn't it?"

Rivotra shrugged as he got into bed. No need to get into the details. "Yeah. It did."

"I thought about that once, going into the army. It always looked so...disciplined and heroic and cool and stuff. Thought maybe I could bring in some money while being a hero, maybe do something with my life. Then I saw what they made in a year. Motherfucker, I was making more than that in three months selling drugs."

"And somehow, we both ended up here."

"Yeah, no shit." Then there was a massive rustling and shuffling up top. "Well, good night!"

Erik was still naive and annoying as hell, but he wasn't really a bad kid, Rivotra reflected. He may have threatened an undercover cop with a gun, but Rivotra was willing to bet that the kid hadn't had nearly the intent or conviction that he'd had at the warehouse. An empty show of force versus foolishly trying to summon evil spirits with some vague notion of vanquishing them.

Even if the inmates weren't all into baseball, the tournament against the officers' team was, hands down, the biggest occasion in the prison. It was almost amazing how much trash talk could be gotten away with between officers and inmates as almost everyone from both sides made passive aggressive remarks about what would happen if one team or the other won.

The officers liked to remind everyone that they had won the tournament for the last eight years. The inmates frequently commented on what they were going to do when they won this year. As the days wound down, the trash talk only got louder and more creative. As long as it didn't come across as a truly tangible threat, no action was immediately taken, although Rivotra was willing to bet that the officers were cataloging who was saying what so that punishment could be doled out later in various forms.

The day before the game, Rivotra headed to commissary to possibly see about some snacks. He didn't care for baseball, but he was not immune to the hype, and this might be fun to, well, listen to. But when he tried to open the door, he found it locked. Before he could process his confusion, someone spoke up, maybe thirty feet from his right side.

"Commissary's closed today!"

"Why?" Rivotra wondered.

"Getting ready for the tournament. Pack a trailer full of goodies, sell them as concessions."

Apparently this event was bigger than he thought. "Are there cheerleaders, too?"

Whoever was talking laughed. "Man, don't even bring that up. Trust me. It didn't go well last time. I mean, maybe you wouldn't care, but we don't need to see the warden in a bikini again."

Rivotra was suddenly glad he didn't have the capability to picture such a thing, although the description was no more flattering.

Considering that nothing in commissary was truly necessary for life and limb, Rivotra had no choice but to leave.

The previous year, Rivotra had been bedridden in the hospital, didn't even know about the existence of this big baseball tournament. He'd assumed that it was like any other baseball game, three innings after dinner.

It was not. After lunch on game day, everyone who was in good standing was given the option to ignore their afternoon chores and attend the first of three nine-inning games which apparently started at one o'clock. Some were not in good standing and had to report to chores. Others were entirely disinterested and went to chores anyway. Some went to chores so they didn't have to sit through the full nine innings.

Rivotra elected to go to the game, if only to do something semi-normal. He almost didn't need his cane to get around, just follow the noise. Shouting, cheering, banging on the metal bleachers. He ran into the concession line first, took his place, and waited.

Such a special event was apparently not special enough to warrant a sale on concessions, but neither did it command a premium. Rivotra got his snacks—beef jerky and a bag of M&Ms—and made his way, slowly, to his seat in the top corner.

The previous year's losers, that is, the inmates, were first to bat. The announcer on the PA informed everyone that the first batter was 955463, Jared "Indigo" Wells. After one strike, Wells managed to score a double, to the delight of the inmates in the stands. The next batter was Carlos "No Mañana" Rodriguez. After three foul balls, he at least got a respectable single base hit.

Rivotra wondered if the nicknames the announcers was espousing were the actual nicknames, or just ones he made up. Although the number of long-standing inmates who didn't have a nickname were few, they did exist, and they tended to be the well-behaved ones who were able to keep up their sports privileges for months and years.

The next batter managed a good hit, and Jared crossed home plate, but the officers were quick enough with the ball that they outed the other two. The next batter up was a quick one-two-three-strike.

The teams switched positions.

No matter how bored someone might be, baseball was still a very long game. Rivotra finished his snacks by the fourth inning—and that was forcing himself to not eat them at times—and was soon mentally looking around for something else to do. The officers were up 5-2, and the sun was merciless with not a cloud in sight according to a few nearby observers.

"Next up to bat, Lieutenant Remy Oswald!" the announcer said.

Rivotra turned his attention back to the game, a sudden idea in his head. It would be easier if he could see, but maybe he could do this by feel. His first thought was to manipulate the ball, except it was too small to find quickly. If he'd thought about this sooner, he might have prepared, but there was nothing to be done about it now. He got lucky that Oswald only nicked the first ball as a foul, and he turned his attention to the lieutenant. After months of having him fairly close by, he knew him well enough that he could find him with a Band with little effort, in spite of the crowds and unfamiliar, blind landscape.

He Slow Banded the lieutenant first. It wasn't a lot—with any luck the man wouldn't even notice anything amiss—and he kept the Band variable so the lieutenant couldn't potentially compensate for the time differential. The next pitch was thrown to a grandiose whiff of a strike. Next, Rivotra Fast Banded the lieutenant, again, just strong enough and with just enough variance to throw off the ball-eye coordination. This time he did manage to hit, but the shortstop caught the ball in short order and whipped it to first base who tagged the lieutenant.

This caused quite an uproar among the inmates, clamoring to deride Oswald and his magically disappearing home runs.

Now amused by his own little game, Rivotra began targeting players at random. A pitcher appeared to throw the ball faster. An outfielder had a sudden burst of speed as he tried to intercept a fly ball. A batter swung too early or too late. It wasn't every player, nor on every pitch or hit, but just enough to make the game interesting, and he even gave the inmates a little leg up. In the end, the inmates won 6-4.

This proved to be a ridiculously big deal going into a late dinner and the noise alone gave Rivotra a headache. Erik didn't make things any easier, and once lights out came around, there was no escaping the overly-excitable teenager as he tossed and turned and took it upon himself to give Rivotra a play-by-play descriptive account of the game.

The following morning at breakfast, Rivotra learned that for at least the last six years, the tournament had never even reached the third game; the officers always swept the first two. For the inmates to have won at all was a huge deal.

So, that afternoon, Rivotra decided to see what would happen if things were forced into the third game. He continued to have a little fun with both teams, Banding players briefly here and there, just enough to spice things up. He didn't give the officers too much to brag about, however, as the final score for the second game only came out 7-6.

Despite the loss, dinner was another madhouse. The players on the inmate team were treated like national celebrities and men willingly gave up portions of their dinner to ensure the players were fed well so they could kick some ass the next day. Other men bartered general prison favors—good clothes from laundry, picking up chore shifts for a day or a week or a month, doing school homework for a week, discounts on goods in commissary, various legal and illegal goods from unnamed sources—in hopes of both easing any mental stresses and currying favor so any man could say he was a personal friend of such-and-such celebrity.

If any psychologist wanted to conduct any kind of sociological study, prison was the place to do it, Rivotra reflected, returning to his bunk. He wondered if any civilian staff were allowed to go to the games and what they thought about all of this. Did the social workers root for the officers to win, because they were employed by the prison? Or did they root for the inmates because they were patients in need of constructive rehabilitation? Did they take the easy way out and just root for both?

"Man, I can't sleep," Erik said overhead. It had only been five minutes since lights out. "I am just so pumped for the game tomorrow!" There was rustling and Rivotra knew he was leaning over the edge, looking at him. "What's it take to join the team, you know?"

"I have no idea," Rivotra told him. "That would be something to ask your social worker."

"Yeah, he told me about it early on when I first got the tour and all my papers and schedules and stuff, but I didn't pay much attention. But if this is like, you know, the Superbowl, that means it's the end of the season, right?" Rivotra didn't know American sports, but he had a suspicion that the Superbowl was not related to baseball. "Which means I couldn't join until the spring." He made a sound and rolled back over on his mattress. "Man, that's bullshit. I have to wait how many months?"

"It means you won't be distracted during your studies," Rivotra told him. "And doing well in your studies will let you keep up your sports privileges so you can play in the spring."

"Yeah, I guess. School is boring, though. Like, with your help, it went from impossible and boring, to just boring."

Erik was still talking as Rivotra drifted off to sleep, and the kid was awake and talking when morning count came around. Had he slept at all? It didn't seem like it. Going to breakfast, Rivotra wondered if he was the only person who had gotten any sleep. Everyone was talking excitedly, inmate and officer alike. Even those who were largely disinterested in baseball were getting into the conversation.

Morning chores were still required, but he doubted much got done that was not necessary. If he had to compare it to anything, morning chores, and even lunch, were like the gates in a horse race. The horses were raring to go, ready to burst with speed and strength and adrenaline; they just needed to hear the bell and launch out of the gate.

Other than places where meals had to be delivered, such as the nursing home, the Fishbowl, and the Hole, takeout was not an option at mealtime. All food had to be consumed inside the cafeteria. There was also a rule that all food taken had to be consumed, no food waste allowed. While normally a somewhat flexible rule, there was little need for it at all today. Men went with half portions just so they had enough to not be ravenous, but not so much that they were slowed down any more than they needed to be. Besides, they would just get more snacks from the concession trailer if they needed to.

Rivotra got his normal food and was intentionally one of the last to the game, taking his seat just as the first pitch was thrown. The inmates, as the losers from the previous day, were up to bat first. The announcer could barely be heard over the roar of the crowd, and the PA system could not be turned up loud enough to even whisper above the cheers when the first hit resounded across the landscape. Even if it only earned the team one base, it was still forward progress.

Rivotra elected not to do anything until the fifth inning. By then, the inmates were actually up 5-2. He considered not doing anything at all. Maybe losing the first game and being currently behind was breaking the morale of the officers. Maybe he should let things progress on their own, let the inmates score a natural win.

Then Oswald got up to bat and hit a home run that put three guys over home plate, tying the teams at 5-5. Any cheering from the officers was drowned out by the resounding boos from the inmates.

Rivotra managed to sabotage the rest of the lineup, but he knew the inmates wouldn't be happy unless they won. Some shift in the atmosphere was very reminisce of an antsy army that's about to mutiny and unleash holy hell on anything in the vicinity if they weren't given another, more desirable task quickly. The last time he had felt this shift was when Julianna led her coup against him, taking three-quarters of his men with her.

He had no choice but to interfere now, and he enjoyed himself far less this time around. Suddenly, for him, it was no longer a game within a game, but a mission to prevent a potentially very serious issue, maybe even save lives. As the fifth inning turned into the sixth and seventh, he couldn't help but think that maybe he shouldn't have interfered in the first place. He was dealing with men who had no real control over any aspect of their lives and who weren't always known for keeping their aggression in check, especially when it came to things like anger, disappointment, and failure.

The ninth inning started, the inmates up to bat first, the score favoring them at 7-5. Rivotra elected not to do anything here, and they managed to score two runs, bringing things to 9-5 as the officers stepped up for the last time. Wanting to get this over quickly, Rivotra sabotaged each batter. The first two struck out easily. The third managed to get in a good hit despite the Band and took off for first base. Rivotra Banded all of the inmate players, unsure who was actually in a position to catch the ball and not really caring. But, whoever it was, he caught the ball for an automatic out. Three outs, end of the inning, end of the game.

The crowd erupted like a volcano, complete with an explosion of men jumping to their feet, and the thunder of their return as they landed, causing the stands to shake. They might have run down to flood the field and congratulate the players, except access to the field proper was strictly controlled, and the best the fans could do was press themselves against the fence or wherever they could find room, yelling and shouting and roaring for no real reason other than to express victorious jubilance in the most primitive manner possible. Rivotra remained where he was, grateful to be able to breathe fresh air and not body odor cooking in the hot sun, although the noise, excitement, and stress of the moment had planted the seed of a headache in his brain, and every passing moment was only giving it water.

After a minute or two, he got the bright idea to make a quick exit. If he was lucky, he could get to dinner early and possibly even finish before the bulk of the masses returned.

He was not the only one to have this idea, and he was not the first to reach the cafeteria. By the time he did walk in and get in line, news had clearly reached the cooks who were all in a frenzy over the inmates' victory over the officers. The noise of clanging pots and pans, coupled with raised voices in a comparatively small area only fueled Rivotra's headache.

He was only about halfway through his meal when the bulk of the inmates burst through the doors. Now thoroughly annoyed and with a headache that was not getting any better, Rivotra hurriedly finished his meal and retreated out of the cafeteria, making a beeline for the genpop building. Other than the posted officers, the place was eerily empty, yet mercifully quiet.

"Rest of 'em behind you?" the desk officer wondered as Rivotra entered his neighborhood and crossed the floor to his house.

He shook his head. "No, they're still celebrating in the cafeteria."

"Hm."

Suddenly the officers didn't seem too friendly. Somewhere in the back of his mind, he found a bit of smug satisfaction at the officers being knocked off their eight-year pedestal, but he was not able to enjoy it at the moment on account of his headache. The near-silence of the building was currently preventing it from turning into a migraine, but that wouldn't last unless he could fall asleep before the mob arrived.

He lay down, thought a minute, then got up and headed off to take a shower. That would help some, in more than one sense. Air conditioning physically existed within the prison, although it was tepid relief at best. Being out of the sun helped, but being cooped up in stale, stuffy air with hundreds of other warm bodies only negated that relief.

Despite the victory, curfews were still strictly enforced. Rivotra had managed to reach a heavy doze, just on the cusp of blissful unconsciousness, when the rest of the neighbors made their entrance, and he was dragged back to wakefulness. Three of his neighbors were on the baseball team, and he could hear their adoring fans still metaphorically kissing boots and other body parts. Then Erik walked in, whooping and making other nonsensical noises far past their celebratory usefulness.

"That—was—one—hell—of—a—game!" Erik shouted, his voice echoing uncomfortably in the tiny house. "Woo! My daddy woulda loved that!"

"Keep yelling like that and you can tell him all about it in person," Rivotra grumbled.

"Man, that was exciting! I am definitely going to try out in the spring!" Erik clambered up into his bunk as noisily as he possibly could, sighing obnoxiously and rattling off a string of highlights from the game, most of them having to do with the inmate pitcher striking out the officer at bat. He finished with, "You know, man, I think I'm going to be okay."

Rivotra did not ask what he meant, nor was he inclined to ever ask, but the kid volunteered the information anyway.

"You know, I got a four-to-twelve sentence for my setbacks. Didn't sound like much, especially 'cause, you know, parole and stuff, but then when I got here, it was like, reality hit. Four to twelve, if I'm lucky. And then the drugs and the rehab and the school and the everything else, and you know what I mean? I didn't think I was going to make it. You know, lot a y'all are pretty cool, ain't no one tried to kill me yet, an' I figure that suckin' dick is a small price to pay for—"

"Good grief, you think I want to hear about that?" Rivotra cut in.

"Hey, no homo, man. Gotta do what you gotta do. I got too many classes and groups and shit to get a job and make money. Commissary and tattoos are expensive." He added quickly, "At least you don't have an imagination no more. Don't gotta see it, don't gotta picture it."

"I still don't want to hear about it. And if you do what I think you're about to do, you're going to lose it."

But the teenager, still hyped up from the game and now apparently thinking in his drug-rotted brain that annoying a man with a headache was a funny idea, did it anyway, gleefully exaggerating the noise from pulling his pants down and his cock out.

Rivotra, head pounding, got out of bed, reached up, and dragged Erik off his bunk, letting gravity do the work for him. Then, once the teenager was down, he gave him a lop-sided kick between the legs to parts that were ostensibly clear out in the open air. The teenager could only make a strangled sound of pain, sputtering incoherently.

"I don't want to hear it," Rivotra repeated sternly.

Still groaning, Erik finally found his voice. "Come on, man. You can't be that old. You can't tell me—"

Rivotra knelt beside him as best he could. "You're right. I'm not telling you. One way or the other. Because, quite frankly, in your own slang and vernacular, telling is homo, isn't it?"

Erik let out a breath and did not reply. Rivotra waited as the whimpering teen pulled himself together and shimmied his way back up to the top bunk. Then he lay back down, closed his eyes, and finally found sleep.

The following morning, the prison was still abuzz with excitement and activity. Any officers who hadn't worked the previous day were informed of their defeat, whether by the previous shift or the inmates as they headed to breakfast—now with seconds—and morning chores. Any officers who had been on the team were reminded of it constantly throughout the day.

Nothing truly bad had come of the celebratory crowd that had, at times, bordered on a riotous mob, although there were reports of several inmates whose rowdiness had become excessive to the point where they earned themselves a trip to the Hole.

After morning chores, Rivotra decided to try his luck in the weights area. Walking into the recreational building, however, he was greeted by a voice he did not expect. It was Oswald, his words and tone, as well as the click of a phone in its receiver, suggesting he was just getting off the phone.

"What's a lieutenant doing on desk duty?" Rivotra wondered, approaching the desk.

"What do you think?" Oswald asked, tone grouchy.

"You hit a home run and put three guys over the plate."

"Still lost."

"And this somehow warrants punishment? Isn't being locked up in here with us punishment enough? And being reminded constantly of your loss?"

Oswald's chair squeaked. "I think I told you once that warden likes things orderly and predictable. Well, he's also a big baseball fan. Literally the only reason we're allowed to have a team. And we are expected to win."

Rivotra shifted his stance. "Sports may have rules, but they aren't something I consider to be orderly and predictable."

"I'm not the one to talk to about that." Now the man's tone was testy.

"How long are you on desk duty? If we get one day of second helpings, you almost got one free day off of work, so, one day on desk duty?"

"Yeah." Another squeak of the chair. "Could be worse, I guess. Desk duty is massive rank-busting for me. But for the desk officers who don't have a rank to bust, they get to be on toilet duty."

Rivotra made a sympathetic noise. "Oof. That's bad. That is punishment."

"I shouldn't take it to heart, I know, but I was kind of looking forward to that extra day off."

"At least you didn't get a day taken away, right?"

"That is true." Yet another squeak. "All right, off with you. Whatever you were doing."

"You're not going to interview me again to assess my propensity for violence?"

"If you were going to do something, yesterday would have been the day to do it. And I'm guessing you don't want to risk anything with your appeal coming up next month."

Rivotra frowned and made a sound not unlike a scoff. "You seem to have more faith than I do in that."

"A lot of appeals do get rejected," Oswald acknowledged. "The majority of those that do go through, well, the person's kicked back here after they're found guilty in a retrial. But you never know."

"You sound oddly optimistic for the appeal of a cop-killer."

The chair again squeaked obnoxiously. "The turnkeys who turn over the fastest are those who walk in every day with a cocky, badass attitude, believing they are God and you are the devil, and they have a chance to beat the ever-living fuck out of you any time they want because you deserve it."

"So you know Francisco."

The lieutenant ignored him. "Those turnkeys end up one of two ways: unemployed, or dead. On the other hand, you have some turnkeys who are better off being social workers because they believe too much in the good of humanity. They, too, end up unemployed or dead.

"The ones who last the longest, who get where I am, are those who are willing to see you guys as human beings. Now, we got some very, very bad people in here. They deserve to be here because if they're not here, they're going to go straight back to doing what they were doing that got them here. Those guys, you don't turn your back on them. You know that. Then there are others who should serve punishment for a crime, but it may very well be that they can be more productive if they are allowed back into normal life. Now, that's not a very popular opinion in this line of work, and it's why I'll probably never be anything more than a lieutenant, but I stand by it. You can dodder around here, watering chickens and folding laundry, and ultimately achieve fuck all. Or you can go home and help your people."

Rivotra frowned. "What about the...paying a debt to society?"

"You're not doing shit for society except for being out of the way and not bothering them. Once a sentence is passed, the general public couldn't give two fucks what happens to you. Here for one year, five years, twenty years, whatever, the only thing they care about is the media sensation, the verdict and hearing that there's a nice, long sentence. All they want is gossip. Two, five, ten years go by, no one remembers you even exist. Not too many people care when an inmate is released, or why, or how, or any of that."

"You don't think that my victims would care if my appeal goes through and I go home?"

"They might. But again, all you're doing here is taking up space and consuming resources. You're not paying any debt except being away from them. It wouldn't really matter whether you're here or on the other side of the world."

"And you're sure I won't just go out and murder more people?"

"We've had model inmates go out and kill five people their first day free. I can't be sure of anything. As I said, I'm popular for my skill in baseball, not politics."

Rivotra nodded. "I can understand why." He tapped the desk with his cane. "Enjoy desk work."

"Fuck off."

The group in the weights area was an accommodating one, and they let him in. As always, one of his first stops was the pullup bar.

He didn't know much about the American judiciary, but he'd heard from other inmates that crime victims were always notified of goings-on with their criminal. Death, parole, a successful appeal, certain other circumstances, the victims were legally obligated to be notified. Whether this always happened, that was up for some debate, but, by and large, it was a reliable process.

He could respect that he wasn't supposed to know anything about his victims, where they were, what they were doing, and so on. And yet, with Tommen dead and Owain moved so far away that his location was unknown even to the lawyers, would they still try to contact at least Owain? If Josina had approached the man under the pretext of investigating his, Rivotra's, death, what would he make of a notice stating that his dead adversary had just been granted an appeal? Mistaken identity? Practical joke? Would he ignore it? Investigate it? If he really was learning the Akari now, Rivotra would place a bet that investigation was more likely.

Would Owain take it upon himself to exact revenge? How long before the news of his survival made its way to Julianna? All things considered, he was surprised he had lasted this long. A year and a half since his murder, and it seemed as though no one suspected a thing.

No one, except the Krydik who knew the truth. They were only keeping quiet because they wanted sole rights of judgment. But what if, playing devil's advocate, what if Nendawagan chose not to execute him? How much loyalty did she command? Would anyone seek personal revenge, regardless of any punishment they might incur? Or would they just let it slip that he was alive and let someone else finish him off?

The bench press opened up. Rivotra dropped to the ground and made his way over.

Of course, how long had he lived *without* such a threat hanging over his head? If it wasn't his stepfather, it was one war or faction or another. Other than a few reprieves here and there, most of his life had been lived in danger, with and without Time and the Akari. And still he lived.

Eventually, Rivotra made his way to most of the machines, taking his time and cutting into the standard lunch period. That was all right, though. His chores were not so labor-intensive or mentally-complex that he needed every spare minute to accomplish them. He could be the last one to lunch, the last one to afternoon chores, and still finish with plenty of time to spare. He finally left the cage about one o'clock and made for the cafeteria.

Lunch was less cacophonous than breakfast, although conversation still rested squarely on the game and the second helping reward. No one asked for his opinions, and he volunteered nothing. Of course, he wouldn't have much to say. Everything he knew about the game, everyone else did, too. The only thing he knew that they didn't was how their team won, and he wasn't about to give that up.

Afternoon chores came and went, and dinner was much of the same.

And still he continued to live, he mused. Intergalactic armies and petty street thugs, and that was just in the last few years. He should be dead one hundred times over. But each time, he had just enough. The Runner's pickax, his swing just off enough that although he may have blinded Rivotra, he didn't kill him. Aklaq's knife in his chest, off just enough that his heart was unharmed and, in an odd turn of events, the wound itself may have actually played a part in saving him. Murdered by his generals yet found by inmates who miraculously cared enough to try and save his life, with just enough time to spare to actually bring him back.

Losing the entirety of his inheritance, yet the government official who bought the farm maintained just enough sympathy to offer him a place to live and a chance to do what he'd always wanted. It wasn't perfect, it wasn't his ideal, but it was just enough.

Spiritual eyes, he told himself. Rifun wanted wealth and power. Rivotra needed to learn to be content with just enough. Erik wanted goodies from commissary and various illegal tattoos, and he was literally putting his mouth on other men's penises to get those things. He was whoring himself out in order to get ahead in a place that was the bottom of the proverbial societal barrel. He was going nowhere. He had nothing coming. If Rivotra could maintain even the most basic of personal and social standards, why shouldn't he be able to do the same in the spiritual sense?

He finished dinner, returned his tray and utensils, then headed to his support group. One day at a time, they were talking about. It didn't matter if their goals were only one hour in advance. If that was all they thought they could achieve, then make that goal and strive for it.

Rivotra knew that mantra. One more hour. Just one more hour. How much longer could a soldier endure traumatic hardship? At least one more hour. Pretty soon, one hour became two, then three, then six, then twelve, then a whole twenty-four hour day. Just one more hour. Just enough to trick the mind, just enough to get by. And live.

The session ended, although most of the men were neighbors in one of three neighborhoods, and they returned to these neighborhoods in groups. Rivotra walked with four other men, the desk officer—another failed member of the officers' baseball team—not bothering to greet them as they walked by. The group broke up, and Rivotra made his way to the showers. It didn't hit him until later, but for the first time in over a year, he was not anxious about going into the showers. He did not have an underlying dread that something bad was going to happen.

It wasn't much. Just enough.

Despite knowing full well that it was all a dream, and the fact that Anagalisgi had been nothing but professional all throughout this alleged healing process, there were still some areas of the body that Rivotra was uncomfortable with people touching, no matter how necessary. Actually, he was very sensitive to touch everywhere, but he could suppress most of it. This did not include places like his groin, buttocks, knees, or Achilles tendon, and it took everything in him not to lash out at the Native man, or else try to run away.

"Learning to use your spiritual eyes takes time, but I think you are starting to understand the concept," Anagalisgi said conversationally.

"It's not about evaluating others and discerning their motives," Rivotra said stiffly, unable to take too much attention off the needle that danced around his left ankle. "It's about looking at myself and discerning mine."

"When it comes to the sins of others, we are the world's harshest judges. When it comes to our own sins, we are the world's most argumentative lawyers." Anagalisgi gently poked the needle through the skin just over the tendon. "It is not wrong to judge others and call out their sins, but we must do so from the correct perspective. Not one of hypocrisy, but loving warning, because we have walked those roads."

"Because sometimes there is no reward. Only death."

"Mhm."

Rivotra swallowed as the needle made another successful pass. "Have you given Nendawagan this lecture?"

Anagalisgi laughed. "You don't need to worry about her just yet."

"But have you? She's not exactly what I'd call an impartial judge."

"No, but you have said it yourself, is not the offense between the two of you and no one else? Who has the right to judge?"

"I offended the entire Krydik tribe. It's me against all of them."

"And the judge has been chosen," Anagalisgi stated, his tone still smiling. "One more hour, Rivotra. One hour at a time, one day at a time."

Rivotra sighed and tried to force himself to relax. This was not fully possible until the man declared the wound healed and the needle did not touch that area anymore. Cautiously, he straightened his leg and flexed his foot.

"I don't have the Akari, but Time has been serving me well enough where I am," he said, turning his head in the direction he believed the man to have gone. "But will I ever get my Akari abilities back? Will I ever be able to heal myself fully in real life?"

"That remains to be seen," Anagalisgi replied, not far off. "Of him who is entrusted with much, much is expected. He who can be entrusted with little, will be entrusted with more. Right now, you have been entrusted with a little. What are you making of it?"

Rivotra took an even breath and considered this. "I sabotaged a baseball tournament, realized that may not have been my brightest idea. So I suppose it might be a while before I am entrusted with much more than that."

Anagalisgi laughed again, once more approaching and kneeling now on his other side. "You have been entrusted with hardship, confinement, a broken body, and deprivation of senses. Any one of these things, men would tell you to be bitter and mournful. Yet here you are."

"I don't want to be entrusted with hardship."

"No one does. But, although I do not know specifics, I do know that you will be entrusted with more in the future."

"Then I am going to survive Nendawagan's judgment?"

Now the man sighed dramatically and touched Rivotra's right ankle, feeling along the wound there, looking for a place to stick his needle. "Focus on the present, Rivotra. One more hour, one more day."

"But—"

"One more hour, one more day. Right now, you should be focusing here, on the work being done in this cave."

"I'm focusing more on not throttling you." Rivotra flinched as the needle punctured skin.

"How long has it been since you've had a fully healed, fully-functioning body?"

Rivotra paused and thought about that. Well, he'd taken a pickax to the head in 1923, when he was twenty-six years old. Before that, he might consider any time he had managed to escape his stepfather's wrath for a few consecutive days.

As if reading his thoughts, Anagalisgi asked, "Have you ever considered what you are going to do with your body when it is healed? I don't mean your physical body in the waking world, I mean this one. Your eyes have been returned to you, and your wounds are almost all stitched up. What comes after the healing?"

The question caught him off-guard, if only because he'd never quite considered himself in such a way before. He knew what he would do with his physical body. He would work. He would farm. But what would he do with his spiritual self? When Anagalisgi finished his work and dismissed him from the cave, what did he expect to do? Stay here forever? Where could he go? What could he do?

"The spirit requires nourishment and exercise just as much as the body," Anagalisgi went on. "And if you consider that all have such a form, what would you expect someone in good condition to do if he came across someone who was just as broken and helpless as he was?"

"The last time I tried to help people spiritually—"

"You were just as broken as they were, crawling around in the dirt, believing that killing them was a mercy because healing was not possible. Now you know that is not true. Now you are almost healed, getting stronger, and will become more capable with time." Anagalisgi's needle again threaded its way closer and closer to a very sensitive area, and Rivotra struggled to focus on the man's words. "The question becomes, are you out to conquer the mountain once for glory, or to help those who have fallen in their own futile attempts?"

Fourteen
Preparation

August rolled into September. It did little for the heat in general, although the rain was starting to provide mild relief rather than only add to the humidity.

Work at the farm started ramping up for the fall harvest, and Rivotra was able to keep his chores for yet another month. He was told that toward the end of the month, he might be tapped as extra help sorting vegetables. Vision helped, true, but if he could differentiate a tomato from a cucumber based on feel, he could get in some extra work. And this was in addition to ensuring the chickens were ready for butchering, which would take place in October. After Rivotra finished cleaning the coop in the afternoon, he would help to catch the chickens so they could be inspected by the agricultural students. He didn't chase any chickens, but he could hold a board to prevent their escape in one direction, or generally hold a net for them to run into and become tangled.

With all this excitement on the prison farm, Rivotra found himself almost sick with anxiety over his impending appeal. Was he putting too much hope in this, too much faith in the American judiciary? At his trial, his lawyer had pressed hard on American politics in regard to his race, religion, and foreign background, pulling every emotional heartstring he could. And it had worked, for the most part. Appeals didn't involve such arguments; they were concerned with the procedures and technicalities of the trial itself. Bartlett was seizing on some odd happenings with the jury selection, and Josina was arguing the lack of communication to Madagascar, plus whatever other "irregularities" she had uncovered. But would it be enough?

Anagalisgi wanted him to focus on the present moment, which happened to be afternoon chicken coop cleaning. But always his mind slid ahead to the impending arguments. He hadn't gotten any notices from either lawyer about when they were going to visit, and he couldn't decide if no news was good news. Even if Josina wouldn't hypothetically be in the United States for a few more days, he might have expected as much advance notice as possible. On the other hand, what did it matter to him? There was absolutely nothing he could do from here. All they wanted to know was if he had anything more to add, and if anyone else wanted to lay claim to his head before this appeal got pushed back again.

His mind also conjured up the fear that something happened on the part of the state, whoever was representing the judiciary. What if something happened to that lawyer? What if he requested more time and won? Was that a thing? Rivotra really didn't know how appeals worked on a technical level; he'd avoided inquiring because he didn't want to get himself too trusting or too depressed about the process. Maybe he could ask Bartlett, if and when the man showed up.

Once the chicken coop was clean, he headed out to help the students round up another batch of chickens. They would take the chickens, examine them for any potential health problems, separate any sick or injured, determine which ones were three years old, then clip their wings to make it easier to catch them for butchering.

For as good as the food was here—hardly his mother's cooking, but miles better than other prison cuisine, according to such aficionados—Rivotra hoped he wouldn't be around for the fresh chicken dinners. If he was planning correctly, and assuming all went well, even if it took the full few weeks, he could be walking out of here the week before those dinners started. As a bonus, he wouldn't have to fight a mob of southern black men for a plate of fried chicken, nor would he have to be present for the fallout if that fried chicken was not made perfectly.

Grim humor was the only humor he was entertaining these days, and it was difficult to maintain any sense of optimism as he walked into the cafeteria for dinner and was subjected to another day where the biggest conversation still revolved around the baseball tournament. One thing about prison, with so little excitement, any and all news was whittled down to the bone before being let go.

This wasn't to say that there was no other news circulating, but most of it was of the common variety. This person put a hit out on that person. So-and-so was the unfortunate recipient of a little friendly reminder because of such-and-such incident. One officer or another was being a particularly annoying shithead today and needed to be shanked in the face.

There was some good news, too. Someone was confident that he was going to make parole this year; his meeting with the parole board was in three weeks and he was already planning where he wanted to go for dinner with his parents. Someone else's kid had turned eighteen and was now making a visitation appointment after their mom kept them away for so many years.

The evening was uneventful and Rivotra returned to his cell for a quiet night's sleep. Erik was in the Hole again for drug-related offenses. It gave him a reprieve, but when he got a letter the following morning, he had to take it to the desk officer to have it read.

"Your lawyer is coming for a visit next week," the officer summarized. "Both lawyers, I should say."

"When?" Rivotra asked.

"Next Thursday, three o'clock."

"Anything else in there?"

"Nah, it's a short letter."

He nodded, thanked the officer, returned to his cell to put the letter in his tub, then headed off to breakfast. He tried to keep calm, but his heart was racing. He shouldn't be this invested in his appeal. Most of them were rejected, why should he have so much hope? After the Author had taken everything away from him so suddenly, why should he think that she would give it all back so soon? No, he was fairly certain that he was going to be sitting here awhile.

And even if it did go through, he still had to face Nendawagan and the Krydik. That wasn't going to go well at all. Actually, thinking about it, that was probably what was going to happen. Earth-side justice had been satisfied just enough, but the Author wasn't going to cheat the Krydik of their justice, too. So, she'd get him out of here, then deliver him unto them for ultimate execution.

He had been brought back for a reason, and maybe it wasn't so he could live out a nice life back home, even if it was as a servant on his own farm. Maybe it was just enough to bring him back around, deliver him from Shadows to Whites, then let him go on good terms as it were.

He mentally nodded to himself around a bite of soy-infused sausage. He could accept that. He could even appreciate it as a gift. He couldn't be allowed to live and continue his horrendous antics, but he had been given one last chance to go out well. Yes. That he could do.

His thoughts on the matter wavered severely over the course of the week, sliding back and forth to ever more erroneous extremes as the date of the meeting drew closer. And he knew it wouldn't improve once they'd gone. Likely it would only get worse until the date of the appeal, and then worse still until the verdict was finally delivered. After that, who knew? The first appeal was always the most likely. Would he hold out hope for a second? Would his lawyer really take it all the way to the Supreme Court, of the State of West Virginia or the United States? Was his case really unique enough or interesting enough to warrant the attention of the highest court in the land? Somehow, even he didn't think so.

Erik returned from the Hole, and his naive and boisterous presence did a decent job of distracting Rivotra, at least in the early morning and late evening hours. The kid swore up and down that he didn't do it and wanted to get clean and improve his life with a GED and baseball, then immediately turned around and made comments that basically admitted that he had not only done the drugs, but quite enjoyed it. The teenager's petty problems were almost a welcome relief, but no less annoying.

"I don't know, man," Erik mused Wednesday night after lights out. "I mean, I go and do all the things, all the meetings and stuff, but you think there's something more I could do?"

"Are you still sucking cock to make money?" Rivotra asked, unsure if he wanted to know the answer, disgusted that he even had to ask the question.

"Yeah."

"Maybe try not doing that."

"What am I supposed to do for money?"

"Suffer a little while, get your GED, then you can get on the chore rotation."

"I don't know, man. I mean, I got this unfinished tattoo here, and it looks like shit until it's finished."

Rivotra rubbed his face. "I've heard fasting can help break addiction."

"Prison don't allow that. You've seen the turnkeys go apeshit 'acause someone didn't finish their dinner."

"I'm not talking about food. I'm talking about material goods. Tattoos, candy, whatever the hell you keep buying in commissary. Stop buying it. And I don't mean stop buying it because you're in the Hole, I mean, intentionally pass it by. Tell yourself no. Give it six weeks, see what happens."

"Six weeks?!"

"Fine, start with four."

Erik just groaned and muttered some protests which soon slid into snores.

Rivotra didn't get much sleep that night. He told himself it was stupid. It was just a meeting with his lawyers. Even the actual courtroom arguments weren't for another week or so. He couldn't let himself get so worked up over this; it was going to make him sick, or else he was going to be so distracted that he or someone else was going to get hurt.

The next thing he knew, it was morning count. As soon as they were released, he decided it might be a good idea to get in an early workout. Maybe he could work off some of the stress he was feeling.

It helped, but only after he pushed himself in both weight and quantity; by then, he was more focused on not killing himself under almost two hundred pounds of weight than worried about an afternoon meeting.

But, as he put the weights away and made his way to breakfast, a new worry sprouted in his mind. Now he was going to be sweaty and odorous in front of Josina. Sure, he'd been working out and doing hard work, which he hoped would impress her, but it wasn't something he needed to, well, overwhelm her with. And his afternoon chores involved the chicken coop, which was not going to add anything pleasant to the olfactory senses.

After finishing up his morning chores, he approached the team leader in the greenhouse.

"What's up?" the man asked.

"I have a meeting this afternoon with my lawyers," Rivotra informed him.

"What time?"

"Three."

"Hm...it's noon now...figure after lunch..." The team leader huffed a frustrated sigh. "You couldn't have told me this sooner?"

"Sorry."

"You know what? Go find Rocky and help him for another hour or so. You'll be on the tail end of lunch, but you won't be wasting any time between lunch and your meeting."

Rivotra nodded once and left to find Rocky. The agricultural student was busy harvesting tomatoes. Rivotra followed him around, carrying the basket full of tomatoes, and swapping out full baskets for empty ones. It was mind-numbing, but it passed the time.

After a late lunch, he had just enough time to get in a quick shower before being summoned to the meeting.

"Well, well, look at what we have here." Again, Bartlett was the first person to open his mouth when Rivotra walked in the room. "Walking and talking and working, or so they tell me. All things considered, you're looking good. Now if only we could do something about that gray hair."

"Gray?" Rivotra echoed, finding his chair and sitting down.

His thoughts suddenly tilted sideways at the word. Gray hair? Since when? He wasn't old, not bodily anyway. He might feel like it some days, but his spirit was strong. Was he really that stressed?

"It's not a lot," Josina told him.

"And it's not why we're here today," Bartlett went on, jumping into business. "Now, to my knowledge, there haven't been anymore headhunters coming after you, right? The only other entity we're competing with is the Krydik?"

Prison gangs probably didn't count, but even Ramone and the Pinto Gang had agreed to a ceasefire. "Correct."

"Good. I would hate to think Miss Zitha flew all this way for nothing. As it is, we are still on track."

"What do you need from me?"

"We're going to be arguing a lot of points. Tainted jury, the void of communication between us and Madagascar, and also possible witness tampering."

"Witness tampering?" Rivotra wondered. "Which witness?"

Tommen was the most likely candidate, seeing how he'd testified for both prosecution and defense. He was quite surprised when Bartlett said, "You."

"Me?"

"You got beat half to shit the night before your testimony. Witness intimidation."

"Except I had already beaten them," Rivotra pointed out.

"In self-defense," Bartlett insisted. "On the surface, it looks like regular jailhouse roughhousing. In context, maybe they were there to ensure you couldn't talk. Or maybe they were just bought off by an outside entity to the same effect."

"Is a judge going to buy that?"

"We're going to find out, aren't we? I pulled your medical records from the incident. Roughhousing is when you broke a couple arms after they tried to harass you. This was straight-up attempted murder. And again, it came the night before you were supposed to testify. Plus you were murdered while here in prison. Very plausible witness intimidation and attempted cleanup, I think."

It sounded like a stretch, but he wasn't going to tell the lawyer not to use the argument.

"I got a rundown from the warden here about a little issue you had with a prison gang recently. Watched the footage, too. Holy shit, that was some wild stuff. You taking on five guys and winning? Except, of course, when they flashed a light in your eyes to exploit your seizures, very similar to what happened in jail."

"Except the guys here had a different—"

"Petty gangbangers, already in for life so it's not like they have anything more to lose, possibly contracted to finish the job," Bartlett cut in, his tone telling Rivotra to shut the hell up and stop defeating all of the arguments. He heard the shifting of a chair. "You are a very tough man to kill. I respect that. God must like you."

"Someone does," Rivotra agreed evenly.

"And, really, other than these incidents, which are all entirely self-defense, you have a clean record here so far. A little misunderstanding once, I think, but, you know, you're new, you make mistakes as you try to figure things out." The lawyer's tone was a shrug. "Nothing I'm concerned about. Between the witness tampering and intimidation, these incidents here in prison, your character is shaping up to be impeccable. And that's important."

"Why? I thought appeals had more to do with the trial procedure itself."

"Oh, sure, but if we're trying to argue that a jury was tainted in order to skew their view of you to one of some savage, third-world marauder, but that's exactly how you act in here, well, were they really all that tainted? Just like in the trial, after you got beat to shit and had to give a taped interview. You remember? If I had let you walk out of the hospital that same day to testify, you would have been seen as this terrible person who could shrug off pain and keep on bulldozing his way through a hail of bullets. Instead, you had to stay and be seen as a sympathetic soul. This is no different."

Rivotra nodded uncertainly. He wanted to be out of this place, but this whole thing felt like a scam. Was this meeting really necessary? He would have been very happy to just wake up one day and be told that his appeal was granted and he was going home.

"Mr. Bartlett is also going to tie that in with the communication delay," Josina added calmly. "Either no one knew that we were supposed to be contacted, regardless of your decision, which is a serious court malfunction in its own right, or they did know. Then they either did not know that the message never got to us, which is negligence at best, or they actively concealed this blackout."

"And which do you believe it is?" Rivotra wondered.

"I have the paperwork indicating that you had been offered the chance to contact the embassy, and the paperwork saying you refused. I have the paperwork that was sent out and reached my office, thus starting the ball rolling in this investigation, and although it was dated with the correct dates for the trial, it was not postmarked until March of the next year. It hadn't been sent out until after your alleged murder."

"Paperwork doesn't print, sign, or send itself."

"Correct, but all of the people involved, who mean anything to this case, more than just a hand to pass through, are now gone. And that's another element that we are using in our arguments."

"What do you mean, gone?"

"They skipped town shortly before or after your murder," Bartlett answered, "and no one seems to know where they went, even their own families. Believe me, the more we've dug into this, the more questions come up. As far as your case, I think we have more than enough to overturn your conviction."

"It is, however," Josina went on, "drawing more eyes in the realm of international judiciary and investigation. INTERPOL, the CIA, Mossad, all of those agencies. It's less about you specifically and more about the group you were involved with, this Cult of the Akari. In Jezik is being tossed around, too, again."

"Am I going to have to testify to something?" Rivotra wondered, knowing a moment of fear at the thought of being interrogated by the CIA.

"Not yet," Bartlett told him. "First we have to get through this appeal. We haven't heard much more from the Krydik; apparently some issues at home have their greater interest right now. But if they don't make a move before you walk out, well, I imagine Miss Zitha can easily fight any extradition orders from the comfort of her office at home, and you can relax under a tropical sun."

Rivotra nodded slowly, then Banded himself and Josina. "How many people know I'm alive?"

"Myself, the Krydik," she told him, her tone uncertain. "There are Time Agents in the CIA and other organizations. They are few in number, but greater than zero. I've managed to do a little detective work of my own, managed to keep them out of this case. I've also been able to obscure your name specifically, either through classification and redaction, or by shifting you to the past tense. Using your former name helps, too. Getting rid of the properties and closing out those cases has allowed me to better erase your name from—"

"What did you say?" Rivotra cut in. "What do you mean, getting rid of the properties?"

Josina made a kind of strangled sound and paused. Then, "The Mahitsy properties had already been decided, or were close enough. The people wanted the houses destroyed, the land cordoned off as haunted by vengeful

349

spirits. There was nothing anyone could have done short of an executive order from the president or National Assembly."

"And the farms around Fianar?" he demanded hotly.

"Your claim was the only thing holding up the process. It could have stayed that way just fine, until our investigation for this appeal started to really get the attention of all those international agencies. If you wanted to remain dead and out of sight, you had to be dead and out of sight. A dead man claims no inheritance."

Rivotra stood angrily and hobbled away from the table several steps. "Handling my appeal at all is going to alert them to my not being dead!"

"I am here investigating your death," Josina said sharply. "That is all the international community cares about on my end."

"And Bartlett? He's here to spring me. Is he trying to get my body exhumed for some reason?"

"It's not perfect, but I'm trying. How often are people murdered for money, power, influence, or land? You stood to inherit a lot of land. Maybe this terrorist group was interested in the land, so killing you and your family provided some opportunity. I don't know. Do you know how hard it is to convince two international conspiracies that the other doesn't exist? The CIA wants to look into your terrorist connections, but they don't know the Akari or Julianna or the intergalactic community exists. Julianna wants to go on a murder spree and will use any means necessary, including terrorism, and she can't be allowed to know that you exist. I imagine it is only a matter of time before I am under serious investigation as well."

Rivotra ran his hands through his hair, a stray thought floating through his mind about how much of it was really gray, or if his lawyer was just pulling his leg. After a moment, he sighed and turned in her general direction, though he did not return to the table. "Did the farms go to good people?"

"They did, yes," Josina answered quietly. "And even now, the houses and land have been cleaned up and the soil tilled once more."

He let out a breath and nodded. "And do you know who got the family farm, the government official? He can't be that bad if he's willing to let me live there as a hired hand. Assuming this appeal pans out."

"I do know. She's not living there yet."

"She? The official's widow, then, I assume."

"No, no, she is the official. She's still based in Tana. But she expects that once this case is over, due to the size and nature of this lie, she will either be forced out of the job or she may voluntarily resign. Contacts at the University of Fianar are in talks to have her teach law there next year."

Rivotra blinked. "You bought the farm."

"It was the only way to try and save it for you. No Merina official would care so much about what this farm means to you. They might work it as a farm, yes, pass it down to their children, but it's just another home to them." She hummed a sigh. "If this appeal goes through, that is where you will live, if you want. Once I start teaching at the university, I will give the farm back to you."

He didn't know what to think. It almost felt too good to be true. "But why? Why not just live there yourself?"

"I figure it would only be temporary anyway." Her tone was dismissive, if sad. "Teach at the university for a while, try to put time and distance between me and this case, earn back some money—the farm did not go cheap, you will be happy to know—and then probably return to my family. Fish, farming, and family. And you will have your farm back."

Rivotra still didn't know what to think. He didn't know what to do. What he could do. The best he could manage was to return to the table with an awkward, "Why do you think you will have to leave your job? Are you under investigation?"

"Not to my knowledge, but I suspect it is only a matter of time. There's plenty of corruption in the government, you know that. But the Senate doesn't like when that corruption is potentially exposed to international investigation. In order to protect you, I have to lie. A lot. Bigger and more often than I could have imagined." There was the sound of shifting in her seat. "And if I'm going to track down Julianna, it would be better if things were quiet."

He nodded absently. "Why help me this much? You're a lawyer representing her client, conducting an investigation. We've spoken half a dozen times at most. Or is this just something you routinely do for your clientele?"

She laughed. "Hardly. No, I..." She hummed as if searching for the right words. "I'm not here to solve one puzzle and move on to the next one. I'm not just here to collect a paycheck. Your murder has been solved. We know who did it. But it's not enough. I want to make things right. If the *ampanzaka* understand anything, it is inheritance, legacy, and dynasty. When my family was murdered, I at least had a home and family to go to. I want to help you get your life back and restore your family name. And I will do that, even if it costs me my job with the Senate. Obviously, I can find work, whether it's in Fianar teaching at the university, or maybe in Nosy Be as a lawyer, or just at home with the farm and the fish."

"I..." He shook his head. "I don't know what to say. Thank you feels...so inadequate."

"Don't worry. I understand."

It was still a long moment before he considered dropping the Band, but he could barely remember what the conversation before had been. Something about his appeal, sure, but what were they discussing? Did he care anymore?

"I'm going to leave here the day after the appeal," Josina told him. "When I get back home, I'm going to take a few days to travel to Fianar and start cleaning up the house, making sure it's clean and ready for your arrival."

"You really think this appeal has a chance?" Rivotra wondered, his brain slowly coming back around to the present moment. "From a legal standpoint, do you really think so?"

"This isn't the first time I've interacted with the American legal system, for either trial or appeal. And I won't lie, appeals are tough. The system is remarkably rigid, and lawyers are very quick to point out and close loopholes for both law and procedure. You can't just bribe your way through like you can back home."

"You can, it just requires a lot more than we can come up with."

She chuckled. "All right, fair enough. But the fact remains, the legal system here is pretty tight. However, I do think we have a very good chance. Mr. Bartlett certainly knows the ins and outs of the system and a good argument."

Rivotra nodded. "I guess the best I can do is hope and pray and leave it in your hands."

Reluctantly, he dropped the Band. He still couldn't remember just where the conversation had been, but he figured it was safe to ask what the next step was.

"All that's left is the argument itself before a judge," Bartlett replied, entirely unaware of the earth-shattering conversation that had just taken place. "Now the good news is, that won't take long. Actually, they're timed. No more two-week trials and whatnot. Of course, that's just for the oral arguments. We also have to submit a lot of paperwork, all of our evidence that we've gathered about the proceedings and irregularities, et cetera, et cetera. That's really what takes so long for a ruling, because the judge has to go through it all.

"Anyway, once the judge makes a decision, we go back to court for what basically amounts to a coffee break. He tells us his decision, everyone agrees to it. If he rules in our favor, warden gets a call, we get in a car to come pick you up. If he rules against us, you'll get an official notification in the mail, and we start filing paperwork for a new appeal. Do you have any questions for us?"

He thought a moment, but nothing was coming to mind. Well, he had a lot of questions, but nothing that was going to make any difference in the moment. First he just had to get through this appeal. All the same, he turned his head in Josina's general direction and asked, in Malagasy, "Why did your letter say that the new owner of the farm was offering me a place to stay if things with my appeal worked out? Is the offer rescinded if it doesn't? Or were you just trying to throw me off?"

"I didn't know what was going to happen," she answered, her tone not quite an apology, "how closely I was being investigated, if at all. And I still don't, on either count. As far as I'm concerned, if I own the property, it is still yours. But if something happened, either with my position or this appeal, if I wasn't able to communicate with you, I didn't want to get your hopes up too high."

"How closely are you being investigated?"

"I just said, I don't know. Right now they're just comments in emails and phone calls, at least for me. If anyone else is being asked questions about me, I don't know."

Rivotra found this mildly disturbing, but he said nothing about it. What was he going to do, anyway? He wanted to do something for her, protect her the way she was protecting him, he just didn't know how at this moment.

"Let's get through this appeal and see what happens," Josina suggested, her tone returning to business. There was the sound of chairs scraping over the floor, and Rivotra followed suit. "I imagine it's going to be the only thing occupying your mind for the foreseeable future, so there's no need to burden you with anything else."

"We'll get you out of here," Bartlett said. "One way or another. Just keep your eyes and ears peeled. And if you have any questions or if you think of something that might help, don't hesitate to give us a call."

Rivotra thanked them and was made to wait. The lawyers were escorted out first, then he was permitted to leave.

And that was that. Unless Josina returned for another meeting for some reason, that was the last he was going to hear from them for at least a few weeks. Then he would either get picked up and whisked away, or else he would receive a letter in the mail very formally informing him that things hadn't gone well and they were pursuing other avenues of appeal. All the way to the Supreme Court if they had to!

He should have asked Josina if she had learned how to open portals yet. He was ready to go home, one way or another. At the same time, there was that whole, international manhunt business. It sounded like this case was already very popular in some very uncomfortable ways; he really didn't want to make things worse. If he did escape, there was every chance that he wouldn't spend more than one night on the family farm because someone was going to come for him. He had to keep his head low.

He wanted to go home.

As he made his way toward his afternoon chores, he found that he was just so...unenthusiastic about them. He was tired of this, tired of being here. He was tired of the people, both inmate and officer. He was tired of the same routine every day. Even the monthly rotations had become dull and exhausting. He was tired of the food, tired of the clothes, tired of the yelling, tired of the constant threat of danger, tired of being in the midst of all these Americans. He was tired of his support group. He wanted to be back among his own people, his own culture, his own routines, his own personal space. He wanted to decide for himself.

And, returning to his cell that evening, he was very tired of his roommate.

"Hey, hey, hey. I don't suppose you can help me with my history test?" Erik asked immediately upon Rivotra's entry.

"Depends on what kind of history," he replied absently.

"American history. We're going over the colonies and stuff, American Revolution. Cool stuff, man, I think I remember learning some of this stuff in fourth or fifth grade."

"I'm afraid I don't know much about it," Rivotra informed him, sending up a silent prayer of thanks that there was finally a subject the kid couldn't badger him about.

"Oh." The teenager sounded genuinely disappointed. "Well, yeah, I mean, I guess that makes sense. You're not from here, so why would you know? But that leaves me shit out of luck!"

"There aren't any tutors you can utilize?"

"Yeah, but, you know, they're all, like, outside staff or the admin guys, you know?"

"And...?" Rivotra waited for a response but didn't get one. "Do they intimidate you?"

"No!" Erik answered, too quickly. Then, just as quickly, "Maybe a little."

"Why do they intimidate you and I don't?"

"'Cause you're my cellie! You're down here in the mud with me! The instructors and staff tutors, they're, like, you know, do-gooders and stuff. And the admin inmates are all uppity about being admin, you know?"

"So you don't want pity, and you don't like pride, and you're willing to fail at life in order to avoid both."

"Oh, sure, make me the bad guy," Erik said, his tone legitimately shocked by the accusation.

"If I have to," Rivotra told him. "And don't think I don't understand. I was murdered last year, spent months not being able to wipe my own ass, and then I spent several more weeks having to pee like a woman. But I couldn't refuse the help because I needed it. If you don't think you're desperate, then either figure out the material on your own, or just wait until you are."

Erik spent the next twenty minutes angrily shuffling papers and making pathetic sounds whose purpose Rivotra could not identify. Growling self-motivaton, whimpering and pathetic self-pity, nonverbal smarmy remarks about his, Rivotra's, counsel, some kind of carousel that hit each mood in turn as it jumped through the teenager's brain?

At the same time, once lights out rolled around, Rivotra found himself almost wishing that he could have helped Erik, not because he was all that invested in the teenager's grades, but because it would have helped to distract him for a while.

An idea sprang to mind, and all next day as he went about his chores, he could see very clearly that it was nothing more than instant cosmological karma. He didn't want pity, and he didn't like pride, but there was one good way he could think of to keep him distracted.

That evening, he again found Erik in the cell, worrying over his history assignments.

"I think I know a way I might be able to help you," Rivotra said, sitting on his mattress.

"What's that?"

"Teach me what you're learning."

"I don't get it." Erik's tone was empty cluelessness. "If I don't know it, how can I teach it?"

"You'd be surprised how often such a phenomenon appears in schooling. The point remains. Teach me what you're learning. What are all those papers you're constantly shuffling around?"

"Oh, well, one of them is a timeline I have to study. The other has, like, biographies of famous people I'm supposed to know. And then—"

"Why don't you read me the biographies?" Rivotra suggested. "Tell me about these people. Who were they?"

Papers rustled, and he thought he heard Erik murmur some kind of doubtful sentiment. Then, "All right, man, whatever. I don't know what you're talking about, but I'll read them to you. Maybe you'll learn it better than me and learn me back."

Similar to his math skills, Erik couldn't read past a second year level, and what started as a simple reading assignment and history lesson quickly morphed into tutoring on basic reading skills, such as how to sound out big words, which did not go nearly as well as either of them might have hoped, although Rivotra had a suspicion about that one.

"Have you ever been tested for dyslexia?"

"Yeah, like the second week of class," Erik admitted. "They told me I got it. I said I knew I had it and it was no big deal, but..."

"It was a lie?"

"Yeah."

Rivotra wanted to ask how the kid had ever made it through school, but it was probably the same way he had made it through with only rudimentary math abilities.

So what started as a history lesson and turned into basic reading skills, metamorphized again into the letters of the alphabet and basic word sounds like one might find in a first grade class. Rivotra had an amusing thought that if Erik copied him letter for letter and sound for sound, he was going to end up with a Malagasy accent, too. Or else he was going to lose his accent, having to articulate some of these English sounds.

"Man, I don't know what I'm going to do when you're gone," Erik told him after lights out. "I'm gonna fail school."

That was quite likely, yes. "What makes you think I'm leaving any time soon?"

"You got your appeal, don't you?"

"If your lawyer is worth anything, you have an appeal, too. Besides, most appeals are rejected."

"I don't know. I mean, yeah, you hear that, but that's so the general public thinks the courts work like they supposed to. How much you think people would believe in the courts if they knew that convictions were constantly overturned?"

"And the fact that I can count on my deficient hand the number of times I've heard of an inmate here getting a successful appeal and not getting shipped back here after another trial?" Rivotra questioned.

"Well..." Erik fumbled.

"I want to believe. I really do. I might even get the appeal. But I have other enemies waiting for me."

357

"Oh. Well, I wouldn't know. It's bad for you folks who went to trial, but for those of us who just signed the confession, we got even less of a chance."

"You're not in that long anyway. By the time an appeal went through, you'd be looking at parole."

"Yeah, but to get that, I gotta finish school and the rehab program."

"Sounds perfectly doable."

"I know guys my age who's got military service and two college degrees. You're teaching me how to read like a kindergartener, and I'm racking up time in the Hole like debt to my drug boss."

"Have to start somewhere," Rivotra offered with a sigh. "You have to decide what you want. You can either get control of yourself and your behavior, or you can walk out of here no better than you came in, and chances are good that you'll be coming back here in short order."

"Yeah..." Erik murmured. "But then I think about it, and it's like, at least that sounds sorta exciting, you know?"

Rivotra blinked. "I don't know that 'exciting' is the word I would use to describe prison, no."

"No, I mean, the danger, the thrill, the change, sticking it to the man. I mean, like I said, I was making good money. I'd watch my honest neighbors —you know, they got a nice, respectable job somewhere and a legit paycheck —and they didn't seem to be in any better standing than I was. Same trailer house, same car problems, same bill problems, same family fights. Difference was, I didn't pay no taxes; I got to keep my money."

"So what do you call giving your boss his cut of the drug money under penalty of death?"

Erik did not respond to that. "So I figure, why not have a little fun? Why not do all this shit? It's exciting. Why do I want to go out and work a nine-to-five at the grocery store for less than half of what I was making?"

Rivotra ceased to engage in the conversation as it plummeted below his tolerable IQ level, and he drifted off to sleep.

The following morning, Friday, was as busy as ever. Morning count, mail, and visitation requests. As they inched toward the holidays, inmates were more intent on their visitations for Thanksgiving and Christmas. Erik received a visitation request and was immediately ecstatic.

"It's my girl!" he cried. "She's gonna come see me! Shelly still loves me!"

Rivotra wondered if Shelly knew her boyfriend was sucking dick for meth.

"Aw, man, I can't wait!" Erik went on, pacing back and forth in front of the bunks. "I ain't seen her since once in jail." He paused. "Aw, man, what am I gonna say to her?"

"Hello is usually a good start," Rivotra offered sarcastically.

"Yeah, but, do I tell her I love her? What if she's got another man?"

"Why would she visit you if she found another man?"

"Maybe she feels sorry and doing the proper thing to tell me in person."

Rivotra considered this, then silently admitted the kid had a point.

"I'm sure she's going to tell me all about her maw and memaw," the teenager went on, his tone turning mildly dreamy. "I mean, I don't like her maw much, but her memaw's a good cook. Good ol' mountain stock in her. When I get out, we're going to get married and have little mountain babies together."

"Is Shelly as much a drug addict and dealer as you?" Rivotra wondered, unsure if he wanted to know the answer.

"She does weed sometimes, but mostly she's, like, the pretty leverage, you know? Having her around keeps things civilized. No one wants things to get ugly in front of a lady. And she knows people. She makes arrangements."

Ten bucks said she was already seeing someone else and possibly making mountain babies with him instead.

Rivotra got out of bed, intending to head out for early chores and leave Romeo to pine for his lover alone.

He left the neighborhood before he could get wrapped up in another pathetic conversation. He knew exactly how this was going to go. Erik would be an insufferable hopeless romantic for the next two weeks until his visit. At that visit, Shelly would effectively break up with him, whether or not she was already seeing someone else. Afterwards, Erik would become an insufferable, hopeless romantic with no partner to swoon over.

With any luck, he wouldn't have to deal with that for very long. Hopefully, his appeal would go through, and then he would go home.

Somehow, his brain still couldn't process it. Josina herself had bought the farm. Of course, it made sense now, in a poetically ironic kind of way. He could almost hear Anagalisgi laughing behind him. Rivotra could understand why she might not want to disclose such a thing in a formal communication, but what excuse did the Native man have? A lot of mental anguish could have been avoided if he had explained all of this to Rivotra earlier. Josina was going to buy the farm to keep it out of the hands of less sympathetic government officials, but her full intent was to give it back to him. Would that have really been so difficult? Would it have really altered the future?

And yet, there was so much more to it. This went beyond her scope of legal practice. From working with international agencies—and trying to keep everyone on both sides blissfully unaware of each other as much as possible —to buying property, really, on his behalf from her own money. Culture was power, but there was no obligation he was aware of that could have compelled her to help him in such a way. Even if she was sympathetic to his situation and everything that had happened, it was just...mind-boggling.

His appeal had to go through. He needed to get home so he could repay her in some way. It didn't sound as though she intended to stay long, just long enough to start teaching at the university, make back some money, and then return to her family in the northwest. He thought she might have mentioned Nosy Be, the island city that was effectively the capital of the Sakalava, much like Fianarantsoa was the Betsileo capital.

He didn't know what he could do for her. He really wasn't going to have any money; anything he managed to take with him out of this prison, while worth much more in Madagascar, was going to have to be used for his own immediate needs. He didn't expect that he would be able to afford any cattle to present to her or her family. Maybe, if he did well enough and worked hard in the *tanimbary*, he could at least give her some real Betsileo rice. It wasn't much, but it was better than nothing.

Well, he would have a little time to think about it. A few weeks here still, and it would take a little time for him to get a feel for things at home. He would have to get to know the house again, explore the land and figure out what kind of shape it was in. After a couple years with no cows to pasture and no one to till the fields, he would expect it to be remarkably fertile and overgrown. He would have to work quickly to take advantage of that. Very likely the neighbors' ducks were still enjoying themselves in the unworked *tanimbary*, so pests shouldn't be a problem.

One part of his mind wanted to plan out the first five years, figure out which fields were in what shape, how he could work and rotate them, how to get everything back the way he remembered. Another part of his mind was happy to remind him of his blindness, seizures, and other disabilities. Exactly how did he expect to do any of this? Neighbors might help, if they didn't mind his dishonor, but this was still his farm. He needed to be out there, too. But he couldn't just wander off through the fields or else he could be wandering for quite a distance. Half the reason he was assigned to the same stupid chores on the farm here in prison was because he couldn't see to help with anything else. That wasn't going to change just because he was in a more agreeable location.

And still another part of his mind said he was getting too far ahead of himself. He could not afford to get his hopes up so high. What if his appeal was rejected, as statistics dictated?

He mentally shook his head. A little faith went a long way. A little dreaming never hurt anyone. And besides, if Josina was going through all this trouble to keep him out of the spotlight and keep competing interests separate, who was to say that she wasn't going to rig the appeal a little? He didn't know how, since it was a judge's decision, but maybe there was something she could do. After all, if his appeal was granted, he could disappear. If it got rejected, then Bartlett was going to keep pushing and pushing, making a bigger and bigger spectacle out of it. It was more beneficial if it just went through the first time.

He couldn't decide whether that line of thought was actually viable, if Josina was ethically capable of doing such a thing, or just the product of a stressed mind on the cusp of a psychotic break. Whichever it was, and whatever the outcome of this appeal, he decided he would be very happy once it was finally over. Then maybe he would be able to go back to cleaning the prison's chicken coop in peace.

With exception of a few wounds here and there, most of the wounds on Rivotra's body had been stitched up, the skin fresh and new and remarkably smooth. But tonight was not about stitching up more wounds, only sitting by the warm fire and eating delicious stew.

"Why didn't you tell me Josina had bought the farm?" Rivotra asked.

"Contrary to popular belief, the gift of foresight does not lessen anxiety," Anagalisgi began. "In fact, it often makes it worse."

"What does that have to do with it?"

"You've been in the United States long enough, I assume you are aware of the taboo, the great sin of 'spoiling the ending' as it refers to movies, books, and so on?"

"I am very well aware of that *fady*."

"I know the ending. If I only told you the ending, then although you may know what happens, you won't know how, or, more importantly, why. And if I try to explain the why, then what is the point in watching the movie or reading the book?"

"That's fine when it's fiction. How about real life? Maybe I would have had a different reaction."

"But she needed to tell you," Anagalisgi told him. "She had to communicate things in the way that you would both understand. You had to work through this issue with her, not me, because she is the one who did it. And she had to be the one to explain it, as much for herself as you. There are two parties involved, and I wasn't one of them."

Rivotra shook his head slightly. "Then why tell you at all? Why...lead me on?"

"What good is a gift of prophecy if I don't know anything?"

"If I recall correctly, Tommen found this attitude infuriating."

"He did say that on a few occasions, yes."

Now Rivotra shifted position, stretching his legs. "And what good is prophecy if you never tell anyone anything? Why not warn people of what's to come?"

"I do tell people such things, and yet they remain surprised by the consequences of their actions. People want to know the future, but they somehow don't consider themselves part of that future. I could have told Tommen any number of things about the battle for the Akarin fortress, the battle on Brelix, or other, smaller incidents. He was always very eager to know the future and try to avoid as much war and death and bloodshed as possible. Yet he failed to factor in the most important element: himself.

"The concept of time and one's relationship to the past and future...they're not quite native to mortal beings. Even I have only an elementary grasp of such a thing. We make plans for the future, we reflect on the past, yet we fail to consider ourselves as having real agency within these temporal environments. You glimpsed this very briefly as you considered the relationship between Rifun and Rivotra, but that is all it was, a glimpse. Now you look ahead, desiring to know what will be, but failing to insert yourself as an agent who is already there and already knowledgeable of such things."

Rivotra blinked. "I don't understand."

"Fifty pages ahead, there you are, acting as an agent in that time. Fifty pages previous, there you are, acting as an agent in that time. Even now, you are acting as a future agent to the past, and a past agent to the future. Remember what I said about prophecy. It's not about what will happen, it's about what you've already done."

"Fate is fixed."

"Something to that effect. And it's difficult to warn people who do not take agency of themselves in the present, never mind the past or future."

Rivotra nodded, even if he still didn't fully understand what the man was talking about. "So, how do I repay Josina for this kindness she's shown me? Does this mean my appeal will go through?"

"What would you like to give her?" Anagalisgi inquired. His tone was a blatant tease. He knew something, and he was flaunting the silence.

"Cattle is the most obvious gift," Rivotra answered. "If I remember right, the Sakalava royalty prize certain colors and patterns as being inherently royal or spiritually bound, and gifting those types of cows would be a tremendous gift."

"All right. And besides cows?"

"Given that the Betsileo are the best rice growers in Madagascar, rice would also be a solemn expression of gratitude. And there are other trade goods that are highly regarded."

"What about things that aren't trade goods? Unless you plan on stealing, you don't have a lot to your name."

"I could work for her family for a season. Labor is not easily turned down."

"Is your family farm really only worth one season of work?" Anagalisgi's tone was mock-offended, but Rivotra still couldn't figure out the joke.

"I have to work my farm, too. Or else it will still only rot, regardless if I am here or there, owner or hired hand."

Anagalisgi made a sound saying he understood that Rivotra wasn't catching on to whatever he was trying to hint at. "And what about Josina? What does she want or need?"

"She says she's going to be staying in the area for a little while, if she gets the job with the university. Unfortunately, even though she needs to make money so she can return home, whether to her village or Nosy Be, she still has more than I do."

"Does she, though? If she does give the house back to you, that's quite a bit of wealth by your own standards. Listening to you talk about this farm nonstop for months now, it sounds like a veritable castle."

Rivotra chuckled. "Well, not quite. But it is worth a lot, in money and memories."

Even as he said it, something in his mind clicked. He paused, soup spoon halfway to his mouth. He set the spoon back in the bowl of stew and looked in Anagalisgi's general direction.

"So that's what you're referring to."

Anagalisgi's tone was gentle. "What does she want or need? What do you want or need?"

Fifteen
Appeals

Not that Rivotra was keeping track, but he knew when it was two days before his appeal was argued in court. He might have hoped that Josina would come for a second visit, but even he knew it was too late now. He wasn't even sure if there was anything more he could offer, as far as their arguments went. Tainted jury, well, he'd had nothing to do with that. The withholding of papers from the Senate wasn't something he had even been aware of until recently. Witness intimidation? He wasn't sold on it personally, but then, he might have been too close to the situation. If Bartlett considered that to be a viable argument, by all means, let the man pull all the records and all the transcripts he thought he needed.

Anxiety had become Rivotra's constant companion over the last few days, and he knew it wasn't going to improve any time soon. He didn't drink coffee with his breakfast, and he now found himself leery of even the orange juice. Who needed caffeine or sugar when your future was at stake a hundred of miles away? But he needed something to wash down the dry biscuits, and he didn't especially enjoy the tap water.

As he made his way to morning chores, he likened the situation to being trapped in a soundproofed room that was, in fact, quite noisy. He was going insane inside the room, but no one outside the room had any idea what was going on. They didn't hear the noise or see the chaos, and he was presently unable to imagine the room being quiet again.

A commotion got his attention before he made it, his thoughts immediately switching to fight or flight as he tried to quickly size up the situation.

There was no immediate threat to his person, and the commotion was not reminisce of brewing violence. But neither was it joyful. Instead, it seemed to be simple shock, multiple men expressing disbelief.

Curious, Rivotra abandoned his course and followed the noise. His path took him back to genpop where officers were saying something about keeping clear and letting medical personnel do their job.

"Someone get shanked?" Rivotra asked of the air.

"Nah, man," someone replied. "Typo got the big one."

"Typo?"

"Head librarian."

That was the most information Rivotra was able to get, and, seeing how this was just a spectacle over nothing—the medical staff confirmed the man's death, then took him out in a black bag—he departed.

He knew he had visited the library once, at least he thought it was the library here. It could have been a different library, actually. But even if it was the one here, he didn't think he'd ever met Typo. Heard his name a time or two, always in a good or neutral manner, but never officially met him. Since going blind, he'd never had a reason to go to a library; he doubted it carried too many braille books. He couldn't even read braille, so it didn't do him any good anyway. He could have bought a CD player from commissary and inquired about audiobooks, he supposed, but, somehow, the thought just didn't appeal to him. He wasn't the most popular inmate here, and he didn't want to deprive himself of any more senses he might need to detect danger.

It was too bad, though, because there was actually a decent selection of literature here.

But how did he know that?

Probably something he'd learned in that short period before his attack. But did that mean he had met Typo at some point? He couldn't remember. At the same time, he apparently classified people according to their language, so if he only knew Typo for a few days, it was possible that the man had simply vanished from his memory.

Rivotra knew a moment of guilt about that, though he couldn't explain exactly why. Maybe they'd been friends for those few days and he couldn't remember, although he couldn't recall that Typo had ever spoken to him after the attack. Maybe this was just some form of twisted pity over a man dying in prison with only the other inmates to mourn him. Did he have any family who cared about him?

Rivotra found his thoughts going back, or maybe forward, to his life back home. Forget the farm; it was a foregone conclusion that he knew what he was going to do there. Crops, animals, all the usual stuff, in whatever manner he was able to do it the way he was. But what about himself as a person? What was he going to do? Who was he going to be, really? A man was defined by his people and his family. He knew the former, even if they didn't really know him. He knew their routines, their customs, their *fady*, all of that. But what about family?

He knew he wasn't going to go running off to avenge his family against Julianna. She would kill him. Flat out, she would kill him. He knew that. But while he might be able to lie low and farm, well, either an accident would do him in or age would eventually catch up with him. Same result, no more Andilans. He was the last one. He couldn't let that happen.

Anagalisgi, are you sure? he wondered silently. *If Josina fails to keep me hidden, or if something else happens and Julianna finds out I'm alive, could I really endanger a wife and children? A woman may be able to put up a fight, but children are helpless, and I'm not in so great a shape anymore either, not against the likes of Julianna and the Order.*

Could his trust really extend so far? Could he really believe that he might have years of peace in which to raise a family? Would God or the Author really give that to him? Considering he'd had such chances before, he couldn't come up with a plausible reason why not, except he really didn't deserve it. Even if it was just an effort to keep him happily occupied and so less likely to jump back into the intergalactic arena...

He paused, then nodded to himself. Whether it was true kindness or telling him to just sit down and stay in his own damn box for once, it was an offer he could not refuse. He would not refuse. This time, he was going to take the hint and just settle down.

The morning was uneventful, at least outside his head. If anyone were to take a look inside, they would still find woeful anxiety and metaphorical nail biting. The afternoon passed much the same way. He finished chores early and made his way to the library before dinner. He paused where he knew the desk officer would be.

"So, what happens now with Typo gone?" he inquired.

"Officers are taking turns being the head librarian," desk officer replied, his tone suggesting it was not the first time he'd answered the question that day. "We'll have a replacement in a week or so, once the social workers submit their recommendations."

Rivotra nodded. "What's going to happen to him?"

"Contact his family, see if they want to ship him out for burial. If not, he'll go to the prison yard outside the fence."

"Outside the fence?"

"Don't read into it. We've had sick fucks dig up graves before and steal the bones."

That didn't surprise him, actually. He thanked the officer and headed out. He might have asked about audiobooks or braille books, but somehow, that felt very...long-term. Even if the check-out time was two weeks, and he knew he had at least two weeks to wait, he didn't want that kind of commitment, or another thing to try and remember to do. He didn't need to come back to prison because he forgot to return an overdue book.

Dinner, shower, then a return to his cell where Erik was busy trying to sound out a reading assignment.

"Hey, man, you know this word?" the teenager asked.

"What word?" Rivotra sighed.

"This one."

"I can't see, dumbfuck. Sound it out or spell it out."

"In...gen...jen...ingen...oo..."

"Ingenuity?"

"I-n-g-e-n-u-i-t-y."

Rivotra had to think for a second before finally nodding. "Ingenuity."

"What's that mean?"

"Do you know the word ingenious?"

"No."

"Genius?"

"Yeah! Like Einstein!"

"Ingenious and ingenuity are derived from that. Ingenuity means creativity and inventiveness. You can take mismatched pieces and make something new and clever from them."

"Like pork rinds and ranch?"

Rivotra blinked. He blanched at the thought, considered correcting the kid, then decided on, "Yeah, sure, I guess."

"Ben Franklin's in-gen-u-ity," Erik read slowly, "con-tri-bu-ted to many sci-en-ti-fic fields and ad-van-ces." He paused. "So he was a really smart dude."

Rivotra pinched the bridge of his nose and settled for, "Yes, he was."

There was no sleeping until lights out, and even then, Erik appeared to be absolutely starved for conversation during the day because he couldn't stop talking.

"So we're reading about all these guys from history, and they're like, really smart guys. But some of them are my age, you know? And they got degrees from, like, Harvard and stuff, and they know a buncha languages and stuff. Right?"

"Yes," Rivotra replied shortly, knowing the kid wasn't going to get the hint.

"You think there were stupid people back then, too? People on drugs and alcohol and stuff? People getting violent and whatnot?"

"I can say with absolute confidence that there were. Why?"

"Well, I was just thinking...if that's the case, nothing really changes, does it? You got your smart people, you got your dumb people. Smart people do smart things, dumb people do dumb things. But being a smart person back then doesn't mean that your kids today won't be dumbshits. And being a dumbshit back then doesn't mean your kids today couldn't be smart."

"Right...?"

"So then, like...what's the point? We eat, we sleep, we fuck, few years we die. Don't matter what we knew. Does it really matter at all?"

It was the most thoughtful and philosophical Rivotra had ever heard from Erik, and he was almost sorry the teenager decided to cut his line of thought short right there. As a matter of fact, that line of thought took hold in his own mind and followed him through the night into the next day.

He had visited with multiple generations of his own family, from his *nenibe* to those who could have been his grandchildren and even great-grandchildren. In one day, he had seen Faliarivo as an awkward teenager who

371

had trouble looking at girls, and then as a grown man in his fifties with children and grandchildren. He had seen his cousin Lalao as a beautiful woman of not quite thirty years, and then again as an old woman near seventy with children and grandchildren. Some of those had turned out remarkably well, others less so. Some were perfect copies of their forebears, others perfect opposites.

So, did it really matter? Did it matter that Rivotra had been to spectacular places and done amazing and unspeakable things? In a purely historical sense, yes, he was significant. And his experiences both good and bad would contribute to his actions as a husband and father. But did it really matter? Something would do him in. Death was inevitable. Time Agents and Akari-bearers just had a little greater advantage when it came to the natural lifespan. But sickness, war, accidents, all other manners of death, it would reach him eventually. And then what?

He considered his ancestors. His *nenibe* and *dadabe*, their grandparents, their grandparents. Each one greatly removed from him and the modern world, yet so essential for his life now.

Perhaps, then, the *razana* was less about a literal, physical or metaphysical force that could be harnessed and manipulated. Rather, it was the life force that created and sustained all living things. It brought two people together in love and marriage, and it brought forth children, sustaining the life of the family. The *razana* was not a separate, abstract power over life and death. Rather, it was simply life. It only knew how to create and sustain. Stifling, strangling, or trying to force it to work for nefarious means, that was what killed the *razana*. It was not a matter of choosing the correct force, for there existed only one life. All else was death.

Faith and Force, Whites and Shadows, angels and demons. However it was perceived, there was only one life, one choice.

He chose life. His life, his renewed life, springing forth as Rivotra, had undone the death that was Rifun. And now, he would choose life again. Maybe life on a farm wasn't as exciting as stars and monsters, kingship and treachery, but it was life. It was caring for the earth and, with a little luck, caring for a family, bringing life to a family tree Julianna had tried so viciously to uproot.

He just had to get through this appeal.

That word, "appeal," and the thought of being late for lunch, broke his philosophical trance and brought reality crashing back down around him. He was still inside, and life was still outside. Josina and Bartlett would be arguing for his future tomorrow, and there was absolutely nothing he could do about it from here.

He wished he had some inkling of how it was going to go. He wanted to actually hear the arguments, see the case laid out, hear the state's rebuttal—did they get one? He honestly didn't know—consider the reaction of the judge. He wanted to be in the courtroom. Could he ask about it later? Could he have a transcript read to him? Even if appeals were considered privileged, well, he was the client in the middle of all of this.

Josina had said she would be leaving the day after the arguments, but maybe she could stop by the prison first, just to let him know how things went. How did she feel about the arguments? Did she think they were good and strong, or was there a sudden surge of doubt as the judge overruled something?

Rivotra didn't think it was possible to be any more anxious about this appeal, but apparently he was wrong. He had simply reached the summit of one peak and now found himself looking at a much taller second peak. And so far, none of his usual calming activities were even remotely appealing. Farming, working out, just taking a walk, nothing was working.

He got through his afternoon and returned to the cafeteria for dinner. After that, his usual shower, and then off to see what Erik was panicking over tonight.

"What does 'pre-mortem' mean?" the teenager asked.

"Before death," Rivotra answered, sitting down on his mattress. "More history again?"

"Nah, this is from another group my social worker's got me in. Supposed to help with long-term planning and goal-setting. Group leader said that after we decide on a goal, we need to do a pre-mortem, said we first have to think about our plans failing." There was some shuffling of papers. "Man, what kind of shitty motivational advice is that? Ain't he supposed to tell us to keep our eyes on the prize and don't give up and shit?"

"Actually, it sounds like very good advice," Rivotra told him. "What do you do if you fail to meet a goal? How did it fail? What could have been done differently? What can you do to avoid some common obstacles? What can you do to try again and do better the next time?"

"Okay, but why is that the first step? If my goal is to get clean from drugs, why is my first step to toss that goal in the trash?"

"It's not tossing it in the trash. It's just assuming, correctly in your case, that you will fail. But why did you fail? How can you avoid failing the next time, assuming you do want to get clean?"

"I don't know. It just seems contraproductive to me. And I learned that word in school, you should be proud."

"The word is 'counterproductive' but you still used it correctly, so I'll give you that."

"Whatever, man. So, what should I list for my pre-mortem? I need three reasons why my goal might fail."

Only three? Rivotra could list at least half a dozen. "You stop taking the placebo pills, you hang around other inmates who do drugs, and you are a mule for others."

He liked to think Erik was shocked that anyone could come up with such reasons so quickly.

"Do you enjoy doing drugs?" Rivotra asked.

"Well, kinda, I think? I don't really remember a lot when I'm on them, so I don't know."

"You're just in it for the money, aren't you?"

"It's good money, man, no arguing that."

"So maybe you can overcome your first obstacle by keeping up the placebo pills and just focusing on the money. You don't have to do drugs to sell them."

Erik hummed thoughtfully. "And it might save me a little trouble, too, if I don't palm some for myself every now and then."

"There you go, make it a business venture," Rivotra suggested.

He didn't know how he felt about actively encouraging the kid to sell drugs and continue being a mule, but maybe if he could just get off the drugs and kick that addiction, he would eventually recover his wits and shutter that business. At the same time, money was still a very powerful motivator, and Rivotra knew of half a dozen officers who trafficked drugs in order to bring in a little extra cash. One little transaction could equal half their weekly paycheck if he understood it right.

"Maybe you're right," Erik was saying. "You know, there's a lot of talk about states legalizing drugs. I mean, everyone knows weed, but some places are pushing for crack, meth, heroin, PCP, LSD, shrooms, all of them! Maybe when I get out of here, I'll become an activist, get everything legalized, and then start my own chain of drug stores!"

"If that's your goal..." Rivotra sighed. "Just don't forget your pre-mortem."

"Well obviously the biggest obstacle is that drugs aren't legal. And lots of people would be against it. But...in order for my business to be successful, lots of people would have to be on drugs." Erik's brilliant train of thought predictably came to a stop at the station of reality. "Maybe I should think this through first."

Rivotra silently agreed, determined not to say anything that might fuel any more bad ideas. He swung his legs up into bed and managed to get to sleep, at least for a little while. Then, at some point in the middle of the night, he jolted awake. He only knew it was still night because Erik was snoring up top and he didn't hear anything going on outside.

He got up to relieve himself, then settled back in, hoping to get back to sleep. Within about two minutes, he knew that wasn't going to happen. His brain had figured out that today was the day for arguing his appeal and latched onto it with deadly ferocity. Surprisingly, he wasn't especially anxious about it, compared to the last few days, but it remained, stubbornly, the only thought in his head.

Today they were arguing his appeal.

Today they were arguing his appeal.

Today they were arguing his appeal.

He blinked and came back to himself as he heard footsteps outside the door, but it was just the desk officer making his hourly rounds. Step up to the door, brief pause as he glanced inside, then move on to the next house.

Today they were arguing his appeal.

Yes, but not right this minute, he told himself, suddenly frustrated and desiring to get back to sleep.

Today they were arguing his appeal.

They were. Not him. He wasn't going to be there, and he had full faith in Josina and Bartlett to do as well as they could. Bartlett had the personality and knowledge of the American judiciary, and Josina had the personal ambition and an abundance of evidence in both local and international matters.

But the voice in his head didn't seem all that concerned about the arguments or the people or the this or that and what ifs. Instead, it was fixated on the singular fact that today was the day they were arguing his appeal. Absolutely nothing else about the process mattered except that fact.

Rivotra decided he could live with that. Even if that was the only thought in his head today, it was still better than the days and even weeks of nebulous anxiety he had been warring with.

Making peace with the voice in his head let him get back to sleep for a couple hours until morning count. From there, he headed to the gym for an early workout.

Today they were arguing his appeal.

It was the only thought in his head, but it provided a useful rhythm and helped him keep track of his reps. It helped him get through morning chores, and, for some reason, took him to commissary before lunch.

"And what do you want?" Ramone asked, his tone more bark than bite. Rivotra could hear the stunted movements of a knee that didn't work quite right anymore.

"Need a pair of jeans," Rivotra told him. "Preferably ones that fit."

Ramone hobbled off to grab a pair of jeans, whipping them at Rivotra when he returned. "You know, couple of my boys spotted your lawyer the other day. Pretty thing."

"If you think Kevin Bartlett is pretty..."

"Not him, you fuckwit. You know who I mean. The lady. She's pretty. Looks like she already had a little run-in with trouble, kinda like you."

Rivotra chuckled lowly. "That...that's from a terrorist bombing. Someone tried to murder her and her family for political vengeance. Yet here she is."

He shook his head. "She may be pretty, but I don't think she would have any problem taking on some low-level punk like you, or your friends. What is it some of the skinheads like to say? Ain't no world like the third world? Please. Try to start something with her. I don't even think I would have to get involved."

Ramone did not reply, but Rivotra could feel the seething hatred coming off the man. He turned away, new jeans in hand, and left the building. He half-expected the gangbanger to throw something at his back, be it pencil or shiv, but it never happened.

Even though Josina was obviously not going to visit again—and even then, he still had his other pair of jeans—Rivotra decided that he should probably have a couple changes of clothes, assuming he was able to walk out of here. The standard issue uniforms, those had to be returned, but anything he bought in commissary was his to keep. Two pairs of jeans, a few pairs of socks, a few pairs of boxers, a couple undershirts, he wouldn't be completely destitute. There were no regular shirts available in commissary, but that was all right. If nothing else, he could wear his *lamba*.

Today they were arguing his appeal.

He had to stay positive. At least with a quieter mind, it made it easier to focus on what he was doing. For now, that was returning his new jeans to his bunk and then going to lunch.

"I don't recall you having a visit this week," the desk officer observed as he walked into the neighborhood.

"Just trying to stay hopeful for my appeal," Rivotra told him, approaching the desk.

"You do know your chances, your real chances, are next to nothing, right? Even if it goes through, a new trial will just kick you right back here. I see it all the time. And you guys talk; how many guys pinned their hopes on an appeal that never panned out?"

"Plenty. But I have to hope, right?"

"Hope is fine. That's what the chapel is for. Appeals are just to make you feel good, try to soften the blow of how long your sentence is."

Rivotra nodded. "Well, I can't give up yet. Maybe if it comes back negative, then I'll think about it."

The officer scoffed and Rivotra had a notion of the man waving his hand dismissively. "Power to you, but don't come crying to me when it doesn't work out."

Rivotra left the desk and made for his bunk. In reality, he wasn't feeling half so hopeful as he was trying to portray. Any hope he did have was basically anxiety in disguise, tempered only by that singular thought.

After stowing his new pants, he headed out for lunch. A promising autumn morning was quickly giving way to a dreary afternoon, and he considered whether he shouldn't have grabbed his coat. They were getting into that time of year where sunshine was comfortable, but any blockage of those beams produced a near-instant chill. A calm wind that was growing more forceful wasn't helping things either.

He silently prayed that this wasn't an omen about his appeal. So much hope to begin with, things looking bright and promising, only to turn stormy at the last moment and give way to a long season of tragic darkness.

"You always were a dramatic actor," Anagalisgi had told him once.

Rivotra mentally blushed and admitted to himself that maybe the man was correct in that assessment. All the same, he couldn't shake that association now that he'd made it. Was he being too optimistic about the situation? Was he putting too much faith in mortal elements? Where did faith end and foolish hope begin? Where did foolish hope end and pure naiveté begin?

Ducking inside the cafeteria, the stark difference in temperature informed him that he really should have grabbed his coat. Well, he could pick it up after he ate, before he went to afternoon chores.

There was no real interesting news currently circulating, at least, nothing out of the ordinary. Someone was in the Hole, someone just got out, someone was picking up some extra chores for more good time before a parole hearing, someone had a special visitor lined up this week, someone had a hit out on someone else, all of it fairly common. And, of course, the baseball game was still a prevalent topic.

Absolutely no one, within earshot, was talking about appeals. Not that they had one in the works, that they wanted their lawyer to get one started, or even that one had recently failed. It was almost as if the process just didn't exist. Yet it was the only thing that consumed Rivotra's thoughts. Was he really that hopeless? Was he just too ignorant of the American judiciary? Was the desk officer right, that appeals only existed to make him feel good, give him a sliver of hope to keep him afloat in the early days of a very long sentence?

He truly did not know what he ought to be feeling, and it frustrated him as he made his way to afternoon chores. His first prison term, back in Madagascar in the 1920's, had only been five years. That was doable, for an invincible teenager or twenty-something, and he had ultimately been pardoned. His second prison term, a captive of the French though still in Madagascar in the 1950's, he had been sentenced to death. Even that had been tolerable because it had been so absolute. No appeals, no parole, no arguments, just waiting for his turn to die.

This was somewhere in the middle. Too long to be merely an inconvenience, but not so absolute that it blocked out all hope. There was just enough, just enough, to make him want to hope, even as reality seemed to dictate that he shouldn't.

After dinner was his PTSD support group.

"So, how is everyone doing tonight?" the group leader asked. "Rivotra, you look a little less anxious than normal. Something good happen?"

"My appeal was argued today," he answered. He hadn't actually brought it up before, other than he had an appeal pending. "It will be a couple weeks before I hear anything."

"Don't get your hopes up too high," someone murmured.

Before anyone could say anything else, the leader jumped in. "What's your opinion of the appeal process? As an outsider?"

"You mean, based on my experiences with my own people, my court martial, and everything else?" Rivotra inquired. "I would like to believe that American courts are less corrupt than they are at home, that this isn't all just for show. But if the appeal is rejected, is that because the arguments did not have merit, or because of corruption? Who is to say, and what is there to do about it?"

"What do you think about the prospect of freedom?"

A bit like a caged animal, really. An animal who has been beaten and abused, skittish around others, mistrustful, unsure if the door really is open, or whether the land beyond is truly a better place. It can't stay in the cage, but it doesn't know where it wants to go.

Well, he knew where he wanted to go. He wanted to go to bed, maybe sleep off the nightmare that had encompassed the last few weeks.

"You know, in an odd sort of way, being here isn't all that bad," another guy said when it was his turn. "Uniforms, routine, officers yelling at you, little shits who think they're all that and a bag of chips, it's really not unlike the service. My ex-wife said I came home a completely different man, and I don't disagree. But being here the last few years, I feel better now than I did in that six months between when I got home and when I killed that guy. Honestly, I think I could walk out of here now and be more well-adjusted, than I could before, and that's with all the transition programs and bullshit."

The guy was a decorated veteran, purple heart recipient, successful in school, all around good guy, wife and kids, up until he got into it with someone at the bar and killed a guy in a drunken rage. As far as Rivotra was concerned, this guy had better cause to be given a second chance than he did. Yet his appeals failed. What would it mean, then, if his, Rivotra's, appeals went through?

Rivotra returned to his neighborhood after the meeting. For the first time in weeks, there were no racing thoughts in his mind. As a matter of fact, the only thing in his head was just the filtering of sensory information to help him get around. Even that singular thought from the morning had faded to a dull sense of disquiet. He wouldn't describe himself as calm, but he might agree to "unsettled."

The appeals had been argued, and that was it. There was nothing more to be done until the ruling. It could be a few days, it could be a few weeks. The only thing left now was hope and patience.

"You're back finally!"

Rivotra sighed and sat down on his bunk. "What do you need help with now?"

"I got a history test tomorrow!"

"Well, I need to take a shower. Figure out your questions and—"

"I mean, I can follow you and—"

"No."

"I need to wash up, too, and—"

"That's great, but you're not doing it near me, and you're not asking me questions."

The nice thing about the showers was that, because they serviced hundreds of inmates, and water demand in general remained high throughout the entire day, warm water was not in short supply. And at night, after the kitchens were shut down and everyone started heading for bed, the water temperature could even qualify as being hot. It was entirely possible, therefore, for Rivotra to buy himself some time just by staying under the showerhead and enjoying the hot water.

"All right, ladies!" the desk officer called, walking in the room to a couple of whistles. "You all look beautiful, now wrap it up!"

Within five minutes, everyone was out of the showers, and Rivotra was back in his cell for evening count and lights out.

"Man, I was getting worried," Erik said, crawling into his bunk. "Thought maybe you died again or something."

"Granted, I don't remember anything about that time, but I think there might have been a little commotion over such a thing," Rivotra told him.

"Can you still help me with my history test?"

"How is that?"

"I don't know. Ask me questions you think might be on the test."

Considering how much Rivotra had been helping him lately, this was not as difficult as it may have first sounded.

"Who was the first president of the United States?" Rivotra asked.

"That's easy, man, George Washington," Erik answered. "Come on, I know I'm dumb, but I'm not stupid."

"When did George Washington cross the Delaware River?"

"Uh..." The teenager paused. "You know what? Maybe we should go back to the easy questions."

"This is an easy question."

"Man, I'm not good with dates."

"So skip the women and focus on the history. When did he do it? I'll even give you a hint: it was on a holiday."

"Oh! His birthday!"

381

Rivotra sighed. "How do you remember George Washington's birthday is a holiday, but you don't know when he crossed the river?"

"You didn't know that either at first," Erik whined.

"I'm not an American. I don't have to know things like that. Come on. Which holiday? Another clue, it's in the winter."

"St. Patrick's Day? Were they all drunk?"

He sighed again. "Christmas, Erik. It was Christmas."

"Christmas? But he crossed the river and beat the shit out of the British. Why would you do that on Christmas?"

"Because no one would be expecting it. He needed the element of surprise. War Strategy 101." He might have asked if the kid had ever read *The Art of War* or heard of Sun Tzu, but he knew immediately how that conversation would go.

Erik scoffed. "Still, man, that's kind of a dick move."

"Next question," Rivotra went on, "name three of Benjamin Franklin's inventions."

This continued for about two hours, pausing only when the officer came around for his hourly rounds. After the second round, Erik said, "All right, I'm going to sleep. I don't know what I'm going to do about this test tomorrow."

Rivotra found himself briefly wondering how much of this infantile learning was due to a poor educational system, and how much was due to other factors like his dyslexia, poor home learning environment, personal lack of interest, and drugs rotting his brain. The best tools in the world couldn't help those who didn't want to be helped. When Erik really wanted something, he found a way to get it. Right now, he wasn't wanting it.

But, that wasn't Rivotra's problem. He would help as requested, but he wasn't the kid's father. And if his appeal went through, well, he wasn't exactly going to be making daily or weekly trips back to make sure the kid had a project for the fourth grade science fair. Actually, all things considered, Erik probably had a pretty firm grasp of science.

As consciousness began to fade, Rivotra couldn't decide if he wanted to talk to Anagalisgi or not. He had an inkling that the man knew how the judge would rule, had probably known long before the arguments. He also had a feeling that the man was not going to disclose those results, citing something about learning patience, having trust in the Author, and examining himself and his motives during a time of uncertainty. There would be a lecture on emotional, mental, and spiritual resilience.

And he would probably also mention something about how Rivotra was not the only party invested in this. Josina would be just as eager to know the results, not only so she would know if and when she had to return, but how to plan things for herself. It sounded like this was going to be her only work on this case, or else it was going to be the only work she did as a lawyer, resigning all other cases she might be working on. But then there was this thing with her future at the university or maybe Nosy Be, plus her training with Time and the Akari; she needed to know how this was going to go, too.

Rivotra could not quite explain the phenomenon, except to say that his soul prayed despite the silence of his lips. There was simply nothing left. His thoughts had deserted him, words were doomed to fail, yet his soul still yearned to be heard. And this was the last thought he had before finally surrendering to unconsciousness.

He did not meet with Anagalisgi that night, nor did he have any notion that he had been anywhere near the man's cave. Oddly enough, he was just fine with that. The man likely knew what happened, could maybe even repeat the arguments word-for-word, but he wasn't going to tell Rivotra anything.

As the officer came around for morning count, handing out mail and visitation slips, Rivotra tried to put himself in Anagalisgi's position. He pretended that he knew what Erik was going to do for the next three days. Maybe he didn't know every detail down to the last breath, but he knew generally how the kid's weekend was going to go. Would he tell him everything?

Pretending that he did tell Erik everything, the most likely response was disbelief—whether simply dismissive or hostile opposition—followed by a perfect track to go out and do everything he had just described. A Greek tragedy at its finest.

If something good were to happen, would foreknowledge of that good thing somehow undermine its importance, either the achievement overall or on a personal level? If something bad were to happen, would foreknowledge allow for a chance at avoiding that thing or only enhance the devastation when it came to pass?

Prophecy isn't about what you're going to do, it's about what you've already done. Two hundred pages from now, there you are, doing that thing. Two hundred pages back, there you are, doing that thing. If fate is fixed, then anything else is simply a wish. I might say that I am going to dance my way to breakfast, but it is only a wish until it happens. I have not truly changed anything, either turned a walk into a dance or a dance into a walk, only proven myself a liar or a fool or both, which I already was when I lied and made the foolish statement.

Anything done outside of that fixed fate, then, is done outside of the razana, *outside of the force of life, and is just as tainting as any theft or murder. Because it is foolish speak, using life and air to expel stupidity.*

Not that he didn't expect to say a few stupid things throughout his life, or even that day, but it was something to consider as the officer came around. The officer proved that he could count to two and recite their numbers, then handed over a stack of envelopes and slips, leaving the two of them to figure out whose was whose.

"All right, most of this is mine," Erik said. "But here's a slip for you."

"A visitation request?" Rivotra wondered, taking the paper in hand.

"Nah, slip for today. Josina Zitha? I say that right?"

"You said it fine." Rivotra waved him off. Once count was finished and everyone released, he approached the desk officer.

"Visitation slip for today, Josina Zitha," the officer repeated.

"I didn't get a request."

"Please, lawyers make their own rules." The officer made a scoffing sound. "And warden put out a special notice that we have to be extra nice when dealing with international ambassadors."

"Nothing like bad PR," Rivotra commented. "What time?"

"Noon. You'll have lunch together, I imagine."

And that was exactly what happened. After morning chores, Rivotra returned to his cell to change into his jeans and was shortly thereafter retrieved for a lunch meeting with Josina. He stood when she entered the room.

"You don't have to rise," she told him. "I'm not a judge."

"Then I'll do it out of general respect," he replied.

They sat to eat, a couple of boxed lunches comprising the meal. Candles were replaced by armed guards, but every restaurant had its quirks.

"How did the arguments go?" he asked, figuring it was best to just get it out there.

"Well, I think," she replied, her tone carefully neutral. "Appeals focus primarily on the court process. Was the process just, fair, and conducted according to established rules and procedures, and if not, how much bearing could any irregularities have had on your trial and conviction? This international debacle is certainly a prime candidate for how things broke down procedurally, but the jury selection is perhaps the stronger argument."

"What about the witness intimidation?"

"Hard to say, seeing how you were witness and defendant. Does admitting witness intimidation really change the trial's outcome? Theoretically, yes, but in your favor, since it may have been what won you favorable verdicts in the officers' deaths. Fortunately, American law does not allow the overturning of not guilty verdicts, but does it have the potential to weaken the other arguments? Maybe."

Rivotra frowned and took another bite of food, swallowed. "Nothing to be done now, except hope and pray. When do you leave for home?"

"This evening. I have a flight to New York, then to Johannesburg, and then to Tana."

He Banded the two of them. "You haven't learned portals yet?"

"No, not yet," her tone was amused but also sad. "Believe me, I would very much enjoy not having to deal with twenty hours of flying, plus all the customs and security. Or even hotels. To be able to return to my own bed at night would be..." She cleared her throat. "I'm sorry."

"What are you going to do after this appeal? Whether it goes through or not?"

"No matter what, I have to sell my apartment. I'm kind of bouncing back and forth here and there, between Tana and Fianar. I've been cleaning up the farm, the house anyway, making it clean and livable again. I admit, I'm kind of using it for storage, too, of my things, until I find a place in Fianar."

"Are the villagers treating you well?"

There was a nod in her voice. "Oh yes. They are very happy to see the farm is being cleaned and restored, that someone is caring for it again. Some are still leery of evil spirits, but most are all right. And everyone has been very kind to me."

Rivotra nodded. "That is good to hear."

"I haven't told them anything about you. I didn't want to get their hopes up, just in case things didn't work out."

"If they didn't, then I would just wait until you had learned how to open portals, and then have you break me out." He said it with a laugh to try and make the idea sound more palatable, like a joke, although he was sort of fishing for her thoughts on the idea.

"Maybe," was all she said.

He coughed once, took a drink, and hastily moved on. "And what else are you going to do? Are you teaching at the university?"

"I will be, yes. I expect that, starting in January, I will be an assistant to a professor teaching law. Then, if I do well there, I may be able to teach my own class the next spring, in September."

"I don't think you will have any trouble. What about going home to family?"

"No matter what, I need some money for that. Either I will have to pay my way there, or learn portals." She laughed. "Whichever comes first."

He grinned and leaned back in his seat. "So, in all of this international espionage between INTERPOL and the CIA and all these other agencies, has anything more maybe surfaced about your family's murder?"

She hummed a sigh. "I admit, I've reopened a few files and made a few phone calls, but nothing has really come of it."

"Just more death threats?"

"Not even that, just silence. I imagine that with so many agencies around, they're being a little more cautious. It's funny, in a way, but frustrating that I still can't make headway."

Rivotra nodded slowly. "What if you could?"

He got a notion of her raising a brow. "More intergalactic espionage, or universe-bending secrets?"

386

Now he shook his head. "No secrets here, no espionage."

"Do tell."

He sat up. "You want justice for your family. I want justice for mine. Right?"

"Yes."

"Our enemies want to see us destroyed, completely obliterated if they could."

"Very true."

He leaned forward on the table and folded his hands. "One day, death will find us all. Old age, sickness, an accident, something will inevitably do us in. And them. If they die, ultimately, nothing comes of it. We know the courts aren't fair, assuming they could be bothered. And if we die, our enemies may have a short gloat about it, but it won't matter much either. And what justice has really been done? Justice for our families, mine and yours, *is* family. Justice is life." He could feel his heart thudding in his chest. "I don't have much to give. All I have to my name is a couple changes of clothes and a few dollars." He made a gesture. "You own my house!" He was grateful for his blindness in that moment, that he didn't have to look her in the eye. "You said you would give it back to me, but I would offer it to you. Together. With a family. What do you say we get revenge on our murderers, together, by simply living. As one."

The silence stretched out much, much longer than he was comfortable with. He would not have been surprised if she had Banded herself to buy herself more time to process what he'd just said, but this was still a very uncomfortable moment.

Finally, after a few false starts, the confident, argumentative lawyer failing to find words, she replied, "I don't know."

Rivotra blinked. "There were only two options. That wasn't one of them."

She chuckled nervously. "I don't know. I mean..." She made several sounds he could not identify, nor compare. "I mean I guess I...you're a client of mine...then I wonder why I've done all of this extra...and I do...it's very improper...but I'm resigning my position anyway...and I...just...don't...know." She huffed another anxious laugh. "I don't know. At the very least, I need to call my aunt."

He nodded and leaned back. "I understand."

Two options. Outright refusal, or consulting the family. Her family might reject him for any number of reasons, or she could later decide to refuse, but it was a positive start.

He dropped the Band. They finished lunch in an awkward silence, then Josina thanked him for his time and gathered her things.

"Safe travels," he told her, hoping to sound at least friendly.

Then she was escorted out.

Sighing, Rivotra stood.

"You know, I thought I was pretty good at reading people," Oswald said from the corner, "but then there's you two. And I don't think it's just a culture difference."

"What do you mean?"

"I mean, you start out fine, everything's great, but then it's like...someone flips the switch and the whole atmosphere suddenly changes. Night and day, right in the middle of a conversation that suddenly ends, yet everyone seems to think and act as if they've had a much longer discussion. I mean, I've never been to Africa, but I feel like there's something going on here."

Rivotra took an even breath. "Well, if you're a praying man, you might start praying that something does happen."

With that, he gathered up the empty lunch boxes, took them to the trash, and headed out for afternoon chores.

Had that really just happened? What was her family going to think about it? With his family gone, there was no one back home to negotiate on his behalf. And how long would it take to make a decision? For the Betsileo, it could be a few days, a few weeks, even a few months. He didn't know much about the Sakalava or their nobility, but he had a feeling that no king wanted to see his princess marry a blind pauper.

Marina: Hello?

Josina: Auntie, Auntie!

Marina: Oh, Josina! Oh, it's so good to hear from you! How are things in Tana? Or are you in the United States again?

Josina: I just got back yesterday.

Marina: And it sounds like you have good news. Did your case go well?

Josina: We argued in court, but it will be a couple weeks before the ruling.

Marina: I see. So what has you all excited? Are you teaching at the university?

Josina: No, but...

Marina: Josina, you are thirty years old but you talk and blush like a twelve year old girl. What is it, love?

Josina: All right, I know I don't tell you a lot about my cases that I'm working on. This one that I just argued has to do with the Betsileo murders, the Andilan family.

Marina: From a year and a half ago?

Josina: That's right. The last living relative is imprisoned in the United States. The group responsible tried to kill him, too, but failed. I've been arguing his case internationally, but I won't bore you with the details. Anyway, you remember that I bought the large Andilan farm outside of Fianar?

Marina: Yes, although I can't understand why. You were active enough for a farm, but always so set on the city.

Josina: Justice, Auntie. I went to school to become a lawyer so I could find Mama and Baba's killers.

Marina: Still sitting in their palace, no doubt.

Josina: I told the relative—his name is Rivotra—

Marina: Rivotra? What kind of name is that?

Josina: It's the one his mother gave him. Anyway, I bought the farm to keep it out of the hands of another bureaucrat. I figured I could teach at the university to make some money, and find a place in the city, and I would give the farm back to Rivotra.

Marina: Foolish girl, he's in prison! Innocent or guilty, he can't live in a house from there! You bought that house months ago and just argued the case a few days ago!

Josina: It was a chance and I took it. He's the only surviving Andilan; that farm is his inheritance. It's been in the family for hundreds of years. I couldn't bear to see him lose it.

Marina: And what about our family, hm?

Josina: Well, that's the good part.

Marina: Are you going to say what I think you're going to say?

Josina: He asked me to marry him. He knows he doesn't have much. All he can offer is a farm and a family.

Marina: Yes, there is a distinct lack of fish in the highlands. What did you tell him?

Josina: I told him I had to at least call you and consult the family.

Marina: Oh, well, it's nice of you to think of us.

Josina: Auntie...

Marina: He's a highlander!

Josina: And he's half-French.

Marina: Ah! Well, that makes everything better, doesn't it?

Josina: And I'm half-Tswa.

[pause]

Marina: What's he in prison for?

Josina: Kidnapping a boy and attempting to murder a police officer.

Marina: Do you think he was wrongfully accused or convicted?

Josina: I believe he's changed.

Marina: Did he tell you so? People lie, you know.

Josina: People lie, but God does not.

Marina: And He told you that this man, the wind, has changed?

Josina: Yes.

Marina: And you know it was God?

Josina: Yes.

Marina: And you brought this up over the phone so you wouldn't have to deal with all of us in person?

Josina: I'm coming to visit in a few days, but...yes. Maybe you could talk it over with Uncle?

Marina: What is there to talk over? This man has no family. You own his house. Sure, he might be able to give you children, but any man can do that.

Josina: Auntie!

Marina: I'm being realistic, child. You're doing well on your own. You have a home, a good job, you make money. Any suitor should be at least a little comparable. What is he going to do when he gets back? Farming takes time, hard work. He won't be able to contribute anything for a while.

Josina: If nothing else, the Andilan name still carries weight. They were the pillar of their community, prominent among the Betsileo and even the

Merina, and he has every intention of repairing that pillar. But he is the only stone holding it up.

Marina: I don't care who the Merina esteem. [sigh] But the Betsileo are known and welcome here. And a good family name is nothing to dismiss lightly. All the same, a name is only a name. Has he acted accordingly?

Josina: With me, he has, yes.

Marina: [sigh] I suppose your uncle and I will have to discuss the matter. You've ignored our suggestions in the past, so the fact that you've found anyone at all is something of note. Has he made any foolish promises about finding your family's killers?

Josina: No. In fact, he suggested that the best revenge that either of us could get, would be to live and ensure that our families continue.

Marina: Hm. An interesting proposition. Funny that you should consider such advice coming from a stranger and not from your own family.

Josina: Auntie...

Marina: Come visit us, child, and we'll talk about it. When did you say you were supposed to hear back on his case?

Josina: It could be a few days or a few weeks. With everything that went on, I'm guessing it will be a few weeks.

Marina: Excellent. Plenty of time to try and dissuade you.

Josina: Oh, honestly.

Marina: I'm only trying to look out for you, child. The Sakalava have never bowed and our nobility remains strong. I am simply trying to ensure that we don't voluntarily go headlong off a cliff.

Josina: But wouldn't it be better to think of it as negotiating an alliance between Sakalava *ampanzaka* and a strong Betsileo family that is near-nobility status itself?

Marina: You're too much of a lawyer, I think. We'll see you in a few days, child. Bring your best arguments.

Sixteen
Ruling

Rivotra did not expect a quick response on his appeal. Given that the arguments were made on Thursday and he met with Josina on Friday, he slipped through the weekend with hardly a thought given to the appeal. He fully expected that nothing would happen, and his emotions agreed to go along with it.

Even as they rolled into October the next Monday, the time passed with relative ease. Judges had other things to do, and care and attention should be given to each affair. All of it routine and understandable, very much within the realm of the benefit of the doubt.

It wasn't until Wednesday that he felt his first twinge of nervousness. He told himself it was stupid. Barely a week since the argument. It could be three or even four weeks, and his case had international elements to it that probably required an extra layer of scrutiny. Why bother to get excited now?

Halloween, he told himself. He wasn't going to be worried until Halloween. That was well over four weeks after the arguments. If he didn't hear anything by then, he would assume that his appeal had been rejected, and he would plan accordingly.

That line of thought didn't hold much weight, but it got him to morning chores at least. He was back in laundry, washing, drying, sorting, listening to the desk officer's incessant whining about anything and everything in the daily newspaper.

"Man, just once, I wish he'd shut the fuck up," another inmate growled. He stood a few machines down from Rivotra, dragging out one set of wet clothes and shoving another load in behind them. "I wish my biggest complaint was some black and white ink about something someone thousands of miles away did. Or the fact that someone dared to critique my favorite food, or change the recipe."

Given that the food in the prison was heavily critiqued, both for making changes and not making changes, it was a fair shot as far as Rivotra was concerned, though he did not respond.

He didn't need to, for another nearby inmate spoke up. "No shit, man. Like to take that newspaper and shove it up his ass, maybe light it on fire."

"He's so full of shit, he'd probably explode."

The two conspirators got a good chuckle out of that.

"Maybe you should bribe the postal workers to not deliver his newspaper," Rivotra suggested casually. "It might force him to do his job."

He had a notion that the pair exchanged a glance. Then one of them said, "Or, we bribe them to deliver the paper to us instead. Then we make a little paper mâché statue of him, light that on fire." There was a noise like the slap of palms, as if for a high five. "Thanks for the idea, PJ."

That was not quite where he'd been going with that suggestion, but he supposed it was better than setting the man himself on fire. Although burning in effigy was considered almost as bad and would probably result in an extended vacation to the Hole.

"Maybe we can get some of the afternoon guys to help us," one conspirator said, his mind evidently latching onto this pyrolytic idea. "When dipshit gets off shift, afternoon guys can bring the paper to us. By the time the postal workers stop delivering, we'll still have a good supply of paper."

"And I'll get with the guys in the kitchen, see about getting their used oil at the end of the day," the second man added. "We can use that to bind the paper together, and it'll light up nice."

Now Rivotra was actually curious about this idea, and he kind of wished he might be able to see it, assuming this was a short-term project, say, within the next week.

"How big we gonna make this? Won't take but two days of missed papers for him to come snooping."

"Maybe we don't divert the papers, just have the afternoon guys bring them to us at the end of the day."

"We can work on this thing at night after count. Long as the Dirt don't mess shit up, we can take our time."

"Sounds good to me. Then we can make it as big as we want."

Well, Rivotra figured, that probably extended the timeline past when he wanted to be here. On the other hand, if he was telling himself Halloween, he had a suspicion that these two, plus any more they recruited, would somehow work that timeline into their project. A midnight effigy burning on Halloween, wouldn't that be fitting?

Lunch was uneventful, and in the afternoon he was back to sweeping, mopping, and vacuuming the admin building. Here he did not have to be party to any effigy burning schemes, but was instead subject to common office gossip among the social workers. He really couldn't decide which was worse. Effigy burning such as had been discussed earlier was potentially a threat, but it was also an intriguing, short-term arts and crafts project born of frustration and boredom. Office gossip tended to be dull, long-term backstabbing and manipulation.

The general rule was that if a door was closed, and it wasn't the weekend, don't open it. Come back to it later to clean. A closed door represented a private conversation, in person or on the phone. That didn't mean that those conversations couldn't still be heard through that closed door.

"Babe, I told you not to call me at work."

Rivotra scrubbed irritably at a spot on the floor with the mop.

"No, I haven't talked to him yet. Yes...yes, I know."

He went over another large swath of floor again, just in case he'd missed something in his blindness.

"I haven't had time! I've been working! No—now you know—you know that's not true. No, it isn't. I'm not just a shoulder to cry on. These men don't cry. They routinely threaten to rip my head from my shoulders and use it as a bowling ball."

And that was one of the nicer threats, Rivotra thought, turning around to mop another large swath of floor.

"I know! I want a raise, too! I know kids are expensive. I know. I—I know. Babe, come on, don't be like that. Don—don't—"

There was a pause, then the slam of a phone back on its receiver. Rivotra moved on from his position in the event the social worker came storming out of his office, which he did after a few moments. Rivotra heard the squeak of his shoes on the freshly mopped linoleum, but they quickly paused.

"If you had to choose between the rock and the hard place, which one would it be?" the social worker asked.

"Isn't the point of the metaphor that you don't get to choose?" Rivotra wondered.

"Humor me."

"Rock. At least you know what it is. Hard place could be a lot of things. A tree, the ground, another rock..."

"All right, point taken."

As the man walked away, Rivotra had a notion that such personal calls were not technically allowed except under emergency circumstances, and the female of that equation had probably exaggerated or even outright lied about whatever that emergency was. He had another notion that the social worker was first going to the telephone operator who directed those calls and telling them to not let his wife or girlfriend do that again, and then maybe going to his supervisor or the warden or whomever to inquire about that raise.

Inmate or civilian worker, everyone was trapped within the concrete and steel, Rivotra mused, carrying on with his mopping.

That was basically the life and times of Mt. Olive Correctional Complex, and it didn't get any better as a string of bad weather started to roll through the area, really taking hold over the weekend. Crisp, beautiful autumn days quickly turned into a hellish nightmare, complete with high water. Coats went from a suggestion for the weak to a requirement for the tough.

As the rain came through with more than occasional rumbles of thunder, small lakes began to form in the fields and anywhere that was just below grade. Soaking shoes and socks and pant cuffs became the norm, to the dismay of everyone, inmate and officer alike.

"This is off that big hurricane that came through the Gulf," someone commented at breakfast. "Fucked up Texas something fierce. Louisiana, too."

"Who cares about them? We're gonna be fucked up here pretty quick," someone else said.

A third inmate sighed dramatically, and Rivotra had a notion of him rolling his eyes. "This isn't the first hurricane tail that's come through. We survived them before, we'll be fine now."

"Yeah, but, this is like...really bad."

"We're on top of a mountain. Do you know how much water it would take to really put this place in danger? A lot more than this little sprinkle."

He wasn't wrong, Rivotra knew. Indeed, the bulk of the rain had basically subsided by Monday night. Tuesday remained overcast, but the worst that happened was a mild drizzle. Wednesday, the sun was out again, though it would take a few days to dry up the soaked ground.

In laundry, the effigy conspirators were making good progress on said effigy. They had been collecting not only the desk officer's papers, but papers from other inmates who also got newspapers delivered. With a good supply of oil from the kitchen, this effigy was well on track to being life size. If they got enough newspapers, Rivotra wondered if they were going to make more effigies and burn a whole army come Halloween.

He almost wanted to see it, or at least be there when it was lit up, but he kind of wanted to be out of prison more. It was now going on two weeks since the arguments, and he had heard nothing. He wondered how long the wait was between when his lawyer sent out a letter and when it reached him. Three days? Four? Longer? How long did it take the workers in the prison post office to sort through, read everything, then pass it off to the correct delivery man? Would such a notice have to go through the warden first, so he could stay apprised of the situation?

It was the international element, Rivotra told himself. The judge had to weigh the international implications of the appeal. If he approved the appeal, did that mean admitting to potential terrorist activity in the area? Did he have international agencies breathing down his neck, telling him to approve the appeal so they could swoop in and take over some kind of jurisdiction? Or were they pressuring him to reject the appeal in order to preserve the image of integrity within the American judiciary?

He kind of wanted to call Josina and ask about it. What was her experience having to deal with the likes of the CIA? He suspected it wouldn't be good. On the other hand, he knew that the call would inevitably turn to other things, and he still didn't know if he was ready for that answer. Sure, he'd asked the question, but he'd also known, at the time, that if he didn't ask it when he was thinking about it and had the most courage, he probably never would have. He could probably let that answer sit in the dark a little longer.

And that just left him in prison, doing laundry in the morning, then sweeping, mopping, and vacuuming in the afternoon.

By the end of the second weekend, everything had basically dried out. The effigy was coming along nicely, and the social worker was in no better disposition than he had been the week before.

"So, did you get the raise?" Rivotra asked casually Monday afternoon, again mopping outside the social worker's office.

"Not yet," the social worker replied with a sigh. "He said he would 'think about it.' "

"I'm sorry to hear that. But it sounds like you got a kid on the way, so that's good."

"How did—? Well, I guess everything gets out eventually."

"I won't tell, I promise. Congratulations, though."

"Thanks. But congratulations are needed less than prayers and patience. You ever dealt with a pregnant woman?"

No, but with some prayers of his own, he might be. "Can't say that I have."

"Well, all that beautiful and glowing talk? Bullshit sold by Hollywood and major consumer industries. No, she's not beautiful, and the hormone changes are hell. But of course, if you say that—"

"She starts threatening to rip your head off your shoulders and use it as a bowling ball?"

"Exactly. Some of you guys are angels compared to her. Sometimes."

"So you come to prison for a little vacation from home?"

"Well...it's not all bad. I mean, she still cooks. She is still nice to me occasionally."

Rivotra nodded. "Well, congratulations anyway. Good luck."

"Yeah, no shit. Thanks, man."

Ideally, inmates weren't supposed to know anything about the civilian staff. Marriage status, family status, residence, pastimes and hobbies, none of it. The leverage potential was too great. But that information tended to get out anyway—often through admin privilege inmates or those, like Rivotra now, who worked in the admin building—and it was usually how they got roped into drug and weapon smuggling for the gangs.

Assuming anyone else didn't know this information, Rivotra could sell it for a very high price. Wife and kids was pretty good leverage, but a pregnant woman could typically edge that out to take the top position.

He had no intention of giving out such information, or selling it either. He just continued mopping, following the routine he had established, and finishing without flourish. The desk officer apparently trusted him enough that he let him go without needing to follow up and get after him about missed corners. This may have had to do with many of the social workers commending his cleaning job, often with remarks about how a blind man did it better than some of the sighted inmates.

With a little free time on his hands before dinner, he made his way to the gym. He found a friendly group in the weights area and joined them, rotating around the machines as they opened up.

"So, PJ, what do you think?" someone asked. "You going to join the wickerman party on Halloween?"

"Is that the one where they're going to light these newspaper effigies I keep hearing about?" Rivotra wondered, adding weight to a machine.

"The very same."

"I haven't decided."

"Why not? I heard it was your idea."

"It was not my idea. I just suggested taking away the newspaper from the desk officer in laundry. Everyone else came up with this idea of the effigies."

"Whatever, man. You gonna come or not?"

"I haven't decided."

"It's only two weeks away!" someone else insisted. "Come on, you gotta come. Okay, maybe you can't see it to enjoy it, but it'll still be fun."

"Is this an official or unofficial event?" Rivotra asked.

"What?"

"Do the officers know?"

"They will eventually."

Rivotra didn't answer. He didn't want to be here come Halloween. But with each passing day, his hopes of his appeal going through grew dimmer and dimmer.

"What time does the mail come in?" he asked, changing the subject.

He had a notion that the other men exchanged glances. Finally one answered, "Dunno. Why?"

Rivotra elected to cut his workout short and pay the post office a visit to find out.

The prison had its own post office and postal code. They even had an official government post master to oversee all of the working inmates. Tucked away in a small building that was connected to the admin building, they were fifteen minutes to quitting time when he walked in.

"What do you got for me?" the inmate at the desk asked.

The room was small, carpeted, and not unlike commissary in many respects. Although it was a post office, it probably didn't have the same friendly feel as the post offices on the outside. Like commissary, everything was kept under guard, and patrons had to specifically request everything they wanted; there was no browsing, no perusal, and no impulse thefts.

"Just a question." Rivotra told them. "When do you get mail in?"

The man's tone changed to one he recognized as having to give the same rehearsed speech to multiple people. "Mail comes in every day at two o'clock sharp. Gets sorted in the afternoon, junk mail gets tossed, special mail is set aside, regular mail is read over, then it gets delivered out the next morning."

"What's considered special mail?"

"You ought to know," someone else nearby scoffed. "Shit's gotta get translated."

Rivotra bobbed his head in acknowledgment. "How long does that take?"

"For you, just have to wait for Cameron. Why, you missing a letter from your girlfriend?"

"No, just curious."

"Listen, man. As soon as we hear about your appeal, you'll hear about it, too." The desk inmate slapped his palms on the desk, causing Rivotra to flinch. "If it's rejected and you're just getting a courtesy letter from your lawyer, you'll get it the next morning, same as always. But, dig this. If your appeal goes through, well, first, warden gets a call. But if the letter arrives first, it gets delivered right away. No need to spend more nights here than you got to."

Rivotra nodded. "So if I get morning mail, it's a bad sign. Afternoon mail, it's a good sign."

"Absolutely positively. That's how it goes."

"Yeah," the second inmate said. "Now we see how you can go, because it's quitting time."

Rivotra waved a hand dismissively and left the room. Although he knew he hadn't taken up fifteen minutes of their time, as soon as the door closed behind him, someone came out to lock it.

It was a nice bit of information, at least. Now he knew that if he didn't get any mail in the morning, he still had hope for another day. So, the next morning, when he didn't receive a letter from his lawyer, he could confidently breathe a sigh of relief. He could eat breakfast and spend his morning in relative calm. At lunch, he could almost look forward to the arrival of the mail. Two o'clock it came in, got handed off.

Junk mail was sorted out first. Sales advertisements, political flyers, all of it straight into the garbage. After that, sort out the special mail, the stuff that had to be translated from various languages and anything else of particular importance. Then, once all mail was read and confirmed to not be harboring any evil secrets or dastardly schemes, it made its way into bins to be delivered to the appropriate neighborhood the following morning.

That meant, pretending that things were as chaotic as he believed them to be, he could be notified of the success of his appeal some time between four and six in the afternoon.

But Tuesday passed, and nothing happened either way.

An absence of mail Wednesday morning gave him hope.

Then the afternoon came and went and he again went to bed disappointed.

Hope sprang forth once more as he was mail-free once more on Thursday morning.

Heading to breakfast, he scolded himself for getting so caught up in this. If he brought this up at the group tonight, he knew exactly how it was going to go.

He had been held captive and tortured, how had he survived that? Had he really been trying to fool himself into thinking that help was coming at any minute, any second? That was how prisoners of war died, because they held so tightly onto a hope that they conjured in their minds. It wasn't the captivity or the torture that killed them, it was often suicide, because they believed in something impossible. He couldn't rely on this short-term hope. He had to dig in and prepare himself for the long haul, and then be happy if rescue came.

Still. He had been here for only a year and a half, maybe a little longer. He had eighteen more years before parole, assuming Josina didn't break him out or he didn't regain his ability to conjure portals, though both options were still out of the realm of real possibility for him.

Off to another day of laundry, then. Thursday meant he was able to pick through all the stacks of clean clothes and choose the ensemble that he liked the most. For him, that just meant they fit well and didn't have holes. He would prefer if they didn't have stains, but the best he could do was trust the others when he asked questions along those lines. At least he didn't have to wear the recycled boxers and socks, only pants and shirts.

"Hey. Week and a half until we burn this motherfucker," one of the original effigy conspirators said, elbowing him in the ribs. "You going to be there?"

"For my sake, I hope not," Rivotra sighed.

"Why not? Come on, man, it was your idea!"

"It was not my idea! I just suggested taking his damn newspaper away. You're the ones who came up with this whole effigy idea with the used oil from the kitchen and whatever else you've got going on."

"But you were that spark of inspiration. We're just giving credit where credit is due."

"Thanks, I prefer to remain anonymous."

"But aren't we supposed to give all credit to Jesus for good ideas?"

Annoyed, Rivotra turned and swung at the man, his fist connecting squarely with the conspirator's nose.

"Aw, shit!" the man groaned.

A chorus of "Ooh!" resounded throughout the immediate area.

"Fuck, man. Aw, shit, I think it's broken."

"Stop calling me that," Rivotra told him. "I'm tired of asking."

"All right, all right. Fuck, man, now I got blood all over my new shirt."

"So pick out another."

"What's going on over here?" It was the desk officer, the old bear roused from his slumber and no happier for it.

There was the sound of a number of inmates suddenly returning to work.

"Well?" the officer demanded testily.

"Nothing, C.O.," the man with the broken nose murmured.

"Nothing? Your nose just broke itself and started bleeding?"

"Cold weather, dry air," Rivotra told him. "Happens to the best of us."

"Uh-huh."

The officer walked past Rivotra to the bleeding man. He heard groans of pain, probably as the officer checked on the wound. Then, "Get over to the clinic for some packs and shit so you stop bleeding everywhere." His vocal attention turned toward Rivotra. "And you can accompany him, since the blood on your hand suggests you tried to help him already."

Right. That's what he did.

It made for an exciting morning anyway as he accompanied the man to the clinic.

"Fuck, man, you didn't have to do that."

"I'm tired of being called Prison Jesus, and I'm really tired of asking."

"Why? What's wrong with being compared to Jesus?"

"Because I'm not Him. Not even close. And I don't think He enjoys the spotlight being taken away."

The man made a congested noise, then spit to one side. "Man, half the guys here don't even know who Jesus is. Last time they went to church was probably Christmas or Easter with their memaw when they were eight. All they know is he was a special baby had angels singing over him and kings visiting, did lots of good things for lots of people, talked back to the man, was killed and then rose again.

"I don't know about you as a baby, but you got international lawyers coming to visit you, you defended a cop, you helped some other people, you got warden dancing for you on some things, and you was killed and came back to life. You're the closest thing to Jesus a lot of these guys have ever seen." He made another noise. "You could take it as a compliment at least, maybe even a challenge."

"I've never claimed to be a Christian. I don't like them much either."

"Good, 'cause lot of the guys don't like Christians. Guys from the Bible college, inmates who are enrolled, lot of them get to be uppity bastards. Better bet is to stay down here in the mud with us, but that don't mean you got to be an ass about it. We're all stuck here."

They reached the clinic. A broken, bloody nose was hardly an emergency, so the man was made to wait. Rivotra got a few wipes to clean his hands, then returned to laundry.

"Where's Mike?" the desk officer demanded.

"At the clinic getting his nose looked at," Rivotra said.

"I told you to accompany him."

"And I did. He'll be fine. I'm not his mother."

The officer grumbled something and went back to his newspaper.

Suddenly, Rivotra did want to go to the burning of the effigy.

Mike did not return before the end of shift, and Rivotra did not hear anything about the incident at lunch either. That was to be expected, and it didn't bother him.

Actually, it was Mike's comments that bothered him more. He didn't want to be compared to Jesus. He wasn't a Christian, didn't like them much, but he still felt it was a mockery of their beliefs. At the same time, wasn't it the highest compliment a Christian could hope to receive? If he was getting that compliment and they weren't, did that really mean something, or was it just foolish association by men who didn't know better?

He could probably ask Jeremy about it. Maybe he would sign up for church this weekend and talk to the chaplain understudy about it afterwards. He wasn't all that uppity.

After lunch, he made his way to the admin building, past the desk where he gave the officer a brief hello, and finally to the small cleaning closet. Another weekday, another day of intruding on the social workers in their offices, and making his way around a menagerie of desks, chairs, and assorted office furniture. Weekends were much easier, when everyone congregated in the visitation hall and he could do what he needed.

But that was neither here nor there. He grabbed the vacuum and made his way down the hall. Habit alone got him where he needed to be, an office that was soon empty, its occupant saying he would take a quick bathroom break so Rivotra could clean. He thanked the man, tapped around, found the outlet he was looking for, then bent to plug in the machine. He did not turn it on right away, but tapped around the room for a couple more seconds, locating everything in his way. Satisfied he understood the room, he pocketed his cane and flipped the switch on the vacuum.

Almost exactly one minute later, he was finished. He couldn't say that there were neat lines in the industrial carpet, but he knew he had gone over every square inch he possibly could. He used the attachment to clean off the chairs, then wrapped up, unplugged, and moved on to the next office.

One by one, down one hall, up another. By the end, he was sneezing something fierce. Who had dumped a truck load of dirt in the offices today? Maybe it was just mud from all the recent rain, drying and turning to dirt and dust. Sweeping the halls was probably going to produce a lot more dirt than normal, too, but at least it shouldn't kick up so bad.

Sweeping was uneventful, and he returned to the closet to make up his mop water. One cap of cleaner, one gallon of water, extrapolate appropriately. As he rolled the bucket out into the hall, he heard a cluster of approaching footsteps. Such a thing never bode well, and he wondered which sorry sap was about to get an unwelcome visit.

"981436."

Rivotra recognized the warden's voice. He paused in his walk, straightened, and turned in the direction of the footsteps. "Sir?"

Three pairs of boots got within striking distance. Again, the warden spoke. "Just need you to confirm your number and name."

"981436, Andilan, Rivotra."

He felt an envelope get pressed into his hand and heard the warden say, "Roll up. You're out of here."

Rivotra blinked, initially unable to process the man's words. Then he clutched the envelope tight. "My appeal—"

"Went through. Now roll up."

"Should I finish—"

"Roll up, damn you! I'm not repeating myself! Leave the fucking mop and go roll up!"

Rivotra was too stunned to be offended, and he did as he was told. He abandoned the mop and bucket of water, positioned his cane, gripped the envelope, turned, and made for the door. A moment later, he heard someone fall in beside him.

"I knew you could move fast if you wanted to." It was Oswald.

"Every man can move quickly at the prospect of freedom," Rivotra told him.

In the middle of the afternoon, everyone was still at their afternoon chores or classes or whatever occupied their time. Few were out and about in the complex, and the neighborhood was empty.

"What are you—?" the desk officer began. "What is he—?"

"It's fine," Oswald told him.

Rivotra entered his cell and grabbed his tub. He paused at a tap on his shoulder.

"I know you got some good clothes. Change into those, and we'll get you a shirt on the way out. Keep the coat for the time being. Here's a bag for the rest of your stuff. There's a process we have to go through, so we're not heading for the exit right this second."

Rivotra nodded, tempering his excitement just a little, just enough to lessen his chances of making a fool of himself, like putting his pants on backwards. Oswald also took the opportunity for one last strip search, which, predictably, produced nothing.

"Warden didn't sound too happy back there in the admin building," Rivotra observed mildly, slipping his undershirt back over his head.

"Good Lord, I had the misfortune of standing right there when he got the call," Oswald said, standing in the doorway, chuckling humorlessly. "He doesn't like you; I don't know if you caught on to that."

Rivotra left the uniform shirt on his mattress and tied the *lamba* around his shoulders. "If I did, I didn't give it much thought."

"Fucking murdered, and you wouldn't give up your murderers. I mean, yeah, maybe you don't remember them, but it still pissed him off. And then there's all this international bullshit going on. You meet with your pretty lawyer a few times, but there is holy hell raining down behind the scenes. FBI, CIA, NSA, DHS, fucking INTERPOL, all those damn agencies."

"And what about you?"

Oswald made a sound that was a shrug. "Remember what I said about me not being very popular in politics and probably never getting promoted to captain or beyond? I mean, it kind of sucks, but it also means I don't have to deal with the whole circus. Lieutenant keeps me pretty well square over day-to-day operations without getting into administration."

Rivotra stood and shoved the rest of the contents of his tub in the plastic bag the officer had given him. "So you do like me. I'm flattered."

He followed Oswald out of the cell, grateful he wouldn't be coming back to it tonight. He briefly wondered who was going to tutor Erik for his next big history test, then decided it wasn't his problem. The kid was going to have to make his own way.

Oswald kept talking. "I like a lot of the guys here. You respect me, I respect you. If this prison wants to tout rehabilitation, well, retraining people in basic decency and respect goes farther than just yelling at them all the time. Yelling is necessary sometimes, but when I can, I try to be a decent guy."

Rivotra nodded. "I appreciate that, always have, even in the nursing home."

"Good news is, we don't have to go there. First stop is the clinic."

"The clinic?"

"Outgoing physical. That way if you fuck yourself up in the near future, you can't blame it on us. And if you fuck yourself up, the doctor or hospital can call and there will be at least some medical record of you."

Made sense, he supposed.

They walked in the clinic where Rivotra gave his number and name and Oswald expedited his wait to no time at all.

"Your lawyers are on their way right now," the officer told him, "assuming they're not here already. Miss Zitha is just fine to work with, but Bartlett's a piece of work. Warden hates him more than you."

"I got that impression from a lot of people during the trial. But he's obviously worth his pay."

"Oh, I am not disagreeing that point. *Pas du tout*." (Not at all.)

"Still working on your French?"

"You know, it's been kind of interesting to talk to Cameron in another language so others can't eavesdrop, but he hates that I have 'the wrong accent' and he's been trying to train me in 'proper French.'"

Rivotra just laughed.

Once in the room, it was only a few minutes before the doctor came by.

"Outgoing physical, eh?" he began. "All right, let's see how you are walking out of here."

Compared to when he arrived, his condition had deteriorated. Some of it was to be expected: the blindness, the vertigo, the lack of proprioception, and all of the other disabilities his numerous recently-acquired head injuries had graced him with. Others were not so expected. He had put on weight, and not all of it from muscle. In spite of working out as often as possible with a fairly impressive routine, being forced to eat regularly had easily outpaced his body's Time-induced nutritional efficiency. That was something that would be just as easily corrected once he was back home.

His vitals were normal, heart rhythm normal, every basic measurement and test concluding that he hadn't left the prison with untended, catastrophic wounds.

"All right, good to go," the doctor pronounced. "Good luck."

Rivotra thanked him and followed Oswald out of the room. "Where to next?"

"You don't have any overdue library books, do you?"

"I hope not."

"Anyone you want to say goodbye to?"

He was ready to say no, then thought better of it and said, "Jeremy, the chaplain understudy."

From the clinic, the two of them made their way to the chapel and back to the offices. Rivotra could hear an inmate talking to the head chaplain, the tone suggesting he was trying to schmooze some kind of good word or recommendation out of the clergyman. A few steps beyond, Oswald tapped on a door to a muffled, "Come in."

Rivotra walked in the room. He did not sit down.

"Well, what can I do for you?" Jeremy inquired.

"Come to say my goodbyes," Rivotra told him.

"Your appeal went through?"

"Yes, it did."

There was the movement of a chair across the floor, and Rivotra felt a tap on his arm. He cautiously held out his hand, and Jeremy found his grasp. "Congratulations. I guess you'll be going home, then."

"As far as I know, that's the plan."

He had a notion of the understudy nodding. "I wish you well. Good luck on the farm. I'm sure you'll have it up and running in no time."

"Thank you. Take care of yourself in here."

"I always do."

"And good luck returning to your home as well."

"Thank you."

With that, Rivotra followed Oswald out of the chapel.

"Anyone else?" the officer asked.

Maybe it was different for men who did spend five, ten, fifteen, twenty years or more behind bars. Like the military or any other captive community, there were bonds forged in this fire, some of them unbreakable. Rivotra hadn't been here long enough to boast of any such bonds, or even the beginnings of one. At the same time...

"Am I allowed to say goodbye to someone in supermax?" he wondered.

Oswald sighed. Then, "Yes, briefly."

Supermax was very reminisce of the nursing home, Rivotra thought. The cells were bigger, seeing how the inmates were not allowed to leave but once a day for one hour of heavily supervised yard time, and there was a perpetual smell to the place that just wasn't pleasant. There wasn't enough movement in the building to dispel the lingering odor of humanity.

His cane tapped Oswald's boot as the lieutenant stopped. A moment later, a heavy door rattled open.

"What—?" the occupant wondered. "It's not yard time."

"All right, say your goodbyes," Oswald said.

Rivotra stepped forward, guided lightly by the officer.

"Goodbye?" Vin questioned. Like Jeremy, a tap on Rivotra's hand alerted him to a handshake, this one more doubtful. "Where are you going?"

"Home," Rivotra said. "My appeal went through."

411

"Your appeal?" Vin cursed, and it wasn't in a supportive way. "You shoot Walt, kidnap Tommen, do all this other bullshit, and your appeal goes through? *And I have to wait for parole?!*"

Rivotra blinked, shocked by the outburst.

Vin yanked his hand away. "Get the fuck out of here! I hope your fucking plane crashes."

He spat some other nonsensical things as the door rattled shut.

"Clearly not the reaction you were expecting," Oswald stated, his tone suggesting he was a little surprised, too.

"Not exactly."

"Well, you can't win them all. Anyone else you need to say goodbye to?"

"I don't know that I want to take my chances."

"Fair enough. Well, let's head to the admin building for some paperwork, and then the warden gets to give you a goodbye speech."

Thus they crossed the complex yet again, this time heading for the admin building. Someone had come through and finished mopping, and their shoes squeaked on the clean floor.

The next step was an exit interview with the prison psychologist. The man admitted that the results could be skewed because of the prospect of freedom, but it was required by the state in order to have a record of an inmate's mental state before his departure from the facility.

Once the psychologist was satisfied that he was leaving in a good mental state, the next visit was his assigned social worker, Andrew. This was less about a teary goodbye and more about signing paperwork and receiving a fairly standard letter of recommendation generically addressed to any employer that Rivotra had good work ethic and could be considered reliable and hard-working. He was also given a small wad of cash, seventy-seven dollars and some change as the sum of his prison account. Rivotra was surprised; he didn't think there was any actual money involved, but apparently there was. Then the social worker wished him well and sent him on his way.

Next was a quick trip to one of the staff administrators who took his tub and gave him some more paperwork to keep track of. His bag of stuff was growing quite full. Hopefully he wouldn't acquire too much more.

"All right, come on down this way and I'll show you to the wardrobe," Oswald said, guiding him along. "Shirt, shoes, coat, and we might have an actual backpack you can use instead of that plastic bag."

The wardrobe was a small room, perhaps a converted closet, with a rack of clothing, a stand filled with pairs of shoes, a chair, and a mirror.

"Where does all this come from?" Rivotra wondered, feeling over the clothes.

"Honestly, the ladies bring in their husbands' old clothes they want to get rid of. Here, try this."

It was a simple T-shirt which Oswald described as being long sleeve, gray, with a faded construction company logo on the breast and a larger faded logo on the back.

"It's just to get you out of here," the lieutenant told him. "Once you leave, you can go to Walmart or JCPenney and buy whatever you want. Here's a coat. Give me that one back."

Rivotra donned the shirt, momentarily surprised by the feel of cotton on his skin. It was thicker, softer, and warmer than the industrial things he'd been wearing for the last almost two years. He then traded out the standard issue coat for one Oswald handed him from the rack. It was thicker and warmer and he was even able to leave it unzipped for the time being.

The tennis shoes which replaced the slip-ons were nothing remarkable, perhaps because they were very well worn and broken in for another man's feet. But, as Oswald said, it was only to get him out.

There were no backpacks available, so he would just have to make do with the plastic bag.

"All right, fashionista, this way now. Time to go talk to the warden."

"That's not a good thing, is it?" Rivotra questioned.

"He's not usually cranky about the going away speech, but I wouldn't expect the handshake and well wishes."

Down the hall to another wing which Rivotra had been in only once, covering for another inmate who had been out sick and had been assigned to clean this area. He had a vague notion of where they were, and, a minute later, they were in a room. It was not an office, and he was unable to discern the purpose of this room at present.

"Well well, Prison Jesus," the warden said as he walked in and was shown to a chair. "Taking a plane and now ascending into Heaven."

Rivotra elected to say nothing.

"You had quite an impact on this place in the short time you were here. See, normally this speech is for those who have served their time or made parole. Rarely does it go to someone with a successful appeal, and even more rare is the inmate leaving on a successful appeal who doesn't come back. Now, this isn't a state-mandated speech, not like the outgoing physical or psych eval or anything else you've done on your walk of fame. This is just something I started doing, in hopes of reminding you about what's just happened and maybe help you to avoid a repeat.

"You've just spent time in a maximum security prison. Your routine has been dictated to you, your meals dictated to you, your clothing choices dictated to you, every action scrutinized, every word recorded. Maybe you got roughed up, maybe you made friends, I don't know. But you're about to step outside these walls for the first time in quite a while.

"Chances are, you'll get to decide most or all of your daily routine from now on, where you go, what you do, what you wear. You can choose the food you eat, when, and where. You are free to associate with whomever you like, and you're not irrevocably stuck with those who may wish you harm.

"The freedom to choose is a precious thing. It is a privilege. Abuse that privilege, and it gets taken away. No one forces you to commit a crime. You choose it. Outside these walls, there are thousands of choices waiting to be made. Some good. Some bad. No one can make those choices for you. Remember this and you just might make it."

Rivotra had a sneaking suspicion that there was supposed to be some kind of cheerful wrap-up on this speech, the handshake and well wishes as Oswald had said, but it never came. The warden was reciting his speech out of habit and some self-proclaimed duty, but, as he said, it wasn't a mandatory thing.

"All right, Remy, take him out," the warden said gruffly. "I got the signatures from the lawyers while he was out appearing to the masses one last time."

Oswald said nothing, just guided Rivotra through the room to another door.

The acoustics of the room beyond caused a massive shift in his mind as multiple puzzle pieces clicked into place. They were on the other side of the visitation hall. They had effectively come full circle through the building. Not that it mattered now since he was leaving, but he enjoyed the sudden understanding.

"There he is!" Bartlett's nasally voice echoed in the empty room. "It's about time!"

"Celebrities require long goodbyes," Oswald said smartly.

"Very funny," Rivotra told him.

A last tap on the hand, and Rivotra shook hands with the lieutenant.

"Take care of yourself on the farm," the lieutenant told him sincerely. "Good luck."

"Thank you," Rivotra replied, equally as sincere. "Take care of yourself in here."

Oswald did not leave, merely took up an unobtrusive post at the door to watch their departure.

"Are you ready to go home?" Josina asked, offering her arm to guide him out. On his other side, Bartlett took his bag full of papers and the sum of his worldly possessions.

"Are we going right now?" he wondered.

"Well, not quite," Bartlett butted in. "As soon as the ruling came down, I called up Calhoun to cash in on his promise to buy you a plane ticket home."

"I'm guessing he refused?"

They left the visitation room and made their way through an outgoing security checkpoint. There was a non-invasive patdown and bag check, and then they were on their way again.

"Oh heck no," Bartlett went on, answering the question. "I badgered him until he gave in. Matched all of Miss Zitha's flights, though you may not be sitting together. Honestly, though, when you're in the terminal waiting for your flight, just talk to one of the agents, they'll do whatever you want, especially with your disabilities."

"The first flight doesn't leave until ten o'clock tomorrow morning," Josina told him. "We'll be staying in a hotel tonight."

Rivotra just nodded awkwardly.

"But first, I think some dinner is in order!" Bartlett declared. "Are you hungry? What do you want to eat? My treat, of course!"

No, he wasn't hungry, hadn't been hungry in quite a while, and apparently he was getting fat. On the other hand, if this wasn't cause for celebration, he didn't know what was.

"Why don't you pick?" he suggested, turning his head toward Josina. "You know what's good to eat around here."

First they had to go through a second security checkpoint, and the room beyond, although empty besides a quiet receptionist and another desk officer, had a much different feel to it. It was still industrial security, but there was something almost normal about it. The carpet was a little nicer, more sound was absorbed in cloth cushions, and a breeze rustled the leaves of a fake plant in the corner.

It was just as cold outside the prison fence as it was on the inside, but there was something different here, he thought. The air logically couldn't be any different, but he might be convinced that there was a hint of freedom on the wind.

His brain still wasn't quite processing that he was free. Right now, he was simply of the mind that he was being shuffled somewhere because someone else wanted him to go there. But, as Josina guided him to the car and he got inside, sitting behind her, his stomach gave an involuntary lurch as he suddenly recalled, with sickening detail, his trip into the prison.

"How well does Bartlett drive?" he asked her in Malagasy.

"Well...this is a fast car. And he knows how to drive it," she told him with some trepidation. "I think he's been trying to show off to me—he likes to brag about American muscle?—and I have a suspicion he's going to want to do the same to you, maybe try to cheer you up."

"I think I'm just going to Slow Band my way to the restaurant."

"That might be a good idea."

Rivotra didn't care if he annoyed Bartlett by ignoring any questions or comments. He didn't care if the lawyer thought it rude or suspicious that he did not react to anything. All he cared about was surviving the trip. Condensing an hour of hellish mountain roads into roughly three seconds was the only way he saw to do that.

As he got out of the car and took Josina's arm again, he still wasn't thinking "freedom." He was thinking "chow time." He was still prepared to walk into a noisy cafeteria, grab a tray, accept whatever was given to him, eat all of it, then return everything and wait for the tines on his fork to be counted.

Walking into the restaurant stirred something in his mind, put a small crack in this rigid mentality. He did not go to stand in a line, but was greeted by a hostess who sounded like she was sixteen years old. She inquired if he would prefer a braille menu. Completely caught off-guard by the question, he couldn't answer. Josina answered for him, accepting the offer, then they were shown to a booth which, reportedly, had a great view of the river.

Rivotra was not consciously doing anything at this point, although he knew to open up the utensil roll and place the napkin on his lap. He touched the menu, felt the bumps, and stopped.

"I don't actually read braille," he admitted.

"Burger, pizza, steak, fish, chicken wings, salad, what's your fancy?" Bartlett asked, his tone distracted.

"I don't know," he told Josina, again in Malagasy. "I'm not hungry, honestly, but it is a celebration."

"What have you wanted to eat but couldn't in prison?" she posited.

He thought a moment. With the culinary school in house, the prison menu was surprisingly varied and complex. Then, "Real meat, not some second-rate cut mixed with eighty percent soy."

The waitress approached the table with glasses of water and inquired after their orders. Again, Rivotra almost didn't know what to do. Only out of habit was he able to order a medium sirloin and side salad. More cracks were appearing in his rigid mental order, but freedom still wasn't quite his reality.

"All right, is there anywhere you want to go after here?" Bartlett wondered. "Once I drop you two off at the hotel, you're on your own."

"That's fine," Rivotra told him. "I really just want to go home."

"I picked up a couple changes of clothes for you," Josina said, "and some other essentials to get you through to Tana."

"Getting through" seemed to be the name of the game right now, Rivotra thought. Get through dinner—which was far more delicious than anything had a right to be—get through the evening, get through the night, get through the flights, everything a stepping stone from here to there.

It wasn't until later when Josina opened the door to the hotel room that something truly jarred in his mind. The room was bigger than his cell, the bathroom was a separate room and fully accessible, he had full control over the temperature and air flow, the bed was comfortable. There was a window. No one was telling him when he had to be in bed, no one was going to walk around every hour and look inside.

"There is one detail I should mention," Josina said. She was still by the door while Rivotra was feeling the bed that had a real mattress and real blanket.

"What's that?" he wondered, only half paying attention.

"Netami is going to meet us in Tana. She is going to take you to trial on Hlohi."

Rivotra paused, his mind momentarily frozen, wondering what to do. He was free. His appeal had gone through. He was no longer in prison, and the prosecutor was declining a retrial. He was going home, but he was going on trial again.

"Well that's some very inconsiderate timing," he stated.

"I know, but I think it's for the best. You are free and clear of this place, but you are not yet established at home."

Well, at least he was going to make it home.

Rivotra had been looking forward to the day when he could sit in Anagalisgi's cave as a free man, but he found that he couldn't enjoy it. Maybe because his mind still wasn't fully out of prison. Maybe because of the impending series of flights he was going to have to endure. Maybe because he knew what was waiting for him at the end of those flights. Whatever the case, he could not appreciate the clothes he now wore over his healed body, could not enjoy the warmth of the fire or the deliciousness of the stew as much as he had been hoping.

"You're worried," Anagalisgi stated.

Rivotra took a bite of stew in order to avoid replying right away. "Almost."

"Hm?"

"Almost. Maybe it would take a day or two to snap out of prison mentally, but even if that does happen in the next few days, I'm only going straight back."

"Still convinced that the Krydik are going to execute you?"

"Execute, enslave, either one."

"Would you rather have this hanging over your head while you work on the farm?" Anagalisgi questioned.

Rivotra sighed. "I suppose not, but...I would have liked to have spent just one night back on the farm."

"It hasn't even happened yet and you are already speaking in the past tense."

"Aren't you the one who likes to say that prophecy isn't about what you're going to do, it's about what you've already done? Two hundred pages ahead, there I am, doing the thing?"

Anagalisgi chuckled. "There is that, but it is intended to help you worry less. Things will happen as they will. It is not about apathy or pacifism, simply faith and trust."

"Do you know what's going to happen? You're a little too calm for my comfort."

"I do know."

"But you're not going to tell me."

"Perhaps you should ask the one who made the arrangements."

"She can't know how Nendawagan is going to rule, can she?"

"You should discuss it with her, if nothing else. If you can't talk to her now, it's not going to get better when you need to have serious discussions as a married couple."

Rivotra scoffed. "Well that's not going to happen either, I think."

"Why not?"

"If I'm executed, obvious reasons. If I'm enslaved, I can't do that to her. She has too much going for her to be dragged into that."

"If your primary concern was having children to carry on your name, well, slaves procreate, too."

"Better an anonymous *andevo* than a disgraced Andilan."

"Oh, for goodness' sake, Rivotra." Anagalisgi sounded genuinely annoyed. "Just because Rifun isn't in control anymore doesn't mean you have to give up all optimism. Reject his arrogance, yes, but optimism and confidence are good things. And just because you may be a slave does not mean your descendants would be slaves forever."

Rivotra sighed and took a bite of stew. Then, "I know. I should be grateful to be out of Mt. Olive at all. Even this afternoon with Josina was...nice."

"Your body has been healed, your eyes restored, your name reclaimed, your freedom regained." The man's tone was gentle now. "There is but one more thing to do before you can step into the life the Author had planned for Rivotra Andilan."

A long silence stretched between them. Anagalisgi was looking for a particular response, some kind of affirmation that Rivotra was grateful for said restoration and he was ready to step into this new life. But Rivotra wasn't ready to give that response just yet.

"Why did my mother stay with Vala?" he asked. "Why didn't she return to the family in Fianar?"

He heard Anagalisgi shift position. "The Shadows do not know the plans of the Author, but that is less important than knowing that there are plans at all. And all they really have to do is follow concentrations of White activity. They tried to get your mother to abort you, but they failed. They tried to get her to kill you at birth, and they failed again. The best they could manage was simple disruption, tearing you away from the Whites that would have taken you to Fianar, and holding you in Mahitsy."

"And all the abuse was just for the entertainment of the Shadows, to predispose me to their point of view, their goals, so that when the shaman divined that prophecy, my choice was all but written for me."

"That's right."

Rivotra shifted position. "Why, though? Why were the Whites so weak? Why didn't the Author send reinforcements or do something else? Why do the Whites lose battles at all?"

"Sometimes, when dealing with the chaos that is the universe, perfect is not an option," Anagalisgi said somberly. "Sometimes, perfect can make things worse. And sometimes, the best we get is only the least bad. I don't have those kinds of insightful answers, not to the degree that you want them. What I can tell you, though, is that the end is fast approaching, and you were a catalyst for it. And yet, somehow, that is a good thing. I can't explain it. I wish I could. But there are stirrings even around me and my life. My time as a mentor is nearing its end."

Rivotra scuffed his foot in the dirt. "Doesn't sound like a promising picture of a future family. For either of us."

"Maybe. But it is what will be. And has already been."

"Fate is fixed."

He finished off the stew and set the bowl and spoon aside. Across the fire, noises indicated that Anagalisgi was likely doing the same.

"So," the Native man said. "With all of that, are you ready to step into the life written for Rivotra Andilan?"

Rivotra took a breath and slowly let it out as he nodded. "Nowhere to go but forward, I suppose. What is the last thing I have to do?"

He could feel Anagalisgi's penetrating gaze, and his heart raced as he waited to hear the answer.

"Die."

Seventeen
Justice

G etting through airport security was possible only because of Josina's diplomatic status. She had acquired a Madagascan passport and visa for him under his new name, but the security database had a lot more information on him, none of it good. Multiple phone calls were made and they were detained for a few hours as people of rank were woken up early in the morning, but they were ultimately permitted into the airport.

"All of our flights have some layover time in case this happens again," Josina explained, guiding him to a chair in the proper terminal.

"If Netami is meeting us in Tana, why couldn't she meet us here?" Rivotra whined.

"Because certain agencies want a record of you leaving the country. There may or may not be undercover agents who are also on these flights in order to ensure that you leave the country."

He groaned into his hands and leaned forward, elbows on his knees.

"Honestly, Rivotra, the last time you were on a plane was 1923, right? Things have improved a little bit since then. And you can Band yourself anyway, like you did in the car."

There was that, yes, but the prospect overall was still unpleasant.

The PA in the waiting area chirped. "Delta Airlines, flight 2607, Charleston to Newark, thank you for your patience and your decision to fly with us today. Our flight this morning is on time and we will begin boarding in ten minutes, beginning with the elderly, disabled, and first class patrons. Thank you."

Josina was not important enough to warrant a private jet, but she was still considered a diplomat and did not fly coach. In fact, she was approached even before the first boarding announcement and told she could board when she was ready. Grabbing Rivotra and their carry-on bags, the two of them were escorted onto the aircraft. Rivotra noted that there were a lot more footsteps than just the two of them and the hostess.

Rivotra sat next to Josina and tried to get comfortable in the plush chair. It was roomier and more comfortable than the planes in 1923. It had leg room and reclining capabilities. He didn't care about the larger TV screen and declined all food and beverage offerings. He just clicked his seatbelt, asked not to be disturbed, closed his eyes, and Slow Banded.

Five seconds later, Josina was touching his shoulder, letting him know they had arrived. He released the Band, momentarily startled as he felt the plane moving.

"Ladies and gentlemen, welcome to Newark International Airport," the pilot said over the PA. "The time is 11:47 Eastern Daylight Time, weather forecast partly cloudy at fifty-two degrees Fahrenheit. On behalf of the pilots and the crew, thank you for flying Delta Airlines, and we wish you safe and happy travels on your next flight or in the city."

Again, Josina and Rivotra were the first ones permitted to move. She grabbed their bags, and he held on to one as they squeezed out of the plane and entered the Newark terminal.

This airport was much, much bigger, with thousands of people clamoring here and there, and a wash of noise in dozens of languages.

"Our next flight is in three hours," Josina explained, "and the flight itself to Johannesburg is fourteen hours."

Sounded like an excellent reason to Slow Band, Rivotra thought. Indeed, that was exactly what he did, both to pass the time until boarding—which was delayed an hour for unspecified reasons—and again to get him through the flight. Or that was the plan. Less than one second in his Slow Band, and Josina was touching him.

He dropped the Band and tilted his head, unsure what was currently expected of him.

"We have grilled chicken with vegetables, an eight-ounce sirloin, or, for our vegetarian option, a squash and carrot soup," a stewardess inquired.

"Nothing, thank you, I don't fly well," he told her, hoping the excuse was plausible. Apparently, it was not.

"In my experience, it's better to have a full stomach than an empty one."

Sighing, he elected for the soup.

"And to drink? We have an excellent selection of wine—"

"Water, please."

The stewardess acknowledged his requests and moved on to the next patron.

Rivotra turned to Josina next to him. "When do we take off?"

She laughed. "We've been in the air for a couple hours now. It's almost seven o'clock, dinner time."

"Really?"

He didn't feel anything, certainly nothing more than a low, humming vibration from the engines. Maybe flying had improved in a hundred years.

"I told you, it's not so bad," she said, nudging him in the arm.

"All right, fine, it's not horrible," he admitted. "When do we land?"

"In theory, seven o'clock in the morning, whatever it is local time."

"Oh."

"Most people sleep through it. We can Band through it."

"I fully intend to. But since I'm here and have some time before dinner arrives..."

"Yes...?"

He let out a breath. "Before I'm condemned to death or enslavement to the Krydik, I'd like to know. What did your family say about...me? Us? What did they think?"

Josina cleared her throat. "Ah. Well...they...needed some convincing, but eventually they agreed. To talk to you."

"Oh. Well, that's good to know." Couldn't even use that excuse to make himself feel better. "And what about you? Would you marry a man about to be a slave?"

"You're not going to be a slave, Rivotra."

"You don't know that. My head or my life. What else is Nendawagan going to do?"

"She could spare you."

He shook his head. "No. I don't know that I would accept that. Evil spirits or not, I don't deserve that, not after what I did to her."

"Isn't that why it's called mercy?"

427

"I still don't believe it."

She made an exasperated sound. "Rivotra, I admire humility, but self-flagellation is not an attractive quality."

"I'm just being realistic."

"Pessimistic."

"You're a lawyer, you have to be optimistic."

Now she really laughed. "I am trained to find avenues of attack and defense or else create them. Clever and industrious are not necessarily synonymous with optimistic."

"But you have to believe those attacks and defenses will work."

"Confidence."

"Optimism."

"Faith." When he did not reply immediately, she added, "And I know yours has been wavering the last few years."

He hummed a sigh. "Well, you're not wrong."

"Things will work out. I know they will."

The stewardess returned with their meals. The smell-taste of Josina's chicken made Rivotra wish he had ordered that instead, but there was nothing to be done about it now. He picked up the spoon, got familiar with the setup, and started eating.

The food was good, he would admit. And this flight was far less traumatic than his last flight almost a century ago. But he wasn't keen on experiencing the next twelve hours in real time, so, once dishes had been taken and everyone started settling in for the night, he Banded again.

The plane landed in Johannesburg, South Africa, early in the morning, but they were not the only plane coming or going, and the airport was respectably busy. They had less trouble here getting through customs and were soon heading for the terminal for their last flight to Antananarivo. He noted the departure of their less-than-subtle entourage.

"This is a three-hour flight, but it's easily the nicest," Josina was saying as they hopped on an escalator and headed down. "Now that we're back where they serve real food and use real manners."

Rivotra couldn't help but smile. He was going to his death, but she was happy, at least. No more constant flying back and forth to the United States—

by the ancestors, how had she done this multiple times, back and forth to see him?—no more running here and there bound by impossible schedules, living out of a suitcase. Resigning from the Senate and going to work at the university would do her well in more than one respect.

From the terminal, they took a bus out onto the tarmac and loaded into a much smaller plane. There was no first class here, but it was comfortable regardless.

Interestingly enough, now that they were on this flight, Malagasy and French no longer worked to keep conversations private, but he was quite tired of using English all the time. It was actually a relief that he was returning to his home country where the people spoke a real language.

He decided to forego the Band during takeoff, just to see what it was like. His head did not agree with this decision, and his vertigo made itself well-known. His only saving grace was that it was only his vertigo and not a seizure, too. Once in the air and leveled out, he decided that he'd had enough excitement and promptly Banded.

A few seconds later, Josina touched his arm. He dropped the Band, stunned as he temporally realigned with the plane and involuntarily jerked. He couldn't even be sure he didn't black out momentarily as the next thing he knew, the plane had come to a stop and people were shuffling past with their carry-on bags.

"You had a minor seizure," Josina told him.

"I thought so," he breathed, head still pounding.

Maybe his stumbling off the plane would evoke some pity from Netami. If they were literally going straight to court on Hlohi, maybe it would sway Nendawagan. Maybe airsickness would be what saved his life.

Josina was well-known in customs, and her ease of access rubbed off on him. Then the two of them made their way through the airport to the front lobby. Josina walked confidently while the best Rivotra could do was put one foot in front of the other, his coordination with his cane severely lacking as he relied heavily on her movements.

"Welcome home," a familiar female voice greeted. "How were your flights?"

"Very long, as always," Josina replied. "And he doesn't fly so well."

"He does look a little pale." Netami did not bother trying to hide the smugness. "Well, come with me, and let's get this over with, hm?"

It was all a show, Rivotra thought. A spectacle. A performance. The decision had already been made; he was just going through the motions, the audience to be entertained and shocked by things the actors knew by heart.

Well, might as well get it over with. At least he had set foot back in his homeland.

He did not resist, did not question, just kept his hand on Josina's arm and followed wherever she went. As they exited the airport, he paused just long enough to breath in the smell of warm, tropical air. The smell of home.

Then they were moving again, and, shortly, he felt the tug of a portal. It wasn't so much a tug as it was the compression of every atom of his being into an infinitesimally small piece of mass followed immediately by the elongation of said atoms to stretch out across the entire universe, then being deposited on foreign soil as an incoherent blob of Matter that was, somehow, still him.

Portal travel had never been easy, but it was still better than twenty-four hours of flying.

The air here was not tropical, but it was warm, in that fresh-out-of-winter sense that he remembered from prison. And there was a purity to it he could not describe. There were no cities on Hlohi anywhere, no industrialization that he was aware of. There was only nature, only the mountains and the valleys and the trees.

With some help, he got to his feet. He'd never actually been to Hlohi, knew it by description only. He didn't know what he could be looking at, which direction he was facing. This was about as blind as blind could get.

"We're just down the mountain slope," Josina said softly as they started to move. "We're going up into a...like a bowl, and the ridgeline looks like—"

"A wolf lying curled up on her side," Rivotra stated. "With a river pouring from the side of her mouth. In her belly lies the protected town of Aktiya Waya, The Wolf Watches Over It."

"That's right."

Not that he knew what it actually looked like, but the description combined with this sudden hiking adventure was a statement in itself. And the fact that he could feel eyes on him. And why not? If things had been arranged this far in advance, why not bring in the welcome wagon? One could argue that this could be standard defensive procedure with what they were dealing with against the Order, but he didn't think that was the case. If things were bad, they'd just open portals directly in and out of the city. This walk of shame was purposefully coordinated.

The old city of Aktiya Waya was set deep into the mountain, so that only the waning sunlight would penetrate the farthest corners. Years of war and migration and internal strife had seen the city grow so that it now started spilling out onto the outside slope. From what Rivotra understood, reading the Books of others, many in Aktiya Waya lived in the old city during the winter for protection from the elements, then moved to the city on the slope during the summer for light, warmth, and a summer breeze.

The path hugged tall cliffs to their left but was open to the right. He heard the many sounds of daily village life: general conversation, children laughing and playing, animals vocalizing their opinions, the rustling of pots and pans and other goods. He noted that the vast majority of adult voices he heard were feminine. He had a suspicion that most or all of the men, those who weren't away fighting, were either gathered in a central location for the trial, or else escorting him now.

He could feel Josina's pulse through her arm, and she was nervous, whatever strong face she was putting on for the people around them. How much did she know about what was going to happen, or was she as blind to this as he was?

The hike up the slope to the old city was the longest, most difficult hike Rivotra had done in a while. Considering it was nothing more than the average walk down the road for any of the residents, he felt even more ashamed of how out of shape he'd gotten.

The air and sunlight out in the open was warm enough, but, like the weather in the United States, as soon as he was out of that direct sunlight, it was cold again. The stone was freezing, and the air, with almost no breeze to circulate any of the outside heat to the inside, was absolutely frigid. He couldn't suppress a shiver, and Josina reacted similarly. Neither one of them made a comment about it, nor did anyone in their escort party.

The Krydik had not built the old city; it had been left by an ancient people from long before, perhaps even the beginning of time. If there was any rhyme or reason to the layout of the city, Rivotra was unable to pick up on it. The buildings seemed to work well enough for the Krydik, but he was forced to wonder, briefly, if they bore any resemblance to any human dwelling, or if any such renovation had come later.

"Here," Netami said quietly, stopping the walk. "When you go in, do not speak, and do not sit until told. Josina, you will stand by me."

Josina murmured an affirmative and Rivotra just bobbed a nod.

The building they entered was blessedly warm, and Rivotra had a momentary notion of being in Anagalisgi's cave. The crackling of the fire provided a soothing ambiance to soften the tension. Not everyone who had escorted them entered the building now, but he could tell there were plenty of people in attendance. Josina guided him to a certain spot near the fire, then put a couple fingers under his hand. He gave her arm a gentle squeeze, then released her, pressing his white cane into her palm.

Suddenly alone amid a sea of questions and hostility, Rivotra prepared for anything. He had read Sabelu's Book once, knew he had been put on trial also. But how similar would his trial be now? Sabelu's trial had been a kangaroo court, his guilt and sentence predetermined, leaving only pomp and circumstance and flourish. This was, in theory, a proper, formal trial. Although, given that Nendawagan had had years to consider what she wanted to do to her son's murderer, and months to prepare for his arrival, was this trial just as much a performance?

Fate is fixed, he told himself. *Whether or not Nendawagan has made a judgment doesn't matter; the Author already knows. It has already been written. Two hundred pages ahead, there you are.*

But what if there aren't two hundred pages left? What if there are only two?

What was written was written. He wasn't going to change it from within the story.

Standing there, waiting for something to happen, Rivotra briefly wondered whether it was better to have a fixed fate or the ability to change things. What if he knew he met a terrible fate and could change it? But then, he ran into the traditional paradoxes of, if that fate no longer existed, how would he know to change it? Then there was the classic butterfly effect. And what if it was better for him to die? Sabelu had certainly believed in such a thing for himself. Maybe he was on to something.

He flinched as someone approached, tossed a few logs on the fire, then began shuffling the logs and coals. He heard the whoosh of air and felt a rush of heat on his face. Then he heard the sound of creaking and shuffling, as from moving furniture. He heard something move behind him, didn't know whether he needed to move, elected to remain exactly where he was, as ordered. Then the noise behind him ceased, and footsteps walked away. Maybe someone had brought him a chair, but he would stay standing until permitted to sit.

There were more footsteps, and Rivotra detected a shift in the disposition of the crowd. Perhaps the judge had arrived. Unsure what was going on exactly, he decided the only thing he could do was come to attention, just as he'd been trained in the army, or as close as he could physically get.

A man began to speak in a language Rivotra did not know. He presumed it to be the Krydik tongue, and the intonation was prayerful in nature. It went on much longer than Rivotra had ever heard the prison chaplain pray, sometimes with long pauses, and he was not aware that it had ended until Nendawagan spoke.

"Sit."

Rivotra pushed one foot out behind him and found the leg of a chair. He sat cautiously, amid a sound of many others also sitting down or otherwise getting comfortable.

"We come together today, at last, for the trial of Rifun Ndolo for the murder of my son, Sabelu."

The murmuring in the crowd was to be expected, but Rivotra wondered just how many spectators truly didn't know that was why they were gathered. What were they expecting when the council or the priests were summoned and Nendawagan chosen to preside over this ceremony?

"Do you have anything to say before we begin?" Nendawagan inquired.

There were any number of things he could say, but he wasn't here to plead innocence. "No."

More murmurs, these ones more genuinely surprised.

Rivotra would admit that he was curious what the Krydik thought of him. The last time they had interacted was when he was helping to plan the defense of Earth and all human worlds against a potential Borelian invasion. Only a handful had showed up to the attack on Ancrath, and they had been under Aklaq's command then.

What did they make of this man in the room now? Blind, disabled, defeated, saying nothing at his trial so far. How many were envisioning his execution or enslavement? How many were eager for it?

"Very well," Nendawagan stated slowly. "The trial begins."

The only knowledge Rivotra had of Krydik trials came from Sabelu's Authored Book. There he was brought before the priests on charges on heresy, blasphemy, and similar crimes. There, the head priest had acted as the prosecutor, judging on behalf of the spirits and spiritual welfare of the people. Now, Nendawagan was acting as prosecutor, judging on behalf of her dead son and the physical welfare of the people. Assuming this trial was of similar procedure and not entirely for show, he figured he could expect some lengthy speeches, some questions about what he did and why, and then given a brief opportunity to defend his actions or somehow prove that it wasn't him.

"Approximately three years ago, my son, the prophet Sabelu, was murdered. He was shot in the back, first by a handgun to take him down, then five more times with arrows to pin him to the ground and drain his life into the earth. This tragic crime may have gone unsolved but for the Authored Books."

Rivotra knew that the Krydik were divided over the Authored Books. Many cared only for the Books that were about them. Others believed them all fantasy, and still some believed all of them were authentic. Did Nendawagan believe in all of them, or was this merely a convenient manipulation of evidence?

"The first Book, Sabelu's own, *Lone Wolf*," she went on. He had a notion that she was holding it up for all to see. "Sabelu knew well in advance of his death, yet he went anyway, to confront the evil spirits and the hand of death, although this hand is not explicitly named."

A pause and shuffling of items on a table. "The second Book, one of Tommen Forbes' Books, *Free Time*." Again, he suspected that she was holding it up for the crowd. "Although his death is not described, Rifun Ndolo is named as the murderer, and he confesses this in order to intimidate a boy."

He couldn't be sure, but Rivotra had a notion that a boy was considered a man, physically if not socially, when he went through puberty. Tommen had been at least sixteen at the time.

"Finally, the third Book, the one belonging to Rifun Ndolo, *The Hand Holding the Knife*. Rifun Ndolo is not only named as the murderer, but there is great detail in how he plotted and carried out the murder, including the dark ritual used to bind Sabelu so he could be sacrificed."

The murmuring intensified to concerning mutters and low growls which were likely threats of some form.

"You were once known as a powerful wielder of the sorceries, which you call the Akari." A change in acoustics suggested she turned to address the crowd. "Rifun Ndolo raised up the First Order to power, this same group that now threatens us on a daily basis."

Now the people no longer bothered to smother their suspicion and loathing, but made their hatred well known. Nendawagan let them carry on for a long minute before calling for silence. The audience was remarkably responsive in spite of their anger, but how long would that last?

"This is the gun used in Sabelu's murder," Nendawagan went on. "It is known as the gun which Rifun Ndolo favored. It is described in these Books as belonging to him and as the one used here. Am I correct?"

Someone approached him and stopped before him. He reached a tentative hand and found the weapon in question. It certainly felt like his revolver. He felt the wheel. One, two, three, four, five, six, seven rounds.

"To the best of my knowledge, yes," he confirmed.

"And do you know which bow was also used?"

"Sabelu's own, with his own arrows from his own quiver."

"Do you deny doing any of this?" Nendawagan asked of him.

Rivotra took an even breath and answered, "No."

Another outburst of anger from the Krydik. It was almost remarkable, he thought, that they were so offended now when virtually no one outside Sabelu's family and lover had mourned for him. No one among the Krydik had really liked the bad-tempered dark seer; he was tolerated at best, even by some members of his own family. Now that his murderer was on trial, though, suddenly he was a beloved prophet whose murder demanded swift, strict closure by his flock.

Rivotra hoped Anagalisgi could see this, or at least knew what was going on. If it were possible, he hoped Sabelu could see this, too.

On the other hand, it was possible that the people had come to appreciate Sabelu more once he was gone. Whether they had read his Book and knew what he had really done for them, or maybe they needed the services of such a dark prophet but couldn't get them anymore, or just because they gave it a little bit of thought, it wasn't impossible that there was some genuine, post-mortem love nestled within this otherwise disproportionate outrage.

Or, in his honest opinion, it was simply outrage over the murder of one of their own. Didn't matter who he was or what he'd done or didn't do, Sabelu had been one of theirs, and they were socially and culturally obligated to defend him.

"Is there anything you would like to say," Nendawagan inquired, "to defend yourself, refute the charges, or attempt to prove your innocence?"

If they were following the same script, as it were, as in Sabelu's trial, he had this one opportunity to present his side of the story, to defend or refute and all that, and then the judges would retire to deliberate. This included both examining the evidence and consulting the spirits. Rivotra could only hope they were consulting the right spirits these days.

"Your word choice," he began, having nothing prepared because he had been prepared to say nothing, "is not lost on me. Rifun Ndolo has a Book. Rifun Ndolo raised up the First Order. Rifun Ndolo favored that gun and used it to murder Sabelu. And yet, I am not Rifun Ndolo."

Now the murmuring turned into confused whispers.

"Please, explain," Nendawagan said levelly.

"I, too, have read Sabelu's Authored Book. I am aware of the troubles he experienced, the things he saw, the horrors he endured. I know he saw into the spirit world and interacted directly with the Whites and Shadows. Often

436

he described them as being attached to people, influencing their actions, maybe even controlling them entirely in some cases.

"Rifun Ndolo was my Shadow, and a very powerful one—"

"You would blame this on an evil spirit, then?" someone, perhaps a priest, cut in. "That you were corrupted and controlled by witchcraft?"

"I can no more shrug off blame than I can shrug off my head. Friends may influence us to do things, but we still choose to do them or not. You may ask a child to do something, and he may have great respect, fear, or love for you as a parent, but he may still be prone to mischief, prone to disobey. Or, he may be prone to obey in spite of every voice telling him no.

"It was once told to me that prophecy is not about telling what you are going to do, but what you have already done. Two hundred pages back, there you are, doing something. Two hundred pages ahead, there you are, doing something. Sabelu knew well in advance that he was going to die in horrendous fashion. He knew when, where, how, and even who. He was asked not to go, to stay and continue doing good work, yet he refused. Because he knew that his sacrifice would bring about a greater good.

"His sacrifice would crack the armor in which Rifun Ndolo had shielded me from meaningful White influence. It would ultimately lead to his expulsion from my soul. And finally, I, Rivotra Andilan, could breathe, redeemed from his terrible influence."

He shifted position, unsure quite how far he wanted to press his luck by invoking Sabelu's Book.

"According to Sabelu's Book, he was confronted by many who wanted to kill him. One he had no choice but to kill. Another he forgave, in spite of knowing that such a person would never be free of his Shadow. And one he willingly gave himself to, knowing that it was for the greater good. Perhaps the only good it achieved in my life was redeeming me before death. For that I am grateful.

"I am not trying to prove innocence, for I cannot. Two hundred pages back, there I am, killing your son. I cannot defend such an indefensible action, for it was not merely bad but born of evil spirits demanding a human sacrifice which I provided, foolishly believing that I was doing good. And yet, where Rifun Ndolo was born of fire and pain and fear, he was washed away when Rivotra Andilan was born of blood and mercy.

"I do not know how to punish an evil spirit; perhaps that is something only the Whites or the Author can do. Just as it is only the Whites and the Author who can separate a man from his Shadow. If someone must be punished for Sabelu's murder, then it should be the one whose finger pulled the trigger. But if I may make one plea for mercy, it may be that if the Author is capable of restoring me, under whose influence are you seeking to destroy what she has rebuilt?"

There was a long moment of silence, then Rivotra could hear the priests murmuring to each other in their own language. The crowd was unusually quiet. Rivotra knew that most of Wolf Clan spoke English, as they were the ones tasked with traveling back to Earth. The Akari also granted its user the ability to understand any language and, in many cases, be understood. Was that the case here? Was everyone here hearing these proceedings in their own tongue, or in English because they understood it? It was an odd thing to think about, but it was on his mind for some reason in the midst of this heart-pounding exchange.

"Is there anything more you would like to say?" Nendawagan asked finally. "Before we retire to deliberate?"

He gave a mild shake of his head. "No."

"Very well. You will remain in this room under guard." Her vocal attention turned elsewhere. "You may remain with him."

With that, court was recessed. The masses departed, talking eagerly amongst themselves. The priests and Nendawagan moved from their spots and, if Sabelu's account was correct, made their way to an adjoining room.

He felt a touch on his shoulder.

"Do you want to stay here or sit somewhere else?" It was Josina.

"If I'm right, chairs are in short supply here," he told her.

"They do seem to be a status symbol."

"Do you want the chair?"

"I'm not keen on sitting in the position of accusation."

He held out a hand and she helped him to his feet. He took her arm and she led him to a particular spot where they sat along one wall. The ground, as expected, was uncomfortably hard, and, in spite of the roaring fire warming the room very well, still relatively cool to the touch.

"And now we wait," he sighed.

"You have no idea how hard it is to be a lawyer and have to watch this with no chance to jump in and argue," Josina said nervously.

"In many courts, the defendant has the right to self-representation. Here, it seems to be an obligation."

"In a place where you don't know the laws, rules, customs, or people."

He shifted position, trying to get comfortable. "Oh, I don't know. Maybe I don't know the specifics, but things do seem to be fairly straightforward. They accuse you, present evidence. You defend yourself, present evidence. Consult the spirits, hope the spirits are on your side."

"Just as susceptible to corruption as back home," Josina told him.

"And the structured, rigid American courts aren't susceptible to corruption? Literally the reason you were tipped off about my case was because someone corrupted it."

She made a sound like a sigh but could not refute the point. "Maybe it's just as well that I'm resigning my position."

"Instead, you're going to train up a bunch of little minions to take your place."

"I don't know. Am I? Are you going to let me?"

"Why wouldn't I?"

"Your injuries have given you many strange abilities, but pregnancy and lactation aren't part of them."

He made a noise of assent. "All right, so you may have a point. That doesn't mean you couldn't teach one class. One class, twice a week, a few hours each day. You could handle that."

"Yes, because teachers do nothing when they're not in the classroom."

"It would give you a break from the farm. I still think you're more inclined to the city, whatever you say."

She touched his hand but didn't quite hold it. "I think you're going to be all right. Nendawagan isn't unreasonable."

He still had his doubts, but he couldn't deny that something felt off. He hadn't thought about it in the moment, but now that he was not actively being questioned, he could think about it a little more.

Nendawagan had used the name Rifun Ndolo, but she had never quite explicitly ascribed it to him. She had never called him directly by that name. Of course, she had never called him Rivotra Andilan either. But throughout the entire exchange, she seemed to speak of him or of Rifun in the third person, as if he weren't in the room. It was almost as if she were asking him, Rivotra, questions about a different person.

He could be reading too much into it. Nendawagan didn't get to Earth often, so far as he knew, preferring to stay with her people and be active in political matters, now more than ever with the Order against them. Maybe it was just a symptom of having less command of the English language. Except, he argued to himself, she hadn't had any problems when she had visited him in prison. An accent, maybe, but her use of the language was on par with his own, maybe even better at the time.

Maybe she had been speaking in the Krydik language, but the Akari allowed her to be heard by him. That didn't feel right either. He might believe that if she were using a piece of technology, the translators from the Wheel for instance, but the Akari was smarter than that. It would translate not just her words, but, to a small extent, her intent. If she was referring to Rivotra, he would know it. If she were referring to Rifun, he would know it.

So why did it sound as if she were separating the two? Could it be that she understood the situation, that she really was distinguishing between Rifun and Rivotra? Did he dare hope for mercy?

And yet, in the back of his mind, Anagalisgi's comment lingered. The next step in becoming Rivotra Andilan, he had to die. No matter how he turned it over in his head, he could not come up with any way it might be a cheeky metaphor. Grow, be humbled, examine, submit, even survive, those words could all be used metaphorically in various ways. Dying could be metaphorical, too, but he wasn't seeing how it could be applied in such a way here. Nor could he see how it might be interpreted as a future event.

"So what did your family actually say about me?" he asked, trying to take his mind off the immediate situation. If nothing else, he did want to know her answer. If she accepted his marriage proposal, well, he could die happy, if unmarried. If she rejected it, whether her own reasons or because of her family, well, he wouldn't be walking away from a promising future.

Josina cleared her throat awkwardly. "Well, the initial phone call was...not very receptive. And when I first visited, that conversation did not go especially well, either. It may have been a bad idea to call ahead, because it gave my aunt time to rally everyone together."

"Blind, epileptic, disabled, dishonored, unemployed, nothing to my name, I can understand why they might not like me."

"Maybe, but at least part of that was not your fault. And it wasn't as though I were fighting a tsunami. My aunt told me that, as a lawyer, I should bring my best arguments. So I did. And at least a few members of the family were on my side."

"How so?"

"First, you're not Merina. That would have been an absolute no from everyone. But, seeing how the Betsileo never bowed to the Merina either—"

"Either? If I recall correctly, the Sakalava were subjugated by the Merina."

"That's what they call it to make themselves feel better. Their kings formed an alliance with our kings. We never bowed."

Rivotra had his doubts, but he knew better than to voice them aloud.

"As I said, because the Betsileo never bowed, you were given high regard in that sense. And, as you said, the Andilan name still carries weight. Granted, it is a bit tainted with the massacre, but your...will to live and your determination to restore your family did not go unnoticed."

"Will to live. Because my life so far is a little less noble than that?"

"They appreciated your military service, but there were some questions about your prison time, both in Madagascar and the United States. Also some questions about your political loyalties and...religious zeal."

Rivotra let out a breath. And no one from his family had been there to negotiate on his behalf. Only Josina had any idea what he'd been through—both in reality and the story he told to account for his apparent age—and her information was incomplete at best.

"I told you I was raised Muslim," she went on. "The Sakalava have historically had great Muslim influence in their beliefs, which made it easier for my mother to convert. My mother's family are actually more inclined toward Catholicism, often mixed with traditional animism."

"Not unlike some in my family," Rivotra commented. "They were more traditional a century ago, almost exclusively animist. But Fianar has always been more of a multicultural hub, and some of those beliefs changed over the years."

"Some questions I simply couldn't answer. But those that I could, well, it made some members more friendly toward you and others less friendly."

"How about your aunt and uncle, who I believe are the bestowers of blessing here?"

"My aunt was concerned, but more inclined to favor you. My uncle...he's a difficult man to read sometimes. Honestly, I think he was more concerned with how you would be able to farm and also whether you would be inclined to work for him for a time, seeing how you don't have any cows."

Rivotra nodded. "That thought had crossed my mind as well. It couldn't be too heavy of an arrangement. The home farm needs work, too, or else it will never produce anything of value again."

"I said the two of you could discuss that in person," Josina said.

It was about the best he could hope for in such a situation, he supposed.

There was some commotion nearby, some muffled voices.

"So," he said, trying to keep his tone even, "before I am sentenced to hang for my crimes, was any final decision made or allowed to be made?"

"Asking for my answer?" Her voice was tight, on the verge of tears he thought, though she tried to force a tease. She managed a nervous laugh as she touched his arm and helped him to stand. Then she lowered her voice and whispered in his ear. "Yes. I say yes."

He took a breath as she led him back to the chair. Nearby, he could hear the priests and Nendawagan returning to their spots between him and the fire that still crackled noisily.

More spectators gathered to hear the outcome of the trial. As expected, there was a brief period of conversation, the people placing bets while the judges got in any last second comments, reminders, or requests.

Then one of the priests, presumably the head priest, stood, and began speaking. Again, Rivotra did not understand, but the tone was prayerful in nature. The man finished, but this time, no one gave permission to sit. After another moment of silence, Nendawagan spoke again.

"It would be dishonest to say that this trial has not been going on since Sabelu's death," she said, quieting the audience. "Before the murderer's identity was known, he was on trial. After his name was known, he was on trial. In many ways, he was convicted a long time ago, sentenced even before I laid eyes on his face, before all evidence was formally gathered, before one word of testimony was given before the people and the spirits."

None of this surprised Rivotra. He remembered well how Rifun had laughed at this very notion, that everyone knew he had done it but could not touch him on account of the Author's favor. It had not been the Author's favor, merely one Shadow protecting another. Now that the Shadow was gone, it was time to punish the flesh puppet.

"And yet, many here remember the turmoil of Sabelu. We remember his statements and convictions, that every man is guilty of harboring his own Shadow. It need not be big and grandiose, just a quiet secret tucked away. If any White were to find it, they would seek to tear it from us. And we, comfortable with that Shadow, would invariably resist.

"We are also not unfamiliar with the concept of names and a person's true being. Many of you keep your names tucked away from all but your closest family members, knowing that your real self is precious and should not be exposed to anyone who may use it maliciously. Some of you have seen what happens when the self is discovered by those who would do such terrible things. If you have witnessed this in a family member, you know it is not your loved one who is acting out. And if you have been that person, you have known a deep and terrible violation of your self beyond your control."

She paused for a tense moment. Rivotra would admit he was a little confused. Was this mercy talking? Could he hope for that much? He swallowed nervously.

"It is true," Nendawagan went on, "I do not know how to punish an evil spirit. But a crime cannot be overlooked simply because we hope that something good comes from it."

There it was. Rivotra could feel the hope draining from his heart.

"This man before us, be he Rifun Ndolo or Rivotra Andilan, servant of Shadows or Whites, will be punished for the ritual murder of the dark prophet Sabelu. He will be taken to Sabelu's grave and sacrificed in the same way he sacrificed my son. And we will leave his fate in the hands of the spirits. Let the ones he serves fight for him or not."

Oh. No. No, this was much worse than anything he could have come up with. He was right. These people could be savage when they wanted to be; such was the nature of keeping to the old ways.

Someone came forward and grabbed his arms. His first instinct was to resist, and this was met with more hands grabbing him. Compared to these hands now, Oswald and almost anyone at the prison was an elderly woman. There was absolutely no hope of breaking out of the grip that held fast his arms to bind his wrists together. Even the rope felt stronger than any handcuffs he'd been bound with the last couple years.

No one came alongside him to try and guide him, warn him of any changes in terrain. Once he was bound, his wrists were jerked, and he stumbled forward. Unable to get his legs straightened and balanced quick enough, he fell to the ground. Someone came on either side of him and hauled him back to his feet. Behind him, the spectators had turned into a mob and were quick to follow the guilty procession.

Stumbling outside the building, the cold hit him like a slap in the face. He puffed a huff of surprise but could only continue forward. He did not know where Josina had gone, wondered if she would be there to witness his punishment. He didn't know if he wanted her there as one last semblance of comfort, or if it might be better to spare her the gruesome details. He also did not know where Nendawagan was. Was she the one on the other end of the rope, pulling him along? It might make sense, but it was hardly his biggest concern right now.

The ground in the city was not level or smooth by any means, and he tripped frequently, unable to control limbs he could not consciously feel as his concentration had deserted him in favor of fight or flight. He felt pain but largely could not localize it. Even pretending that he survived this, he was going to have bruises all over his shins and arms.

Then they were outside in the sun once more, and he knew a brief moment of warmth. That moment was swiftly snatched from him as his bonds were yanked again and he hobbled over ground that was even less friendly.

If there was any reprieve, it was that a good portion of the angry mob did not follow them past the edge of the old city. They stood on the threshold and continued to shout for a time, then he figured they dispersed to continue about their day, satisfied that appropriate justice would be dispensed by those in power. When their noise had faded, he counted only half a dozen sets of footsteps including his own.

Then they turned off the main path and Rivotra stumbled so often that his captors finally decided to just carry him the last distance to his final destination. They dumped him on a patch of ground covered in sharp rocks that cut him and embedded into flesh.

"Stand up," Nendawagan ordered.

It took some doing, and no one offered any help, but Rivotra struggled to get to his feet. He got his legs shifted around where they needed to be and slowly relaxed, letting his invisible legs bear his weight.

"Turn to your right."

Standing on a slope, Rivotra concentrated, then turned, step by step, to his right.

"Do you know why you're here?"

Something in the tone of her voice caused Rivotra to know instantly that she was intentionally quoting her son. It was one of the last things Sabelu had said. He had known, easily. He just wanted to hear Rifun say it.

"Because I murdered your son," he said quietly.

"Do you want to know why you're really here?" she asked, tone uncomfortably level as she quoted Sabelu again. He heard the hammer on the revolver click into position.

He took an even breath. "To die."

Then he was falling forward. He fell before he heard the shot. His lower body went dead instantly, and his bound wrists did not allow him to catch himself even if he had been of a mind to attempt such a thing. Then the pain started rushing through his upper body. He could feel his heart racing, body and mind struggling to figure out what just happened.

He cried out involuntarily as something sharp penetrated his left shoulder blade and pinned him to the ground. His lung was ripped open and he weakly spit bloody foam onto the sharp rocks. A second blade struck through his right side and did the same. He knew there would be three more in time. Some he knew he would not feel on account of the paralysis. If there were any above that line, well, things were starting to blur and no longer matter.

He could hear crying. He could hear footsteps. Someone knelt beside him. In Sabelu's Book, Anagalisgi had come to the dying man, to guide him into the afterlife. Who would come for him? He closed his eyes and waited for a voice. As unconsciousness took hold, he could not identify the person, but he was able to make out two words.

"To live."

Anagalisgi sat alone in his cave, poking at the coals, his heart disturbed. Like everyone, he wished he knew more. The difference was, he understood the price of knowing. Perhaps, then, he did not wish for knowledge, but for wisdom.

At the front of the cave, he had built a cabin-type room, maybe more of a sheltered observation post. It had wooden walls, large windows, and a door. This door was not directly in line with the cave, but on a perpendicular wall, so it was not quite possible for the cave to become a straight wind tunnel when the door was opened. The door was also not visible from the fire pit.

He looked up, startled, when he heard the door open. Never in all his decades and centuries of being here had anyone entered this realm without his knowledge. And never had anyone come to him in his cave whom he did not intentionally summon. Even the Whites, of whom he was constantly aware on a subconscious level, announced their presence long before. And most had other means of entry beyond the front door. He was halfway to his feet when he saw who intruded upon his abode.

"Sabelu," he whispered.

His nephew, three years dead, walked in the door. He looked just as he had in life, including his near-perpetual scowl. He even bore the scars of the wounds that killed him: one bullet wound and five arrows. He wore what he had been buried in, and his bow was strapped to his back as one might expect. Behind him, Yawi and the White Wolves padded silently.

"You're dead," Anagalisgi stated. "How is this possible?"

"You were my mentor, and you have to ask that?" Sabelu wondered, his voice, tone, intonation, and sour attitude all just as they had been in life.

Cautiously, Anagalisgi approached his nephew. He reached out a hand and touched him, put a hand firmly on his shoulder. Solid. He glanced at the wolves, already aware that they were authentic. They said nothing and seemed to hold an odd deference to the man in their midst. Anagalisgi had never claimed superiority over any of the Whites, although he had given them orders a time or two in specific situations. Now, though, Sabelu held a kind of equality among the pack. Maybe not pack leader, as that fell to Yawi, but he was more than a familiar acquaintance.

Anagalisgi took a step back. "Are you alive?"

His nephew shrugged. "Yes and no. Did my body in the waking world rise from its grave? No. Do I have agency to move about here and in this time? Yes."

"In this time," Anagalisgi echoed. "I don't understand."

"And that's what I'm here to fix. You've done all you can. You have guided and advised and mentored well. But the days of prophecy are coming to an end. The pages are much fewer in number than they used to be. The Timekeeper awaits."

"The Timekeeper."

Sabelu sighed and rolled his eyes. "Yes, now I understand how frustrating it is to be the mentor."

"You're from the future," Anagalisgi stated, shifting his stance uncertainly.

"Not the future. The end. Of all things."

Anagalisgi had a thousand questions, but none of them would articulate properly in his mind, never mind on his tongue. The best he could manage was, "How long do we have?"

Sabelu brushed past him toward the fire. "Long enough to prepare." He sat down and looked at Anagalisgi. "Not long enough to waste."

Anagalisgi cautiously approached the fire and took a seat a respectful distance from his nephew. "Why are you the messenger?"

"Two messengers," Sabelu corrected. "One servant of the Whites. One servant of the Shadows."

Anagalisgi frowned. "No." He shook his head. "No."

"Regretfully, yes."

"I mentored that boy. For years. I tried to stop him, I..."

"He made his choice." Sabelu's tone was gentle, compared to his normal attitude, but not what someone who didn't know him would call empathetic or compassionate. "And this today was the last piece of the puzzle."

"The death of Rifun. The birth of Rivotra."

"Willingly dying to self. And now the pieces have been set."

"But what makes this different? You destroyed the Sacred Zukatopa and the Sacred One of the Desert, you and the Whites brought the Shadows to their knees. The Krydik, though battered, still stand strong. Is that going to change?"

Sabelu's expression turned unreadable. "I've learned a lot of things, being dead. Most of it I can't put into words, I admit. But this, I think I can. What aspects of the universe do the sorceries, the Akari, encompass?"

"Time, Matter, and Energy."

"Many Advancing species in the universe have discovered this, but have you heard of the law of the conservation of matter, or the same one regarding energy?"

"It cannot be created or destroyed, only change form," Anagalisgi recited.

Sabelu nodded. "Why would the same not be true of Time?"

Anagalisgi blinked.

"All the Harvesters who take Time from those at the end of life, or those who consume Time Capsules to extend their lives, a simple yet balanced equation. But all those Timekeepers, Banding for every frivolous thing, imbuing themselves with Time itself. Some of this is offset by those affected by accelerated aging, but not all."

"The Whites and the Shadows know what's coming," Anagalisgi stated. "The end of all things, the end of Time. They're preparing for one final push on humanity and the universe. That's why Julianna was pushed into power, and it's why she's going so hard after those with Authored Books."

"Rarely has it ever been about the mortals and their squabbles, though they are the prize to be won," Sabelu affirmed. "It has always been about the Whites and Shadows."

Anagalisgi nodded. "What do we do? What is my role in this?"

"A period of mentorship," his nephew told him, shifting to a more comfortable position. "The people will be fine for now. When that changes, you need to be ready."

Eighteen
Home

Rivotra did not know what kind of afterlife awaited those who questioned the ancestors yet still did good and honored the family and traditions, or those who hated Christians yet were compared to Jesus. But, he figured he must have done something right because he was fairly certain he had reached the "good side."

There was no pain. Not in his head, nor his eyes, nor his back, nor anywhere in his body. Furthermore, his body had weight to it again, in the sense that there were no invisible spots. He could feel his arms and legs, every shaft, every joint, and none of it hurt. He could willfully bend his knees, move his hips, bend his arm and wrist. No questions, no shifting to get invisible muscles to cooperate, no pain, and if he was right, the metal rods and screws in his arm were gone. Even his left ring and pinkie fingers cooperated as they were supposed to. He mentally startled when he realized he had all five fingers on his right hand again! Cautiously, he pressed thumb and fingertip together. It was real, solid. He could feel every natural sensation. He could curl his fingers, ball his fist into a normal shape, run his thumb over the digits. And there was no questioning the movement, either. He didn't have to think about it, didn't have to relearn; it was as if they had never been missing.

Turning his head, a few things surprised him. First, his head rolled normally, smoothly. There were no bumps, lumps, or divots. No pain anywhere on his skull, no headache anywhere in his brain. His head felt grounded, no sloshing, no auras, no fear at all of a precursor to either vertigo, seizure, or other betrayal of his body or brain. He knew that he lay on his back on some kind of mat, a blanket over him, and every sensory input from all over his body confirmed this. And he knew he could be confident in that assessment.

Second, he could smell smoke and wood. He wasn't tasting it, wasn't mentally gagging on something that did not exist how his brain thought it did. He was actually smelling it, a sweet aroma rising into the air and sending the sensory information from his nose to the correct part of his brain.

And the third thing that surprised him, he could see light against his eyelids. It was faint, but it was there. Even when he'd had blindsight, he could not process such a thing. He didn't know why that thin stretch of skin over his eyes made so much difference to his head injury, but it had made enough of a difference to shock him now.

Cautiously, he opened his eyes.

He was, indeed, lying on his back, inches from a stone wall, looking up at a stone ceiling. A blanket covered him up to his chest.

Was it possible that he was alive? But how? He very clearly remembered being shot in the back, remembered the paralysis, remembered the arrows going through his body to pin him to the ground, remembered spitting bloody foam onto the rocks. He knew all of that had happened. So where was he? And why was he? What kind of "good place" was this? After a minute or two, taking stock of his body and quietly listening to his surroundings, he decided there was only one good way to find out.

He sat up. Again, there was no pain, no vertigo, nothing in his body screaming at him to stop moving. And his sight traveled with him. There were no blind spots, nothing blurry, no having to wait for his brain to catch up with his body, or vice versa. Everything responded exactly as intended.

He put a hand to the back of his head. His original head injury, that damn pickax from almost a century ago, was gone. There was no perpetual low-key headache, no deformation of the skull, no scar tissue, no bald spot. The same was true for every head injury he had sustained in the prison attack. Healed, as if it had never happened. He could see, he could smell, he could taste, he even felt like he could think clearly for the first time in a very long while. It was as though there had been some sort of very quiet noise in his head, easily dismissable as simply ambient room noise, and yet even that had been quieted. His head was his own again. His body was his own again.

He looked down at his body, found he was shirtless. Every injury, every wound, every scar, erased. No more twisted, pitted, wretched scar tissue, just brand new skin, some hair; his burned nipples were normal again as well, healed from electrocution burns. His neck, where they'd tried to strangle him with a red-hot chain, normal. The areas where he knew the arrows had gone through his body, there was no evidence of it, not even a mild scratch.

Glancing at his right hand, he confirmed there were indeed five fingers there. One, two, three, four, five, perfectly functional and responsive, with hardly a conscious thought on his part.

As he twisted, several loose hairs tickled his nose. He pushed the hairs out of the way, then gathered a lock and brought it forward so he could see. Not fully gray, but it was noticeable against the brown. Well, he had been under a lot of stress; why wouldn't dying twice in two years cause a few gray hairs? At the same time, did "heaven" or wherever he was, have gray hair? The rest of him seemed to be restored, so why not the gray hair, too? Was he really, truly alive?

He lifted the blanket and glanced under, knowing he had no clothes on whatsoever.

Circumcision was practiced by many Malagasy, and those in his home village of Mahitsy were no exception. It was a rite of passage for a boy to become a man, some time between the age of ten and fourteen when he started to mature. Vala had denied him this ceremony, and it had been a major contributor to their falling out. When he'd joined the VVS at age sixteen, they had insisted on circumcising him as a show of loyalty to the Malagasy people, and he had readily accepted the blade.

That was now clearly reversed, along with every other injury he had ever sustained in that region.

And on it went, all the way down both legs, both feet. Everything functioned better than it ever had, or better than he ever remembered. Head to toe, he was healed. Everything Anagalisgi had done in his cave in the dreams, was now manifest.

He dropped the blanket and looked up, finally taking in his surroundings. There was a fire pit not far away to his right, the fire starting to burn low but still very hot. The room was maybe twelve by sixteen, seven feet tall, all stone construction with some added wooden elements for aesthetic and privacy. He saw a few tables at the far wall in front of him along with a few chairs. This couldn't be the room where he'd been tried; it wasn't nearly big enough. Perhaps this was the side room where the priests and Nendawagan had deliberated.

Well, he figured he could confidently say that he was alive and not in some afterlife he had never imagined or heard of. But then the question came back: why was he alive? He had been sentenced to death. And, assuming that he was alive, that they'd decided to keep him alive for some reason, why had they healed him so completely? Fixing up the gunshot and arrow wounds they had just inflicted on him, fine. But to regrow or reattach fingers, to heal his brain, that was dedication, that was commitment. That was a level of compassion he had, at no time, felt from any of the Krydik present. Not from the spectators, not from the priests, and certainly not from either Netami or Nendawagan.

With all of this information, then, what was he supposed to do? He didn't think they would just let him walk out of here. Even pretending that he had gotten some kind of pardon, which was already doubtful, that didn't mean that everyone in town was going to honor it. That mob had been too intent on his execution for someone not to try something.

If nothing else, whatever he did, he would need his clothes, and he didn't see them in front of him. Looking around, however, he was shocked, and a little embarrassed, to find Nendawagan, sitting not five feet behind him, working on some small leather project in her hands. Her gaze was turned down to the leather, but he knew that her real attention was on him. She hadn't said anything because she just wanted to see what he would do.

He stared at her, unsure if he should move or just lie back down.

After a few seconds, she reached beside her and lightly tossed him a bag. Inside, he found a change of clothes.

"Put them on," Nendawagan said, her tone neutral. "Then sit down."

He obeyed without a word and with no problems at all. His body responded as he needed it to, no need to shift or balance a certain way to get pants on or anything. Jeans, which he had bought in prison commissary. Socks and undershirt, the same way. The button-down shirt was brand new, likely something Josina had bought. The *lamba* he had been given in prison turned out to be deep green in color with some decorative brown designs at either end. The shoes were also new, a pair of simple slip-ons. Once everything was comfortable, no chaffing from poor sizing or because of twisted skin, he sat down again on the mat.

"You never met Sabelu," she began, still not looking at him. "Not really. Everything you know about him comes from his Authored Book or what others have said about him. What do you know?"

Rivotra nodded slowly, trying to appear nonthreatening. "I know he was troubled, difficult to get along with, pragmatic, honest to a fault, but also incredibly loyal. He looked at people, saw all their hopes, dreams, fears, flaws, and faults, and he loved them anyway. But knowing so much about people also drove him up a wall and made him...difficult."

Nendawagan pulled a bone needle threaded with sinew through the leather she held in her hand. "A nice way of putting it, but also entirely correct. He did love the people, in his own way. Their disregard for the truth about themselves, the brewing trouble with the Shadows, was very discouraging to him. They wanted to hear...what they wanted to hear. They wanted to believe that everything was good, that we had left all our problems behind us in the Old Land, that we were special because we were separate, because we had hidden ourselves away. But he wouldn't tell them that, couldn't, because it wasn't true.

"When he was finally able to get that point across, the people still didn't quite get it. They were expecting a singular entity. There was one evil person or perhaps a small group. There was a tangible thing that could be rooted out and cast aside like a troublesome weed. And, while true, they still didn't understand the nature of how such things occur."

She fell silent for a moment, and Rivotra wondered if he was supposed to say something. He didn't think anything she had said had been intended as a question or similar cue, but he couldn't be entirely sure.

"If Sabelu were here," she went on, "he would be able to tell us which Shadows lurked over our shoulders. Envy, Anger, Pride, Doubt. Fear was my companion for a long time. Everyone has at least one. It may be as small as a gnat, whispering in our ears, or it may be as large as any of the monsters we know from childhood stories. Without a White to keep it at bay, it will only grow and consume us.

457

"You were correct in your assessment, that we are heavily influenced by Shadows and Whites. A Shadow of Envy may begin as simple, harmless want, but it can very easily turn into Rage, Desire, Lust, Resentment, and can lead to horrible deeds. But a White may also whisper in our ear, speaking Peace, Gratitude, and even Charity. And you were right. We all make our choices, to follow the Shadow or the White, to feed one or the other."

Now she looked up from her work. Her expression was hard, sculpted from months and even years of worrying over her people and her family. Yet her gaze was almost compassionate.

"What many people misunderstand is that choice. It takes many years of feeding a Shadow for it to take over someone so completely. We may react more quickly to a familiar Shadow's whisper, but it remains a choice. Even among Sabelu's most ardent adversaries, I believe only one may have been under such total Shadow control that his own will had been supplanted. Otherwise, everyone still has a choice. Even if heeding a voice becomes reflexive, that reflex can be broken. And that goes for Whites as well.

"Those who do have a basic understanding of such a thing, then, fall short of its full implications. We may use it to exonerate ourselves, but we still apply heavy judgment to others. We do not understand the fight of someone who has wronged us. Maybe it was a great crime, but it is rooted in something. It started out as a gnat and was never addressed. A choice may have been made, but something put that desire there. Something presented that choice.

"We must also consider how we treat those who have shaken off their Shadows. In the Old Land, alcoholism is a plague among many of our brothers and sisters. When one shakes off those bonds, it is cause for celebration! Yet, somehow, this is not so when it is almost any other vice. We focus only on the wrong, only on the hurt. Much ado is made about changing ourselves, improving ourselves, but we have difficulty applying this concept to others. This, again, is the work of the Shadows, seeking only to sow anger and resentment and division, feeding and watering these seeds as often as possible."

There were a few comments Rivotra wanted to make, but he bit his tongue.

"Anagalisgi came to me a few years ago, after Sabelu's death. He warned me of trials coming to the people. He warned me of trials coming to my family. After losing my second son, I didn't know what a worse trial would look like. And at first, when the Order made their push against those with Authored Books, among other targets, I assumed that was entirely what he meant. I thought he was trying to warn me that I was going to lose even more children. I have not, thankfully, but it is a possibility every single day that we are at war.

"Then we started getting messages from the Old Land, and it came to light that you were alive. What's more, you were in some kind of trouble or you wanted to move against Julianna. It took some time to discern exactly what was going on. But when you made it known that you had apparently had a change of heart and wanted to undo all the treachery you had wrought, I knew that was what Anagalisgi was talking about, for my family.

"How could he? How dare he? Was he claiming to be able to bring back the dead? What terrible plan did he have now? What power was he searching for? I was indeed very angry."

"I don't blame you," Rivotra told her.

"Seeing the state you were in, hearing what you had to say there in the prison, I really wasn't all that convinced. Even after Josina told me what had happened to your family, all I could figure was that you just intended to go out in a blaze of glory, one last heroic act to draw attention to yourself and try to make yourself a martyr for the universe."

She took a breath and huffed a sigh.

"Anagalisgi and I had many conversations. Netami and Josina have also been in constant contact; Netami is teaching Josina the sorceries, what you call the Akari. And it has been a battle to discern your intentions, your sincerity, if you have changed and to what degree. My faith in the Author is not as strong as Anagalisgi's."

"So what convinced you?" Rivotra wondered.

"I was not convinced until such time as your execution," Nendawagan informed him. "What could I do to Rifun Ndolo that he has not already endured and only become more entrenched in evil? Then, considering the conversations I had with Anagalisgi, I decided on one simple concept: self-sacrifice. Dying to self, as he put it. A trial where you are entirely guilty and worthy of death. What would your defense be? Of course, you had endured similar trials before, but how would you react to your fate being left to the spirits? What if you knew you had something waiting for you that you could not have?"

He blinked. "Wait, so...did you have Josina say yes to me...just to make it so I might have something to look forward to?"

Nendawagan's expression turned puzzled. "Say yes about what? Whatever you talked about during deliberation—"

"I asked her to marry me. Did you coerce her into saying yes just to test me?" He didn't know if he was angry at Josina for going along with it, or angry at Nendawagan for putting her up to it.

But the matriarch's gaze softened. "We had no idea you had asked her to marry you. She's never said anything about it, just that you intended to return home and reclaim your family farm. We were under the impression that you were simply friends, by virtue of her helping you with prison and your blindness and everything else."

He shook his head. "No. She saved the farm from government bureaucrats, to give it back to me. I asked her to marry me, and she said yes. You promise that it wasn't you?"

Now Nendawagan's expression turned guilty. "I promise you, it wasn't me, or any of us. We had no idea."

He let out an even breath. "Would it have made a difference if you had?"

Her expressed guilt became more obvious. "No." She shifted uncomfortably in her seat. "Sabelu could have done a lot of things. When things came to head, around the time of his trial, and when he returned from exile, he could have told even the greatest Shadow to dance, and it would have. But he knew that he was just one man, and when he died, if he had continued to lead, the people would be lost. They were counting on physicality, but they needed to learn spirituality.

"His greatest mission was the individual. The person, the couple, the family. Make them strong, teach their children to be strong, and that spiritual strength would continue for generations, long after he was gone." She nodded slowly. "Perhaps, then, I was in the wrong."

460

He shifted position. "You did exactly what I expected you to do. I wouldn't trust me either." He shifted again. "But why heal me, if you were so afraid of treachery?"

"Rifun carried his scars as a source of demonic pride and anger and resentment, a constant reminder of everything that had been done to him, each one a reason to hate and to keep doing what he was doing. But if Rivotra is to live his life as the Author intended, as she wanted for him, then it's only right that he should be rid of everything that Rifun had done to him. All the hurt, the pain, the anger, the sorrow. All the mistakes and the burdens."

He nodded as he lifted his right hand, resting it on his upright knee. He expected to see only nubs where the index and middle fingers had been, yet he was not shocked when all fingers were present and accounted for. It was almost as if the last four years had been little more than a temporary inconvenience, despite all the trouble it caused him.

"Something we learned from Nathan," Nendawagan told him. "Something we have had to make great use of in this war."

"Is Nathan alive, then?" Rivotra questioned. "I heard he was missing, presumed dead."

"He is believed to be dead, yes, but there were instructions in Tommen's final Book, when he used the technique to heal Micaiah and restore his missing leg."

Rivotra frowned. "Too little, too late."

"Just enough at just the right time."

He huffed a sigh. "I said I wanted to make things right, and you have restored my body so I can do so much more than I have been able to in the last two years."

"Julianna is intent on wiping out those with Authored Books. She very nearly succeeded. She thinks she succeeded with you."

"If I go after her, she's going to kill me. Different day, same result."

Nendawagan nodded. "As I said, Sabelu believed in the individual. And the family. Your marriage to Josina is exactly what he would have wanted. And I would agree. Restore your family. Live the way the Author intended for Rivotra. Not Rifun."

461

Rivotra agreed. "No more stars and monsters, no more kingship and treachery, no more walking along the edge of a knife."

"Sometimes, the best way to prove you've changed, is not to try and draw attention to it and flaunt yourself, but to simply sit down and live quietly."

Rivotra bobbed a nod. "And that's what I intend to do." He paused. Then, "How long has it been? Since, you know, you killed me?"

She scoffed a laugh, eyes glittering with amusement. "A few days. And it was my other sons who executed you, as was their right. Afterwards, you were brought back here, still alive I will add, where Netami and I and a few others went to work on your healing. As I said, with the war, we've become proficient in many things. Your brain was the hardest part, and I cannot guarantee there won't be some potential side effects, but we did the best we could."

"I can see—actually see—for the first time in almost a century," he told her. "You did great."

Nendawagan smiled for a moment, then grew serious. "As far as most are concerned, you were executed and we brought you back here to rummage through your pockets and prepare you for burial. Assuming that Julianna does find out that you survived her attack, the best she will be able to do is learn of our judgment on you. Like most, she will not believe that you could have escaped certain death here.

"But that is now entirely dependent on you. If she thinks she wiped out you and your entire family, or that we got to you, then living quietly on your farm should be no trouble at all. You are free to marry, have children, and go about your day without fear of intergalactic threats."

He nodded again. "That sounds...perfect."

She stood and he followed suit. No vertigo, no nausea, no purposeful shifting and sorting of invisible limbs. Everything exactly where and how it was supposed to be. She was a good head shorter than him, but there was no doubt who still had command of the conversation.

"I believe I see in you now what you should have always been," she told him. "It is not a glamorous life of stars and monsters, but it is a good life."

"Thank you." He didn't know what else to say.

"There is, however, one thing I will tell you about that. Being good does not mean you do not fight. It means you fight with the correct motivations for the correct reasons. With Julianna still pushing, there may come a time when you have to fight again. And the Shadow who is Rifun will come back to whisper in your ear." She nodded. "Don't listen to him. Fight if you must, but do it for the right reasons."

He dipped his head. "Wise words." He shifted his stance. "And on that topic, do you know, really know, what happened to Godwin and the Miaramila?"

Now she frowned. "I don't know the specifics. What I do know is that the Miaramila intercepted a plan to attack Yonhi, to the west, as part of Julianna's major push against the Authored Books. It was a much larger attack than anything we had endured before, and I believe that their interception and willingness to come to our defense is why Yonhi still stands. But it came at great cost, with many being captured and taken away to slavery."

Rivotra nodded slowly.

"If the dragon's goal is to wipe out those with Authored Books, then it will find a way to do so, or at least try," Nendawagan said. "When you did not go along with these plans, it simply raised up another pawn. It could have been anyone. Blame does not rest solely on your shoulders."

He mulled this over, trying to convince himself of it. He wanted to help, but there was nothing he was going to be able to do.

"I assume, then, if everyone thinks I'm dead, that Josina went home?"

"She knows you're alive, and she was sent home to wait for you."

"Are you going to escort me to make sure I go home?" he wondered, remembering the federal agents who had not-so-discreetly accompanied them on the plane.

Nendawagan smiled. "No, I think you can go home just fine on your own."

He gave her a look. "Maybe Josina didn't tell you, but I don't have my Akari abilities anymore."

She raised a brow. "Are you sure? Have you even tried?"

Curious, he glanced at his right hand and touched his thumb to his index finger. Like riding a bike, he was able to Feel the new finger. He could tell the bone was not originally his, but his body was nearly finished replacing all of the cadaver bone with his own cells; in the big picture, he couldn't tell the difference. The nerves were fresh and new, and the muscle and skin had been reformed from Matter elsewhere on his body.

"How did you know?" he wondered.

"A hunch only," she told him.

"Hm."

"Your bride-to-be is waiting."

It was a kind way of saying he could see himself out, and also, he had overstayed his welcome.

He met her gaze. "Thank you."

"You can thank me by living by the principles Sabelu showed us. You owe him that much."

"No, I owe him a lot more."

He took a step back and considered his options. Josina had probably returned to the farm outside of Fianar, if she knew he was alive and was waiting for him. That would be his first stop. He should probably start outside the back door, that way he wouldn't be seen stepping out of a door in thin air by the rest of the village; he wouldn't completely spook her, wherever she was in the house; and so he might take in the landscape for a moment before going in for a long conversation.

Taking a breath, he opened a portal. It was just as difficult as he remembered, having to punch through the fabric of the universe. But there, on the other side, exactly what he expected to see: shrubs, trees, greenery and mud from heavy rains that poured down even now in the evening hours.

He did not give Nendawagan a second glance as he stepped through. Despite his restored abilities and enthusiasm, it was still as traumatic as every other portal he'd ever walked through. His whole being was stretched into nothing, then compressed the same way, before depositing him ten feet from the back door of the house.

His blindsight had allowed him to see everything as an impression on his mind, like how one might picture something familiar. It worked well enough and he knew how and where everything was, but having real vision was, to use an expression, a sight for sore eyes. To see everything as it was in real time, all of the colors in their full brilliance and not washed out, was beauty beyond description. How could he put words to the joy and relief and beauty of restoration? He couldn't be sure if it was just the rain on his face or if he was actually crying.

He was facing south, down the path that separated the animal pasture to the east and the crop fields to the west. All of it was grown up from disuse, although he noted that there were proper sprouts in the fields, seeds that had fallen and germinated or roots that had propagated in spite of any destruction wreaked by Julianna's marauders, now in their second year of haphazard life. It was a good sign, and a good project to start on, bringing everything back into proper order.

Turning around, he was presented with the home of his ancestors, the Andilan farm. Originally built like any other home with only a couple basic rooms, many generations had made many changes. More rooms were added for more generations of larger families, electricity brought in from the city. In the brief period that the French had seized control, construction was modernized, more modern amenities had been added or updated, running water, sewer, kitchen appliances. The exterior, originally simple wooden boards like everyone else, had been covered over with adobe and stucco, the roof replaced with clay tiles. Overall, the place was almost too nice and modern compared to the rest of the village houses, but it still wasn't quite on par with new houses in Fianar.

But it was home. He stepped up on the porch and approached the back door, noting that it was brand new, likely replaced after the old one was destroyed in the attack. He cautiously tested the knob. Unlocked.

Rivotra knew a moment of disappointment as he walked inside, into the main living area. He had known, of course, that everything had been destroyed, yet he still somehow expected to see all the familiar furniture, the decorations, the walls and floor. He would have even settled for new pieces in the same arrangement. This was not the case. There was still obvious damage to some of the walls and floor, or notable areas where repaired damage had not yet been painted or sanded to match the surrounding area. The amount of furniture was greatly reduced, limited to a few chairs and the wooden frame of a couch with no cushions. A handful of boxes were stacked in the corner, contents unknown. To his right were three doors, all closed. One led to the private bedroom of the head of the household, another to the room for children under twelve, and the third for any other household members who were married. To his left, in the kitchen area, there was a table and two chairs. There was a small refrigerator and a wood stove, as before, but not the same, just replacements for something damaged. To the north, there were three more doors, also closed. The one in the middle was the bathroom. On either side were the bedrooms for unmarried men and women. A staircase led to an attic space which could be used for storage or any extra guests, if a gathering truly got that big.

The door to the master bedroom opened, and Rivotra was stunned by the sight.

Oswald's description hadn't done her justice. She was indeed tall, with a figure that was just as beautiful to the eyes as it had been to the hands. She had replaced her formal Western court attire with more casual clothing, a short sleeve shirt with a red and blue *lamba* tied around her chest as a simple dress. In true Sakalava style, she also wore *masonjoany*, a traditional face paint depicting intricate, decorative flowers and designs around her cheeks and forehead. She bore more African features than the Austronesian-descended Betsileo, and she kept her tight, curly hair short.

On seeing him, she crossed the room in only a few strides and threw her arms around him. He pulled her close, remembering her paint at the last moment and moving his head so he didn't smear it. She seemed to recognize this move, laughed, and moved to take a step back. He loosened his grip, but continued holding her hands.

"You look good," she said, clearly nervous. "Better than...I've ever seen you."

"And you look...amazing," he told her, mentally hitting himself for such a lame compliment. "I never would have been able to imagine something so beautiful." He could feel the heat in her skin. As he squeezed her hands, he noted that the right one was different than last time. "The Krydik healed you, too, didn't they? I don't see or feel any scarring."

She nodded. "They did, yes. Nendawagan told me that I needed to let that go and live as I was supposed to."

"She told me something similar."

She looked down and played with his hands, touching his restored fingers. "I was so worried. Healing the body is one thing, but when they started working on your head...no one really knew what would happen. Would it harm you more? Would you remember anything? Would you even be you?"

He made a strangled sort of noise. "I think you were more worried about that than they were, in the sense that, they probably wouldn't have cried if something went wrong."

She laughed nervously again. "Maybe so." She looked back up. "But you're here, and alive and well, and that's what matters."

He pulled her close and hugged her again, enjoying the feel of her against him. After a moment, Josina cleared her throat and made a noise that was almost like a giggle. "But we might have to have a talk about *that*."

Now it was his turn for his skin to flush with embarrassment, and he didn't have quite enough melanin to fully conceal it. Nor were his jeans thick enough to conceal his fully restored libido.

"Why don't you go sit outside a minute?" she suggested, letting go and stepping away. "I'll make up some tea."

He nodded wordlessly and headed for the back door, turning on the porch light. Outside was still pouring rain, but it was a nice sound, a welcoming sound. To his left were two chairs with plain cushions, an upright log acting as a stand. He chose one and spent some time simply enjoying the view. There wasn't much to see in the growing dark, but he was grateful for what he could see by the porch light. At one point, the porch had been screened in as protection from mosquitoes, but it was gone now. He could see where the broken frame had been cut so as not to be a minor hazard.

Some minutes later, Josina joined him, carrying a plate containing a steaming teapot and two empty cups. She set it on the stand, poured the tea, and they each helped themselves to a cup.

"For a while, I was beginning to think I would never see this place again," Rivotra said. He sipped at the tea. It wasn't traditional tea leaves, but had a berry and citrus flavor.

"I'm sorry I didn't tell you sooner," Josina told him. "I really was trying to keep everything as quiet as possible."

"No, I can appreciate that. What more do you have to do as a lawyer? Are you still working with all those international agencies?"

"There is still a bit of work that I have to do to wrap up your case as it relates to your actual trial in the United States. I already put in my resignation with the Senate and I am supposed to start work at the university in January."

"Were you able to sell your apartment in Tana?"

"Oh, easily. Housing is difficult enough to find as it is, and where I was staying was an excellent location."

He nodded and took another drink. "So which bedroom, specifically, were you sleeping in?"

She gave him a knowing look. "In some Sakalava villages, simply moving in together is all that's required, though a couple isn't really considered married until their first child is born."

He raised a brow. "Was that something you wanted to get started on right away, then?"

Josina burst into laughter so suddenly she nearly threw her teacup. The worst she did was spill some of the contents, though she couldn't stop laughing long enough to care right away. Rivotra wasn't sure if he should laugh with her or feel embarrassed again. Instead, he just watched as she gathered her composure, finishing off what remained of the tea in her cup then refilling. This time she placed her cup back on the plate on the stand.

"I'm sorry, that was rude," she said, avoiding his gaze though her tone was still laughing.

"I am not accustomed to dealing with Sakalava royalty," he told her.

"Not royalty, *ampanzaka*. We used to be royalty, but now we just have that association."

"Do I still have to bring your family a chicken and some cows?"

"Some cows, maybe, but what is the chicken for?"

"We take a chicken with us when I formally ask for your hand. If the chicken survives the trip, it's a good omen of things to come. Then it is butchered and prepared as part of an acceptance feast."

She shook her head but she was still smiling. "I've never heard of such a thing, must be unique to the Betsileo." She shifted in her chair. "Do you have it where the first coupling must be in the home of the bride's mother?"

He shook his head. "No such thing. Although any children should be born in the mother's home village."

"We have that also. And...forty days until presentation?"

"Forty days?!" Now it was his turn to be startled. "We only wait seven!"

"So short?"

"So long?"

They stared at each other in disbelief, then started laughing.

"What am I supposed to do for forty days?" Rivotra asked mildly.

"Work for my uncle," Josina answered very matter-of-fact.

"Forty days..." He sipped at his tea and refilled the cup. "We may have to discuss that."

"There won't be much to discuss if we're in a Sakalava village for the birth. Everyone around you is going to enforce that forty days."

He let out a breath and took another drink. "Cutting the hair ceremony?"

"Mhm."

"First rice ceremony?"

"Mhm."

"Circumcision?"

Now she shook her head. "Expressly forbidden."

He nodded wordlessly. He had been very intent on such a thing when he was younger and desiring to become a man. But now that it had been completely reversed, he wasn't so keen on subjecting himself to that again. Ideally, the only one who would know would be Josina, and it sounded like that was not only a preference, but a requirement. He decided he could live with that.

"Have you known a man?" he inquired.

She looked at him and shook her head. "No, never."

"Mm."

"I know that you have known women. Your Books give you away. But that was Rifun. And you are Rivotra now. Rivotra has not yet lived or known women."

"Known his wife."

"Fiancée. Girlfriend."

He shrugged, trying to shake off the sudden awkwardness. "So, I guess, tomorrow, we'll be making a trip to your village where I can officially meet your family and ask for your hand."

"But you don't have a chicken," Josina giggled.

"I still have seventy-seven American dollars, I think I can buy a chicken." He thought a moment. "I might even be able to buy a couple cows."

"One for us, one for my uncle."

"There we go, this is sounding very promising. But it still doesn't solve the dilemma of who is sleeping where."

"Unless it is *fady* for you, we can sleep in the same bed. We just can't do anything."

That was asking a lot of a man who really hadn't seen a woman in at least a couple years and whose physical prowess had just been restored to its full capacity. And the woman sitting next to him would, with luck, be the mother of his children, which, in itself, implied a few things.

"If you don't think it'll work, I can sleep in another room," she went on, perhaps sensing his uncertainty. "This is still your home, you sleep in the main bedroom."

He would admit, it was probably for the best. He would never rape her, of course, but he could see that she was just as eager as he was. If they did sleep in the same bed and he pressed, even a little, she would give in.

Or maybe not, he decided when he did finally lie down to sleep. Having spent a couple days unconscious after being healed, he wasn't exactly tired, despite the late hour, but after years of thin mattresses and hard metal trays passing as beds in prison—and the mat he had been lying on in the room on Hlohi wasn't exactly the most comfortable thing either—this new bed in the master bedroom was a godsend. His whole body melted, and he fell hard into sleep.

He woke up about mid-morning, initially confused. He had a notion in the back of his mind that someone was going to come around, bang on the door, make sure he was still where he was supposed to be. Then he told himself that was foolish. He was home now.

He glanced to his left where the morning sunlight was streaming in through the window. The window was not original to the house. It was considered bad luck to have windows on the east side of the house, but the French hadn't known that. And they had indeed brought bad luck on themselves, getting kicked out after the Uprising. Although, it seemed, in almost sixty years since, the eastern windows had not caused so much bad luck that they had been removed. And, if he wanted to be honest, he kind of liked having a window in his bedroom. Being trapped in a little box for a room was making him more appreciative of some odd things in life, and being blind for over a year made this the most beautiful sunrise he had ever seen.

He shunned the jeans, instead choosing a simple shirt and light pants, again, that Josina had gotten for him. He would have to see about that as well. Clothes, one or more chickens, some cows, that seventy-seven dollars wasn't going to last long. He was going to have to get out there in the fields and bring those back to rights.

Walking out into the main room, he did not see Josina anywhere, although a faint scent of tea said she was awake. He crossed the room and opened the front door, on the west side of the house.

The village was alive with activity, and why not? With the rainy season upon them, it was imperative to make the most of the periods with no rain. He smelled food, listened to the quacking of ducks and clucking of chickens, heard the lowing of cattle in a nearby field. Children laughed and played or were sent on errands. Women sat in circles working on small projects while discussing the day's news, and men busied themselves in the fields or with their houses. For Rivotra, it was like stepping out of a nightmare that had seized his whole night and walking back into reality.

No more prophecies, no more pain, no more torture, no more impending war and doom of his own making. Life was his to live again. Or maybe for the first time.

He didn't know anyone, but that was quickly remedied as he started walking down the street. He didn't know where he was going. He didn't have a mission. And he was happily distracted by anyone and everyone welcoming him to town, or back to town. Josina had told everyone about this last Andilan who had been found and was coming home, and they wanted to express their joy at having an Andilan back on the Andilan farm.

"The ancestors rejoice!" one old man proclaimed, shaking Rivotra's hand and giving him a near-toothless grin. "I imagine, you will want to hold *famadihana* just as soon as possible, to restore order to the tombs."

Rivotra mentally paused. *Famadihana* was utterly sacred to the Betsileo. Removing the ancestors from the tombs, dining with them, dancing with them, wrapping them in linens in order to make them happy and curry favor for blessings. But was that really what was happening? Or was it just another snare of the Shadows?

On the other hand, the tombs had been desecrated tremendously. Other than a priest, he was the only one allowed to visit and handle the bodies, or whatever remained. He would have to do something about that—another thing on his to-do list. And, truly, was it wrong to at least respect his ancestors? Even if he did not desire their favor, they were his family as much as his future children were his family, and he had to take care of both.

"As soon as possible," he told the old man. "Among many other things that must be done."

The old man laughed and sent him on his way.

He found Josina a little farther down the road. She wore another short sleeve shirt, but her *lamba* was red and brown today, and her *masonjoany* was painted in a different pattern. She was talking to a woman and holding a chicken.

"So, you found a chicken," he said casually, ambling up beside her.

"She told me you intended to ask for her hand," the woman replied. "Was she wrong?"

"No, that's the plan for today."

"Well, she's been helping to take care of my children the past few days, so I thought I would give her something that would help her have children of her own." The woman regarded him. "She said you were Betsileo, but you are light-skinned and wear long hair like the Tsimhety."

He nodded, suddenly conscious of his hair which fell loosely about his shoulder blades. "Yes, my mother was Betsileo. My father was French, but I never knew him. My stepfather was Tsimhety."

The woman frowned and nodded. "I see. Well, an Andilan's an Andilan, and we're happy to have you back."

She and Josina exchanged goodbyes, then Josina followed him on the rest of his tour around town. It had grown up some in the last few years, many newcomers city-dwellers returning to their ancestral roots. She introduced him to people, although most already knew him and congratulated them on their impending engagement.

"You know," he told her, "if we spend all day talking to people here, we're never going to actually get around to getting engaged."

She laughed but did not disagree, and they changed course.

The town and terrain in general did not well allow for large motor vehicles like cars. Even motorcycles, dirt bikes, and mopeds had trouble navigating the stepped terrain. Anyone needing to pass through the town had to utilize a bumpy trail that wound around the outside of the main town and around multiple outlying farms. So there was a parking lot on either side of town where residents parked their vehicles. The most crowded lot was the one where they went now, on the east side of town, the road that led to Fianarantsoa.

"Did you happen to get a cage for the chicken?" Rivotra inquired.

She gave him a look and pulled a cage out of the car's trunk. The cage was made of wood and wire, and a wire latch held the small door closed. He held the cage while she dropped the squawking chicken inside. Then she laid out a cloth on the trunk's floor and he set the cage and the bird inside.

"Do you want to drive?" she asked, her tone impossible to tell how serious she was being.

"You know, to be honest, I don't know that I've ever really driven," Rivotra admitted. "I think the last time I drove was in World War II, taking men and supplies up to Antsrinana Bay before our defense against the British."

Josina sighed dramatically and got in the driver's seat.

"If all goes well and the roads are in tact," she said, starting the vehicle, "we should arrive before dark. And, if all goes very well, we will be having a chicken dinner."

He nodded and shrugged as she pulled onto the road. "All things considered, once we're away from so many prying eyes, we could just Band to get there faster and have a chicken lunch."

There was that, too, although it took much longer to get away from so many prying eyes than he originally thought. The distance between the town and Fianar was much shorter than he remembered, with a lot more people. The road from Fianar leading northwest toward Nosy Be was also much busier than he expected. Even when they reached a point where they could Band, it didn't last long before more busy roads and prying eyes forced them back into real time. Had there always been so many people on this island?

It was late afternoon when they arrived in Josina's village, and they were announced long before the car came to a stop. By the time they opened the doors, relatives had swarmed her side of the car, ready with hugs and kisses.

Rivotra spotted an older couple in the back of the crowd. The woman moved to greet Josina, but the man approached him.

"So, you're the mysterious Rivotra we've been hearing so much about," he said, grasping Rivotra's wrist. "The wind does indeed exist."

"He does," Rivotra confirmed.

He moved to the back of the car and opened the trunk. The chicken, who had apparently settled in for the ride, suddenly jumped to its feet and started squawking. Rivotra pulled the cage out of the trunk and set it on the ground at the man's feet.

"Josina tells me you don't have such a custom," he said, and proceeded to explain the significance of the chicken. The man listened politely.

"A chicken," he stated when Rivotra was finished. "But no cows."

Rivotra cleared his throat. "With respect, sir. They wouldn't fit in the car."

The man stared at him for a long five seconds before breaking into laughter. In his peripheral vision, Rivotra saw Josina breathe a sigh of relief. The man nodded, patted Rivotra on the shoulder with one hand and, with the other, motioned for his wife to take the chicken.

"You make me laugh," the man told him. Still smiling, he grabbed Rivotra's shoulder, turned him, and nearly pushed him toward a particular house. "All right, let us go inside, have this chicken feast, and see what we can work out about your marriage to my niece, hm?"

So they went inside the house and did just that.

May 16, 2020

To: Mt. Olive, West Virginia, United States of America
From: Fianarantsoa, Madagascar

Lt. Oswald,

I don't know how proper it is for an ex-con to write to his former turnkey, but I decided that everyone could use a bit of good news these days. Lockdown is hard enough on the inside, and I imagine that it's especially difficult for you dealing with it on the outside, too.

After returning to Madagascar, I got settled on the family farm with Josina, who you remember was my lawyer who was working for the Senate at the time. A few days later, we visited her family and I asked her to marry me. She and her family enthusiastically said yes, and we were married December 21st, which, for us, is the longest day of the year.

In September of 2018, we welcomed our first son, and in July 2019, we welcomed another. Our third was born only a few days ago, though, because of tradition, it will still be a few more days before I am allowed to see him.

It took some time, but, with the help of some goats, a few cows, and some of the neighbors, much of the land has been cleaned up. We have a flock of ducks (not chickens) and geese which provide eggs and meat and pest control in the fields. The rice and vanilla are producing well. The yield is growing to the point where we are able to provide for ourselves and help others as this farm has always done. This is becoming more important with each passing day during this pandemic as Josina is out of work.

Josina resigned from her position at the Senate shortly before my return and started teaching at the university in Fianarantsoa. Her classes range from political science to law to government to international affairs, and her students and colleagues love her. In the beginning of the pandemic, they took off a couple of weeks, hoping this would pass quickly. Now that more time has passed, they were forced to forfeit the semester. They hope to return in September, even if it is only virtual, although internet service out where we are is spotty at best; most are grateful just to have electricity.

Having to be home all the time now and with three children so far, though, she is considering resigning from her position at the university and simply staying home as wife and mother. Although I have greatly supported her work and do not want to limit her opportunities (and, honestly, it is a good salary), I am hoping that she will do just that. She is an excellent mother, and as we plan on having more children, they will need her. More to the point, I will need her. Simply being home has done wonders for my health, but she is my partner as much as I am hers, and we depend on one another.

With my poor background and lack of fatherly role models, fatherhood has been as much of a challenge as a blessing. And yet, I find it much easier to put myself in their little shoes, to know and understand what they're thinking. They are not contemplating the great mysteries of the universe. They are doing things and waiting for a reaction, something to say that these things are acceptable or unacceptable. I remember looking up at my stepfather with paralyzing fear right before a beating; never do I want my children to experience the same when they look at me. So far, a stern word or look is all that is needed, but we'll see how that changes as the oldest approaches two years old.

I do hope all this pandemic hysteria will clear up soon, and I hope things are going well for you, in spite of it all. Again, maybe that's an odd thing to say. And maybe this letter won't even reach you because it is somehow illegal or improper. So, to whomever is proofreading this, I hope things are going well for you, too.

As we are highly unlikely to see each other again, I do wish to say thank you. Thank you for your faith in me, and thank you for not being one of those uptight, cocky bastards on a power trip. Maybe you aren't popular on account of your political views, but what is needed, and what is right, is not always popular.

If he is still around, please give my regards to Jeremy Long and tell him that he was right about the Krydik. He'll know what that means.

Sincerely,

Rivotra Andilan
Prison Jesus
981436

Authors Note

Many years ago, in one of the earlier roadmaps of *The Timekeeper Chronicles*, this whole book took place behind the scenes. Rifun was going to be tried, convicted, and sentenced in book nine of *The Chivalrous Welshman* (which he was), and then he was going to reappear in book fourteen, twenty-seven years later, still living in West Virginia on parole, changed, married, and just trying to live a quiet life. Because of how far out all of this was, I generally kept the outline, scribbled out a few key scenes to remind me what was going on, then put it on the backburner to be revisited later.

Well, a few things changed as I developed *TKC* into a more coherent narrative and things actually started happening. I made rules, and discovered that I kind of had to play by those rules, many of them relating to who the characters were and what the Akari was capable of. So, the first iteration had to get scrapped.

The second iteration was me trying to be clever. Because Rivotra would be blind for basically all of it, I wanted to experiment with new modes of storytelling. Some of them did survive until the very end, as letters and phone call transcripts. Unfortunately, they work better as interludes than a full story, and the second iteration had to be scrapped as well.

This final iteration did not truly come about until after I finished *The Eleventh Hour (The Chivalrous Welshman #10/F)*. One little detail in that book toward the end informed me how this book was going to get set up and what the overarching conflict was going to be, how everything was going to fit together in the greater *TKC* universe. And yet, the setting was so intuitive to a single novel, and Rivotra's character demanded resolution. In the first iteration, when he made his reappearance in book fourteen, he was going to jump back into the fray, convince Josina to go with him (I hadn't quite

481

decided whether she was going to be exposed to Time and the Akari or not) and go after Julianna and everything else and be the hero. This time around, not so much. And that's okay.

It's not uncommon for authors to become attached to at least one character in their writing, to give that one guilty pleasure a teeny bit more plot armor than the rest of the cast. Rivotra has been that character for me, from his first appearance in *Time to Kill (The Chivalrous Welshman #1)*. Josina only serves to augment this, and I am uniquely delighted to see that he has received the fulfillment of the Akarin mantra, "May the Author write you a happy ending." I am just as delighted that I was even able to give it to him, that all the years, all the books, all the changes, and it still came back to a happy ending.

Now, as for the Krydik, both Nendawagan's parting words and Sabelu's reappearance, if you read this book and you're happy with it and choose to read no more of *The Timekeeper Chronicles*, then I wish you a happy ending as well. Nothing will be missed.

But if you are following along, and you know that there is one last segment of *TKC* to be written, *The Fifth Horseman*, then consider it a little insider knowledge, at least for now. Guilty blood spilled upon a willing sacrifice. An empty husk torn apart. One messenger of the Whites, one messenger of the Shadows, one last push for the End of Time.

\- Brooke Shaffer

www.ingramcontent.com/pod-product-compliance
Lightning Source LLC
Chambersburg PA
CBHW061536190726
48289CB00004B/1066